THE LIVING DOLL

Ellie heard a movement behind her—the sound of a footstep. But it was very soft, like a barefoot child's.

She whirled.

No one was there—except *Zenoa.*

Ellie gasped.

The doll was standing. Ellie had put her in the chair, but now she was standing. *Without support . . .*

. . . halfway across the room between Ellie and the table.

Ellie stared, unable to move, to breathe, to open her mouth and cry out for help. Fear was enveloping her in an icy prison. Her thoughts flashed to Becky and the things Becky had told her. It moves, she had said. It moves by itself.

Now Zenoa stood severeal steps from the chair where Ellie had left her. She was no longer beautiful, she was hideous. Her one eye glared and her red tongue stuck out. Her hair was thin and torn and ratted. As Ellie's eyes remained pinned to her, she saw the right arm raise, and in the hand something glistened.

The ice pick.

RUBY JEAN JENSEN
THE LIVING EVIL

ZEBRA BOOKS
KENSINGTON PUBLISHING CORP.

ZEBRA BOOKS are published by

Kensington Publishing Corp.
475 Park Avenue South
New York, NY 10016

Zebra and the Z logo are trademarks of Kensington Publishing Corp.

First Printing: August, 1993

Printed in the United States of America

BOOK ONE
1870
The Gift

One

"Make it go away! Make it go away!"

Ellie woke, feeling at her back the jerk of her little sister's body in the beginning of one of her night terrors. She cringed, knowing the scream would come next. Then their mother would come . . .

The room in which they slept, and spent much of their time playing in the daytime, had room barely for the pallet in the corner on the floor. A dim light filtered up through the narrow alley below the window, rising from the flickering jet of the street light on the corner. Deep shadows moved in the room. It was like a fight that waged continually between the dark and the light. Ellie could almost see the things Becky said were there. Terrible things that flew, and crawled, and had many arms and claws and teeth, and frightening wings that grew even from the tops of their heads.

Becky had always been afraid. As far back as Ellie could remember, when she was five and Becky three, Becky would disturb the nights with her screams. Then, if their mama was home she would come and shake Becky and yell at her, and slap her and slap her until her nose bled. If she didn't stop screaming, she would take the old razor strop their real papa had left in the house, and beat Becky with it.

Tonight the fog horns moaned, sounding as if they were coming through the walls. Ellie herself had slept restlessly, disturbed by the fog horns, disturbed by the new papa that was in the house. Just knowing he was in the next room, with Mama, made her uneasy. She had gotten used to being alone in the house with Becky. Then Becky wasn't so afraid. They sat on the floor beneath the window, where their bed took up the corner, and played with whatever they could find. Little sticks from down at the dump. Pieces of broken dishes.

For several days now Mama had been very happy. She had even brought them a stick of horehound candy once, to share. But tonight as Ellie stirred uncomfortably in the bed next to Becky she waited, wondering. Would Mama be nicer now?

She always knew when Becky was going to scream. She felt her stiffen, and heard her breath stop and then suck inward, like the wind through the hole in the wall just above their bed. She sometimes turned over and tried to shake Becky. *No, no, don't disturb Mama.* But Becky didn't know she was there.

As the shrill scream ripped through the night Ellie turned away from Becky, covered her ears, and pressed hard against the wall, pretending to be asleep. She had finally learned how to avoid being hit by their mother. Becky hadn't learned yet.

Becky screamed, words tumbling out, sounding something like, *"Take it away make it go away!"*

The footsteps came running from the next room, the only other room in their fifth floor flat. Across the walls somewhere a man's voice boomed, "Shut that goddamned kid up!" and in a lower voice muttered, "Can't get any sleep in this stinking hole."

In another flat a baby began to cry. The apartment building took on a restlessness, like something stirring in its sleep.

Becky kept screaming, one gasping cry after the other.

The floor shook with the running steps. Heather entered the room, her long hair swinging past her waist. Ellie took a quick peek from under her hands and saw her mother like a ghost in the dim light that followed her through the door. Her gown swept back, trailing in gloomy white from her

8

shoulders. Her dark hair swung. Her face was a white blur in the dark, featureless. But Ellie could feel the hatred in her eyes.

The hatred in her eyes.

Ellie had seen it and cringed from it all her life, puzzled by it, crushed by it. Such beautiful eyes that looked with sparkling pleasure at everyone else, especially her friends, looked at Ellie and Becky with that sharp hatred.

"Stop it!" Heather screamed, her hands coming down on Becky with hard slaps. "Stop it! You're waking up the whole house, for Christ's sake. Shut up this minute, Becky!"

Becky settled, crying, and curled into a knot at Ellie's back.

The footsteps left, but a moment later came back again, with a hard deliberation, and preceded by a light. Ellie uncovered her face.

Their young mother carried a candle. She set it on the wall shelf above the hooks that held their two good dresses. Then she came to the bed. Ellie saw she was carrying the leather strop.

Through teeth that had clinched together as if forged by her hatred, Heather told Becky to get out of bed.

"No, Mama, no, Mama," Becky whimpered, drawing back into the bed and huddling so hard against Ellie it pushed her onto the floor between the wall and bed.

"I said get out of that bed. I'm going to teach you a lesson once and for all. You are not going to carry on like this anymore. I'm sick and tired of it. I'm sick and tired of you. You've been a crybaby since the day you were born. Now move! Do as I say. Get out of that bed!"

Becky moved away from Ellie. Her nightshirt came only past her bloomers when she stood up next to the bed. Her legs looked like white sticks. She shook, Ellie saw, her hands shook, her arms shook, so hard that even her head began to shake. She looked so tiny standing on the cold floor next to their mother.

Ellie turned away again as the strop began to fall in a terrible, steady rhythm across Becky's back. Becky's sobs

9

were soft. Nothing at all like her screams when she woke in the night from her dreamless dreams.

Ellie heard heavier footsteps, and then a man's voice spoke from the doorway.

"Haven't you done enough? The child's had a nightmare, that's all."

Heather said nothing, but the beating stopped.

Ellie peeked out from between her fingers. The man filled the doorway, his head bent forward a little. He had a beard, and dark eyes. She had seen him a few times before, and once he had smiled at her. She hadn't known if the smile was kind, but now she knew. Their new papa was kind.

They left the room together, Heather and the new papa. He put his hand on her back as they left.

Becky looked up. Mama was going out of the room with the man. She was carrying in her hand the candle, with its little bright flame. The man had taken the razor strop from her and had folded it in his hands. Becky's back burned where her mother had struck her, burned as if her skin had been peeled away.

She was afraid to move, afraid her mother would see and remember her, and start hitting her again. She remembered not to scream when she saw the black ghost, so clear in the light of the candle. It hovered around her mother's head, like a lot of hair fluffed out. Only the black ghost was darker than hair, darker than any hair was ever dark. It coiled and worked within itself, growing. It was a bad thing, Becky knew. She could feel it in the way her skin tingled.

As the curtain fell over the doorway, Becky crawled back into bed and lay staring at the curtain, afraid the black ghost that was around her mother's head would come back into the room.

"Did you see the bad ghost?" she whispered to her sister, who lay warm and comforting against her.

"Shh, Becky, go to sleep."

"There's a ghost around Mama's head."

"There ain't no ghost. Go to sleep."

10

"Yes, there is. I saw it. It's black."

"Ghosts ain't black, they're white. Go to sleep."

Becky lay still, staring at the old curtain that covered the doorway. Waiting for it to move.

She remembered another place they had lived before they came here to this nicer place. They'd all had to sleep in the same bed then. Aunt Aster had tried to get Mama to come and live with her, but Mama said she wouldn't live with that old biddy if she were dying.

Becky had looked at her mother and asked what an old biddy was, and Ellie reached over and pinched her, which meant she should shut up. But their mother didn't hit Becky. She laughed instead. Still, she never answered the question.

It was always hard to know if their mother was going to laugh or get angry.

Becky didn't know Aunt Aster very well. She thought she might have seen her once, when they went to their grandfather's funeral, but she wasn't sure. So many people were there. Uncles, aunts, great aunts, old, old people. Young ones too like herself and Ellie, all sitting quietly in the stillness. Flowers were heaped on the pretty box that held their grandfather. A casket, Ellie said it was. It was prettier than their mother's prettiest dress, grey, with silver handles, and the inside was grey satin.

She had seen her grandfather before, sitting in a rocking chair, his long, spidery hands holding the wooden arms of the chair. She'd had to sit quietly, and not speak. Before they got to the house, Mama had told her, "Children are meant to be seen and not heard, so shut up." Why, she wondered, were children meant to be seen? Grandfather didn't seem even to see them.

And their mother hated seeing them. They stayed in their room when Mama was home, so she wouldn't have to see them. They played very quietly so she wouldn't hear them. It was much better when Mama was gone. Then she and Ellie could go down the long steps to the outdoors and go look for something to play with. Once, the grocery lady had

11

given them an apple.

Through the wall she heard their voices.

"They've been a terrible burden, Thurman, you've no idea. I know my temper may be short sometimes, but if I'd let her, Becky would cry all the time. She's the biggest cry-baby that ever was born. I think she knew when she was born that she was a terrible mistake."

"A baby is never a mistake, Heather. You don't feel that way about this one that's coming, do you?"

"Oh no, Thurman, you know I don't. A boy, we'll have a perfect little boy. He'll look just like you, Thurman."

Becky heard the change in her mother's voice. A baby boy? Would she and Ellie get to see him? Play with him? No, their mother wouldn't allow that. Where would he sleep? Would there be room for her and Ellie then?

She heard the creak of the bedsprings and the soft mur-murings that seemed to come through every wall in the house, from different people in different flats.

Becky couldn't sleep. Her back hurt. It felt as if the skin was gone all the way from her shoulders to her knees. She lay half on her stomach, and finally almost went to sleep, then it seemed she saw the curtain move. The black ghost entered, a round thing just the size of fluffed hair around her mother's head. She saw it come through the curtain, and rise up against the ceiling in the corner. She trembled.

"Ellie," she whispered. *"It's here. In our room."*

"What?" Ellie muttered sleepily.

"The ghost. The bad black thing."

"Oh for gosh sakes shut up and go to sleep. There's no such thing as a black ghost. Ghosts are *white*, and they live in big empty houses, not in two-room flats."

Sometimes Ellie could sound almost like their mother.

Becky stared at the corner of the ceiling until it grew grey with light, and she could see the point where the ceiling came together with the wall in three lines that ran in different directions.

In the early morning mists Aster went out to work in her

flowers. Beads of moisture hung on the golden petals of the marigolds. Bumblebees nursed at pollen-saturated centers. They buzzed past her, large, black, prickly. Unaggressive. Together they worked among the plants, she and the bumblebees.

The house was grey shingle, with porches and a steep roof angled with dormers. The second floor had three large bedrooms. The front room had been occupied by her parents, and the other two crowded with beds to accommodate the boys in one bedroom, and the girls in the other. Among her five sisters and four brothers she had grown up sharing a dormered room. The oldest girl, she had served also as the maid, cook, general cleaning and washer woman. Her lips had grown thin with the bitterness that came with years. While her brothers left home to roam the world and her younger sisters married one by one, she had stayed. Mama needed her. Papa needed her. Now, alone, her feelings were mixed.

She had gradually grown used to the silence. Alone with her parents the house had seemed morbidly quiet, and then pleasantly quiet. Mama died years ago. Papa last year. In the silence of the house she looked back at her life, her inheritance. The one who had given care to the parents was given the house and a small trust, barely enough for upkeep of the house. While her sisters had families, she at least had a place to live.

The lot was large, as were the others in the neighborhood. The back yard held a huge, old elm tree, and several smaller trees on the west, separating her from the neighbor beyond, whom she didn't know. People bought and sold and moved, and she didn't bother to keep up with them. The northeast corner contained her vegetable garden, grown smaller over the years, shrinking from a plot that once fed the family most of its vegetables, to a place that also held marigolds, dahlias, and hollyhocks among the rows of asparagus and rhubarb. Honeysuckle crawled over the fence, and beyond the boards and wire lived her closest neighbor, whose wife had died just a few months before her father.

13

His name was William Jessup. For years she had called him Mister Jessup. With the horse he stabled in the five acre pasture behind his yard, he'd plowed her garden every year for so many years past that she'd lost count.

He was only Mr. Jessup, the husband of Amy Jessup, the father of the two children who grew up and left home last year. Aster knew him to speak to, but only because they sometimes met at the mailboxes that were on the same post in front of their houses.

Now he had begun to talk to her over the fence, and she found herself thinking of him. What would it be like to be married? At forty-four was she too old to have children? She hadn't reached her change of life yet, but sometimes in the night, when things didn't seem right inside her, she felt herself tighten with dread that she might be too late before Mr. Jessup asked her to marry him.

Perhaps he had no intentions of asking her. Why should he? She wasn't exactly beautiful. She wasn't even pretty, and never had been. She was tall and angular, the tallest of the six girls, and the roundness of figure that was so desirable had somehow passed her by. She had lots of thick, auburn hair, but she also had thick, heavy eyebrows that overpowered her face, and her cheeks tended to be fuzzy. She used to rub them viciously, and even a few times had used her papa's straight razor to get rid of the fuzz. Merle, just younger than she, was small and round, the shortest of the girls. She was a full head shorter than Aster. How could sisters be so different? Having been born of the same parents? But nature had given most of the beauty in the family to Heather, the baby.

Aster was eighteen when Heather was born. Her mother's change of life baby. Aster herself had helped with the birth, had been the one to wrap the infant and place her in their mother's arms.

Mama laughed, that warm night, and said, "My changeling baby. Isn't she beautiful?"

Yes. Even then. Such a perfect head, with moist, dark ringlets, and wide blue eyes.

"Good morning, ma'am," a deep voice said.

At first she thought it was Mr. Jessup, but the man who had crossed off the front walk to stand in the damp grass was a stranger. With fog from the bay swirling about him, he was almost like a dream. Tall, broad of shoulder, young, his dark eyes looked intensely at her.

"Excuse me," he said. "Are you Miss Aster, Heather's sister?"

"Yes." She pushed the front of her bonnet up so she could get a better view.

"I'm Thurman Winslow, Heather's husband."

"Heather's husband!"

She had only once seen the sailor Heather married nine years ago, but her recollection of him was of a man much smaller. And the name was not familiar.

"Yes," he said. "Our wedding was last month. We didn't invite the family. My apologies. It seemed at the time that perhaps it would be better if she and I just went to the city hall."

Aster nodded. It didn't matter. What had happened to the sailor? She didn't ask. "Would you like to come in for coffee?"

"No, no. I have only a moment. Heather doesn't know I'm here." He looked down, turning his cap in his hands. He was a handsome man. He and Heather must make a fine looking couple. Aster waited.

"I've come about the children," he finally said. "I think it would be better if they stayed somewhere else for awhile. You see . . . Heather . . . is . . . well . . . not kind to them."

Yes, she had heard rumors through the family. Heather wasn't the best of mothers. Perhaps it was the family's fault. They had spoiled her. Not only Mama and Papa, but the brothers and sisters who were still at home when Heather was born. Heather had grown up getting everything handed to her. She'd had the prettiest dresses, to fit the tiniest waist, of any of the girls. Aster had sewn stitches until her fingers calloused, to see that Heather was dressed as well as any girl

15

in the city.

At eighteen she married, already looking a bit thick in the waist. At eighteen she had Eleanor, and two years later Becky. Her husband was a sailor, and they lived in various flats over on the waterfront. Aster knew those places only by the growing complaints in Heather's visits. She came home only when she needed money.

But Aster had seen that her children were neglected. While Heather still managed to dress nicely, her two little girls looked like street ragamuffins.

Once Aster had made the mistake of saying so. Eleanor, four years old, and Becky two, had dirty faces and ripped skirts. "Heather," Aster said, when they came into the house, the children trailing behind like small goslings, "can't you do better by your children? Don't you at least have soap and water where you live?"

Heather flew into a rage, grabbed her two little girls by their arms, and left. After that she seldom came home.

Heather wasn't the only one mad at her. Mama and Papa were too, and blamed Aster because Heather no longer came to visit.

Mama saw Heather only once more before she died, and Papa saw her perhaps once a year after that. Only when Heather was desperate for money.

Heather was a beautiful woman with her fine, arched eyebrows and large, catlike slanted eyes. She had a slight overbite, but it only made her mouth more appealing. There was a dimple in her chin, and when she smiled slightly tiny dimples appeared right in the corners of her lips. Her dark hair was thick and wavy and made a luxurious bun on the nape of her neck. She was beautiful, yes, but restless, and had always been. Aster wasn't surprised that she was willing to give up her children.

She looked across the fence, but Mr. Jessup was not in his yard. It didn't matter. He probably didn't want her anyway, children or no children.

"Yes," she said to Heather's husband, "I'll take the children."

Two

Aster checked the room again. It was the room that had been Heather's alone as she grew up and became the only child left at home other than Aster herself. When the boys left Aster took their room because Heather wanted a room alone. They had taken out the other beds, so that only one wide, fat bed was left in each room. Now Heather's old room needed two beds again. Would it be suitable for two little girls? Would they be happier sharing one room, with one big bed, or would they prefer separate rooms? Wouldn't they be frightened to be separated at their young ages?

She found her hands were itching. Nervousness didn't make her hands damp the way it did ordinary people. No, her hands had to itch, like the dry, wrinkled skin of an old maid. And wasn't that what she had become?

She thought of William Jessup, next door. Just this morning she had been out at the break of dawn, unable to sleep. Knowing this was the day she was going after the two little girls had given her the most restless night of her life. She had gone to her roses for comfort. Mists moved among them, visibly, ghostlike. Fog up from the bay was so thick this morning it obscured the trees in the empty lot across the street. Her cat, Sir Thomas, had come from wherever he had spent the night and curled his long yellow tail around her ankle at about the same time a male voice said, "Good morning, Miss Aster."

She had jumped and squealed like someone who had escaped from the crazy house. Then she saw Mister Jessup

17

grinning at her across the fence. She had started to chatter in a way that was not at all usual for her.

"You startled me," she said. "You and the cat, at the same time. It was almost as if the cat spoke to me. Actually," she said, going on and on as she pulled her shawl tautly around her chilled arms, "actually, I came out because I couldn't stand being in the house alone a moment longer. I always turn my cat out at night. He wants to go out, you know. He stays inside and sleeps all day, then at night, just like a man, he's off to who knows where . . ."

She stopped. She bit her lip. How could she say something like that to Mr. Jessup? He never went out at night that she knew about, and her own father had never gone out at night without her mother, so where exactly did she get her information?

"I mean," she said, "That's just the—uh—the—"

"I understand," he said, still grinning. "Tom cats are that way. Maybe you should get yourself a lady cat. She would probably stay at home at night. And keep you company. Though I don't know why you should ever be alone, Miss Aster," he added so softly she really didn't hear it.

"Yes, I'm sure you're right." She looked off through the mists thinking of a lady cat staying home nights, and thinking of a mother who wasn't kind to her small daughters. Somewhere there was the waterfront, where she would be going in a few hours to pick up her nieces. "Actually, I won't be alone after today. My two small nieces are coming to live with me. I'm to go after them in a while. Their stepfather, Thurman Winslow, is a seaman, and is away at this time. He came to see me last week. It seems my sister isn't—uh—well, and he felt the children would be better off here. I wrote to my sister and told her to have them ready to come today. I've been trying to get a room ready for them. I didn't know if they would prefer to stay together in one room, or if they'd prefer separate rooms. When I was growing up there were so many of us we had to share rooms, but now, there's only me, and I could move into the master bedroom, and let each girl have a room of her own, if need be."

18

She was going on and on again. Wasn't it fairly common knowledge that a man didn't like a chattering woman? But then perhaps her information on that was as erroneous as their similarities to tom cats.

"How old are they?" he asked.

"They're really very young. Six and eight, I believe. Yes, six and eight. Becky and Eleanor."

"They'd probably rather be in the same room, coming as they are to a strange house to live." He had stopped smiling. "Is your sister seriously ill?"

"Oh. No, she's uh—with child. And they live in a very small flat." She felt herself blushing. She was telling Mister Jessup such personal things this morning. What was the matter with her?

But he didn't seem to notice.

"Will they be visiting you very long?"

"Yes. Indefinitely."

For a moment they just looked at each other, and she read in his steady stare the question. Why?

Aster cleared her throat, aware suddenly of him as a man. He was medium tall and of medium weight, but he had fine, square, broad shoulders. His hairline had receded more and more each year for many years now, but when he was wearing a cap, such as now, he was very handsome. She hadn't noticed before how attractive he actually was. He was probably fifty years old now, which would be just right for her.

She became aware of herself, and of the forceful beating of her heart. She had been kissed once or twice in her early years by a beau who had walked her home from a school party, but that was all. She drew her eyes away from Mister Jessup's lips, but the memory of the mustache revealing only the full lower lip stayed with her like the image of a light she had been looking at too long.

Sir Thomas curled around her other ankle, dragging with his tail the dew he had gathered as he came through uncut weeds from vacant lots and weedy gardens.

"Heather, their mother, has married again. Recently. She

19

is getting ready to begin a new family with her new husband, and they still live in the flat where Heather lived with her daughters . . ." Because they couldn't afford more, Thurman had told her. She hadn't asked what had happened to Heather's share of the inheritance from their papa. Of course it hadn't been much, anyway. Yet if she had carefully invested it, as Aster had hers, it would have provided her with enough income to have a decent place to live. "So her daughters from her first marriage are coming to live with me."

She was repeating herself. Why should Mister Jessup be interested? In repeating herself it was almost as if she too were trying to understand why a mother would want to give up her children. She was unkind to them, Thurman Winslow had said.

Mister Jessup was nodding, nodding as if he understood. He didn't say, ah yes, I remember Heather. The young woman who flounced in and out of the house on the arm of a different young man every day. Who left when she was very young, and rarely came back. Not many young women married twice at such a young age. But of course Heather would.

"Her first husband died?"

"Yes, he must have." She didn't know. Divorce was rare. But of course Heather wouldn't let that stop her. However, to be fair, he might have drowned at sea, or been stabbed in one of those brawls that sailors get into so often. But then again, where was she getting her information?

"You've got your work cut out for you," he said, adding, "And so do I, and if I don't get on the job my boss is going to find someone else to do it for me."

She noticed for the first time he was wearing blue-grey workclothes. He was a laborer somewhere, she assumed, by the way he was dressed. She nodded good day to him and watched him disappear into the mists. Then she went around to the back porch and crossed it to the kitchen door. She held it open for Sir Thomas.

In the kitchen she fed him. Into one dish she put oatmeal

mixed with tuna, and into the other dish she poured a small amount of milk. Then she went upstairs again to Heather's old room.

It looked so dark. The one window was nearly covered by vines that had grown up over the west end of the house. But the featherbed was fat and deep, and some of Heather's things were still on the dresser, and her small clock was on the bedside table that was covered with a heavy linen cloth with a velvet fringe. Wouldn't the little girls feel more at home living together in the very room that had once been their mother's?

She went back downstairs. If she left now, she'd have plenty of time to find her way to the address on the waterfront. She pulled her shawl close around her neck and refastened it so that it didn't feel as if it were choking her. Then she went to the kitchen, where the telephone hung on the wall. She twisted the handle one long ring for the operator.

When the female voice answered Aster took a deep breath and asked, "Would you give me the hack service please."

She waited. She heard three long rings and two short, then another female voice. The day she had mailed the letter telling Heather she would pick up the girls on Thursday, she also called the hack service and made arrangements to be taken to the address down on the waterfront and then brought home again. One adult and two children.

"Hack service," the woman on the line said, amid cracklings and dimmer voices somewhere on other lines.

"This is Miss Aster Morris. I called last week for a hack for today."

"Yes. I believe he was to pick you up at nine?"

"Yes, well, would you tell him I'm going to walk down to the foot of the hill, and would he mind coming on now and meeting me there?"

I can't stand this another minute. If I don't get this over with, I'll go mad.

If Heather didn't have the girls ready to go when she got there, then she'd just wait. But now she had to hurry out.

21

For the first time since her parents died, she felt as if the house had grown to surround her like a prison, and was closing down, dark and heavy.

She left it gratefully, crossing the front porch, seeing the sunshine slanting through the mists. She drew a deep breath and started down the walk to the gate. It was several blocks to the foot of the hill, but that was all right. The walk would do her good.

"Hurry up, she'll be here, and you won't be ready to go. Ellie, did you brush Becky's hair?"

"Yes'am."

"Well, brush it again. It looks like a rat's nest. It always looks like a damned rat's nest. I don't know why her hair had to be so curly. No one in my family ever had such hard to handle hair."

Becky cringed. Their mother had awakened them while it was only partly light, and told them this was the day. But their clothes were already ready. For several days now Becky's Sunday dress had been folded in the paper sack, and her clean underwear was there too. But this morning their mother had told them to take the dresses out and put them on, and to put their dirty dresses in the bag instead. She had told Ellie to brush Becky's hair then, too, and Becky had huddled with her shoulders hunched up against her ears as much as possible while Ellie pulled and tugged on her hair with the wire brush. It had hurt so much. It always did. Most of the time she didn't have to have her hair brushed, and the knots and tangles would get so bad that sometimes they had to be cut out. She wished her hair could be cut short, like a boy's, so it wouldn't hurt to brush it.

"I don't want my hair brushed again," Becky dared to say, tears coming to her eyes. "It hurts."

Ellie hissed in her ear, "Hush! Do you want her to hear you?"

Their mother's voice was coming at them, on and on,

22

from the other room. But she wasn't very mad today. She even sounded cheerful and happy as she told them again how lovely it would be to live there in the old home, as she called it.

"I used to walk to school. There's a white school house down the road about a half mile away that has a big yard and two rooms. There are swings and teeter totters and merry-go-rounds. I went to school there, and now so shall you. And Aunt Aster keeps a rose garden and vegetable garden. You'll love the rose garden. She'll even let you help her pick roses and fill the vases. Hurry up now, and make sure your hair is pretty and your dress is clean. She'll be here soon. And do you know what? I have a surprise for you."

Becky whispered, "What's a surprise?"

Ellie whispered back, "A surprise is . . . well, it's a surprise, dummy. Don't you know what a surprise is?"

"You can tell me."

"No. Hush."

"Maybe I'll know after I go to school."

But then she remembered. Ellie had never been to school either, so she probably didn't even know what a surprise was, and that's why she hadn't told her what it was.

Then her sister whispered in her ear, "A surprise is something that you didn't know about until it happens."

"Oh. How did you know?"

"I just know. You've heard that word, Becky. You know, like, what a surprise!"

"Oh. Like us going to live with Aunt Aster. Like when Mama said, I have a surprise for you girls. You're going to live with Aunt Aster. Like that?"

"Yes, but also like a gift."

"A gift?"

"Like a present. Like we got that time at Christmas, remember, when Aunt Aster sent us the pencils and the tablet in the mail and it was wrapped in pretty paper? Those were surprises."

Becky hunched under the old wire brush and thought of

23

everything. The white school. The yard with all the things to play on. The rose and vegetable gardens. She thought of living in the very house where her mother had grown up. She remembered being there, but it was like a dream that got dimmer as she woke up. She couldn't separate Aunt Aster from all the other vague faces. She had an impression of a big, dark house that wasn't filled with other flats. It scared her to think about going to live in such a faraway place, such a strange place.

"I don't want to go," she whispered.

"Shhh! Don't ever say that. You'll really get Mama mad if she hears you say that."

She thought about the surprise their mother had for them. Was it a new dress maybe? Now that they had put on their clean dresses, they had only their old dresses in the paper bag. A new dress would be a nice surprise.

The footsteps in the hall outside the flat were the steps of a stranger. Becky was used to all the footsteps that pounded through the hall and the other flats. Children running. Men clumping home heavily. Mothers dragging their feet all day. But the footsteps coming along the hall sounded quick and precise, not heavy like a man's, nor dragging like the mothers'. Their own mother's footsteps were usually soft, for much of the time she went about only in her slippers with the soft leather soles. Becky sat up, dropping her shoulders, and Ellie lowered the hair brush.

They sat still, listening. Becky held her breath.

The steps came to the door and stopped. Then knocks came instead. One, two, three.

Their mother's soft steps came running. She paused and pushed aside the curtain on the door.

"Here she is! Come on!"

Becky stood up. In the front room her mother cried, "Aster! It's so good to see you!"

The other voice was like the voice of the lady at the grocery store down on the corner. Soft, low, and a little quivery.

"Heather. You're looking very good."

24

"Oh I'm feeling fine. Getting a bit heavy now on my feet, but feeling fine."

"I'm a little early . . ."

"That's all right. The girls have been ready for days. They were up early this morning. They're so happy to be going with you. I'm so glad they're going to have a yard to play in. And you'll be sending them to school this fall, won't you?"

"Yes, of course. What books—where are their records—?"

"Oh, no school is available here. None I would send them to. They'd have to walk through some very dangerous neighborhoods, I'm sure. It's time Ellie, especially, is going. She should be in school. She needs to learn to read. I'm so happy you offered to let them come live with you, Aster."

Ellie picked up the sack that held their clothes. Becky saw her hand was shaking. It shook so hard the paper sack rattled. Becky followed her through the doorway, first Ellie's hand then Becky's pushing aside the old, heavy curtain that had long ago lost its color and now was merely dark and dreary like the walls of the flat.

The tall lady stood just inside the door with a black shawl hanging from her shoulders. Her hair was streaked with white and pulled back from her face. She had heavy dark eyebrows that looked full and thick compared to their mother's thin, arched brows, and her eyes were deepset and steady.

But they weren't angry or unkind. It seemed to Becky as she looked up at the tall lady that she saw something sad in those deepset eyes as they looked down at her.

"Hello, Becky and Eleanor," the lady said.

"This is your Aunt Aster, girls, do you remember her?" Heather asked.

Ellie said in a shy little voice, "I do."

Becky shook her head. She remembered the house, so large, with high ceilings . . . but she didn't remember the rose garden or Aunt Aster. And yet, it seemed she did, somewhere in the back of her mind. It seemed the lady

25

wasn't really the stranger Becky had felt she was when she learned they'd be going to live with her. Would Aunt Aster slap her, the way Mama did? So that she never knew if she should talk? Sometimes her mother slapped her when she didn't answer, and at other times she slapped her when she did, so that Becky had become afraid to talk. She never knew if she should speak.

It was better, most of the time, to say nothing. So she said nothing now until her mother ordered, "Becky, speak to your Aunt Aster, for goodness sake!"

Becky opened her mouth, but nothing came out. She saw in the corner of her eye the tightening of her mother's lips. The next moment her hand would jerk upwards and come down against Becky's head, the fingers long and stinging. Becky cringed, drawing her shoulder up protectively against her cheek.

Heather laughed as if Becky's movement had embarrassed her.

"She's a nervous kid, I have to warn you, Aster."

Aunt Aster smiled faintly, and the strange sadness in her eyes increased. Becky thought for a moment she was going to cry. But then she put her hand out, palm up.

"We'll do fine, won't we, Becky?"

Heather gave Becky a shove forward, and Becky put her hand into Aunt Aster's. It was warm, and it closed over Becky's hand. Suddenly Becky remembered her. This was the lady who had picked her up and kissed her cheek. This was the lady who had kissed her!

It was the only time in her life she had been kissed.

She knew it was a kiss because she had asked Ellie about it later, and Ellie told her it was called a *kiss*.

Later she noticed that many of the papas kissed her mother. Right on the lips. But she had forgotten, until now, that once someone had kissed her.

She didn't feel quite so scared about going away from the only place she had ever lived.

As if Aunt Aster read in Becky's eyes the memory of the kiss, she bent down and once again kissed Becky's cheek.

Becky stared up at her in amazement. Then Aunt Aster kissed Ellie, but Becky saw Ellie jerk back as if a wasp had stung her.

"Their things are in the sack, Aster," Heather said. "They have underwear and an everyday dress. We'll try to send something for school clothes."

Aunt Aster took the sack from Ellie and turned toward the door. Becky saw her eyes flit once over the front room of the flat, with the unmade bed in the corner and the colorless rags on the windows and dirty dishes in the pan on the stove. Becky and Ellie always washed dishes, but this morning Mama hadn't called them yet to wash the dishes. Becky wondered who would wash them now that she and Ellie were going away.

Aunt Aster opened the door.

"We should go. The hack is waiting, and the waiting won't be free, I'm sure."

"I have one more thing," Heather said, and there was a smile in her voice.

Becky waited, and she saw that Ellie waited too, while Aunt Aster stood in the open doorway. This was the surprise Mama had spoken of. Becky had almost forgotten about it. A new dress, maybe. She hoped with all her heart it was a new dress. She had seen one in the shop window a few blocks away. A lovely white dress with tiny blue flowers, and lots of ruffles and lace.

"Now don't peek," Heather said, and went to the corner to reach in behind the stove.

Becky looked at Ellie and saw her sister staring with wide eyes.

Heather came back and she was carrying something in a long, narrow box. She was smiling, looking at Ellie. And then she looked at Becky, and she was still smiling.

"We were only able to get one. It's very expensive, so you'll have to share. But since Becky is the youngest, I thought maybe she would like to carry her."

Heather opened the box.

27

A little girl! So pretty. So much prettier than she or Ellie. Lying so still with her eyes closed, as if she were in a casket, dead.

No. Not a little girl, not real, but a beautiful doll. Ellie's mouth opened but she said nothing. Even Aunt Aster was very quiet, no longer moving as if she were in a great hurry to leave. Becky stared at the most beautiful doll she had ever seen. It was prettier even than the ones she had seen in the window of the dollmaker's shop. His dolls were quite ordinary. This doll had long golden-red hair, parted in the middle with little pink velvet ribbons high on each side. Bangs hung down to her pale, lifted eyebrows. Heather tilted the box and the doll's eyes slowly opened. They were large and brown, like Heather's, only the doll's eyes were round. She had a mouth that looked like Heather's too, with the upper lip protruding a bit over the lower. Mama called it her overbite, because her upper teeth pushed out just a little. The doll, Becky saw, looked so much like her mother it might have been her when she was a little girl. Only the hair was different, and the shape of the large eyes. There was even a dimple in her chin.

"Isn't she lovely?" Heather said, holding the long, white box out to Becky. "Her name is Zenoa. She's an exotic doll from a faraway port. Thurman bought her because he said she reminded him of me, and I think he's right, don't you? He bought her for me, but he said it would be all right if I gave her to you."

Becky put her hands behind her back as she stared at the doll in the box. Heather tipped the box upward and the doll's eyes opened even wider. She stared directly at Becky.

"It certainly does look like you, Heather," Aunt Aster said. "Amazing. What a lovely present, girls."

Heather removed the doll from the box and held it out to Becky. Its long, lacy dress fell to black high-topped shoes. Ellie poked Becky in the ribs with her sharp elbow and hissed, "Take it!"

"This is my surprise to you, Becky," Heather said. "Zenoa is to make sure you never forget me."

28

Becky drew back. Her skin tightened across her cheeks, the way it always did when something bad was going to happen. She stared at the doll. The black ghost that showed at night around her mother's hair was now shadowing the top of the doll's head, like a bad moon rising. Becky saw it growing behind the golden hair, making a circle around the top of the head. *Couldn't they see it?* The black ghost, like black fog, the dark halo just like the one that surrounded her mother's head at night when the lights were dim. The bad thing, the bad, bad thing that hated her and wanted her never to have been born.

The doll came at Becky, pushed by the hands of her mother.

"No! No!" Becky screamed. "Take it away! *Take it away!*"

But it came nearer, nearer, shoved angrily by her mother's hands, its dark eyes round and large and staring at Becky with that terrible look, just like her mother when she was hating Becky. It came at her with the black and terrible halo arched over its head the way Christmas angels wore their white and silvery halos, but this was not an angel, this was a terrible thing that wanted to kill Becky.

"Take it away! Make it go away!"

Three

"What on earth's wrong with you now?" Heather screeched.

Ellie stared from their mother's face, to the doll, to Becky. Mama was angry and disgusted. She stopped trying to get Becky to take the doll. With a short hollow laugh she added, "Good God, can't even give the brat a present. Here, Ellie, you take her."

Ellie looked at Becky, and slowly accepted the doll. Becky's face was white and quivering, and she stared at the doll as if she were seeing a real ghost. Ellie thought she understood. They'd never had a doll before. And the doll did look something like their mother. She was a little glad Becky didn't like it, for that meant the doll might be hers.

"It's okay," she said. "I'll carry the doll for you, Becky." She looked at Heather to see if she had said the right thing.

"It's your doll too," Heather said. "Aster, I have to warn you about Becky. She's the most nervous child. She's scared to death of everything. It's really exasperating. She cries at everything."

"Yes, well . . . I'm sorry. That must be very difficult . . . for her, too."

Aunt Aster looked puzzled by everything, and perhaps a little disgusted too, but Ellie wasn't sure what about. Maybe she was only surprised that Becky was afraid of the doll.

She started out the door again. "We really should go now."

Then she did something strange. She reached back and took Becky's hand, pulling it out from behind her and holding on to it even though Becky looked as if she were trying at first to pull away.

Then they were going out into the hall and down the long flights of stairs, Aunt Aster in the lead, her long brown skirt dragging the steps behind her, and her arm reached back holding firmly to Becky. Her other hand clutched the sack and the railing as if she were afraid of falling. And you really did have to be careful on these stairs. The woman who lived next door had warned Ellie and Becky many times through her open door. "Take your sister's hand," she'd say to Ellie. Now, Ellie saw that Aunt Aster's white glove was already looking soiled from the bannister.

Ellie followed, the large doll pressed possessively against her. Hers, it was all hers. Becky didn't like it. The doll was heavy, but she was used to going up and down these steep steps and it didn't bother her. She could have laughed at Aunt Aster. She reminded Ellie of a kitten trying to get down from a tree.

When they reached the bottom Ellie turned and looked back up. Their mother stood at the distant top, five flights up, looking as tiny as a doll herself. The shadows of the hall suddenly engulfed her and she was gone, as if she had become part of it. A pang of something went through Ellie, like a sliver of coldness, of fear, or pain. She couldn't identify it. She felt sad. Would they ever see their mother again?

Then Aunt Aster was opening the door to the outside, and the noises of the street drew Ellie forward.

Just beyond the curb, parked on the rough cobblestone street, was the hack Aunt Aster must have hired. It had a black canvas roof and two seats. A man sat in the seat up front, the reins of the horses' held loosely in his hands, his elbows on his knees. He turned his head and spat stringy, brown tobacco juice into the street. All the men did that. Flies immediately collected on it. One of the horses shifted his weight from one leg to another. Their long tails swished at flies and shooed them up from their brown, shining rumps.

"Ready to go?" the man asked.

"Yes, we're ready."

There were steps, and places to enter, but no doors that opened and closed. The man didn't get down to help them up, so Aunt Aster lifted Becky into the seat. She slid across to sit on the far side. Ellie stepped forward, transferred the doll to the curve of one arm, and pulled herself up and into the seat to sit beside Becky.

Aunt Aster climbed in and settled on Ellie's right, and had barely sat down when the driver lifted a whip and cracked it over the horses backs. They began to trot. The buggy wheels bounced over the cobblestone and Ellie glimpsed tiny sparks, like the Fourth of July fireworks she had seen only last week. Ellie bounced too, her teeth clicking together. It was great fun. People she had known all her life paused on the boardwalk and watched them go by, but none of them waved. She knew them only because she saw them on the street, or on the stairs or in the hallway, not because they were friends. She didn't know their names. She wouldn't miss them, and they wouldn't miss her.

They headed away from the waterfront. For awhile Ellie watched the shops they passed with curiosity. Then they came to fewer shops and wider streets. She began to see big trees in empty lots, and large houses. Sometimes the houses were small and ugly and unpainted, then they'd leave that street and the houses would be white and pretty, with porches and rocking chairs on the porches, and sometimes people would be sitting in the chairs watching them go by. The horses trotted, and they left the cobble street and came to a smooth dirt street on which grass grew outside the tracks made by the hacks and buggies and wagons.

Ellie looked at the doll. She felt the doll's hair. It was soft and fine, and Ellie knew it was real. The brown eyes were as changeable as her mother's, with flecks of lighter brown within them. They were made of glass, they *must* be made of glass, but they seemed so real. It was as if all the while Ellie was looking at the doll, the doll was looking at Ellie.

"Zenoa," Ellie said aloud, to feel the name on her tongue.

Aunt Aster must have thought Ellie was talking to her.

She looked down. "Yes, it's a very unusual name, isn't it?"

Ellie nodded.

"And she's so beautiful," Ellie said softly. "Just like Mama. Look! She even has a tiny dimple in her chin, like Mama does."

"Yes, it's very strange how much she resembles your mother. Especially when she was your age."

"Do you think that's her age now? Zenoa's age? Eight, like me?"

"I think that might be very possible," Aunt Aster said with a smile. "At least we can pretend so, can't we?"

"Yes. I like that."

Ellie ran one finger down over the doll's pink cheek, and into the corner of the slightly parted lips. She hadn't noticed before, but four tiny white teeth were barely visible, and the tip of a red felt tongue. The doll's eyelashes were long, thick and very black. Just like Heather's. How odd to have such dark eyelashes with such golden hair. Ellie's own eyelashes were fair, so fair they were almost invisible.

She glanced sideways at Becky. She had felt Becky pull away so that her shoulder was no longer pressed against Ellie's side. Now she saw why.

Becky was staring at the doll again, and Ellie was at first stunned, then annoyed at the look in her eyes. There were times when she understood exactly how their mother felt. Especially when they were alone and it was up to her to make Becky behave.

"What's the matter with you, Becky?" she demanded. "The doll ain't going to hurt you. It's only a doll. It can't hurt you. It can't even twist its arms, see?" She twisted the arms for the doll, and discovered they did indeed move, just like her own. They moved forward and up over her head. She tried to put them out sideways, and heard something rip.

Aunt Aster said quickly, "I wouldn't be so rough with it if I were you, Eleanor. I think you've torn the sleeve."

Ellie had a sudden urge to force the doll's arm backwards, all the way back, the way Mama sometimes did Becky's, but

33

saw Aunt Aster watching her. She sat still, the doll between her knees, standing on the floor.

Aunt Aster leaned forward and looked beyond Ellie at Becky, and Ellie cut her eyes sideways to see what Becky was doing. Her mouth was puckered as if she were going to cry. Oh no, Ellie thought with her patience gone. Not now, not here, Becky. What if Aunt Aster hated having her crying the way their mother did? Becky would be whipped and then . . . what would Aunt Aster do to Ellie for not making her behave? There wasn't a room now to make Becky go to, no room where Becky would have to stay all the time, to do her crying alone where it wouldn't get on everyone's nerves. Ellie felt herself cringing away from Aunt Aster. Every movement made Becky jump and dodge, and Ellie's anger at Becky increased.

"Stop that, Becky!" Ellie lifted her right hand, reached around and slapped Becky on the side of the head. "Stop acting like such a scaredycat!"

Becky lifted her arms to protect her head, but didn't cry. Suddenly, to Ellie's surprise, she felt her own arm clutched, between the wrist and elbow, very hard, by a dry, warm hand. She looked up into Aunt Aster's angry eyes. Her aunt spoke without unclenching her teeth.

"Don't you ever do that again! Eleanor, do you understand me?"

Ellie forced a smile at her aunt. No, she didn't understand, but she nodded. She wanted to explain. Mama hit Becky all the time, and sometimes she told Ellie to hit her. If Ellie didn't, Mama would hit both of them. There were times when Becky had to be disciplined about her whining and crying and being so scared of everything. Didn't Aunt Aster understand that?

Aunt Aster released her arm, then reached out again, and Ellie dodged, lifting her right arm against attack. But instead of slapping her, Aunt Aster simply reached across Ellie to get hold of Becky.

She said in a gentle voice, "Come over here and sit by me." She pulled her up and over, and made room for Becky

34

on the other side. Ellie couldn't believe it. Aunt Aster was actually sitting with her arm around Becky.

"She's only a baby," Aunt Aster said. "She's barely six years old. The doll is too large for her. When we get home, sweetheart, we'll see if we can't find some of the old dolls. I know of one for certain that I think you might like. It's only five inches tall, and it's called a china doll. Do you know what china is?"

Ellie barely listened as Aunt Aster explained that a china doll was very fragile, that it could be broken because it was made of something like glass, but it was a nice little doll, and was her very own, and now could be Becky's.

Ellie twisted the doll's arm, but slowly, barely moving it, so that Aunt Aster wouldn't notice. She turned the doll's back to Aunt Aster and examined the face. She tugged at the long eyelashes, and a few came out in her fingers. She wiped them carefully off against the cracked leather seat of the hack. She gripped the tip of the little red tongue and pulled. She felt it give. In her fingers it grew longer, coming visibly out of the doll's mouth.

"What are you doing, Eleanor?" Aunt Aster asked. "You must take very good care of your beautiful doll. When we love something we take good care of it. You should pay more attention to where we are. You can play with the doll later. We're almost home. This is where your mother grew up. You're going to be in her old bedroom."

Ellie rubbed the doll's rounded cheek, and smiled up at Aunt Aster. The doll stared at her. It wasn't a real smile on the doll's lips, Ellie noticed, it was more like a smirk. And now the red tongue stuck out as if she were sticking it out at Ellie. She must be punished for that. Later. When they were home, and Aunt Aster wasn't watching.

To please Aunt Aster Ellie paid more attention to their surroundings.

They seemed to have left the city behind. The houses were farther apart, and there were large trees and large gardens. Then the driver was pulling to a stop in front of a tall grey shingled house that had a front yard and a walk going up to the porch. On each side of the walk were roses. On the porch was a porch swing and rocking chairs. The house had many sharp peaks in the roof and long, narrow windows.

"Here we are, children," Aunt Aster said.

This time the driver got down and came to the side of the buggy. He helped Becky, then Aunt Aster, and then Ellie with her doll.

"My," he said. "That's some doll you got there."

He didn't seem to notice the tongue.

"Yes," Ellie said. "Her name is Zenoa and she looks exactly like my mother."

"You must have a very pretty mother."

"Yes. She's—" Ellie stopped. She'd been going to say that her mother was going to have a new baby, but then she thought it might not be a proper thing to say to a man. Especially a strange man.

That was the reason Heather could no longer keep her and Becky, Ellie told herself. The new baby had to have their room. But there was another reason too. Mama hated them, especially Becky. Becky was such a crybaby that their mother couldn't stand having her around.

Ellie went up the walk, following behind Aunt Aster and Becky, whose hand was still held firmly in the white, soiled glove. But Ellie could tell by the tilt of Becky's head and the lift of her shoulders that she was scared. How long would Aunt Aster put up with Becky being a baby before she got angry, like Mama?

At the door Aunt Aster turned loose of Becky's hand, and Becky wanted to grab it again and hold it, forever, to be safe. But she waited instead while Aunt Aster took a key from a handbag that had been covered by her shawl, and unlocked the front door. The door had an oval glass in it that was made of all different colors, blue, green, yellow, and figures that looked like fat, naked babies flying, their wings almost too tiny to hold them up. Becky looked at them closely, searching for horns, for forked tails, but then she decided they were really angels. Maybe that meant this would be a good house, where bad things didn't fly through the night and hover over her bed. But she would have to wait and watch, and be sure. '

She was afraid to enter this strange place, even though it had angels on the door. The doll was here, bringing with it the black ghost. Every time she looked at the doll, and she tried hard not to look, she saw the black ghost that was like gauze over its hair. Why did no one else see it? But only at times did Ellie see the things Becky saw.

The door opened, as if it were pulled from something invisible that was waiting inside. Aunt Aster entered, her long brown skirt sweeping the raised threshold. Becky felt Ellie push her, and she went forward into the hallway.

A stairway rose, going up one flight and stopping on a landing. Becky saw darkness there, and in the darkness there were eyes on the walls. Faces, framed in heavy frames, some of which were gold and some dark wood. Aunt Aster began climbing the stairs. The railing she moved her hand along was sleek wood, polished and clean.

Becky followed her. She looked behind to make sure Ellie was coming too, and looked directly into the face of the doll. It was staring at her, its straight lips tucked into dimples in the corner, its red tongue sticking out. The black ghost floating over its head was thicker now, making Ellie look as if a veil hung in front of her face.

Couldn't Ellie see it?

Becky turned quickly away and hurried to catch up with Aunt Aster, going into the strange house that looked so large and so dark. The rooms seemed to go on and on, doors opening onto other rooms, instead of being stopped by walls that separated flat from flat, the way she had always been used to.

Aunt Aster took them into a bedroom that had a bed that stood up off the floor on fat, glossy legs. A heavy, loosely woven bedspread covered it, hanging almost to the floor. Over the bed was a framed picture of the doll that Ellie carried.

37

Becky cried out, then remembered and clamped both hands over her mouth, shutting off the cry.

Aunt Aster said, "That's your mother, when she was a very small child, Becky."

Becky blinked and looked at it again. It still looked just like the doll.

"This is your room, girls," Aunt Aster said. "This was your mother's room when she was still at home."

Ellie said, "The bed is so big. Our bed at home was on the floor."

"Then you have to be careful not to fall out," Aunt Aster smiled.

But the smile looked as if it weren't real. It stretched her lips, leaving her eyes with the sadness. And, Becky thought suddenly, that was the way with the doll. Its lips were stretched, as if it might smile in a minute, but its eyes weren't smiling. They weren't sad, though. They were just *watching*.

"We'll put your things right over here in the dresser drawer. Eleanor, you can put your things in this drawer, and Becky, you can have this one." Then she looked into the sack and said, "But first, we'll have to launder them."

Becky looked around. The room was so big. Bigger than their whole flat. It had two windows, but they were covered with lace curtains. There was a rug on the floor that had strange figures woven in it. The furniture was so big and dark. And there was the picture on the wall just above the bed where it could look down at her when she slept.

She backed toward the door. "I don't want to stay here."

Ellie jabbed Becky with her elbow. "Hush!"

Aunt Aster looked carefully at Becky and asked, "Why not, dear?"

Becky pointed at the floor. "What are these things on the rug?"

"Why . . . they're only roses, with stems, and leaves."

Becky lifted her eyes toward the picture on the wall above the bed, then looked at the doll in Ellie's arms. Both the doll and the picture watched her, eyes round and large, mouths so much alike, with the upper lip fuller than the lower, and the tiny dimple in the chin a dot of darkness.

The picture didn't have a black ghost, but the doll . . .

Becky tried to talk, and couldn't. She wanted to tell Aunt Aster about the black ghost that had been part of her mother and was now part of the doll, but words didn't form.

Ellie spoke for her, as always, "She didn't mean that, Aunt Aster. She likes the room."

As always, too, she got it all wrong.

Four

She felt nervous, anxious, yet oddly stimulated to action, as if she had a houseful of company that she had to feed and entertain. First, after looking into their pitifully few things, she found them so soiled they had to be taken down to the laundry room and put to soak. The children trailed along. Then she had to prepare lunch. Sir Thomas came out from hiding, and Becky looked at him and screamed. The cat ran to hide again.

"It's only a cat," Eleanor said, with that tone of impatience she often used with the younger child.

Aster sighed. Becky, the poor child, was, as she had been warned, afraid of her own shadow, so to speak. Aster put her hand gently on the child's head. Her hair was thick and curly, but it was also brown and lustrous, darker than Heather's had been when she was that age, and much darker than Eleanor's pale, thin hair.

"Come on Sir Thomas, let Becky see you. She won't scream again, she promises, don't you Becky?"

Becky nodded. Her mouth, still almost formless, like a baby's, was held in a pucker, as if to release it would allow it to tremble. Her chin too, puckered.

"Come on, kitty, kitty, kitty. Help me call him, girls. This is his home too, and you three must get used to one another."

They called. Eleanor got down on her knees, the thirty-inch doll held awkwardly in the curve of her left arm. She looked beneath the pie safe.

"He's in there," she said.

"Call him, Becky."

Becky said tremulously, "Kitty, kitty."

40

Sir Thomas peeked out, his big yellow head filling the space between the bottom of the safe and the floor. His eyes were wide and alarmed, but he was settling down.

"Pet him," Aster suggested. "He's very gentle. Cats won't hurt you, if you don't hurt them. If you hurt a cat it might scratch just to defend itself, but all cats are very eager to be friends. Wouldn't you, if you were that small and had no hands?"

Becky nodded. Then she squatted, her plump knees round in their white, soiled stockings. Aster made a note to relieve her of them and put them to soak too, along with her own gloves and the rest of the children's things. Tomorrow, she thought to herself as Becky and Eleanor made friends with the cat, they'd go shopping and get material to make clothes.

She brought out a cold lunch of cheese, bread, and milk, and felt again the awkwardness of being responsible for people other than herself. Especially such small, vulnerable people.

"Now you set down right there, and you behave," Eleanor said very crossly, "and don't you move or I'll knock your head off."

Aster whirled and looked at Eleanor, but she was talking to the doll, not Becky.

"What a terrible thing to say," Aster said. "Even to your doll."

Eleanor smiled faintly at Aster, but didn't answer. It was the same timid, apologetic smile Eleanor had used when Aster scolded her for slapping Becky earlier, but Aster had a feeling it was only a surface smile.

The children weren't comfortable either, Aster saw as they ate. Both girls kept looking at her as if they were afraid of making the wrong move. Becky watched her carefully as she reached up to pick up her glass of milk.

"Be careful," Eleanor warned in the low, hissing voice Aster had noticed she used with Becky. "Don't spill it."

Aster got up. "Perhaps the glass is too large. Wait, I'll get a smaller one."

She poured the milk into a small glass, and was rewarded by a touching look of gratitude.

What kind of treatment had these poor children been used to, she wondered. What terrible kind of tension had they lived under? What had Heather transferred to Eleanor? The older sister acted like a harsh disciplinarian herself.

With a guilty twinge Aster found herself longing for her chair and the silence and privacy of her room. Yet here she was responsible for two little girls who didn't seem to know what it was to be treated with love and kindness.

"After lunch do you take naps?" she asked, hoping they would say yes.

Eleanor and Becky looked at each other, but neither answered. Aster had a sudden notion they didn't know what naps were.

"A nap," she explained, "is really a period of daytime sleep. Or just rest, sometimes. It helps your food to digest if you rest quietly for an hour after the noon meal."

That might be a slight exaggeration, but Aster felt desperate for time alone. The girls might as well become adjusted to taking an hour's rest after dinner.

She led them to the washroom and showed them how to use the sink for washing. They had to use the long-handled dipper and carefully ladle the water into the sink, after the stopper was in place. After washing, she showed them where the towel hung. Then she took them into the backyard and showed them the outhouse, hidden among vines and trees. Eleanor was carrying the doll again, and Aster had to hold it while Eleanor went into the outhouse to relieve herself. When it came time for Becky to go she began to cry.

Eleanor hissed at her, "Shhh. It's just a little place, there's nothing to hurt you."

Aster gave the doll back to Eleanor and took Becky by the hand. She showed her the interior of the outhouse. It had been whitewashed, and was clean and smelled of the lime that had been put into the dug-out space beneath the seat with the two holes. She opened the cover on one hole and explained to Becky that it was really all right. Reluctantly, Becky accepted the outhouse. As Aster stood waiting, she wondered what toilet arrangements were made at the flat where they had lived.

But she didn't ask.

When she finally got the children back upstairs and took them to their room for their naps, Becky clutched at her hand. Aster looked down into the small face.

"Please," the child said in a voice so low it was almost a whisper, "can I go with you?"

Surprised, Aster said, "Wouldn't you rather stay with your sister?"

Becky looked at the doll in Eleanor's arms, then back up at Aster, her face filled with pleading. "Please?"

Aster sighed and relented. "If it's all right with Eleanor."

Eleanor shrugged.

Aster hesitated, looking at the small girl who held the large, lovely doll in her arms. Alone, Eleanor might have looked very pretty with her wide-set hazel eyes. Her hair was not as pretty as Becky's, but it could be prettier if arranged better. It fell in a bang over her eyebrows as if it had been cut recently, and was tied into two pigtails, unbraided. The ends reached past her shoulders. Her face was too thin for an eight-year-old child. Aster made a promise to herself to fatten them both.

"I like this room," Eleanor said. "I'm not afraid. Not like Becky is."

Becky clung even tighter to Aster's hand. She wasn't going to be alone after all, not even for an hour of rest. Aster felt the strangeness of the child trotting along so willingly at her side. In the bedroom she lifted the little girl onto her own bed, to lie on top of the white, crocheted spread. She had made it herself, as she had the one in Heather's room, and it had taken a year. The child yielded to her every touch, eager to please. Aster pulled the edge of the summer comforter up from the foot of the bed where she kept it folded on top of the bedspread. She covered Becky's bare feet, and noticed how dirty they were. As if the child hadn't been bathed in a month. And now here she was lying on her pure white spread. Ah, but, so what?

"Now close your eyes," Aster said. "And try to sleep."

Becky closed her eyes obediently.

Aster went to her chair by the double windows. She pulled aside the old lace curtain that had hung there as long as she could remember and pushed up the window. Soft, summer air eased in, touching her face with warmth. She sat back in the rocking chair and put her feet up onto the footstool. A small cushion attached to the back of the chair had developed a curve that fit the shape of her head over long years of use.

She closed her eyes, hoping the children would sleep. Sir Thomas came to sit by her chair and purr. She put her hand down to caress his head.

The silence lulled her. This was what she was used to. Daily, since she was young, she had come to this chair after dinner for an hour of rest. After the other children had moved away, after Mama and Papa grew old, the silence grew more profound. After their deaths the silence was broken only by the purr of the cat, and by birds singing outside the window, and sometimes the rattle of a carriage or buggy on the road and the clip-clop of horses' feet. It was a silence she had grown used to and, she realized now, had depended upon.

Ellie stared at the closed door for a long time, then she turned and looked about the room. The bed took up the middle of one wall. Above it hung the picture of Heather. She saw as she looked more closely at the picture that it was mainly the doll's mouth that was like the girl in the picture.

Ellie carefully placed the doll on the bed, stretching to reach the middle. She leaned it against the pillows and then stood back. The picture smiled just a little, the doll almost smiled, but not quite. Zenoa only had a look on her mouth that in a minute she might smile. Her red tongue stuck out at Ellie in a very sassy way. Sometimes Ellie ignored naughty behavior. But later, she'd punish her, just in case she thought she was getting away with something. Right now, Ellie was busy looking at the room.

Across from the bed was a dresser, with a large, oval mirror. On the dresser was a white scarf, edged in lace, and there were pretty little bowls with lids, that looked as if they might hold something that smelled nice. She opened them and looked in, and found nothing.

There was a tall chest that matched the dresser against another wall. The windows were covered with white lace curtains that had no rips and tears. Ellie went to the window, parted the panels of lace and looked out. Down below was a garden, and a fence that separated it from the yard next door. A large tree threw its shade onto the edge of the garden. There were flowers in the garden, but other things too that Ellie had never seen before outside a market. Tomatoes hung red and ripe on a vine that reached up over a fence. But behind Ellie was the strange, still room, and the silence in the big house in which only Aunt Aster lived.

She turned and looked at the door. Closed. Leaving her alone in a room for the first time in her life. Becky hadn't wanted to stay with her. Becky was gone, somewhere in the house.

Why did you go and leave me?

Why has our mother given us away?

Her eyes found the doll on the bed, with the large brown eyes and the sassy tongue still sticking out between her lips.

Ellie's own lips tightened.

She ran to the bed, grabbed the doll by the arm and yanked it toward her. Her hand raised and came down, hard, on the side of the doll's head.

"I wish you'd never been born! I hate you! I'm going to find another place for you to live!"

Rage fired by action surged through Ellie. She trembled with her rage, and she felt the satisfaction that was released in striking the doll. She raked her fingers down across its cheek the way she had seen Heather do Becky one day. Blood had beaded along the scratch on Becky's cheek, but the scratch on the doll's cheek merely showed something white beneath the pink skin. The doll looked at her, the half-smile curling the corners of its mouth inward, and the slight overbite pushing out the upper lip, and the tongue sticking out at her. *Yah, yah, yah, you can't hurt me.*

"I'll show you, you terrible child!"

Ellie slapped it, again and again. She put her fingers into its hair and pulled. A large clump came out, revealing white scalp with tiny holes. Another clump of hair came out in Ellie's fingers, and another.

"You bad thing, you terrible thing, I don't know why you were ever born . . ."

She pushed her fingers into the eyes, and felt them go back into the head as if they were on springs. But they were real eyes, and Ellie pushed harder. *I'll make you blind. You'll never look at me again.* Heather didn't want to look at her. *Get out of here,* she'd said so many times Ellie couldn't remember them all. *Get out of my sight, you're the ugliest thing I ever saw. At least Becky was born beautiful. Get out of my sight.*

Ellie sat on the floor panting with exhaustion. Zenoa lay face down. Ellie didn't want to see her face. But as she got up she saw the clumps of hair on the floor.

She gathered them up and stuffed them between the mattress and springs.

Then she picked up the doll, and smoothed down what was left of the hair. In the gloomy light she saw that one of the doll's eyes wouldn't open. She began to pick at the eyelashes, trying to pull the eye open, but it remained shut, the lashes black against the scratched cheek. Carefully, Ellie tried to make the doll look right again. She brushed its hair with her hand, and she brushed its cheeks.

Zenoa.

Not *the doll*, but *Zenoa*.

It was as if the doll had whispered to her.

Aster suddenly felt tense, as if a door had closed somewhere below. She remained in her chair, listening.

She heard the soft, even breathing of the child sleeping on her bed. She heard the soft purring of the cat, and then she heard the purring stop.

Then, in the growing silence as even the cat listened, she heard the other.

"What did I tell you? Didn't I tell you to be still? Didn't I warn you what would happen if you didn't mind me? I'll knock your ugly head off. Do you hear me? I'll kill you. You bad, bad girl. You don't even deserve to live. I don't know why you were even born."

The voice came as if from somewhere far away, it was so

soft, but the anger and the words spoken jolted Aster as if she were in a nightmare.

She stood up. The sounds of slapping, or hitting, followed the sound of the voice like a funeral wake.

Aster glanced at Becky. The little girl was still soundly asleep. She had turned. With one hand under her cheek, she looked so young, even younger than her six years.

Aster hurried out of the room, closing the door softly behind her. The sounds of disturbance were clearer in the hallway, coming from Heather's room.

She opened the door.

Eleanor stood by the foot of the bed, leaning over the doll. She was slapping it viciously, her hand striking the side of the doll's head, jolting it so hard it looked as if the head should fall and roll.

"I hate you, I hate you! I wish you'd never been born!"

"Eleanor!"

Eleanor jerked around, staring at Aster, her left hand holding the arm of the doll. It hung in her hand with the head twisted sideways, the hair looking as if it had been pulled and disarranged. The ribbon that had held it back on the left side had come untied and now strung down against the cheek limply.

Eleanor straightened, smiled at Aster, and then began to brush the doll's hair gently.

"What on earth were you doing?" Aster asked, a sick, helpless feeling starting somewhere deep in her heart.

"Nothing," Eleanor said.

Aster felt her own heart pounding. She should do something, she felt, but what? She didn't know how to handle children. And this was something she had never expected. What on earth did it mean?

"You were beating your new doll?"

"No, I wasn't."

Aster decided against arguing with her. She crossed the room and took the doll from Eleanor's hands.

She was shocked at its appearance. The doll had been ruined. In such a short time, how could a young child have done

47

so much damage to a doll?

The cheeks were scratched, hair had been pulled from all over the head, leaving patches of scalp like sores. But most hideous, one eye had been shoved inward so far it now appeared to be permanently shut. The other eye stared open and unscathed, surrounded by dark eyelashes. The dress was torn.

Aster did not understand this kind of destruction, and it scared her.

"You have ruined your doll, Eleanor. You don't deserve to have it, so we'll put it up and you can't play with it anymore."

Eleanor's mouth opened, but it was a moment before she began to cry. She reached her hands up for the doll, her fingers waving and wiggling. "No, no, no. Please, let me have her, let me have Zenoa. *Please. Don't take her away from me.*"

The child's eyes held a desperation that seemed only a deeper step into this strangeness that had come so suddenly into Aster's life. She felt the doll should be removed from Eleanor for a few days, but she didn't have the heart to do it. Slowly she lowered the doll. Eleanor snatched it and buried her face against it, weeping hollowly.

"You must be kind to your doll," Aster said. "Look, we'll fix her hair again, and try to make her pretty. You want her to be pretty, don't you?"

"Yes."

Aster retied the ribbon, and used the hair brush from the dresser to try to arrange the hair to cover the bald spots. But it would take a needle and thread from her sewing box to repair the sleeve, and there was no way she could undo the deep scratches on the doll's cheeks or open the one eye. The mechanism behind it must have broken.

She looked at Eleanor, and saw the little girl smiling up at her innocently, tears still clinging in drops to her lower lashes.

Five

In the days that followed Aster tried to get used to having children around. She managed to recover from somewhere long in her past the ability to care for them. She braided hair, even Becky's curls, and she washed faces and hands and gave baths and saw to it they washed themselves. She cooked meals she thought they would grow healthy on, and took them to the store with her and bought material and began the long and tedious chore of sewing new dresses. School would be starting in a few weeks, and they would need at least four dresses.

She went into the attic to look for old toys with the girls trailing along. Becky peered timorously over her shoulders at the deep shadows that skulked behind the light of the candle, while Aster tried to keep her mind on the adventure. They uncovered a small tea set that had belonged to Heather, and which was destined to become one of Eleanor's favorite playthings. The three old dolls also came downstairs, and the child-sized table and chairs that were so old Aster didn't know what child had owned them first. She carried the table with one hand, the candle held carefully in the other, while behind came Eleanor with a chair and a doll, and Becky with the other two little chairs. When they reached the girls' bedroom and set the table and chairs up in the space between the foot of the bed and the dresser, Eleanor happily arranged the tea things, tiny cups and saucers, and set her dolls to having tea.

But Becky wouldn't stay. She never stayed in the room in

the daytime, preferring to go wherever Aster went. Nor did she seem interested in any of the old dolls, even the small china doll. She looked at everything with that same fearful look that seemed to frustrate Eleanor so much.

Aster offered her the china doll. Becky put her hands behind her back, looked at the doll's old face, and said, "I don't like its face."

"Very well, I'll make you a doll, Becky, when I have time, after I finish your new dress. Would you like that?" Aster added, "Eleanor can add the china doll to her tea party."

Becky looked at her wide-eyed and said nothing. There were times when Aster understood Eleanor's frustration with Becky. The child seemed afraid to talk. Yet at other times she would suddenly start screaming, nearly scaring Aster out of her wits.

In the middle of the first night, when in her sleep Aster had forgotten the children were there, that tortured scream woke her.

Aster stumbled out of bed and in the dark ran down the hall to try to find the source of the cry, and by the time she reached the door of Heather's old room she remembered the children.

She entered the room where a pale light flickered from the candle she had left burning so the children would not be so afraid.

Becky was trying to climb the head of the bed, staring over her shoulder at something that terrified her. Aster took the child in her arms, felt the stiff, trembling body, and saw the direction of the gaze. She was looking at the dresser, where the candle flame was reflected in the mirror. But the doll Heather had given them was also on the dresser. Aster had set it there when she had tucked the girls into bed.

"What is it?" Aster asked. "Is it the candlelight?"

Eleanor had sat up in bed, wide-eyed. Becky was still screaming, and Aster asked Eleanor, "Is she afraid of candlelight?"

Eleanor shook her head.

Becky pointed. *"The doll. Make it go away."*

Aster turned Becky's face against her chest so the child couldn't see, and said over her head to Eleanor, "Put the doll out of sight on the floor."

Eleanor slipped out of bed and took the doll off the dresser.

In Aster's arms Becky went back to sleep.

The next night Aster moved the doll before the children were put to bed. She placed it in the corner of the room where the candlelight from the dresser wouldn't touch it. But when Becky's scream brought her stumbling from her room, the doll had mysteriously reappeared on the dresser, sitting against the mirror where Aster had put it the first night.

"Why did you move it?" Aster asked Eleanor, after Becky's screams had subsided. She held the small girl and rocked her, blinking over her head at Eleanor, who had sat up in the bed round-eyed, as if she would never sleep again.

"I didn't," she said.

Aster said nothing. Obviously the child was lying, but the look on Eleanor's face was of such innocence that it only confounded Aster. She had told Eleanor several times to take good care of her once-beautiful doll, and even though she hadn't caught her beating it again, she could see each day by the doll's appearance that Eleanor was still very rough with it. The lovely hair was now thin and ragged. One of the ribbons had disappeared.

On the following night when Becky again was screaming about the doll, and Aster again found it in a location where Eleanor swore she hadn't put it, but which was in full sight of Becky, Aster tightened her mouth and made a decision.

"There, there, Becky, it's all right. Aunt Aster will take the doll away."

She settled Becky back onto her pillow and went to get the doll.

A strange mewling sound started up from the bed and Aster turned. It was Eleanor.

Eleanor's face was twisted, and the agonized cry poured quietly from her open, rounded mouth. She stretched out

51

her arms for the doll, she wept almost silent tears, in terrible contrast to Becky's screams.

"But Eleanor," Aster said. "If you would leave the doll out of Becky's sight, if you wouldn't move it, you could keep the doll in your room."

"I didn't move it," Eleanor sobbed, her voice catching. "Becky did."

Becky shook her head. "No, no, no."

"It will be just outside the door. I promise. And when Becky gets used to sleeping in a strange room, I'll put the doll back."

She would have given in and searched for some other solution if Eleanor hadn't been satisfied with having the doll just outside the door. She stopped fretting, scooted down into bed, and seemed satisfied.

Aster set the doll in the hall. Then she put a new candle in the old holder in the hall and lighted it, so that she wouldn't be stumbling in the dark when the children needed her.

The next day Aster made Becky a rag doll. She seemed to have a fear of doll faces, so Aster made it faceless.

Becky stood at Aster's knees, watching each stitch that went into the making of the doll. Aster cut two pieces of round, white cloth. Then she sewed the two rounds together and stuffed it with old rags. At the neck she sewed on the body, made of a stocking stuffed with rags, and a dress that hung over the armless, legless doll.

When she handed the homemade doll to Becky she was rewarded with such a look of love and wonder that she felt it melting into her heart and bones. As the little girl hugged the doll against her cheek, she knew the change in her life had been worthwhile. The look on the child's face made everything worthwhile.

Then, like a whisper in her ear, a memory struck her.

There's no reason you would ever have to be alone.

Mister Jessup had said that. What had he meant by it? Had he meant that he might be interested in her?

She sat a moment longer mulling it over, then set it aside

in her mind with a tart, well, it doesn't matter now, does it? It was time to start supper.

Becky went out with her to the garden to pick onions and tomatoes, carrying the rag doll.

She kept the rag doll on her lap at suppertime, just as Eleanor always brought Zenoa with her to the table, placing the large doll in one of the empty chairs.

That night Becky hugged the rag doll, and she didn't wake screaming.

For two nights Becky slept without waking, so Aster left the large doll behind, in the corner of their room on Eleanor's side of the bed where Becky couldn't see it.

Aster kissed both girls goodnight, and set a fresh candle on the dresser to burn slowly.

"See the flame dance in the mirror, Becky," she said. "See, you will never be in the dark. Watch it until you sleep."

Becky had seemed especially afraid of the dark, which to Aster was more understandable than some of her other more vague fears, which Becky was unable to verbally express.

At the door Aster looked back. Eleanor's eyes were already closed, and Becky's were drooping. Aster stepped into the hall, leaving the door part way open. Dim light fluttered through the hallway from the candle bracket on the wall. The smell of burning wax was pleasantly aromatic.

She went downstairs, enjoying this moment of being alone. It was like having a load removed from her shoulders when the children went to bed and to sleep. She loved the children, she felt very sorry for them, and she would never wish them to be elsewhere.

But . . .

She felt trapped.

She went back to the kitchen where she had left a candle burning. Then, after pausing, she went outside.

She stood on the long, back porch. Moonlight shone brightly onto the garden in the corner of the yard, and she went down the steps and stopped on the path.

There was a faint light in Mister Jessup's house, in one of

53

the upper rooms. Was it his bedroom?

She felt embarrassed for even wondering, for standing there looking at a window that could be a man's bedroom.

She walked around the house. She passed through deep shadows at the end of the house and beneath the trees, and at the front walked again into moonlight.

The roses looked different in the light of the moon, their colors changed, darkened, made neutral.

She carefully felt along a stem for a place not so peppered with thorns, and attempted to break off a rose.

"Lovely night, isn't it?"

The voice startled her, and she jerked around, her fingers closing over a stem of thorns in the process. She saw the man on the walk beyond the gate, a shadowy figure in the dark beneath the trees. But it was Mister Jessup, no doubt. He must have gone to the mailbox.

"Yes, yes," she said. "Very lovely."

"I was a bit late looking for my mail. I was getting ready for bed when I remembered."

He came closer, with something white in his hands. He motioned it toward her.

"My newspaper. You wouldn't think I'd forget my newspaper since I take it from my box every day and read it every evening, but this evening I worked later than usual."

She nodded, smiled, and nodded.

"How're you getting along with the young ladies?"

"Oh, very well, thank you."

"They're certainly quiet children."

"Oh." She hadn't thought of it before, but she supposed they were. They didn't go outside to play, even though she had tried to show them what interesting things there were to do. The old swing was still on the tree, for instance. But they only looked at it and returned to the house. They played almost too quietly for children, their voices never loud enough to hear beyond the walls of the house. Except, perhaps, for Becky's occasional screaming fits. But, obviously, he hadn't heard one of those. "Yes, they are."

They stood a moment longer. She could think of nothing

to say, and evidently neither could he. She thought he was going to say more, but then he only said goodnight and went toward his own gate. Covertly she watched him go up the walk in front of his house and disappear into the shadows on his porch. She heard his door close.

She turned back to her own door, roses forgotten.

Becky stared at the candlelight in the mirror. It was like there were two candles on the dresser instead of only one. The flame danced up and wavered and moved and settled back, and then danced up again, on and on. In the bed beside her Ellie slept. Becky knew she was asleep because she had covered her head. Ellie always scrunched farther and farther down in bed until her whole head was covered, even on hot nights such as tonight.

The flames danced, one on the dresser and one in the mirror, and Becky closed her eyes.

Her rag dolly was warm and comfortable beneath her cheek, its head a pillow upon the big pillow that was part of the bed.

Becky listened to the quiet world she now lived in. She remembered the sounds of people's voices, of footsteps on the floors of other flats. She remembered the sound of her mother's laughter as she talked to their new papa. She listened now to the silence that was her new world.

This world was as frightening as that. If she opened her eyes she would see ghosts. They rose in dark corners, and floated in darkness beneath the bed. A black world made up of things that could see in the dark. Things with wings that fluttered in the night, and huge eyes that watched her.

She tried to keep her eyes tightly closed, but something slipping softly in the shadows brought them open again. She saw the tall post at the corner of the bed, and the shadows licking away from the candlelight. But she could still hear someone out of sight slipping closer to the bed. *Mama.* Home from the tavern to punish her. No. This wasn't Mama's house. Mama didn't live here anymore. Mama wouldn't come here to punish her. But . . .

Someone . . . *someone* . . . was crouching in the room. Over by the dresser. It wasn't the sound a ghost made. This was real.

A tight, icy band squeezed her chest so hard she couldn't breathe.

Shut your eyes . . . don't open your eyes. They'll go away. If you don't open your eyes you won't see what's there, and day will come again, and it will be all right. She couldn't make her eyes go shut. She couldn't breathe. The sound by the dresser had stopped. Someone was looking at her.

She cast her eyes desperately in search, and then she saw the head of the doll, barely above the high mattress of the bed. It stared at her, its eyes dark and terrible. As she returned its stare it came closer, away from the dresser and to the bed. Its eyes looked at her steadily over the quilt at the foot of the bed. Its head came higher, edging upward, as if it climbed the quilt hanging there. It was coming to kill her. She could see in its eyes that it meant for her to die.

Arched above the doll's head was the black ghost trembling and quivering.

Come here. Come to me, or I shall come and get you.

Becky gasped. She stopped the scream that was bursting in her throat. She strangled on it.

I'm coming to get you, Becky.

The doll edged upward, its head as high now as hers. The black ghost gathered in its hair, moving and stirring within itself, growing blacker and thicker and more powerful.

Becky screamed.

The doll disappeared into the shadows between the dresser and the bed.

Ellie woke, jolted by Becky's scream. At first she was back in the flat, on a pallet on the floor. Then she saw the dresser and the candlelight, and the distance from the top of the bed to the floor. She turned, reaching for Becky.

"Shhh, Becky. Shhh!" Aunt Aster would take her doll out of the room again if she heard Becky screaming. "Shut up,

56

Becky! Shut up! Nothing's going to hurt you here at Aunt Aster's house."

"The d-d-doll," Becky whimpered. "It was coming up the bed. It's going to kill me."

"No, silly! You dreamed, that's all."

"It was! It was! It's hiding now. At the foot of the bed. It was coming up. It was!"

"You're crazy!" Ellie hissed at her in desperation. "Listen, Becky, do you want Aunt Aster to make us go back to Mama's? *Do you?*"

"No. No."

"Then shut up! Don't yell at night. Don't . . ."

Ellie watched the door, afraid. The footsteps running into their room were the footsteps of their mother, and Ellie tried to protect Becky by pulling her down and making her be quiet.

Then she saw it was Aunt Aster, not Mama, with her hair down in a single braid, and her eyes blinking wide.

Aunt Aster entered the room, paused and looked down at something on the floor, then stepped over it and came to the bed. Ellie drew back. Aunt Aster had not slapped Becky even once. But Ellie watched her, nevertheless, expecting any time the hand to reach back, long fingers straight, and then fly forward against Becky's head.

Instead, Aunt Aster gathered Becky into her arms and started patting her on the back, and in a voice that was almost like singing, told her, "There, there, it's all right, it's all right, Becky. Aunt Aster's here, and you're fine. Eleanor is here, right beside you. The candle is still burning. See its flame in the mirror?"

Becky usually never talked much when she had the bad dreams in the night, but this time she pointed toward the dresser and said in a quavering voice, "It was there, coming up the foot of the bed. *It was there.*"

"What was there, dear?"

"The d-doll. It was there, staring at me. It was coming to get me. It came out of the corner to get me."

"No, no, no."

57

Becky nodded her head up and down, up and down, but she said no more. Her face turned and hid against Aunt Aster's breast. Above her head Aunt Aster stared at Ellie, and Ellie saw harsh disapproval in her eyes.

Becky had grown quiet before Aunt Aster asked softly, "Why did you move the doll again, Eleanor?"

Ellie returned her stare. She didn't know what Aunt Aster was talking about. It was like the other nights, before Aunt Aster had started taking the doll out of the room. Aunt Aster thought Ellie had put the doll on the dresser, but Ellie hadn't.

She turned, looking toward the corner where Aunt Aster had left Zenoa.

The corner was empty.

Six

Aster eased the sleeping child down into bed and pulled the sheet up beneath her chin. Eleanor, she saw, was lying down but still wide awake. Her eyes looked huge and round in the flickering light of the candle on the dresser.

Just looking at her made Aster feel a little uneasy. What was the child made of? She seemed to want to comfort Becky. She seemed at times even maternalistic and loving. So then why did she do the things that she knew would terrify her little sister?

Aster picked up the doll. It had lain sprawled on the floor, face down, between the dresser and the bed as if it had fallen off the dresser. She stood holding it a moment, wondering if she should just start taking it out of the room again. No, she told herself. Eleanor must learn to obey.

She took the doll back to the corner on Eleanor's side of the bed and sat it on the floor. When she looked at Eleanor the large, round eyes were watching her.

Speaking softly, so as not to waken Becky, she said, "I need to have a talk with you tomorrow, Eleanor."

She started to touch the child, then decided this was not the time to offer sympathy in any form. Instead she said, "Now close your eyes and go to sleep, and don't get out of bed again until morning."

Eleanor blinked rapidly a few times, but said nothing.

Aster left the room and hesitated in the hall. A deep sadness had invaded her. Why did she feel as if she had just been as cruel to Eleanor with her spoken words as Eleanor's own mother?

She went back to her room and lighted her own candle. She didn't feel like lying in the dark. The clock on the shelf ticked slowly. One-thirty. Was that all? It would be hours before the night ended.

She sat down in the rocking chair and leaned her head back and closed her eyes. Slowly she began to rock. Other sleeping arrangements would have to be made if she couldn't talk some sense into Eleanor. Would giving them separate rooms be better? She just couldn't bring Becky into her own room. She couldn't give up all her privacy. She just wasn't used to having children around. How long would it take her to get used to it?

Ellie couldn't sleep. She lay with her cheek on her hand, her eyes on the doll. Aunt Aster had told her to stay in bed and not get out again until morning. But she hadn't been out of bed, she had wanted to tell Aunt Aster. She hadn't known what to say, she couldn't just say *I didn't put the doll there, I didn't get out of bed,* because if she hadn't done it, who had? Becky? She didn't want to get Becky in trouble. Any minute, every time Aunt Aster came toward Becky, she expected to see the sudden change in her eyes, the lift of the hand, and the hard slaps. Any minute. Ellie watched her aunt for the changes she had seen in her mother. Those swift changes, those sudden movements, and the slaps, the strikes, sometimes with the rolled fist.

But she didn't know who had moved the doll. It was like the other times. Someone did it, but who? She had told Aunt Aster she hadn't done it, those other nights, but Aunt Aster didn't believe her. And all Becky did was scream and cry.

At times that made Ellie so angry she felt like slapping Becky too.

Instead, she slapped the doll.

Without realizing she had gone to sleep, she was waking, and the room was light. Aunt Aster was helping Becky get dressed. Ellie sat up and looked toward the corner.

Zenoa sat exactly as Aunt Aster had placed her, with her round brown eye staring at the bedpost, and her funny little mouth tucked in at the corners as if she might burst out laughing. It was almost as if she was making fun of Ellie, for getting in trouble all the time with Aunt Aster. It was as if Zenoa knew, and was laughing inside.

Ellie stooped toward her and whispered, "I'm going to have a talk with you, later. You won't be laughing then."

She looked up to see Aunt Aster watching her. But instead of Aunt Aster scolding, she said, "Put on your new dress today, Eleanor, and bring your dirty dress and underwear down to the laundry room."

Oh great! She had been looking at the new dress Aunt Aster made since the day it was finished, wondering when she'd get to wear it because Aunt Aster had said it was for everyday. It was what Aunt Aster called plaid, with red and blue stripes crossing and making boxes. Becky had one exactly like it.

Ellie dressed while Aunt Aster brushed Becky's hair. Becky stood between Aunt Aster's knees with the rag doll tight under her arm. Ellie brushed her own hair and then stood at Aunt Aster's knees while the braids were put in. She wondered if maybe Aunt Aster had forgotten what she had said about having a talk with her. She hoped so. Talks were like scolding.

They went downstairs. Ellie glanced back toward the corner, but left the big doll sitting. To punish her. Let her sit in the dusty, shadowy corner, instead of coming down into the big, light kitchen the way she always had before today.

They ate breakfast, and after breakfast the ice man came and brought a big block of ice that went into the top of the ice box. When he was gone Aunt Aster asked Ellie and Becky if they would like some ice.

Becky nodded, and Ellie said, "Yes."

"Yes, please," Aunt Aster corrected.

"Yes please," Ellie said dutifully, and heard Becky repeat her words, as she sometimes did.

They stood watching while Aunt Aster used the ice pick

61

with the long, round, thin blade. She chipped off several pieces. She put the pieces into cups and gave Ellie one of the cups. Ellie stared down at the clear, cold chips. When she turned it just right, the light from the sun entered the ice and made it sparkle with red and blue, almost like fire.

Aunt Aster went out to the garden. Becky always went with her, and Ellie followed. But Ellie didn't like the outdoors. The sun was hot, even with the bonnet Aunt Aster had made her. And there were bugs sometimes, on the plants, in the air. Ellie was afraid they would crawl on her, sting or bite her.

Becky liked to help pick vegetables and pull weeds, but Ellie wanted to be inside the house, the way she'd always been, all her life.

"Can I go in, Aunt Aster?"

"Yes, Eleanor, if you'd rather."

Ellie slipped the last piece of ice into her mouth and went back into the cooler interior of the house. She stood in the middle of the kitchen looking into her cup. There was nothing but water now. The last few chips of ice had melted.

She peeked out the door. Aunt Aster and Becky were in the far corner of the garden.

Ellie pulled a chair over to the ice box and climbed onto the chair. She opened the lid on top where the block of ice was kept. The ice pick lay in a small groove beside the lid. She held it in her hand the way Aunt Aster had and jabbed down.

A large corner of the ice separated from the block. With a hurried glance out the door, Ellie reached in and picked up the chunk. It was too large to fit down into her cup. It barely sat on top. She would borrow the ice pick, just for a while.

Hurriedly she climbed down from the chair and pushed it back under the table. Then, her hand balancing the ice to keep it from falling off the cup, she went into the hall and up the stairs.

"A tea party," she murmured aloud when she felt safely out of Aunt Aster's view. Aunt Aster would never miss the chunk of ice. She hadn't taken that much, she told herself.

Zenoa was still sitting in the corner, but Ellie was no longer angry at her.

"We're going to have a tea party," she said. "Come and sit. We'll have iced tea today, because it's so hot. My, but it's hot."

She moved the little table over under the window, and placed around it the little chairs that were a faded red. She put the cup with the ice in the center of the table and arranged the tiny cups and saucers. Two of the old dolls were already sitting in chairs at the table. She had moved them carefully while they were still in the chairs. All the dolls were there except Zenoa. Ellie went to the corner and picked up Zenoa and took her to the other chair.

"Your hair's a mess. Why didn't you fix up before you came to the party? I'll teach you."

She got a handful of the doll's hair and yanked, hard. The doll fell out of the chair. Ellie jerked her up, turned her face down and spanked her. She brought her hand up high and brought it down hard, the way she had seen Heather do, so many times. The way Heather had done her, so many times.

A feeling of power grew in her, and she struck the doll harder, then sat her up and yanked her hair. "I'll teach you to not fix your hair. How dare you come to my tea party with your hair such a mess?"

She sat the doll in the chair and arranged her carefully. "Now," she said, "we will get on with the tea."

She broke the ice into three smaller chunks with the ice pick, but they were still too large to put into the tiny cups. She left the table and went to the old toy box Aunt Aster had brought down from the attic. On her knees beside the wooden box she looked in. There were only a few things in the box. A broken horse and wagon, one flat piece of wood that looked as if someone had tried to carve something. It might work for a platter onto which she could put the ice.

She heard a movement behind her. *Aunt Aster!* She sat still, as if in being still she would also be invisible.

I didn't do it! But Aunt Aster would see that Ellie had taken more ice and brought it up to the room. She had even brought the ice pick, which children should never touch. I didn't *mean* to do it. Would Aunt Aster believe her?

She waited for the voice, the sound of scolding. The question, why did you do that, Eleanor? Aunt Aster always called her Eleanor, never Ellie. She heard a footstep. But it was very soft, like a barefoot child's, like Becky's.

She whirled.

No one was there except . . . *Zenoa.*

Ellie gasped.

The doll was standing. Ellie had put her in the chair, but now she was standing. *Without support . . .*

. . . halfway across the room between Ellie and the table.

Ellie stared, unable to move, to breathe, to open her mouth and cry out for help. *Please, Aunt Aster . . . come . . . help me.* Fear was enveloping her in an icy prison. Her thoughts flashed to Becky, and the things Becky had told her. It moves, she had said, in the morning after Aunt Aster found the doll in a different place. It moves by itself. Don't be silly, Becky. But now Zenoa stood several steps from the chair where Ellie had left her. She was no longer beautiful, she was hideous. The one eye glared, and the red tongue stuck out. The hair was thin and torn and ratted. As Ellie's eyes remained pinned to her, she saw the right arm raise, and in the hand something glinted.

The ice pick.

Unable to move Ellie stared. The doll took a step, then another, faster. As if she were only learning to walk.

Ellie managed to turn. She went down on her hands and knees. A deep gurgling came from her chest as if it rose from somewhere in the floor beneath her. She heard it, as she heard the sudden running of the small steps behind her.

She had to get out of the room and go tell Aunt Aster. She had to tell her that Becky was right, it was the doll that moved, by herself. There was something horrible about the doll Heather had given them. She had to tell . . .

A sharp pain in her back shoved her forward. She felt it again as she slid weakly to her stomach. She reached out for the door, her hand clawing the rug.

Aster glanced often at Becky. The little girl worked diligently, helping with the picking of the tomatoes. They had enough now to start canning. They needed all the food they could gather and preserve. They must save their money for such things as wood for the winter months, and wax for candles, and salt and sugar and flour.

Becky said suddenly, "My Mama had a black ghost in her hair."

"She what?"

"In her hair. It came up around her head. It growed out of her head like her hair, only it made a ghost around her head."

Aster frowned at the little girl, but the child only kept picking tomatoes, beginning to pull those that were mostly green.

"And then," Becky said, "the doll got it."

"The doll got what, Becky?"

"The black ghost that was my Mama's."

Change the subject, Aster thought. The child shouldn't dwell on bad dreams. "I think we have enough tomatoes now, dear. Our basket's about full. Don't pick the green ones. One of these days we'll cook some green tomatoes, but we don't have time today. We'll slice them, roll them in flour and fry them. Some other time. Come along, it's time for dinner."

Becky ran ahead of her, hesitating only slightly. Aster watched her, wearing her new dress, her small feet bare beneath the long skirt. It was a very simple dress, with a long, loose bodice, no belt. Aster had gathered the skirt so the dress wouldn't be quite so plain, and had made a tiny collar with a red trim. She had used plain white buttons because they were cheaper.

They entered the cool kitchen. The sun no longer shone

through the east window. Aster pushed her bonnet off her head. It hung against her back, the ties around her neck. After she removed Becky's bonnet she would take off her own, wash her face in cool water, and prepare to set out something to eat. Then in the afternoon she would have to start peeling and preserving tomatoes.

"Where's Ellie?" Becky asked.

Was it only her imagination, or was Becky loosening up and talking more? Aster smiled, a thrill of satisfaction seeding a strange new happiness. Perhaps this would work out after all.

"She must be upstairs. Why don't you go get her?"

Aster saw the flicker of fear on the child's face. She was still reluctant to go into another room alone. But those looks of fear weren't coming as often as they had a week ago, as if in being able to talk more, Becky was losing some of the unreasonable fear she had brought with her.

Still, she didn't move to go look for her sister.

"I expect she's up in your room playing," Aster said.

Becky stood without moving. Aster considered going with her, as she had on other occasions when Eleanor had chosen to stay inside, and the house was strange to Becky. Then, with Becky's hand in hers, Aster and she had gone looking for Eleanor. They had found her with her little tea set up in the bedroom, talking to her dolls. Eleanor seemed to have no fear. Certainly not like Becky. But now Becky should learn to go alone.

"It's time you learn to be brave, Becky," Aster said. "There's nothing here to hurt you. Please go look for your sister."

"There's the doll," Becky said softly, "and the black ghost."

"No, there isn't. Not really. If there were, don't you think Eleanor would be afraid too? And I too, probably!" Aster laughed for Becky's sake.

Becky blinked. Both children had a habit of blinking that made Aster want to gather them into her arms and protect them forever from life itself. But she couldn't do that, she told herself. The best thing to do for them was to teach

66

them there was nothing to fear.

"Run along, and get your sister. Tell her it's time to eat. She'll be in her room having tea, probably, with her dolls."

"Ellie ain't afraid," Becky said, blinking.

"Isn't. No. And you mustn't be either. Go now."

Becky went slowly, walking as if her legs were stiff.

It's better that she go alone, Aster told herself as she watched the little girl disappear into the gloomy shadows of the front hall. Too much protection is as bad as not enough.

Still, Aster watched the shadows, long after the child had disappeared. It seemed as she stood alone that the house had swallowed both children, leaving her alone again, as she'd been before they came to live with her. But now with a strange and terrible emptiness.

Seven

Becky stopped at the foot of the stairs and looked up.
Ellie. Ellie. Aunt Aster wants you, Ellie. It's time to eat.

She stood with her mouth open, trying to make her voice work. She was afraid to call Ellie, and disturb the frightening things that lurked in the silences in the house. She looked back down the hall toward the kitchen. The swinging door always closed by itself. It wouldn't stay open.

She had to go up. Aunt Aster had told her to go up and get Ellie. She had to.

The stairs were not like the long, long narrow stairs back at the flat. They went only to the second floor, but they were harder to climb because each step was higher. But most of all was the silence in the upper hall. And the shadows. She could see eyes on the wall looking down at her. They were only pictures, Aunt Aster had told her, of people who were her relatives, but from the bottom of the stairs, and in the dark of the upper hall, they looked only like eyes glaring down.

She wanted to call out for Ellie, but was afraid to release her voice into this deep quiet.

She looked back toward the kitchen, where the swinging door had closed behind her. She couldn't even hear Aunt Aster moving about now. It was as if Becky were alone in the whole house, except for the doll and the strange black ghost, and the things asleep in the shadows.

Slowly she put her hand out and touched the newel post. It was fat and sleek, dark and polished. Even she had helped Aunt Aster polish the railing one day since she had lived here.

She put a foot up, and then another, drawn only by knowing that her sister was up there. *I'm not really alone,* she told herself. *Ellie is here, Ellie is here.* She had to keep telling herself that, for otherwise the upstairs seemed filled with all the ghosts of people who used to live there.

She reached the top of the stairs. There was no sound. The windows were closed. Aunt Aster always closed them in the morning so the house would stay cool, and opened them at night to let the night air in.

Becky opened her mouth. *Ellie.*

Nothing came out. She couldn't make herself break the silence. The closed door of the bedroom was the first one down the hall on the right. She had only a few more steps to go.

She reached the door. Ellie was making no sound. There was no clink of tea dishes, no voice talking to her dolls. Then as Becky hesitated to reach for the knob she heard footsteps, and knew Ellie was in there. The footsteps seemed a little odd for Ellie, as if she were running on tiptoe to hide. Was Ellie going to jump out and scare her?

You can't do that, Ellie. Aunt Aster said you should never do that again.

Becky opened the door and pushed it inward, following it, her hand lifted to the knob. There was the small tea table and chairs beneath the windows, and two of the little dolls. But where was Ellie?

She stopped, looking down. *Ellie? Why was Ellie on the floor?*

Ellie was not hiding, nor was she running. She was lying on the floor with an arm reaching out and the rug gathered in her fingers. Her face was turned away. Her back was stained with something red. It streaked across her dress and disappeared over the side.

Was this a new way Ellie had thought of to scare her?

Becky took a step into the room, then another. Ellie didn't move. She was so still that Becky had a sudden and terrible feeling that Ellie would never move again.

"Ellie!" Becky went down on her knees beside Ellie, her hand touching Ellie's back. The red stuff smeared onto her hand and she instinctively wiped it on the front of her dress.

Suddenly she knew what it was. Blood. She had seen blood coming from the meat the butcher cut. As if the meat once had been a person. Now the blood oozed through the tiny hole in Ellie's dress.

She heard the footsteps again, running lightly, like Ellie on tiptoe.

Becky's stare pulled away from Ellie and she looked up.

The doll came running around the foot of the bed, her head turned a bit sideways, one eye shut as if she were winking. She came at Becky with her right hand lifted. Light from the window flashed on the ice pick as if it were a long sliver of ice.

Becky screamed.

She whirled toward the door, but felt the impact of the doll as it struck her. She recoiled from it, the touch of hard arms, a hard, cold body. She began to fight, flailing her arms to throw it away from her, pushing at it with her hands, struggling and crawling closer to the door.

Her screams rose and fell as her breath waned and gasped again. She felt the hard arm of the doll beneath her hand and the sting of the ice pick through her dress. She grappled, in silence, and with both hands desperately shoved the doll back.

Suddenly she was free. As if the doll had forgotten her it was standing again over Ellie. Becky saw the arm lift high and then lower, swiftly, and the ice pick plunged again into Ellie's back. Ellie's body jolted. The ice pick stayed there, stuck in Ellie, as if the brown handle grew from Ellie's back.

Becky rolled through the doorway and then scrambled to her feet and ran.

Oh no, not again.
Aster had sliced bread on the bread board, set out the

70

cheese, and was at the table slicing tomatoes when she heard Becky screaming. Oh not again, Becky. Her feelings of sympathy had become somewhat like Eleanor's, she was afraid. They were often, especially in the daytime, more impatience and exasperation than sympathy. She put her knife down, turned to the pan of water on the cabinet and rinsed her hands.

The screaming continued.

Aster began to listen. This sounded more intense than Becky's usual daytime frights. Eleanor had, in the beginning, jumped out at Becky a couple of times, making her scream. Aster had tried to talk to her, and found that wide-eyed innocence of which Eleanor was so capable. Still, her scoldings had seemed to work. Eleanor had stopped entertaining herself with scaring Becky.

Until now.

Aster dried her hands. Then she paused again to listen. There was a sudden silence, followed by a dull thumping on the stairs, as if someone had fallen.

Aster hurried toward the swinging door and pushed into the front hall. Becky was just getting up. She had obviously rolled down the stairway. Her face was colorless with terror. She seemed almost to claw the air as she reached toward Aster.

Aster's sympathy rushed to the surface again as she hurried to pick Becky up. She held the trembling child. This was going too far. At times Eleanor seemed very motherly and caring toward Becky, and tried to soothe her fears. Then, perversely she'd turn right around and make a face at her, or jump out at her, or tell her to "Look, Becky, there's a ghost in the corner!" or some other ridiculous thing to start Becky screaming in terror again. Only once had Aster seen Eleanor slap Becky, and that was something that absolutely would not be tolerated. Eleanor seemed to understand that, and hadn't done it again.

But what had she done now?

Aster patted Becky's back and tried to comfort her, but Becky was stiff and shaking convulsively in her arms, her

71

eyes wild with terror. She was unable yet to speak. Her attempts only emitted formless sounds.

"There, there," Aster soothed. "Tell Aunt Aster. What did Eleanor do now?"

Becky shook her head, and shook her head. She seemed to soften, to become less stiff. She pulled around and looked back up the stairs.

"Ellie . . . Ellie . . ." Becky finally managed. "Ellie's dead. *She's dead! It killed Ellie!*"

"Oh no, now this is really going too far."

Aster stomped to the foot of the stairs and began to climb, and in her arms Becky stiffened and began to scream again. She was fighting Aster against going back up the stairs.

Aster stopped and put her down.

"Stay right here. I'll go up and see to Eleanor."

But as Aster turned to climb the stairs Becky grabbed her dress.

"No! It'll kill you too. Don't! Don't go!"

Aster bent and pried the child's hand from her dress. Going again up the stairs she yelled, *"Eleanor!* Eleanor, you come here this instant!"

She heard herself in astonishment. She was sounding just like some of the women she'd heard screaming at their kids in the apartment building where the children had lived. She stopped on the stairs again, with Becky right behind her. But Becky, finally, had stopped screaming, and was again making the little groaning sounds that were almost as unnerving as the screams. Aster raised her voice to a pitch that made her throat ache.

"ELEANOR!"

Her call seemed to echo mockingly from some distant place, and in dying away left an unnatural, deadly silence. She began to listen, and to wonder. This wasn't like Eleanor. *Eleanor's dead,* Becky had cried. If Eleanor were only playing a morbid game, trying to frighten her little sister, wouldn't she have answered by now? She usually came with that peculiar little smile on her face to take whatever

72

scolding Aster could manage. But now a deep uneasiness began to invade Aster as she heard only silence.

She took another step upward toward the hall, and as if Eleanor had finally responded there were running footsteps in Heather's old room. They sounded oddly light, as if the child had tried to run without being heard.

With her growing consternation receding somewhat and turning again to annoyance, Aster stepped up onto the hall and went to the bedroom. The door stood half open. Aster put out her fingertips and gave the door a shove.

"Elean—"

The small figure lay facedown a few feet from the edge of the open door, one arm stretched forward and her hand clutching the rug. Something protruded from her back. A wooden handle. Of something . . .

. . . something . . .

Aster suddenly knew what it was.

The ice pick!

It had been plunged into Eleanor's back, and rivulets of blood trailed away like thin red stripes in the material of the dress. Eleanor lay still. Her light brown braid hung limply off to one side of her turned head. Her legs were bare, and her dress had slid upward when she had fallen.

God, oh God, oh God. The wordless prayer went through Aster's mind, on and on as she knelt by the child on the floor. The ice pick had been buried to the handle in her back. Oh God, oh no. Aster gathered her apron in her hand and wrapped it around the handle of the pick. She pulled, and the child's body moved upward off the floor. With sobs beginning in her heart and throat, Aster pulled again, forced at last to put out her left hand and hold Eleanor's body still so that she could remove the pick. It had a five inch blade, and it had been rammed with great force into the child's back. What strength had it taken for Becky to do this?

Oh my God, what has Becky done?

The pick made a terrible sucking sound as it suddenly came free. Red blood dripped from the point, and Aster

73

quickly put the pick into her apron and wrapped it. On her knees, feeling her bones against the floor yet not really feeling, she turned, and turned again. She didn't know what to do.

Oh God . . .

She saw that Becky had followed. But instead of coming to the door she had pushed against the wall on the other side of the hallway. She stared past Aster to the body on the floor, her face bloodless, her eyes filled with terror. Then as Aster only glanced at her she saw the child's eyes lift and stare past her. The terror in her eyes increased.

Aster turned her head, following the direction of Becky's horrified stare.

But she saw only the children's play table and chairs, and the dolls sitting in the chairs.

Aster got to her feet. She turned, and turned again, and into her mind came the image of a mouse, trapped, filled with fear, and with no way to escape.

With the bloody pick wrapped in her apron, she went quickly into the hall, reached her free hand out and grabbed Becky's hand. Then, pulling the child so fast she occasionally stumbled, Aster hurried downstairs.

In the kitchen she released Becky's hand. The child was silent, as if she were unable to utter a sound. In added horror Aster saw the blood on the front of Becky's dress, as if she had tried to clean her hands there. She had not noticed it before.

Aster leaned over the dry sink. The pan of water still sat there, holding a skim of soap and the dishrag. Nausea crowded into her throat, forcing Aster to stand with her head down and her eyes squeezed shut for a long moment. Then she turned away from the sink, unable to remember what she had intended to do. She went into the laundry room, paused, then noticed she still had the apron wrapped tightly around the bloody ice pick. She couldn't bear the thoughts of ever seeing the ice pick again, but she didn't know what to do with it. She had to get rid of it. Finally she shoved the bloody apron, with the pick, down into the bottom of the laundry basket.

Then again she stood, the nausea rushing up and receding. She swallowed saliva and almost vomited. She stood with her hand over her pounding heart. With her eyes closed she thought of nothing, nothing, just calming down. Becky needed her. And Eleanor . . . yes, even in death, she too needed her.

She went back to the kitchen and sat down. Becky stood with her arms down at her sides. She seemed like a small statue of fear and terror, with no voice, no ability to move. Aster saw again the smears of blood on the dress, and on her hands.

"Oh Becky," she cried in a whisper, "what have you done?"

Eight

Becky didn't answer. Aster hadn't expected an answer.

She put her head down for a moment in her hand, leaning her elbow on the table. She sat with her eyes closed.

She couldn't believe it. If she hadn't seen it, seen the results of it, she wouldn't be able to believe it. Becky, a frail little child only six years old, had stabbed her sister in the back with an ice pick? Oh God, how had such a terrible thing happened?

"Becky," she said. "Do you realize your sister is dead?"

To Aster's surprise she heard Becky speak, but her voice was so low she understood only part of the words. They seemed disjointed and spaced oddly.

"The doll . . . the doll. Zenoa. It killed Ellie. I got away. The doll . . ."

Her voice trailed away to silence. Aster felt if the child had said another word she too would have started screaming.

With a long sigh Aster stood up. She had to go back upstairs and do something about the poor child's body. She had to go get a neighbor to call the doctor. She herself had to call the doctor.

She turned to the telephone on the wall and twisted the handle in a single, long ring. The voice of the operator answered.

"Please, call Dr. Thornton for me. This is Aster—Aster Morris—he knows where I live. Please call him and tell him something terrible has happened. I have a—a dead child here."

She hung up the phone.

She stood in the middle of the floor. The basket of tomatoes, red and ripe, sat at the end of the cabinet. The table was set for three, the bread sliced, the cheese sliced, tomatoes sliced, the pan with the knife and a tomato partly sliced sitting, oddly, on the stove. Why had she put it on the stove?

She hurried to it and pushed it over to the warming oven, away from the heat. But it wouldn't have mattered much, she realized. The stove was barely warm, unused since she had put wood in it early this morning to cook eggs.

She looked around. Sir Thomas was not in his usual place. Then she remembered. The cat hadn't been staying in the house since the little girls came, unless he could sit on her lap or feet. They never bothered him, still he came in lately only to eat and then wanted out again. Everything had changed since the children came.

She stood in the middle of the kitchen. Becky stood a few feet away staring at her with wide, frightened eyes. But she was quiet. No more horrible nonsense about the doll.

Aster looked at her again. The child had streaks of blood, just enough the doctor would notice, and wonder. The doctor must never know what happened. No one must ever know. What would they do to Becky if they knew? Would it matter that she was only six years old?

How can a six-year-old child kill?

She was in a nightmare. A very vivid dream, and soon it was she who would wake screaming, and Becky would come to comfort her, and Eleanor would come and look at her with those large eyes and that strange little smile of innocence.

No, she wasn't dreaming.

She had to hurry. The elderly family doctor lived only a few blocks away. It wouldn't take him long to arrive at her house. He knew she had Heather's daughters living with her. They had met in the market one day last week, and he had stopped to talk, his interest taken by the children.

"And who are you?" he asked. He was small, shorter than Aster, and his hair had grown white as summer clouds, rimming his head, sticking out over his ears in little tufts. The

77

top of his head shone, as if he rubbed it often. And indeed, he did, it had been a habit of his as long as Aster could remember. Back when she had the flu one winter and her mother had called in the doctor she had lain in bed and watched him rub the top of his head. Then, it had a thin layer of brownish hair. He had told her mother, "Feed her orange juice. Boil the rind, and have her drink the solution."

Aster took Becky by the arm and hurried her into the laundry room. She looked around, even as she was pulling the blood smeared dress off the child. What was there to put on her? Her newest dress was now soiled. The old dress . . . the old dress, in the laundry basket. Soiled from being worn several days, it had grass stain, and dirt from the garden. It was wrinkled. What difference did it make, for God's sake? Her sister lay upstairs dead, and what difference did the dress make?

Aster jerked the dirty dress down over Becky's head. Then she noticed the stained hands. Just enough blood in the creases for the doctor possibly to notice. She grabbed up a washrag and began wiping the child's hands.

"The doll . . ." Becky whimpered. *"Make the doll go away."*

Aster threw the rag back into the water, then remembered what she had to do, and grabbed it up again, wringing it. She hurried to the kitchen and took the dishpan from the sink. She draped a towel over her arm and pushed her way through the swinging door.

"Stay here," she ordered Becky, but her last glimpse of the child was of the terrified face and the hurrying to keep her in sight.

At the foot of the stairs she looked back and saw that Becky had come into the hall. Tears were sliding down the thin, white face. Terror in her eyes had seemed to increase, if possible.

"No!" Becky cried softly. "Don't go up there!"

"Stay here!" Aster commanded again, then turned and hurried up the stairs.

She slowed when she reached the bedroom. The door was closed. She couldn't remember closing it, but she must have.

The house was so quiet. She glimpsed a movement on the stairway and saw that Becky was following her. Like a small animal told to stay away, still she followed, keeping far enough behind not to seem too obvious.

What did it matter?

She opened the door and went into the bedroom.

She stopped.

The child on the floor . . .

The sight stopped her more thoroughly than it had the first time. The first time she hadn't known. This time there had lingered within her a dying hope that it was all a mistake, that Eleanor had been playing a trick on both of them, that she would be up arranging her dolls around the small tea table.

The dolls were still there, leaning awkwardly in the chairs, the tiny china doll, as white as the bed sheets, and the old doll with the stiff expression on her face and the thin strands of human hair looking as if some child had combed it too often too hard. And then the doll that had been so beautiful before Eleanor began mistreating it. It too sat in a chair, leaning slightly, its one-eyed brown gaze fixed on the floor somewhere, perhaps even on the body that lay there.

Aster went down on her knees beside Eleanor. She lifted the arm that reached out toward the door and found the skin soft, the hand limber. The little curled fingers released the rug, but rug fibers came away with the hand.

The skin was still warm but growing cool.

Still warm . . .

"Eleanor? Eleanor!"

Aster picked her up and cradled her. She jiggled the child the way she did Becky at night, to rouse her from a bad dream. Eleanor's head hung limply back over Aster's arm and her eyes had rolled upward as if she were trying to see up into her own mind.

Still warm . . . . not dead . . .

"Eleanor, answer me! Wake up, Eleanor. *Eleanor.*"

Aster rocked her and jiggled her, but the body hung limp in her arms. Aster felt tears tickling her cheeks and realized she was crying. In desperation she was trying to bring back a dead child.

She stopped moving. For a long moment she held Eleanor tightly, and wished she had held her this way while she was living. Had she not shown the child enough understanding? Was this in some way her fault?

What would Heather do?

The shock of losing one child would make her want to take the living child home, perhaps. Perhaps . . .

Aster stood up, Eleanor in her arms. She took her to the bed and laid her down gently. When she turned to bring over the pan and washrag she saw that Becky was standing in the hall. Her eyes were fastened on the once lovely doll that had been given to them by their mother.

Aster turned away, and began stripping clothes from Eleanor.

The body was so small and so thin. The ribs stuck out. Aster hadn't had time yet to fatten up either child, round out the cheeks, put meat on the ribs. As she had so wanted to . . . hadn't she?

She turned Eleanor onto her side and began washing the stab wounds. Tiny, bloody pricks. Two of them. Dear God. Twice the ice pick had been plunged into her back. How on earth had Becky managed such a feat? Eleanor must have been running from her. The tiny marks were right below her left shoulder blade, within an inch of each another.

As Aster washed, she realized the marks were becoming invisible. Blood was no longer oozing out. The stabs must have struck her directly in the heart.

Now cleaned, the stab wounds could have been mere freckles, or less. The doctor, unless told, might not even see them.

Aster turned Eleanor onto her back and bathed her carefully, and then she dressed her in her nightgown. It was still very early in the day. She could tell the doctor . . . she could tell him . . .

The knock came on the door then, sounding far away.

Aster hurriedly gathered up the pan and rag and the towel

and carried them back downstairs to the laundry room. Becky stayed behind her, ten, fifteen feet away. Aster hardly glanced at her, even though she was aware of her presence.

Aster poured the bloody water down the drain, then went to the front door. Doctor Thornton stood on the porch, wearing the old black suit he always wore, his bald head bare, the white hair looking even whiter. He rubbed the top of his head.

"I got your call, Aster. What on earth happened?"

He hurried through the door, saw Becky in the hallway, and stopped.

"Upstairs, Doctor," Aster said, and heard her voice trembling. "It's the older child. Eleanor."

She trailed behind him up the stairs. He seemed to know which room, and went toward the open door straight ahead. The children's room, the one where Aster herself had been in a bed there when she'd had the flu. In those days the large room had held three beds.

"What happened, Aster?" the doctor asked as he entered the room briskly and put down the black bag onto a chair he pulled up.

The child lay in the bed, her head cradled on a fat pillow, a summer sheet pulled up and folded carefully at her waist. Aster had crossed her hands on her chest, but she hadn't closed her eyes.

Doctor Thornton bent over her and pulled up an eyelid, peering in closely at her eye.

Aster looked away and laced her trembling fingers together. "She — she wasn't feeling very well, so I allowed her to stay in bed. When I came back up to check on her, she was gone."

Aster had told a lie for the first time in her life, and as it came haltingly from her mouth she felt as if it were she who had committed the murder. She was as guilty now as Becky. She had conspired with her to conceal the truth. But how could she say, I came up and found her facedown on the floor, the ice pick in her back? She had been stabbed not once, but twice. And there was no one who could have done it but Becky, frail, small Becky. The children have lived with me only a week, and I don't know them. They have fears I don't understand, and Eleanor was angry and violent with her lovely doll. Although, as it now slipped quickly through Aster's mind in a kind of blank surprise, Eleanor had not treated the other dolls that way. Only Zenoa.

Aster became aware of soft sobs, and she went to the doorway and looked into the hall. Becky had slid down to huddle with her back against the wall in the corner. Her hands covered her face. She was weeping, softly, her shoulders jerking convulsively. Aster almost went to her, but the doctor's voice called her attention.

"Sometimes we don't know what causes a death, Aster," he said. "But in this case it must have been a blood vessel burst in the brain. Or in the heart. I'm sorry. There's just nothing that can be done."

He straightened, yet still was stooped, as if in examining a dead child he had aged dramatically.

"How old was she, Aster?"

"Eight."

"Only eight. Well, she was still a small eight. She hadn't been fed very well, Aster."

Aster nodded.

Doctor Thornton put away the few things he had taken from the black bag and closed it again. Aster glimpsed bottles of pills and medicines. He had been in this house many times, but rarely administered any of the medications in his black bag. Instead he left instructions for some herb preparation or another. Peach tree leaf tea had been one of his favorites, she recalled. He had wanted her father to drink the tea for many years before his death, and he had lived to be an old man.

Doctor Thornton stood a moment longer at the side of the bed, looking down at the little girl's body. Then he rearranged the sheet the way Aster had it, and turned away.

"It's time to call in the family. I'll send my nurse up to help you prepare the body for burial, and I'll call the mortuary and have them deliver a casket, if you wish."

Aster nodded, then followed it with a quiet, "Thank you."

She followed him downstairs, and closed the door behind him. Through the glass on the door she saw his buggy in the street just beyond the gate, and the old mare who rested with one leg bent and her head hanging.

Aster turned slowly toward the kitchen. Becky had followed her down the stairs, staying, as always, several feet away as if she were afraid to come nearer.

How was she going to reach Heather? And the rest of the family? Their sister, Esther, lived a few miles away, but she at least could be reached by telephone. And Esther had a son still at home, who might be sent to reach Heather.

Aster called the home of the neighbor where Esther said she could be reached, and after long minutes of buzzing lines and poor connections, managed to leave a message that Esther would understand. Heather's older daughter, Eleanor had died, and the family must come. She gave Heather's address, and left a message that Harry, Esther's son, take the message to Heather.

Then she sat down. Becky had come into the kitchen, but had huddled in the corner. Aster put out her arms.

The child came running, her own arms out, reaching, tears glistening on her cheeks.

Weeping hard, Aster hugged the little girl to her. How could this have happened? But it had. And thank God no one would ever know. Aster could no longer wonder how such a small girl could have used such strength. But perhaps . . . it hadn't taken much strength. Perhaps it had taken only anger, the kind Eleanor had turned on the doll.

Becky was murmuring something over and over. At first it didn't register with Aster. Then, with an eerie feeling of horror creeping over her skin, Aster realized what the child was saying.

"The doll, the doll, make it go away. Make it go away. It killed Ellie. Make it go away. I saw it. I saw the ice pick in its hands. I saw . . . the doll . . . hurt Ellie."

Nine

"Hush. Hush!" Aster whispered against Becky's cheek. "Don't ever say that again, Becky. Don't tell that to anyone. Not even your mother."

Becky had grown quiet at her command. Her arms hugged Aster tightly, with surprising strength. Aster had a sudden urge to pull away, to put the child from her. What kind of madness existed in that young mind?

Then, hugging Becky desperately closer, she repeated, "In all your life, Becky, as long as you live, when I'm no longer here to protect you, do not ever say that Eleanor was stabbed. Do you understand? Don't ever mention the ice pick."

The child was silent in her arms, and Aster began to rock her. Then together they wept softly, but still Becky trembled, as if she were so terribly afraid.

The nurse came, and went upstairs to be with the dead child and prepare her for burial. Her name was Opal Purvis. Aster had known her since they both were young. She had married, and had many children. Another time Aster would have inquired about them. She was a short, heavy woman, comforting and motherly. She patted Aster on the arm and said, "I'll sit with the dead tonight. You have the living to tend to."

"I have bathed her," Aster said carefully. Although the tiny pricks on Eleanor's back were hardly noticeable, Aster

84

couldn't take a chance that Opal's sharp eyes might see them. "I've tended to her. She needs only to be dressed."

Opal nodded. Aster saw a flicker of relief on her face. Sitting with a dead child the night before the funeral was difficult enough, at least she would be spared the bathing of the body.

At bedtime Aster saw Becky watching her with silently pleading eyes, and instead of taking the child to the spare bedroom Aster took her to her own and put her to bed there. Becky didn't seem afraid to lie in bed alone, candles glowing in their holders on nightstand and dresser. But her eyes sought Aster often. Aster sat in the rocking chair by the window and looked out into the darkness, and the squeak of the chair as she slowly rocked was like a cry from the mysteries of death.

Becky slept in the bed, and Aster spent the night in the chair. She got up and snuffed out one of the candles after Becky was sound asleep. At each moment, as Aster dozed, she expected Becky to wake screaming, but she slept through the night peacefully. How very strange, Aster thought to herself.

Preparing the body for burial had not taken long. Opal had only to dress her in a white dress Aster had made for church. It was a simple dress with a round lace-trimmed collar. Ruffled cuffs on long sleeves covered half the small hands. The little girl lay on the bed, her eyes closed now, as if she slept.

Death is only God's sleep, Opal told herself as she rocked gently in the dim light of the room. She had buried children of her own, and she'd had to maintain her belief in God and in a marvelous afterlife, or she would go mad. Now, as she rocked, in the middle of her all-night vigil, she saw in her mind's eye the children playing in the most beautiful meadow. Her children, and this child. This thin little girl who hadn't had a chance yet to live. They played. Opal closed her eyes, seeing the flowers in the meadow, seeing the mountains with their snowy peaks rimming the valley, and the sunshine on the heads of the children. Her own little Charlie was there, barely two years old, and Gladys.

Another existence she had been taught since she was a small child came unbidden into her mind. A dark world lighted only by eternal fires, where terrible creatures doomed forever walked in misery, and red devils built of sin and fire carrying pitchforks and dragging long tails behind them herded the doomed ones. She cringed from the image of innocent children, unbaptized, being dropped into that place of—

A movement in the room drew her back to the moment.

She listened, sitting very still, her eyes closed, her breath held. The door hadn't opened. No one had entered the room since Aster left to stay with Becky hours ago.

Her imagination, she told herself, at work, thinking of heaven, thinking of hell and the terrible things that her Bible teacher had said could happen to her.

But she heard it again, soft stirrings in the room, on the far side of the bed, nothing distinct, but *something*, as if it had been here in the room all the time but had remained very still until now. A footstep. *No one had opened the door.* It was as if the child on the bed had risen and begun to move about.

Opal's eyes opened. Without moving her head she stared. A small, strange child stood on the other side of the bed, her head barely visible. Light from the single candle on the dresser flickered and moved, like fingers curling and uncurling, drawing its light in and out, reaching toward the child and receding. Opal stared, and saw one round dark eye looking at something on the bed. The other eye was closed.

Opal's heart pounded. *Who was she?* Where had she come from? This was not the other little girl, Becky. This girl was smaller, with pale hair, tousled and unkempt.

Opal sat forward. Slowly, her hands gripping the arms of the chair, she rose.

On her feet she could see more clearly over the bed, and to her astonishment she saw it was not a child, but a doll. On recognition she felt faint. She put her hand over her heart in relief.

The relief leached away, leaving her staring again at the doll. The doll was standing on its own in a sideway, crooked position, as if one leg were shorter than the other, but it was standing without being held. That was possible, she supposed. A well-made doll, with straight legs and flat feet, could stand without support. But this doll did not have straight legs. Something was wrong with one of them. Still, it could have stood alone, it *was* standing alone, but who had placed it there? No one had entered the room, taken the doll from the chair by the small tea table, and stood it there, halfway between the bed and the wall. Opal had noticed the tea table and the dollies in the chairs. One doll, a china doll, was so small it had been placed on a pillow. How sad, she had thought. The little girl's playthings.

She had seen the large doll, but its face had been turned so that she hadn't seen the closed eye. It had been in the small chair at the tea table when Opal entered the room.

Who had placed it upright near the bed?

The doll's one eye seemed to be staring directly at the child on the bed.

Nonsense, she told herself, go around to that doll and put it back where it was. Someone must have moved it since she had noticed it among the dolls at the tea table. She'd had to leave the room several times, to go to the outhouse once, and to fill the pitcher of water for the dresser. She had been in and out of the room several times. She might not have noticed if the doll had been moved.

With a strange dread stiffening her joints, she went around the foot of the bed. In the shadows thrown by her body it seemed the doll turned.

Opal stopped, watching the doll closely. She didn't believe it could have turned alone, yet it had, somehow, and it now faced the small tea table. Shadows flickered over the doll, over that part of the large bedroom. Opal's own shadow danced and jerked over the doll, throwing it even more into the gloom of near darkness. She saw that one of its ankles appeared to have been broken. The foot twisted to one side, the high-topped black shoe pressing flat against the floor, while the other foot, the other shoe was standing sole down.

She had only imagined the turning of the doll, she told herself. It was like a painting of a face. There was one in the doctor's office. The eyes in that painting appeared to be looking straight at you no matter what part of the room you were in. She and patients who sat waiting to see the doctor laughed about it.

It was that way with the doll.

Opal moved over, so that her shadow did not obscure the doll. She looked at the tea table. The small dolls were still there. The tiny china doll was about to fall off its small cushion.

Opal stooped and straightened it.

She glanced at the doll that stood alone. The room was so large that one small candle didn't light it well enough for Opal to see. She went to the dresser and picked up the candle. This was such a nice house. With real rugs on the floor, and lots of highly polished furniture. So nice, and so large. Aster had lived here a long time by herself. It was good that she had someone now, but so terrible that with the coming of the children to live with her, the one child had passed on, so unexpectedly, without even the preparation of illness. Though a long illness could be devastating on the family, it at least prepared the loved ones for the coming death.

She heard the movement again, a soft step, a whisper of clothing. It seemed she saw the doll turn again and move away from the bed. She even heard the sliding of the broken foot along the rug. Her heart pounded and a dull pain burned suddenly in her chest, bringing upon her that awful weakness she'd been experiencing lately. She felt smothered. She needed to open the window, to get air, but she

88

couldn't force herself to move past the strange, terrible doll.

In the shadows thrown by the large bed the doll—the child—whatever it was—began visibly to walk, one small step after another, over toward the tea table, dragging the injured leg. The sound, soft in the room, screamed in Opal's head. Step, s-l-i-d-e. A whisper of movement as the shoe dragged. A soft footfall, heavier than it should have been, supporting the crippled leg. Then the lingering drag again.

Saliva drained from Opal's mouth and left it rasping and dry. She trembled all over from the pounding of her heart. She hadn't seen right. The candle blinded her. She put up a hand to shield her eyes from the flame.

She saw the doll more clearly now, and she stared, unable to move her eyes away from it.

It had gone to the tea table and bent forward at the waist slightly. It reached for the small tea pot, picked it up and like a child playing pretended to pour something into each tiny cup. It placed the tea pot back exactly in the center of the table. It stood still for a heartbeat then it lifted its right hand and began a vicious stabbing motion at the doll in the chair closest to it.

Opal couldn't breathe. She had to find the door. The room looked strange, as if she had never seen it before. There was no door, no way out. She heard the sound of falling at the tea table. The strange tiny child had knocked the small doll out of its chair.

I have to get out of here.

On the bed the dead child, Eleanor, lay still, dressed in white, her hands folded almost as in prayer. The way Opal had placed her. She could almost feel her rising up and walking, joining the strange tea party with the dolls.

I have to get out of here.

In her confusion Opal found herself facing the tea table again. The large doll—the child—the strange child—was coming toward her, faster, faster in its one-sided gait, its right arm lifted and its fingers curled as if it held something in its hand, though nothing was there. It stabbed at her, and she felt its touch brush her skirt.

With a cry in her throat, Opal stumbled away. Pain ripped through her chest. She had to get to the door. She had to slam the door between herself and this nightmare. She had to get away from this nightmare.

The pain in her chest burst to fire, her knees buckled and she collapsed. She fell, heavily.

The candle rolled out of her hand and onto the rug, the small flame licking at the old, dry fibers.

She lay on the floor, unable to lift herself. She gasped, and gasped again as her eyes stared, wide open toward the door. It grew small and distant beyond the heightening flames.

The smell of smoke reached Aster. Half awake, she at first sat still. A neighbor burning trash at this time of night? She didn't even wonder at the oddities of such an act. Nothing was right anymore. Then she realized the smoke could be coming from somewhere inside the house.

She ran from the room and stopped in the hall. The candle in the holder on the wall burned feebly, leaving the corners deep in darkness.

Aster paused. The downstairs was dark. The smoke did not come from there.

She hurried down the hall and opened the door of the bedroom where Opal kept vigil with the body of Eleanor.

Smoke boiled out into her face. A small flame danced on the floor near the foot of the bed, reaching higher, spreading quickly, eating the rug as if it were a miniature forest. On the floor just beyond the flames Opal lay. Even as Aster moved hurriedly to get the pitcher of water from the dresser, she perceived what must have happened. Opal had taken up the candle, for some reason, and then had fallen. Just minutes ago. The fire was only getting started.

Aster threw the pitcher of water onto the flames, and saw them recede, blacken, and die. With the dying of the flames the room became dark and featureless, smoke curling into Aster's face, choking her. She stumbled toward the door, found it, and went out into the hall.

She stood, gasping. Then she ran to the stairs and went down into the darkness of the first floor. With her hand on the wall she felt her way to the kitchen. She found the candle drawer and then at the stove she removed a lid. Coals glowed within the stove. A box on the floor held wood and kindling. Grabbing a sliver of kindling she got a light, and held it to the candle. With the lighted candle she lit other candles in the room. Then she hurried to the water bucket in the laundry room and carried a full pail back up the stairs. Carrying a candle in her left hand she went back into the dark bedroom. She picked up the wet candle on the floor and laid it on the dresser, then she placed the candle she carried into the holder.

With the pail of water as insurance against the fire breaking out again, she knelt on the floor beside Opal.

Death, again. For the first time, in this room, death had come. And it had come twice in one day. Aster knelt beside the prone woman, her skirt soaking up the wetness of the rug. Then slowly, she rose. She paused to check Becky and found her sleeping, though she stirred uneasily, moaning, not quite awake.

She went downstairs again, and out. She hurried down the walk to the gate and then, for the first time since he had become a widower, she went to Mister Jessup's front door.

As she waited, she looked back at the upstairs windows of her own house. Faint light came from the windows of Heather's room. Curtains hung still. If the window had been open, the fire would have quickly been out of control. She stared at the window. A room once filled with the voices of sisters, more often happy than sad, now held death. A child of one of those sisters. Never, never had she foreseen.

The door opened and Mister Jessup looked out.

"I need help," Aster said simply, and almost collapsed into Mister Jessup's arms.

For the first time Aster understood how it could feel to turn everything over to a man. She wanted to stay in his arms forever and like a child hide her face in the strength of his chest. But she pushed herself back, and Mister Jessup slowly removed his arms from her.

"What can I do, Aster?"

He had heard about the death of the child. The neighborhood knew. News of death traveled swiftly, especially a child's death.

He walked beside her as she tried to explain what had happened. Opal, staying the night with the dead child so that Aster could stay with the living. Opal, fire, death.

They entered her house and hurried upstairs. Opal still lay on the floor, and Aster's hopes that she had only fainted and had come to her senses by now, perished. On the bed, with her arms crossed over her chest, Eleanor lay. In her white dress she looked like an angel.

Mister Jessup said, "You go stay with your other child, I'll take care of this. Do you have a telephone?"

"Yes. Down in the kitchen. But—"

"Now go," he said again. "I'll call the doctor."

Aster went back to the bedroom. Thank God, Becky was still sleeping. Aster walked the floor, from her bedroom to the door of Heather's room, down the stairs, back up. She checked on Becky every few minutes, but the little girl continued to sleep, stirring, moaning, then turning and settling, and for a moment seeming to rest. Mister Jessup remained a comforting source in the house as he waited for the doctor.

The doctor arrived with the deepest hour of night. He bent over his nurse, his skin colorless. He listened for a heartbeat. Then he looked up.

"Opal's heart has been giving her problems lately. I had hoped . . . ah well. I'm so sorry."

With effort he rose. Mister Jessup reached out to help him, but drew back his hand.

The doctor glanced toward the body on the bed. Then with a long sigh he picked up the old, cracked leather physician's bag and led the way toward the door.

"We'll have to have the body removed, of course, as soon as possible. I'll have the mortuary come and pick it up. Her family will have to be notified." He shook his head. "I'm so sorry. She wasn't an old woman."

Aster felt responsible. Opal should not have been doing Aster's job. It was Aster, and Heather, who should have been sitting with Eleanor tonight, not Opal.

Ten

Daylight came, and Becky woke, and though she said nothing Aster saw the memory of Eleanor come into her eyes. They widened with horror and darted back and forth like frightened birds trapped. Aster put a protective arm around her. Becky cringed as she looked toward the closed bedroom door. Aster wondered, what regrets does the child hold? But she saw no regrets, only a silent terror, a look of helplessness.

Remarkably the child had slept through the horrors of the night. Opal's body had been removed in the last dark hours before the dawn. Thank God, Aster had thought each time she checked on Becky, nothing had interrupted her sleep, restless though it was.

Aster held against her the child who had picked up an ice pick and stabbed her sister. Her once peaceful house had become invaded by death and something else she didn't understand. She could not ever have imagined these terrible happenings. She hardly believed it now.

I can't handle this.

But she had to. Who else would?

Of course she had an option. She could tell Mister Jessup the truth, and he would carry the word to the doctor, and something would be done. The child would be removed from her house.

Taken away.

Aster pulled Becky up into her arms and hugged her tightly for several minutes before she released her.

"Today," she said, her throat strained with efforts to keep her voice normal, "you'll wear your prettiest new dress. People will be coming. Your mother will come, and Aunt Esther and Aunt Merle. Others too, I expect." She didn't add, there will be a funeral. The body will have to be buried.

Already there seemed to be a smell of death in the house, mingling with the acrid odor of smoke. Even with the windows opened now, with air circulating, the odors were there.

Tomorrow there would be another funeral, one they couldn't attend because she wouldn't subject Becky to two funerals in two days. Opal would understand. For now she had to act as if the day were normal, for Becky's sake. Perhaps for her own. She would dress Becky, go downstairs, build a fire in the cookstove, and cook breakfast. Oatmeal. Biscuits. Anything, even though her hands shook and threatened to drop whatever she touched.

The family came, in buggies, hacks, carriages. The street outside Aster's front gate was crowded with waiting, restless horses and the vehicles to which they were attached. Heather came last of all, wearing a black veil so that her face was barely visible. She held her head high, and didn't even embrace Becky.

Aster expected that Becky would release her hand and run to Heather, but she didn't. She drew back against Aster, her face against Aster's full skirt, her thumb in her mouth as if she had reverted to babyhood. She stared at her mother. Aster bent to her.

Keeping her voice low so that only Becky heard, she asked, "Don't you want to go see your mother?"

For a while it didn't seem that she was going to answer, then she whispered to Aster, "I don't know."

Aster noticed they were being observed by other members of the family. Folks were watching Heather, watching Becky. They spoke softly to Heather, extending sympathies.

Heather, as she had always been when she was a child, was the center of attention.

Though Heather's stomach rounded against the black gown she wore, and her face was veiled, still she was gracefully beautiful, outstanding in the collection of friends and relatives who had come for the funeral of her child. Aster saw her dark eyes through the veil, and was reminded of the doll upstairs. She found herself hoping Heather would not ask to see the doll.

Aster led Becky nearer to Heather. Heather continued to give her attention to relatives, until at last one of the elderly aunts asked, "Is this your other child, Heather?"

Heather put her hand down toward Becky and motioned her near. Becky went to her, walking with that odd stiff-legged gait with which she entered a darkened room. She stared up at her mother.

"Yes, this is Becky. Becky, say good morning to Aunt Hazel."

"Good morning, Aunt Hazel."

Becky's voice was so faint the elderly aunt bent toward her.

Heather shook her slightly. "Can't you speak up?"

Becky nodded, but said nothing. The thumb went back into her mouth. Aunt Hazel turned away, called by someone behind her. Aster watched Becky, and saw her stare up at Heather again, as if she weren't sure she knew the person behind the veil.

Heather began talking to someone else, and Becky turned, searching for Aster. She came, and grabbed Aster's hand and clung to it, her fingers surprisingly strong, biting into Aster's hand desperately.

They walked to the cemetery behind the horse drawn hearse, a group of relatives and friends of relatives dressed in black. At the sides of the road buggies and wagons pulled over to wait for the procession to go by, and men stood with their hats off.

Aster felt the clinging of Becky's hand. She could not loosen herself from it, even to brush a mosquito from beneath her own veil.

After the prayer at graveside, Aster pulled Becky back, so that she wouldn't see the casket lowered into the ground.

Earlier, after services in the parlor back at the house, where the small white casket stood among flowers gathered from gardens, a well-meaning relative had lifted Becky so she could see her sister in the coffin, and Becky had stared briefly down, then turned and reached for Aster, and had buried her face silently against Aster's neck. Aster carried her into another room. She didn't know if Becky truly realized that Eleanor was dead. She wondered if the child even knew what terrible harm she had done.

I don't know how to handle this.

Time, Aster sensed, would help to solve the problem.

They returned to the house, and people began to leave. Heather was one of the first to go. Aster thought she had completely forgotten Becky, but at the last she came, leaned down, lifted her veil and put her face close to Becky for a kiss. The child dodged away, and lifted both hands to cover her face.

Heather hesitated, laughed shortly and dropped her veil. She turned away without saying goodbye and disappeared among the crowd at the door that was leaving.

That night when Aster sat in the privacy of her room with Becky in her arms, drowsy, yet unable to fall asleep, she thought of the tense moment after Heather had moved away from Becky. Becky had sounded as if she were moaning in fear, and Aster pulled her hands down. The little girl looked around and grew quiet, and then reached again for Aster's hand.

In the silence of her bedroom, Aster rocked Becky gently. The old chair had a soothing squeak, barely heard. Candlelight threw groping hands onto the floor toward them, never quite reaching the rockers of the chair.

"Why," Aster asked, "didn't you let your mother kiss you goodbye before she left?"

Becky replied softly, *"Kiss me?"*

"Yes. She wanted to kiss you goodbye."

Becky shook her head. Aster felt the movement against her chest. "I thought she was going to hit me."

Oh God.

Aster closed her eyes, and leaned her head back against the cushioned rest at the top of the chair. For the first time tears oozed out from beneath her eyelids and trickled down her cheeks. Pain in her heart burned like fire. Pain not for herself but for two little girls, one of them now dead. In anger, Becky must have picked up the ice pick and without realizing what she was doing stabbed at Eleanor with it. Not once, but twice. Somehow it was more difficult to understand the second stab. The first one could be thought of as accidental, even though it had penetrated enough to fatally injure. But the second stab . . . ?

She rocked Becky until she felt the relaxation of the small body. As if the child were boneless. "Hold the baby until she sighs, and then she won't wake up when she's put down," her mother had told her when she was appointed to rock Heather to sleep. Tonight, in a way alone in the world, isolated by the secret they shared, she continued to hold Becky, waiting for the sigh. She rocked gently, rhythmically, watching the fingers of shadows and light moving out from the dancing candle flame.

All the beds in the house were full tonight. Relatives who lived out of town had stayed over. Some of them might stay two or three days. But after that, Aster would have to decide what to do with Becky. She would have to have a room of her own, but Aster couldn't put her back into the room where her sister had died. The only room left was the large master bedroom, where her own mother and father had passed away. But that was somehow different. Natural causes had taken them, when they were old and tired and unable to be healthy again.

Aster felt Becky sigh deeply. She stood up, and carried the little girl to the bed. Then she went back to the chair, pulled up the footstool and leaned back.

The night would be long, as nights were now, and she would rise stiff and tired in the morning, feeling as if she

98

had aged twenty years in the past two weeks.

Aster slept lightly, and woke to hear Eleanor's footsteps in the hallway. Eleanor had a way of running that was different from any child Aster had ever heard. She ran lightly, on tiptoes, an almost silent sound. But Aster had heard it before, on several occasions, and she knew it could be no one but Eleanor, because Becky was asleep, on the bed.

Aster jerked up.

Eleanor!

But the sound was gone, receded with her sleep. She must have dreamed it, and yet it had woke her.

For a long while Aster sat forward in the chair, listening. The candle had burned low. The old house made soft noises, a board settling closer to another, a stair squeaking. As if someone had stepped on it.

Aster rose and went quietly to the door. She opened it and stepped out. The candle in the wall holder had burned low also, like the one in her room. The stairway was in darkness, but if anyone had stood there she could have seen them.

After a moment she went back into her room and closed the door. Then she lay down on the bed beside Becky, still in black mourning dress, crossed her ankles, crossed her arms on her chest and closed her eyes.

With mixed feelings she watched the rest of her relatives leave the next day. Her favorite aunt, Aunt Merle, now looking old and grey, was the last to go. The elderly woman said goodbye and turned her old mare toward the road. She had come in a buggy, driving herself. She was alone now, her husband dead, her children married. But she didn't need Aster. One married son was moving in to live with her. He and his family. He hadn't come to the funeral. Aunt Merle had to hurry home and help them arrange the house.

"Do come see us, Aster. Bring Becky. She will enjoy her cousins."

Aster nodded, Becky's hand in hers.

They stood watching until the buggy had gone out of sight beyond the trees. Until even the small puffs of dust from the horse's hoofs and buggy wheels had dissipated into the weeds at the roadside. Aster looked toward Mister Jessup's house. What would she have done without him? He had come to the funeral yesterday, and stood in silence, just an acquaintance who was a stranger to most of the relatives who had come for the services. Then at the end he had given Aster his sympathies and had gone away.

He would be back at work now, his life returning to the mold it had acquired.

"There'll be tomatoes ripening on the vine," Aster said to Becky. "We'll need to be gathering them and getting them preserved."

"I'll get the baskets," Becky cried, with the first enthusiasm in days.

Aster watched her run toward the porch, up the steps, and across the porch. She started to enter the house, then abruptly she whirled and ran back toward Aster. Her face had lost its enthusiasm, its color, and fear was etched there again. She came in silence to Aster and reached for her hand.

"What's wrong, dear, aren't you going to get the baskets?"

Becky shook her head.

Aster went toward the house, Becky's hand in hers. They had to start living a normal life again, as much as possible. To pretend things were normal might help to make them seem so.

Relatives had taken the tomatoes that were picked, to get them off Aster's hands. That was some help, now, not next winter. Aunt Merle had asked once, when they walked out to look at the old garden, "Why do you keep such a large garden now, Aster, when you're alone?" Then she remembered and added, "Oh but you're not alone now, are you?"

Aster brought the baskets from the house. Becky was forced to let go of her hand. She clutched Aster's skirt instead until Aster handed her a basket. They returned to the outdoors and went down the path between the zinnias and hollyhocks to the vegetable garden. Tomatoes hung like large, red grapes on the vines, overloaded and heavy. Aster began to pick, and beside her Becky picked also, her small hands careful to remove the fruit without tearing the vine.

Aster dreaded going into the house. With the baskets full she looked toward the house and thought of her dread. For the first time in her life the house was not a haven, but . . . something else. The windows looked hooded and dark. The roof lines pitched more steeply, the shingles darkened and almost black, mold and moss growing grey-green in the crevices. The grey shingles on the outer walls had become uneven and wavy, as if the house were no longer stable.

Aster noticed that Becky was looking up at her. Her shadowed face, beneath the brim of the bonnet, was pinched and drawn.

"It's time to go in," Aster said. "Why are we standing here in the sunshine?"

Then Becky asked a surprising question.

"Are you afraid too?"

"Oh no, no," Aster denied. *Yes.* "Why would I be afraid?"

"Because it's in there." Becky looked toward the house.

"Because what's in there?"

"The doll. It's in there. It killed Ellie. It's going to kill me too."

Eleven

Becky was living a dark and terrible fantasy, Aster thought to herself. She knew she had to talk to Becky about that, but didn't know how to start. As she dipped tomatoes in boiling water and took them out again to peel, their skins loosened and falling away, she thought of the simple life she had led. Alone after her papa died, she had concerned herself with thoughts of Mister Jessup and ways she could manage to make herself known to him. Now, as she thought back, embarrassed at having such minor problems, she had thought life was difficult. Alone in her house. Alone with her garden. Only her cat for company.

But now, even her cat was absenting himself. He refused to enter the house. He came to the porch, slept in pools of sunshine until he woke panting, then moved to the shade. He stood at the door in the evening and meowed for food. He peeked through the screen door, looking as deeply as he could into the house, but he refused to enter. His food dish was now on the porch.

The house seemed so quiet without Eleanor, yet there were times when it seemed Aster heard her moving about. A footstep, a sliding sound as if she had pulled something, the little table perhaps, rearranging her playhouse. Aster paused, tomato juice running between her fingers, and listened. Then, knowing it was only the ghosts of her memories of Eleanor, she went back to work

The third time it happened she saw that Becky too had

paused and was still, her head turning slowly upward, as if she could see into the second story.

That action drew a coating of ice around Aster. She felt her skin tingle with the strange new fear that had begun to be a part of her since Eleanor's death. She tried to see in Becky's face some sign of the viciousness that must have been behind the attack on her sister, but saw nothing beyond Becky's own fear, and that made it even less tolerable to Aster.

Her hands began to shake when she worked.

Together, Becky working faithfully like a tiny woman, they preserved twenty quarts of tomatoes that day. It was nearing dusk when Aster said to Becky, "It's time to take them into the fruit cellar, Becky."

She was exhausted. It would take about three trips down into the cellar beneath the house, a kind of half-basement reachable only from the laundry room.

Becky said nothing. Red tomato juice stained the front of the old apron Aster had doubled and tied beneath Becky's arms. Her small hands were gummy with red juice. The cellar would be frightening to Becky. Aster knew where the shelves were and could almost find them in the dark, but she lighted a candle.

She carefully placed seven jars into the bottom of a basket, but then went into the laundry room. She'd leave Becky busy while she was gone, she decided. It would help the child to be less fearful.

"I'll fix your bathwater, Becky, before I take the tomatoes down. You can start undressing for your bath."

She brought in the round, wooden tub that hung on the outside wall on the kitchen porch, placed it in the center of the laundry room and carried hot water in the teakettle and poured it in. Then she pumped a bucket of cold water and poured in just enough to make the bath water tepid.

"You can undress and take your bath, Becky," Aster said again, because Becky hadn't started undressing. It seemed the child was listening to something else, far away, and heard nothing Aster said.

Aster opened the door into the cellar. Becky stood closely behind her, staring at the stone steps that led steeply downward into darkness. Aster told her again to take her bath. Slowly, she began removing her stained apron. She hadn't spoken a word in hours, and she didn't speak now. Her silence unnerved Aster.

Aster felt the need to explain her actions, to try to alleviate at least a part of the fear and worry on the little girl's narrow face. Was she getting even thinner and more pinched looking? Or was it the angle of light, the lack of light in the room, the growing shadows, the oncoming of night. Night that came so swiftly sometimes lately.

"It's getting dark," Aster said. "It's time we lighted more candles."

She went about gathering candles. She left one on the kitchen table, and put two in the laundry room. Their flames, competing with the last slanting rays of a weak sunshine, looked vaporous and insignificant as if they might dissipate into the air, leaving only a thin, dying trail of smoke.

"Then," Aster said, feeling as if she talked to an empty house, a haunted silence, "I'll be carrying the tomatoes down in my basket. It will take several trips. First, I'll take a candle down and set it on the table that's down there. Perhaps another time you'd like to come down and see the cellar."

Becky's large eyes glanced up, but then back down again to the drop into the dark cellar. She said nothing.

Aster picked up one of the candles and started down the stairs.

Becky's voice cried out at her. "Don't leave me!"

Aster paused and looked back. The little girl stood half undressed. She had pulled her dress over her head but it still covered one arm and shoulder.

"I'll only be at the bottom of the stairs, Becky. Come here, you can see the dirt floor just a few steps down."

Aster waited, but Becky didn't move. She only stared, her eyes large and round, reflecting the darkness of the cellar, and the single flame on the candle. Aster attempted a smile. She felt it stretching her lips, an unnatural tightening.

"You just hop into the tub, and you'll forget I'm out of the room. After I get the tomatoes carried down we'll clean up the kitchen and fix some supper, all right?"

Becky bowed her head. "All right," she said in a meek little voice.

Aster went down the steps and set the candle holder in the middle of the old oak cooktable that had been in the basement as long as she could remember. Dampness was gradually ruining what it once had been. The cracks between the boards in the top were wide enough to put a finger through. It listed, a bit farther each year, one leg bending under. In recent years it had been used only to hold the candles.

She climbed the steps. The wavering candlelight left deep shadows beside the steps, beneath the table, in the depths of shelves that had been emptied of fruit and vegetables. She felt icy air pushing at her back as she hurried back up into the laundry room.

Becky was still standing by the tub of bath water. She had removed her red-stained outer clothing and stood in her bloomers. Her little chest looked no wider than the doll's chest. Stringy little arms hung powerless.

This child didn't stab Eleanor.

For one moment Aster glimpsed a horror reflected only in Becky's eyes, but her own needs pushed it away. Of course it was Becky, it had to have been Becky. No one else was in the house. The front door was locked, and Aster herself had been near the only other door that led outside. She had seen no one enter the house. No one, other than Eleanor, then Becky.

Aster went into the kitchen and picked up the basket with seven jars carefully arranged in the bottom. Becky voiced no further objection as Aster carried it to the cellar door and down.

She put the basket down on the cool ground and stood a

moment looking at the shelves. Empty jars took up spaces between jars that were filled and ready for winter. Before the girls came to live with her, Aster had canned early peaches from the tree in the backyard, and spinach from her own garden.

She set about arranging it as she used to, by color. Certain fruits and vegetables looked better if they were arranged just so, and it was, after all, one of her few pleasures to have her cellar artistically arranged. Merle might laugh at her, and Heather would roll her eyes upward, but to Aster it was just part of life.

Green spinach, red tomatoes, yellow squash from last year, then greenbeans from last year, and then the peaches.

Becky stood trembling by the tub of water. She was alone now, and she was so scared to be alone. Aunt Aster was out of sight down in the cellar. It looked deep and dark, like the grave that had been dug for Ellie's casket, only a lot bigger, like a grave that would hold many caskets.

Aunt Aster had told her to take her bath. There was the rough washcloth, and the soap. And the water in the tub. Becky looked at the window where all the red streaks from the sun were gone now and left it black, as if on the outside a big hand had drawn down a black curtain. She looked at the open door into the kitchen. A candle made a little pool of light in the middle of the table. She saw the circle of light, and the dark shadows beneath the table.

She hooked her fingers under the waistband of her bloomers and pushed them down and stepped out of them. She looked around again.

She started to step into the tub when she heard it. The doll, moving. Becky held her breath.

For a long time the doll would be still, like Sir Thomas when he slept in the sunshine on the porch. Then it would move. And sometimes it sounded just like Ellie so that she wasn't sure, and she thought Ellie might be just playing a trick on her. Maybe everyone was playing a trick on her.

Ellie wasn't really dead. Maybe. Maybe she was hearing Ellie. Maybe it was Ellie coming now into the kitchen.

Becky stood listening. She heard the swinging door into the kitchen squeak, the way it always did. Then the slipping along, the footsteps on the kitchen floor, very slow, as if Ellie didn't want to be heard. Was it Ellie, coming back from her grave, or was it Zenoa? She wanted to believe it was Ellie. But she knew it wasn't. It was Zenoa.

Becky stood still, frozen in a stoop, her hands on the edge of the tub. If she held her breath Zenoa might not know where she was, might not ever know where to find her.

Suddenly Becky remembered. It couldn't be Zenoa who had come into the kitchen. The doll couldn't walk anymore! She had forgotten, but Ellie had fixed the doll so that it couldn't walk. The very last morning before she died.

At first Ellie had been mad at Becky, and had scolded her and threatened to hit her. Becky could almost hear her voice again.

"Becky, stop making Aunt Aster come running to our room every night. She's going to get mad like Mama and start hitting you. And you have to stop moving Zenoa at night! She thinks I move Zenoa at night, but I don't, you do!"

"I didn't move her, I didn't! She moves by herself, Ellie. I see her, when it's dark."

"That's a lie. Dolls don't move. They ain't real."

"It's not a lie. I saw her move! She moved from the corner to the dresser, and then she got down from the dresser. She was coming to hurt me!"

"Then I'll fix her so she can't walk."

So Ellie picked up the big doll, high over her head, and threw her down on the floor, again and again. The doll's head made a cracking sound on the floor both times. It kind of bounced, then lay still. Both eyes were closed. She looked dead. Becky wondered in a kind of wordless horror if Ellie had killed Zenoa.

Ellie stood with her hands knotted on her hips and said,

107

"Hmmm. I know what I'll do. You have to be punished, Zenoa. You've been bad."

She sat down on the doll's body, grasped one leg and pulled, hard. She looked up at Becky, her face red with the effort of whatever it was she was trying to do. "Help me," she commanded. "We'll make it so she can't walk."

Becky shook her head and edged away, her hands behind her back. She began to whimper. Her stomach felt twisted and sick. "Don't hurt her!"

Ellie gave her a disgusted look, and scooted down so that she was sitting only on the doll's legs. With both hands she grasped a foot and jerked upward.

Something in the doll's leg made a cracking sound.

In the white stocking, just above the black shoe, the cracked section bulged, and the foot flopped sideways.

Ellie smiled.

She stood up, and lifted the doll to its feet. The doll's one good eye opened, and it stared at Ellie. But the doll couldn't stand. It flopped sideways, and Ellie had to catch it to keep it from falling.

"See, Becky, she won't be walking around now, will she?"

Becky drew a deep sigh of relief, though she didn't feel good about what Ellie had done to Zenoa.

Yet later when Aunt Aster had sent Becky up to find Ellie, Zenoa had been standing, as if her ankle weren't broken. Standing with the ice pick over Ellie.

Becky felt confused. The footsteps she had heard had sounded like Ellie's. Yet much slower than Ellie's, as if she took a step, paused, stepped again.

Ellie might have come back. She might have climbed from the grave. There were a lot of things Ellie could do that no one but Becky knew anything about. She wanted Ellie to come back. It was a constant cry in her heart. *Come back, Ellie.*

Perhaps she had, because Zenoa couldn't walk with her broken ankle, could she? Ellie had promised.

Becky moved slowly toward the kitchen. Hesitantly she peered through at the swinging door. It was closed now.

She could see all of the round kitchen table with the candle, and the big, black, iron cookstove against the wall. She saw the woodbox, with the wood that would be used tomorrow to can more tomatoes. But there was no one standing in sight, not even by the wall between the door and the stove.

She took another step, stretching to see. Ellie?

She slipped silently through the kitchen door.

No one. No one stood anywhere in the large kitchen.

The footsteps started behind her, and this time she heard the dragging step of the broken foot. It made a soft sliding sound that sent terror into Becky's soul.

She whirled. The doll stood in the corner, almost invisible in the deep shadows thrown by the ice box. Becky knew. She had come to get the ice pick again.

Becky's scream seemed to rise from far above. Aster's first thought was of the child in bed, with her sister, screaming in a night terror. Then, even as she automatically turned and began running up the cellar steps, she remembered that Becky was in the laundry room. Yet she sounded so much farther away.

Aster entered the laundry room. The tub of bath water stood empty in the middle of the floor. Beside it lay the crumpled dress and apron, even the bloomers. Becky was not in the room. Her screams were like dying gasps, breathless, weakening.

Aster ran through the kitchen door. She stopped, staring from one face to the other.

Becky stood as far back in the corner behind the table as she could get, squeezed in terror against the wall. On the floor a few feet away, on its stomach, face turned sideways, lay the doll Heather had given the girls.

A thing once so beautiful now was hideous. Both eyes were closed, but one was pushed so far back into the face it was like a black hole. The scalp had bald places, the tiny holes where the hair had been rooted visible in the candlelight flickering on the table.

As Aster stooped to pick up the doll she became aware

that Becky's scream was now a sobbing, *"No, no, no."*

Aster paused.

Becky pleaded, *"Don't touch her."*

Her.

As if it were something with a personality.

"It's all right, Becky," Aster said. "It's only the doll. It's—" And then it occurred to Aster that the only way the doll could have gotten into the room was if Becky had gone upstairs and brought it down.

Everything was all wrong. Why would Becky, so terrified of being alone, so afraid of the dark, of everything, undress and then run upstairs as soon as Aster was in the cellar and bring back this poor, ruined doll? And then start screaming because it was there? Aster felt her lips tighten. She hated what was happening to her. She hated not understanding the mind behind the innocent eyes of the six-year-old child.

She picked up the doll, and tried to straighten its torn clothing. A needle and thread might help. But she could hardly stand to touch it. Its face, once so very beautiful, was now frightening. The one eye turned inward, yet still seemed to be looking at her. Balefully. Could a glass eye in a doll's head hold such an expression?

Aster looked around for a place to put the doll, and finally took it through the swinging door and set it down in the hallway. Very little light came through the glass on the front door, and the hall was almost dark. Aster could see the outline of the stairway, and nothing more. The doll blended into the darkness of the corner.

The swinging door squeaked as she returned to the kitchen.

Becky, now silent, had moved out from the corner. She was naked and shivering, pitifully small and defenseless.

The time had come to talk to her. Aster had to try, even if she didn't know how.

She brought a clean nightgown from the laundry room and slipped it over Becky's head. No matter about the

110

bath, she thought to herself.

She pulled a kitchen chair away from the table and sat down.

"Why did you do it, Becky?"

Becky looked at her. Aster saw the child's chin was jerking. Aster held out her hands, and Becky came forward. But she didn't run as she had before, as if now she had lost some of the trust.

"Why did you run upstairs and bring down the doll? And then stand in the corner screaming?"

"I didn't b-bring her down. I d-d-didn't."

Aster sighed and looked toward the ceiling. It was a high ceiling, almost lost now beyond the candlelight. All the ceilings in the house were high, but especially these on the first floor. Tonight she would rather they were not so distant, and so dark.

"Becky, what did your mother do when you lied? Didn't she ever teach you the difference in pretend and truth? Pretend can be lying, when you don't tell the truth about something."

Becky covered her face with her hands. She began to cry. Her voice came half-smothered from between her fingers.

"I didn't lie. I heard something. I heard Ellie come into the kitchen. And I came to see. It wasn't Ellie, it was *her.* Zenoa. She was coming to kill me, like she killed Ellie. She hates me. She's bad. Her eyes . . . her eye—She hates me because Ellie made her ugly. She was walking, dragging her foot."

"Dragging her foot!" Of all the things Becky had been saying that one thing struck Aster as absurdly ridiculous, yet significant. Of course the doll didn't walk. Of course not! *But . . . dragging her foot . . . ?*

Becky nodded. "Her foot—it's broken."

Aster stood up abruptly, pushing Becky back from her knees. She picked up one of the candles from the table and pushed through the swinging door.

The doll lay on its side, fallen over from the position in which Aster had left it.

111

Aster knelt and placed the candleholder on the floor. She lifted the doll's long skirt and looked at the feet.

Yes. The left leg was broken just above the top of the black leather shoe.

Aster eased the doll down. The quaint little mouth with the slight overbite and the amused half-smile was made now into something grotesque by the protruding tongue. Eleanor had even managed to ruin that.

Aster drew back. The one dark eye stared at her, and Aster could sense an evil hatred. It was as if Becky's beliefs were creating a strange kind of life within the emptiness of the doll.

Twelve

Oh God what am I going to do?

She'd had to bring the child into her own room again, put her to bed on one side of her wide bed. Becky slept now while Aster sat in the rocking chair at the window looking out through the screen into the night. The candle-light disturbed her. Millers fluttered against the screen. She wanted to snuff out the light and yet couldn't bear the thought of darkness in the room.

Now that the funeral was over and the house empty of family and voices and presences Aster felt more trapped than she'd ever felt in her life.

She had to face it. The child sleeping so innocently in her bed was insane. She needed care that Aster couldn't give her.

She had to admit, in the still darkness of the night where sounds seemed exaggerated, the whispering of the candle flame, the soft breathing of Becky, she was afraid. Afraid of every sound, of soft slidings she'd never heard before, of movements in the house like footsteps coming near. Afraid of her own house. Afraid of the darkness now. But . . .

Afraid mostly of the child.

She hugged her arms to her chest, bending forward in the pain that knowledge gave her. Love struggled against fear. And she was yielding to the fear.

What had she done with the ice pick?

Was it still wrapped in her apron, blood still crusted on its handle and turning the metal dark?

She got up and stood at the foot of the bed looking at the

sleeping child. Her face was turned into the pillow, almost buried. One arm hugged the pillow. Her long, white nightgown had crept up onto the backs of her legs, leaving her ankles and feet bare. They looked so small. The child herself looked so very small. Yet as Aster stood looking at Becky it seemed the atmosphere had changed and if she looked over her shoulder she would see what Becky had seen. But she didn't dare turn her head, for that would leave her defenseless against this horror within Becky which she didn't understand. Fear grew, destroying the person she had been, and her relationship with Becky.

She couldn't keep Becky. Aster knew that suddenly and definitively. She couldn't keep Becky any longer.

What was she going to do? She couldn't send her back to Heather, or to any other of the relatives.

She turned away, fear and failure enveloping her like an icy sheet. She wanted to look back to see if Becky had opened her eyes and was staring at her, reading her mind, understanding what she was going to do.

If Becky knew, what would she do?

Don't be ridiculous, Aster told herself. Eleanor had been only a frail child, hardly larger than Becky. But Aster was neither small nor frail. She could certainly protect herself. Especially from one so small. For the time.

But Becky was a growing child. She would get larger.

Aster slid the dresser drawer open as quietly as she could and removed a candle. She lighted it at the flame of the burning candle and then turned slowly. Becky had not changed position.

Walking softly, her slippers whispering on the floor, Aster left the bedroom. She went down the stairs and down the hall toward the swinging door, the candlelight touching upon darknesses she was only recently finding existed in her house.

She stopped.

The doll was gone.

She stood still, bewildered, wondering. When could Becky have moved the doll?

114

After supper they had gone upstairs, and Aster had made up the bed in the master bedroom for Becky. Where was Becky when she was making the bed? In the room, huddled against the wall. But Aster's back was toward her.

Then, Aster had put the little girl to bed in the largest bedroom in the house. The furniture there was crowded and dark. Mama had gathered things during her lifetime. She'd had a passion for fine old furniture and whenever she could find a place for something, and the money, she purchased it. Especially after Heather left home. It was as if she were using shopping to fill the gap Heather had left. Aster saw Becky looking about in her usual wide-eyed terror, and Aster soothingly told her, "This was your grandmother's room. Of course Papa's room too. Papa was your grandfather. You've seen them both, do you remember?"

Becky shook her head.

Aster left Becky in the room.

It must have been then that she slipped from the room and went downstairs in the dark to get the doll.

Yet Aster had only begun to undress for bed when Becky had begun to scream. Aster ran to the bedroom, just across the hall, to find Becky standing up in bed, staring at the doorway and screaming words that Aster finally understood were, "Make her go away. Make her go away."

Aster was unable to comfort her, or to leave her. As Becky grew quiet at last, in Aster's arms, in the rocking chair in Aster's bedroom, she had known. Becky needed more help than she could ever give her. It would take doctors and nurses, and there was no money for a private hospital.

Aster stood now in the hall looking at the place where she had left the doll. Becky must have found enough time to come and get it, and that was the only thing that could have happened. Was she only pretending to be terrified of a doll that was now broken and hideous looking?

Aster went on into the kitchen, and then into the laundry room. She had tucked her bloody apron, with the ice pick wrapped inside, in the laundry basket, beneath other dirty clothes.

She felt for it. Her groping hand touched nothing but clothing.

She upended the basket and dumped the dirty clothes out onto the floor. Her heart wrenched in pain as she saw clothes Eleanor had worn. The new everyday brown dress, as plain as an apron, that Aster had sewn for her, as quickly as she could so the child would have something to wear. There was also a nightgown, and old white flannel bloomers that had become too small and were worn through in several places. There too was the dress Eleanor had been wearing when she was stabbed, with the torn holes in the back. The ice pick had torn the cloth of the dress more than it had the resilient skin of the child. Blood had surrounded each torn hole and run in rivulets, making thin stripes. Blood had been smeared on the dress as if Becky had tried to wipe away what she had done.

But there was no ice pick.

Aster began to shake. Her hands trembled as she anxiously dumped out all the clothing and riffled through it, searching frantically for the ice pick. The apron was still there, on the bottom of the pile, but the pick was gone.

Had she cleaned it and put it away on the top of the ice box where it belonged?

No.

She had wrapped it in the apron and hidden it. Just as a few minutes later she had hidden Eleanor's dress.

To be sure she went to the ice box and looked. The narrow groove that ran around the edge of the lid contained nothing. Although she could see the pick was not there, still she ran her fingers around the groove feeling, all the while wondering what could have happened.

Becky.

Becky had seen her wrap the pick in the apron . . . no, she hadn't. Becky had not gone with her into the room where Eleanor lay.

Someone else? One of her relatives? No one had stayed long enough to consider helping with the weekly wash. No, none of them would have taken the ice pick.

116

Aster searched. She looked through drawers and into the top of the ice box itself where the chunk of ice had seeped away to half its original size. In the crackling silences of the house, in the middle of the night, her way lighted only by a candle, Aster searched. She searched the laundry room, even into the drawers of the chest where she kept folded, ironed linens and clothing.

Finally she had to consider that she herself had, when she was half out of her mind, only thought she had wrapped the pick in her apron. She sat down on the old rickety chair in the laundry room, exhausted. She wanted to think she had misplaced it, but she knew in her mind that she had left the pick in the apron, wrapped tight.

Now it was gone.

Becky must have it. Sometime, somehow. As quietly as the child moved about, usually staying so close to her, she probably had seen more than Aster thought she had.

But now, please God, she was asleep.

Aster had to make arrangements for her to be taken away. She had a letter to write, an explanation to Heather.

Her searching eyes fell upon the small dress on the floor with the torn holes and the brown stains. Eleanor's dress. She was glad now she hadn't washed it. It would be needed to show the doctor. She had to show him that Becky was dangerous, to others and perhaps herself.

Aster stood up wearily, picked up the dress off the floor, and the apron with the dried brown stains.

She took them into the kitchen and hung them both over the backs of kitchen chairs. Then from the drawer she took a sheet of paper and the pen and small bottle of ink.

She sat down at the table and began to write.

Dear Heather,
As you will see, this is the most difficult letter I've ever had to write in my life. But I must. I know that you won't be able to take Becky back into your house. It would be too dangerous. When morning comes I'm going to call the doctor. And then I'm going to call the police. I don't know what else to do. Becky killed Eleanor. She used

117

the ice pick and stabbed her twice in the back. At first I tried to hide
that fact. I cleaned Eleanor's wounds, and they looked only like
small freckles. No one else noticed them, not the doctor nor the nurse,
God rest her soul. But now I think I did the wrong thing. Becky
needs hel—

Aster's head jerked up. Had she heard a sound of movement in the hall or had she only imagined it?

She sat still, listening, hearing her own blood race and her heart pound. The world seemed empty and black, without sound beyond herself, yet filled with ominous beings that crouched behind her with long-bladed ice picks in their hands.

She turned her head, listening.

There . . . again.

A step, soft and light, and then . . . *s-l-i-d-e* . . .

Aster's mouth opened. Her chin hung lax. She stared at the swinging door. She had to turn in her chair to see the door, behind her. Over her shoulder she watched the door slowly open, slowly, slowly. Aster stared, unable to move, her mouth hanging open and her throat dry and parched.

Step . . . slide . . .

Then she saw the tiny fingers that clutched the edge of the door. Not Becky's . . . dear God . . . not Becky's . . .

This is not possible.

God in Heaven, things like this aren't real. They are nightmares, made up of too many fears and too many terrible things happening. The human mind could take only so much, and then it broke down and mixed nightmares with reality. And her mind had broken.

She watched it enter the room.

It was like a specter of madness, half its hair pulled out, its right eye permanently closed, its left eye turned slightly inward toward its nose. Yet still it stared steadily at her as if she were a kind of prey. Its arms had dropped to its sides. It approached upright, stiffly yet with eerie ease, step, slide. It walked on the broken and jagged ankle, the small foot with the shoe still attached dragging along.

118

It came nearer and nearer to Aster, and she watched, as paralyzed as a trembling and helpless mouse in the cage of a hungry snake.

Becky was right.

What kind of horror had Heather let loose on them? Had she known there was something supernatural about the doll? No, no, surely to God, no . . .

Aster's body reacted, at last. She shoved her chair back and rose from it, stumbling backward. The doll turned, stiffly, following in its uneven movements. Aster walked backwards, her eyes on the doll. *Mister Jessup* — she had to get Mister Jessup —

Her heel caught on the braided rug she had made only last winter, a small rug that added a colorful touch to the drab kitchen. She felt herself falling, backwards, her arms flailing helplessly. She lost sight of the doll for that instant. Then she struck the floor. All breath expelled in a painful burst, and before she could rise she saw its face inches from her own.

She reached up to throw it away from her, and felt a cold, repulsive skin, artificial yet alive with something she couldn't bear to touch. She twisted, reaching up for the doorknob, so close, so close . . .

In the corner of her eye she glimpsed the thin slash of the ice pick, candlelight catching on one clean spot of the blade like moonlight on a gravestone.

She felt it pierce her skin and enter her chest, again and again as she tried weakly to lift her arms and push away from her the hideous face that was commanding more and more of her world. The one eye watched her with no emotion, only dark, boundless evil.

Thirteen

The beautiful white box, covered in satin and lace, stood off the floor, satin draped over the stand beneath it. Flowers in large and small bouquets had been arranged around it. Above the raised lid Becky could see the spikes of gladiolus. She knew all about the flowers because Aunt Aster had told her. There was even a flower named aster, and it was that flower Aunt Aster had been named for. It was a delicate lavender flower that bloomed in the fall, and it grew wild along the roadsides.

People's faces, none of them smiling, floated like the flowers around the beautiful satin box. Becky went closer to the box. A casket, a casket, casket . . . the word floated in the air with the scent of the flowers and the faces of the strange people.

Becky looked into the casket. She didn't want to.

Ellie! Ellie!

People stared at Becky when she screamed, stared and stared, cold strange eyes.

Then another face was suddenly before her. The black veil was thin, and now Becky could see the mouth, the upper lip sticking out just a bit beyond the lower, and two dimples at the corners. She could see the delicate nose and the large round dark eyes.

Zenoa. Pretending to be her mother. Zenoa.

What have you done? the voice behind the veil asked, bending closer and closer to Becky's face. What have you done, you evil, evil child? Nobody but Becky saw the smile.

Becky tried to look away from the grownup face behind the veil and her eyes came upon the casket again, and within it, her sister.

But this time, there was an ice pick in her chest, and blood was ruining the lovely white dress.

120

* * *

With a cry Becky jerked awake. Then, seeing the newly familiar surroundings of Aunt Aster's room, she lay still, her head half buried in the thick pillow. She looked at the distant ceiling. It was so high it looked as if there were no ceiling at all, just a distant, dark sky.

Fear made her tremble. She was afraid to move, to make a sound, to draw the attention of things that lurked in the dark. The doll . . . Zenoa. She might have come into the room while she slept, and Aunt Aster might not have known. She had to tell Aunt Aster. Slowly and quietly Becky sat up and looked for her aunt.

She was not in bed. Aunt Aster's side of the bed was still neat, and the pillow fluffed large and round and long, part of it leaning up against the headboard the way Aunt Aster liked it.

The rocking chair where she sat so much at night was empty too. *Where's Aunt Aster?* Becky looked about in the gloomy shadows. She saw the light of the candle, rising, falling. Her ears picked up a soft whisper and she looked frantically for who or what might be making that whispering sound, and looked back at last at the candle. It was as if the flame were trying to tell her something.

Whisper, whisper. Beware, beware. You're alone, alone, alone, except for her, her, her. Zenoa, Zenoa, Zenoa. Shhh, shhh, don't make a sound, or she will find you, find you, find you. Kill you, kill you . . . Heather sent Zenoa here to kill you, kill you . . .

Becky felt the scream in her throat, but she held it back. She had to be quiet. The candle had told her so.

She had to find Aunt Aster and Aunt Aster had gone from the room and left Becky alone.

Where had she gone?

The house was so large . . . and Zenoa was here, somewhere, in the dark house. Zenoa could see in the dark. She could walk, even with her broken foot. Even with one eye she could see. Even if she had no eyes at all she would be able to see Becky in the dark.

121

She couldn't hurt Aunt Aster, because Aunt Aster was big. But Aunt Aster wouldn't believe that Zenoa had killed Ellie, and was going to kill Becky too. Aunt Aster wouldn't make the doll go away, because she thought Becky was lying.

You bad girl, you tell lies, lies!

Her mother's hand was like the shadows that crept ahead of the candlelight along the floor and walls, and Becky cringed. But then it withdrew, like the shadows, and Becky had only the burning memory of the pain.

Where was Aunt Aster? *Come back, please, Aunt Aster. Stay with me.*

Becky sat in the bed with her knees drawn up and her arms clutching them tightly. She stared at the closed door.

"Come back, come back, come back Aunt Aster," she whispered beneath her breath, willing her aunt to return. Maybe she'd only gone out for a drink, for . . .

No, there was water on the dresser. And there was a chamber pot beneath the bed.

Why had Aunt Aster left her alone?

Where had she gone?

Zenoa hurt her, the candle whispered.

No, Aunt Aster was big. Zenoa couldn't hurt her.

And if Becky stayed close to Aunt Aster, Zenoa couldn't hurt her either. Aunt Aster wouldn't let her.

Becky slipped out of bed. Her bare feet touched the rug on the floor. Its woolen fibers stuck her feet, like grass in the yard. Becky had learned the feel of so many strange things since she had come to live with Aunt Aster. The feel of wool rugs, and the feel of grass.

Shhh, shhh, shhh.

The candle hissed, and the flame leaped frantically.

Becky paused, then took another step, then another. Would Zenoa hear her moving, even though she moved without making a sound?

Yes. Yes. She had to hurry and find Aunt Aster.

She opened the door, and the candle flame in the hallway leaped toward the ceiling and then fell back and almost went out as if the darkness there had smothered it. The candle behind Becky kept whispering.

She slipped out into the shadowy hallway. She listened. Aunt Aster was not here. Becky was afraid to open the closed door of the room where Ellie had been killed, and where the nurse who had come to stay with Ellie had died. Had Zenoa killed her too? Even though she was big?

The other bedroom door was closed too. The big bedroom where Aunt Aster had tried to get Becky to sleep, all alone, with no protection against Zenoa.

Becky went to the stairs. She looked down into darkness. Aunt Aster had left Zenoa down there, in the lower hall. For Becky to get to the kitchen where Aunt Aster might have gone, she would have to pass through that hall.

She stood still.

The dark in the hall below seemed to become less dark. Becky could see the big post at the bottom of the stairs, the one Aunt Aster said was the newel post. She could even see the chair and the chest with the long, oval mirror and the umbrella stand. The umbrellas were like black skeletons.

Light! Dim, and far away. Starlight. Moonlight. Coming through the glass on the door. She could go out the front door and around the house to the back door. She wouldn't have to go through the hall where Aunt Aster had left Zenoa.

She went down the steps slowly, quietly, leaving the light of the candle in the hallway behind. With her hands gripping the posts along the stairway, she finally reached the newel post.

She looked toward the swinging door at the end of the hall, and she saw light in the crack beneath the door. Aunt Aster was there, in the kitchen. She wanted to call for her, but couldn't make her voice talk.

She slipped quietly to the door, looking over her shoulder into the dark hall where Aunt Aster had put the doll. Her hands worked at turning the knob. It turned, but the door didn't open.

Locked.

She stood with her back against the door and looked at the crack of light at the end of the hall. She stared into the darkness for an outline that might be the doll. Nothing.

If she ran . . .

She couldn't run. She could still hear the whisper of the candle in the bedroom above. *Shhh. Shhh.*

She slipped forward, one stiff step after another.

At last she came to the place where Aunt Aster had put Zenoa. She slid along the opposite wall, as far away from that place as she could get. She wanted to scream for Aunt Aster to come and let her into the light of the kitchen, but her voice still wouldn't talk.

Finally, she reached the door. No small, long-fingered hand clutched her ankle.

She pushed the door open. It squeaked. But that was all right. She could see the light in the kitchen, and Aunt Aster might be angry that she had gotten out of bed, but Aunt Aster wouldn't hit her.

She entered the kitchen.

Aunt Aster lay on the floor, stretched long and oddly flat, facedown, as Ellie had been. And in her back, was the ice pick.

Becky ran to her and fell forward. *Aunt Aster, Aunt Aster* . . . She could feel the cry in her throat, but nothing came out. She felt the blood on her hands, as she had felt Ellie's blood. She gripped her aunt's arm and tried to lift her.

Her voice broke loose. "Aunt Aster, please, Aunt Aster, get up. Get up, Aunt Aster."

She managed to lift her aunt's arm and shoulder, but then it fell back and lay still.

In the silence she heard a movement. She turned.

Zenoa sat in the corner, as if a little girl had placed her there. Her broken foot stuck out to one side. Her head lolled a bit sideways, but her one eye watched Becky.

BOOK TWO
1969
The Legacy

One

"Lovely day," the neat, thin, elderly man said with a smile when Virginia entered the antique store. A small bell clattered as the door closed. The store had a musty smell, as of thousands of old things hoarded away to gather dust.

"It certainly is a most lovely day," Virginia answered. "Do you mind if I just look around?"

"Browse all you want. That's what we're here for."

How nice, she thought to herself, to have browsing time. This was the first Monday she had not gone to work for eleven years, since her husband, Ted, died suddenly of a heart attack.

Retirement was promising to be interesting, though not at all what she and Ted had planned. There would be very little traveling now, without him. But she could investigate her own city and surrounding areas. At least retirement promised not to be boring. Not as long as there were antique stores like this that were themselves antique, on small, old inner city streets she had never seen before.

The main room was large, filled with dusty aisles and counters with every conceivable item that was once used by people, old combs, costume jewelry now tarnished and dull, handkerchiefs elaborately embroidered and now yellowed, tiny bottles, things Virginia had no idea what their purpose had been. Along the side tiny rooms or booths had been created each by two walls, the fronts opening into the main room. Each individual room held collectibles of different sorts, glassware in one, kitchen accessories in another, even items once used in barns or stables.

A few other people were wandering about in the store, but they all seemed to be avoiding one another. Antique browsing required a certain state of mind, she supposed. Just looking at the sort of things one's great-grandmother used in her kitchen took a person back into a kind of dreamlike state of mind, bordering on nightmare. How people had worked just to live! Yet how great it must have seemed to a great-great-grandmother to be able to replace her old scrub board with the modern machine in which all she needed was one or two of her dozen or so kids to turn the handle and crank the clothes about in the tub. She'd have time then to haul out the automatic apple peeler, get another kid to turn its handle, and peel that basket of apples.

Meantime, great-great-grandpa was out in the yard making sausage with that funny looking old machine. That is, if it were butchering time, in which case he'd have the pig or the calf tied up by its hind legs in the barn, squealing its poor, scared heart out while he sharpened the butcher knife on that old grinding stone and prepared to cut its throat.

Virginia shook her head and moved on. What had made her think she wanted to see antiques?

Beyond stacks of larger antiques she found a door in the back opening into a room with more, and junkier, antiques. Virginia wandered through, looking at dusty glassware behind dusty glass cases. She looked at an old grandfather's clock that was at least eight feet tall. The large pendulum hung still, and had for a century, probably. The wood looked as if it had been out in the weather for at least fifty years.

She moved on, wondering how much of this stuff the owner sold. Were most of the customers like herself, just looking?

She saw through the door in the back a child's doll buggy, and she thought of her youngest granddaughter, Kit. Her ninth birthday was coming up in a couple of weeks, and she'd probably never even seen such a buggy.

128

But it had a broken wheel, and dust had ground permanently into the wicker hood. The handle was gone too. Impractical, maybe even impossible to repair.

This room was much smaller. Another door at the rear was closed. It probably opened into a workshop where some repairs were made, or perhaps it only held even worse junk. She turned, careful to touch nothing. Her hands already felt grimy with dust from touching the doll buggy.

Shelves lined the room, holding every imaginable small thing that would fit, from glassware stacked, to fancy old valentine boxes to toys and dolls.

Virginia started out, then stopped and looked back. The sadly ruined doll on the shelf across the room caught her eye. Her first glance saw the ugliness. Her second glance, the beauty. It had the most unique mouth she had ever seen. Although it had a slight overbite, the lips were sweetly perfect. They were parted slightly, and looked as if she were about to speak. The lower part of its face was incredibly beautiful. But it's cheeks were scratched, its golden hair was dusty and thin, one eye was closed and sunken. The other eye was a soft brown. It turned inward toward the nose. Still, it seemed to be looking straight at Virginia. She felt a strange tingle zip across her shoulders and neck.

She went slowly back and picked up the doll.

It was large, with a firm, molded body, jointed arms and legs. The detailing of the hands was perfect, each finger separate from the other, and slightly flexible with rounded nails. One leg, at the ankle, was broken just enough that it hung sideways. Still, with all its defects, it was one of the most beautiful dolls she had ever seen.

Zenoa.

"Quite remarkable, isn't she?"

Virginia jumped and looked back. The man who had spoken to her at the front door now stood within reach. Virginia's heart pounded uncomfortably. She took a deep breath.

"Yes, she is."

"I can let you have her for less than fifty dollars. She's a real antique, a hundred years old.

"Really?"

"Yes. And quite a history. She was found back in eighteen-seventy in a house where a lady lay dead with an ice pick in her heart, and the only witness to the murder was a six-year-old mute child. The little girl's sister had been murdered the same way a few days before and the little girl was so shocked by the murders, she never spoke another word the rest of her life. She spent it in the state hospital for the insane. Died when she was fifteen. The aunt had been writing a letter claiming the little girl stabbed her sister, but that was discounted by the judge. The murders were never solved. The child was never able to tell what she had seen. My grandfather built this store just after the Civil War, and he acquired the doll right after the murders, and it's been here in the back of this shop ever since. No one would ever buy it. I think he always kept it back here because of its history."

Thinking of the young girl who had died in what was then an asylum, Virginia said, "That's terrible."

"Well, yes, but we always make a point of telling its history just because it's interesting, even though we know it kills the sale every time. People are superstitious." He had a strange little giggling chuckle. "But in the almost one hundred years it's been here, there haven't been any ice pick murders."

"Oh, its history is no problem with me. I'm not superstitious."

"I can even direct you to a good doll repair place."

"Why is it you never had her repaired?"

"Well, it's an antique, and it's better not to touch antiques. Keep them with their defects. But in the case of this doll, if you have a little child in mind for her, that's a different story. The little girl wouldn't care if it's been repaired."

"I can see it has been a beautiful doll. It has the most appealing mouth I've ever seen. And it so happens that I

130

do have a little granddaughter who's having her ninth birthday soon."

"I'll let you have the doll for twenty-five dollars, just for the granddaughter."

Virginia smiled and shrugged. "Why not?"

He carefully removed the doll from the shelf. She followed him toward the counter at the front of the store, paid for the doll, and watched him put it into a large sack. Then he gave her the address of the doll repair shop.

With the sacked doll in her arms Virginia started toward the door, then paused.

"You said her name is Zenoa?"

The man's face went totally blank. He blinked. "Zenoa? No, I . . . I don't think I ever heard that name before."

The tingle rushed again into the back of Virginia's hair. She and the man stared at each other, then she shrugged and opened the door that took her out onto the sidewalk. Her smile died as she walked to her car, unlocked it, and carefully laid the doll on the back seat.

As she drove away she thought of the instant the doll's name had entered her mind. The man had spoken behind her, and she had associated the two. But obviously he had never heard the name before. She had picked it out of the dusty silence in the back room of the antique store.

Oh well, it was a name as good as any.

She checked the address of the repair shop. Another street she had never driven on before. She didn't know the city had so many narrow little streets, themselves antique, business buildings crowding against the sidewalks and no room for widening. Some of them were one way, but these had no traffic problem even though they were two-way streets.

She found the street she wanted, and finally the sign that said merely, REPAIRS. She parked, took the doll from the back seat and went into the shop.

A middle-aged woman wearing a heavy leather apron came from a door at the back of the small shop. Someone else was working back there, out of sight. Virginia heard tappings and buzzings.

"I was told you repair dolls?"

"Yes."

Virginia laid the doll on the counter. "It's an antique, and I'd like her kept as much as possible the way she is. If you could just fix her eye and her leg, and her hair, maybe put her into a new dress?"

The woman became excited as she examined the doll. "Oh, she's fine bisque, a lovely doll. Made in Germany in eighteen-sixty-nine." She touched the cheek where it was deeply scratched. "I'll touch up these scratches just to make her more lovely. She'll want to be as pretty as she can, this doll, she's probably very vain. What miserable conditions she's been under all these years waiting for some attention."

Virginia listened to the woman in surprised amusement. She was talking about the doll as if somewhere deep within its fine bisque there lingered a personality. But what the heck, the woman was, after all, in the doll repair business. She probably needed to feel they were more than just dolls.

"I can make her beautiful again, without removing her worth."

Virginia didn't bother to tell her she'd purchased the doll for only twenty-five dollars.

"It's for my youngest granddaughter," she said. "Her birthday's in two weeks. She'll be nine."

"How lovely. What a lucky child. I promise you I'll have her ready by then."

As Virginia prepared to leave, the repair woman asked, "What's her name?"

Virginia hesitated at the door, wondering if she meant her granddaughter, or the doll. But the woman was still intently examining the doll, and that was where her interest lay.

"Zenoa," Virginia said.

She returned to her car feeling delighted with her purchase. Kit would love the doll.

The sky was perfectly blue, with small, dumpling clouds,

and Virginia felt her first surge of freedom since Ted's death. She recalled feeling this way most of the time when she was eighteen. And that reminded her of Pamela, her son Leslie's second daughter. She was eighteen now, out of high school and entering college in the fall. Pam had a job for the summer as a checker in a supermarket within a few blocks of her home, where she still lived with her parents, little sister Kit and brother Nicky, who was now twelve. Beth, her older sister, was twenty-two, married, and had a baby daughter herself. Virginia had the pleasure of babysitting two-month-old Tresa whenever Beth and Rory wanted a night out.

On a sudden whim Virginia decided to drive over and have lunch with Pam, even though it was across the river and the traffic would be heavy at this hour. She had to get onto the freeway, which made her nervous. She usually avoided it as much as possible, and didn't see the kids as often as she might have for that simple reason. Ted had always done the freeway driving for her. He had done too much for her, she'd decided in the eleven years since he'd died so suddenly. She had always been mother and homemaker, even though after their one child, Leslie, left home there was no one to mother except the cats, dogs, and Ted himself. But that was the way he wanted it. He wanted her at home when he got there, just as Les had when he was a growing boy.

That was the way she had wanted it too. She loved housekeeping, gardening, sewing, all the traditional things. They had bought their older, spacious home when Les was small, and had planned to keep it all their lives. When Ted died, she learned that if she wanted to keep the home, with the big trees in the front yard and the lovely garden spot in the back, the place where she felt closest to Ted, she'd have to go to work.

Now that period of her life had ended too. Her home was secured. The mortgage was cleared. Home paid for with enough monthly income to keep her going. No more seven o'clock openings at the laundry and cleaning service six blocks away, the best job she'd been able to find.

She clutched the steering wheel as she drove over the river and up the access to the freeway. She kept to the outer lane, traffic whizzing past on her left. When a few miles later she saw the exit sign on Roland, she sat back with a sigh, not realizing until then how contracted her muscles had been.

She drove down into the suburb and through less nerve-wracking traffic on streets with fewer lanes. She found the shopping center, which was only a ten-minute drive from Les and Fay's home, and parked. She sat still a few moments to settle her nerves before heading over to the supermarket where Pam worked. She had vehemently determined early on that she would not become one of those nervous old ladies who was afraid to cross an intersection. And she was still determined. Certainly, none of her family was going to see her hesitate.

When she reached the supermarket she found Pamela busy with customers. A slender, petite girl, bright-eyed and friendly, she carried on a conversation with every customer inclined to want one. She smiled readily, looked as if she'd never had a problem in her life, and faced the world with lively curiosity. She liked this job, any job. She had worked part-time during her senior year in high school, and was now working full-time until she started college in the fall. She'd had jobs since she was old enough to work, even though her parents gave her an allowance large enough to take care of her needs. She had worked in a garden center potting flowers, at the Humane Society cleaning cages and petting dogs and cats on the side. She had baby sat. She was just that kind of kid, and Virginia loved her deeply.

As soon as Pam saw Virginia, she raised a hand in a wave.

"Hi Gramma! What a surprise. Just a minute and we'll go for a break."

"I'm too late for lunch, right?"

"That's okay, we'll take ten anyway. I didn't take my break this morning."

134

She reached for the line-closed sign and put it in place.

As Virginia walked back to the employee's lounge with Pamela, she marveled at the beauty of her granddaughter. Did Pam know how lovely she was? Though Beth was a lovely brunette also, and Kit was beautiful too, with long silky blond hair and large blue eyes, Pamela was somehow very special to Virginia. Her hair was thick and dark with reddish highlights, her eyes dark brown. She had Les's coloring, as did Nicky and Beth, but Pamela had the added beauty of her mother's slightly Asian look, with the uptilted eyes, and smooth golden skin. She also had the momentary advantage of being eighteen and perfectly developed with a small waist and shapely hips and legs. She'd never had a weight problem, thank God. So many girls seemed tortured about their size, always wanting to be thinner. Virginia had been listening to the problems of such girls for eleven years, over the counter at the cleaner's when they had picked up their cleaned sweaters, blouses, date dresses, school clothes. They all told Virginia they needed to lose another ten pounds. Those thin little things. Had the girls been so weight conscious when she was young?

"You're not working, Gramma?" Pam asked as she got Cokes for them at the machine in the lounge. The lounge was empty of other employees at the moment, and they took chairs in the corner that had a small table between.

"My first day of retirement."

"Really?"

Pam looked at her with widened eyes and Virginia grinned at her. She could almost see the thoughts in Pam's mind. *Retirement,* when she had just started her working years. An impossible distance between, from the viewpoint of an eighteen-year-old.

"Well, let's say I'm just not going to a job anymore that starts at seven in the morning. From now on I'm going to be busy taking care of the yard, having a garden again, lots of flowers, a few vegetables. And who knows, I may join a bowling group or something like that."

"Mom says she's never going to retire. Not until they

135

kick her out."

"But Fay has a career. She spent years getting her degrees. My career was homemaking."

"I was totally surprised when you walked in today. I'd been thinking about you. I was thinking about coming over and seeing you on my day off."

"You can still do that, can't you?"

"Well, yeah, but Craig was wanting me to go sailing. I hadn't made up my mind. Craig wants me to spend every minute with him."

She looked pleased, and Virginia remembered what a thrill it had been to discover that Ted wanted to be with her all the time. It had been the beginning of a good marriage, ended too soon by his death. But she wasn't going to tell Pam that. She and Craig had been dating since Pam was fifteen, and it was serious enough without encouragement.

"Maybe we can do some more exploring," Virginia said, and told Pam about her morning of exploring some of the stores and streets of the old part of the city, which was more accessible to her home than the suburb in which Les and Fay had decided to settle. She told her about the doll she had bought for Kit.

"It's a hundred years old, and once must have been a fantastic doll. It has a history, not a very good one."

Pam listened attentively as Virginia told her the history given to her by the antique dealer.

"Do you suppose that's true?" Pam asked. "Or did he just make it up?"

"If I were going to make up a history for a doll that's over a hundred years old, I'd choose something nicer, don't you think?"

"Yeah, maybe, like she'd belonged to a little girl who lived during the Civil War, and the doll was damaged by fighting when the North and South met and burned her house."

Pam continued the story until she noticed the time. She jumped up.

"Gosh, Gramma, I have to get back to work. It's great

136

that you came over. Are you going out to the house?"

"No, I'm going home. Tell everyone hi."

"Why don't you come out for dinner, since you're already here? Maybe we could call Beth and Rory to bring the baby over."

"I'd love to, but then I'd have to drive back on that awful freeway after dark." Virginia laughed. "I feel like I could do that only in an emergency. I'll see you on your day off, unless you decide on sailing with Craig. If you do, tell him I said hello, and both of you have a good time."

Virginia kissed Pam's cheek and returned to her car. She sat a few minutes, looking at the trees the builder had left at the end of the parking lot, and the cars entering and leaving.

A strange darkness closed over her mind, as if an inner shade had been drawn. Something terrible was going to happen to Pam. Pamela, whom she loved more than anything in the world, outside her own son. She had an urge to run back into the store and tell her not to drive over on her day off. Stay off the freeway, stay safely at home. Don't go sailing. Don't move. Freeze where she was standing until this terrible threat ended.

No. Impossible. Ridiculous.

It was just her age, her aloneness, her new freedom that was suddenly causing her to feel as if everything were ending now. Anxiety, that was all. Hadn't she read anxiety was common at her age?

She started her car and headed home.

But the feeling of being beneath a great cloud of doom stayed with her, through the night, into the next day. Pamela stayed on her mind.

Something terrible was destined to happen to Pamela, she was certain, and there was nothing she could do to stop it.

Two

The largest of the birthday presents lay at the back of the arrangement, and Kit knew Pam and Mama must have put it there on purpose. The smaller boxes were at the front. They had eaten cake and ice cream, and now it was time for Kit to open the presents. Grandma Virginia, whom she'd always called Gramma Vee, had brought the big box. It was wrapped in white paper and tied with a wide pink ribbon. There were a lot of pink ribbons and white paper.

Even Kit's new birthday dress was pink and white, just like her recently decorated bedroom. The bedroom had been her birthday present from Mama and Daddy.

Her mother said, "You may begin opening your presents, dear."

All her family was there. Her other two grandparents, her mother's mama and daddy, and even her mother's sister, Aunt Cybil. And Uncle Paul. Her three cousins, too, of course. They were all boys, older than she. When they came to visit, her brother, Nicky, didn't nag her to go play ball. Which usually meant just running to get it for him, because she wasn't a very good player.

She was nine years old today, and she had thought it would be great to be nine. Maybe tomorrow it would, but today she felt shy and timid. Too much the center of attention by too many people all at once. They usually came to visit one or two at a time, except for really big holidays like Christmas. Gramma Vee and Grandma were hardly ever here at the same time.

Mama, who was a child psychologist, had said she didn't know where Kit came from, she was so introverted. Kit had overheard. But instead of asking her mother what introverted meant exactly, she asked Pam. Pam had rubbed Kit's head gently and said it just meant she was quiet.

Everyone was looking at Kit and smiling. She wished she could shrink to the size of a bug and slip beneath their feet and away somewhere to hide. She knew and loved every single one of them, but she wasn't used to being right in the middle with all of them looking at her.

Leaning over the table at the end was Nicky, with that gleam in his eye that warned Kit of something about to happen. Maybe he had bought her the present he wanted for himself. A new baseball mitt, or something. Nicky did things like that sometimes.

Even the baby was present. In the moment of silence while everyone waited for Kit to do something with the presents she heard the baby cooing. The sound was almost identical to the sound of the doves in the trees outside the open window.

"Here," Nicky said, shoving a package at her. "Open this one. Do you want me to help you?"

Their mother said, "Shh. Nicky."

Kit heard his deep sigh as he settled back with his elbow on the table. She began opening presents, her fingers fumbling ribbons and paper. Being the center of so much attention had never happened before that she remembered. Her last birthday was so far away she could hardly remember how she felt. Anyway, last year her aunt, uncle and cousins weren't at her small party. There'd been kids instead, playmates she saw every day.

She unwrapped a robe and matching pajamas from Grandma and Grandpa Elkins. Silk. Pink to match her new bedroom. There were barrettes, to match a bracelet, from her uncle. Nicky kept pushing his present over for her to open. It was wrapped in bright red paper, and tied with Christmas ribbon. She could see by the uneven way it was

139

wrapped that Nicky had done it himself. She began undoing the ties.

It was a shiny football. He said, "Wow! How'd I ever think of that?"

It made Kit laugh, and after that there was more talking and she didn't feel as if all eyes were on her.

Beth and Ross's present was a diary with a golden key. The present from baby Tresa was a small framed picture of her to put on Kit's new white dresser or nightstand. Aunt Cybil gave her a satin cushion, pink, with ruffles, for her new bedroom. Pam gave her a necklace, a ring and a bracelet. Grandma and Grandpa Elkins also gave her a savings book with a hundred dollars on deposit, and promised her a hundred more on each birthday.

Another present was a package of coloring and cutout books, with a new box of crayons. She liked that present a lot. It was from Mama and Daddy, even though they had given her the new bedroom and had it finished just in time for her birthday. Before the party had started everyone had gone up, as they arrived, and looked at the bedroom. Everyone said how lovely it was. Except, of course, for the boys. It was like boys were blind sometimes, Kit thought. Nicky had only looked at it too, each day, when Kit insisted. "Yeah," he'd say, "Great. Wanta go out and play ball?"

He always asked, even though she wasn't a very good ball player, and really didn't like to play.

Then she found another present from Nicky, wrapped by himself. She could tell. It was an artist's box of paints, real oil brushes, a palette, a bottle of turpentine, and a small canvas. Kit felt breathless with delight. Nicky knew what she liked after all. He'd only been kidding with the football. She all at once had a great rush of affection for him. He grinned self-consciously when she smiled at him.

Kit looked at the long box Grandma Vee had brought and wondered what it could be. So many of the presents were something for her new room. But what was shaped like that?

The dining room was much noisier now, people talking, moving about. Uncle Paul's flash kept going off as he moved about with his camera taking pictures. Kit came at last to the long box. Pam helped her open it. Kit stared. The beautiful doll lay with her eyes closed, long eyelashes on her cheeks.

"Ohhh," Kit breathed, and lifted the end of the box that held the doll's head. The eyes opened slowly and looked directly at Kit. They were a soft, deep brown. Two perfect little teeth were like white snowdrops beneath the pink upper lip. The lovely golden-red hair was parted in the middle and pink ribbons were tied high on each side, like barrettes. The dress was long-sleeved with tiers of lace. It was a beautiful doll, and her dress was new, but there was something about her that looked very old and fragile.

"It's an antique," Pam said. "Gramma Vee found her in an antique shop over in old town."

For awhile everyone exclaimed over the doll, except the boys.

Nicky asked, "Hey, Kit, can we take your new ball out and try it out?"

She nodded and he and their cousins ran out to play.

"Take it from the box," someone said, but Kit had a strange and uncomfortable feeling about touching it. She said to Pam, "Will you?"

Pam removed the doll from the box, handling it very carefully. Kit glanced over among the papers and ribbons, but all the presents had been opened. The big doll was lovely, but she'd really wanted another Barbie doll, one she could dress and play with. She hadn't told anyone though. She'd just hoped maybe Pam or Gramma Vee would think of it.

"Her name is Zenoa," Gramma Vee said.

"Zenoa?" Kit repeated.

Uncle Paul yelled at the boys to come for a family picture, and then he made sure Kit stood right in front with the new doll in her arms. The boys fidgeted and giggled

141

and made faces until Uncle Paul told them if they didn't be still he'd see to it that none of them ever got a cent of allowance again, including Nicky. Even though everyone knew he was kidding, the boys straightened up long enough for the pictures.

The telephone rang and Pam went into the den to answer it. She curled up on a chair and settled down to talk. Kit could see her through the open door.

People began leaving. Kit stood with the big doll in her arms and thanked everyone as they left. When Gramma Vee started to leave, Kit tugged on her sleeve. Gramma Vee stooped, kissed and hugged her and wished her a hundred more happy birthdays.

"Gramma," Kit said softly, so no one else would notice. "Do you mind if I name her Elizabeth?"

"Elizabeth?"

"Yes."

"Don't you like the other name?"

"No," Kit whispered. She couldn't say why. She didn't know why. But when Gramma Vee had said the doll's name was Zenoa a funny feeling had come over Kit. It was a feeling she didn't like. Almost a scared feeling.

"I think that would be all right. She's yours now, you can name her what you want to. Goodbye dear, come see me."

"I will. Thank you for the doll. She's nice."

Later, when all the company was gone, Kit took the doll upstairs to her bedroom. Last month her walls had Walt Disney characters hanging over her old, narrow bed. Donald Duck, Mickey Mouse, and the cow jumping over the moon. Among the moon and the cow were stars, in gold. Her furniture then had been brown, and her bed small with side rails.

Now her bedroom had gone through what the decorator called a transformation. From a little girl's room to a big girl's room. She had let Kit help with the decorating. The carpet was rose shag, and the throw rugs white and fluffy. There was one on each side of her new white bed and one at the foot. In the corner was a pink satin chair with a footstool the same height as the seat so that they looked like a chaise longue.

The walls no longer had the cow or the other figures, and Kit missed them, even though she had helped pick out the blue, pink and white wallpaper. It was a lovely room, but it was a stranger's room.

She stood at the foot of the bed looking around for a good place to put the doll. The pink satin chair in the corner hadn't been used since it was placed in the room last week. Kit had always sat on the floor, and she still did unless she sat at her new desk. All of her toys and dolls had been put on shelves in the walk-in closet. They used to be on a shelf and in a box in the bedroom, when it was still a little girl's room.

Kit took the doll to the chair and sat her down, then stood back and looked at her. She looked back at Kit, her brown eyes large and round and perfect, her pale eyebrows lifted as if she were asking a silent question. She wasn't quite smiling. She looked as if she would start talking at any moment. Kit tried to feel some love for her, but just couldn't.

With her golden hair and pink and white clothes she fit in the room as if it had been made for her. And suddenly Kit knew.

It was no longer Kit's room. It hadn't been since it was finished last week.

It was *Zenoa's* room.

Kit stood a moment longer gazing curiously at the new doll. Aloud she said, "Elizabeth. Your name is Elizabeth." She always talked to her dolls, but this time it was as if the doll really understood and didn't like Kit changing her name.

Kit wondered, how had Gramma Vee known her name? Had the antique man told her?

Kit went into her closet and turned on the light. On the left wall were the shelves that reached from ceiling to floor. They had probably been built to hold shoes, Pam had told her, but now they held toys and dolls. Kit's two Barbie dolls

143

were there, dressed as if they were going to a party too. But Kit didn't want to play with them now. She hadn't even known how much she'd wanted some real oils for painting, and she was eager to try them. Ever since she could remember she'd painted with watercolors, and drawn pictures with colored pencils and crayons. But the oils meant serious art. She was glad Nicky thought of it.

She took off her frilly pink and white dress and put it back on the padded hanger. Mama didn't like for her to wear clothes she'd had on before, until they were laundered. But the party dress had to go to the cleaners, not into the hamper.

From the shelves beneath the rods where her blouses and dresses hung, she took jeans and a pullover shirt. She sat on the stool and removed her white shoes and anklets, dropped the anklets into the hamper and carefully placed the shoes on the shoe shelf. Her mother had said once, "Kit is the neatest child I've ever had. Both Beth and Pam have a tendency to sling things, they're always in such a hurry. And Nicky, well."

Kit listened to these occasional remarks from her mother, and judged herself by them. Her daddy never said anything about her except that she was his pretty girl. She didn't really believe that. She wasn't pretty like Pam, with her hair like gold over brown, and her face so perfect. Or Beth, with her long dark hair. But that was okay. She knew it meant that he loved her. She still sat on his lap when she was tired in the evenings, and when he was resting in his chair in the den watching television. Those were good times. They watched the news together and sometimes he playfully covered her eyes so she wouldn't see what was on the news. After eight o'clock she wasn't allowed to watch. And she knew a little bit why. Nicky had told her, in a whisper, "You couldn't handle it. Once I turned on the TV after midnight when I couldn't sleep, and take my word for it, you couldn't handle it."

What did he mean by that? She had asked, but he had only shrugged and run off to play ball.

She returned to the bedroom and went to her new desk. Her oils and the canvas looked exciting, just waiting to be used. The tubes of paint were tiny, no longer than her finger. She opened one called prussian blue and squeezed a drop onto the palette. She chose one of the three brushes and then paused. She looked up and turned her head toward the chair in the corner by the window.

The doll was staring at her with that odd expression on her face. It gave Kit a strange, tingly feeling as if she were being stared at by a real person. The creeps, Nicky would have said. She could almost hear him saying, "That doll gives me the creeps."

Kit put the brush down carefully on a sheet of paper, even though she hadn't touched the drop of paint. She wondered what to do with the doll. But there was nowhere else in the room where she could put it that seemed right. The doll belonged in the chair.

She gathered up the paints and put them all back in the little box with the grooves that cradled each tube. She put the brushes back and placed both on the canvas. Then carrying the artist's supplies she left the room, went down the quiet bedroom hall, down the carpeted stairs into the foyer. She paused to look out the long, oval glass on the front door. Street lights were coming on. Shadows beneath the big shade tree in the front yard were almost like night already.

Kit saw a light down the hall in the den.

She entered to find her dad in his favorite chair, reading the newspaper. The television wasn't on.

Kit carried her paints to a favorite location on the floor and put them down.

"Hi Chickie," her dad said. "Going to do a little painting?"

"Yes."

Kit chose a newspaper from the magazine rack, took out a page of advertisement and spread the paper on the floor so she wouldn't get paint on the carpet. Then she placed

145

the paints, canvas, palette and brushes just so and sat back and looked at them.

Just as she leaned forward to start work on the canvas, the doorbell rang. She waited. Footsteps came immediately along the hall, running. Pam. Daddy lowered his paper.

"Pam going out again tonight?"

Mama entered the room at that moment, and said, "She and Craig are just going for a Coke."

"They were out last night."

Kit's mother said nothing more. She sat down, picked up a magazine and began leafing through it.

Craig and Pamela came into the room. He was taller than Pam. The top of her head barely reached his chin. Sometimes he stood with his arms around her waist, her back to him, and rested his chin on her head. It made Kit laugh. She liked him. Everyone in the family liked Craig.

Pam had changed clothes too, and now wore jeans. Craig was carrying a small package. He leaned down.

"Happy birthday, Kit."

"Thank you." She took the gift and smiled shyly up at Craig. She'd be kind of glad when her birthday was over, so she wouldn't be put on the spot so often.

"Open it," Pam said, "before we leave. I'm dying to see what kind of present Craig picks out."

"I did it all by myself, too," he said, like Nicky would have, and the grownups laughed. Kit decided he wasn't serious. She had trouble telling when people meant what they said.

She unwrapped the package. It was a collection of doll clothes for a Barbie doll.

"Oh, hey!" she exclaimed, a big smile starting deep inside and just naturally bubbling to the surface.

"See," Craig said, and poked an elbow at Pam. "I know what little girls like. I have a sister of my own, remember?"

"Thank you, Craig," Kit said. Now she didn't know whether to stay and paint a picture, or go upstairs and dress her dolls.

She heard Pam and Craig leave, she heard Nicky come

146

in the back door. Then the soft sound of the refrigerator door opening and closing. She heard the sounds of her parents' voices, her father talking about work tomorrow at the office, her mother talking about one of her patients, both of them discussing the new man who was running for mayor. With the paints still untouched, Kit examined every item in the small suitcase of clothing. There were even bras and panties, a pair of pajamas, a robe and slippers. Tiny fluffy high-heeled slippers.

Nicky came in, turned on the television and sprawled on the floor. Kit heard laughter, but didn't look up to see what was on.

Almost before it seemed possible, her mother told her, "It's eight o'clock, Kit, time to go to bed."

"Mama, I don't have to get up for school tomorrow."

"Come on, to your room. You can stay awake awhile there."

Kit gathered up her things, kissed her daddy goodnight, and went upstairs. The halls were dark now, and very quiet. But she had been coming upstairs by herself since she was six years old, and had never been afraid.

She turned on upstairs' lights when she reached the foot of the stairs. The upstairs, beyond the railing, was softly lighted, and very quiet. Just like always. But Kit stood still, looking up. There was something different tonight. She didn't know what. But it was like there was someone up there, waiting for her. Someone bad.

She looked back toward the open door into the den. She could hear the laughter on the television. In a few minutes, after she'd had her bath and had gotten into bed, her mother would come up and tuck her in, straightening her sheet and blanket. Sometimes she stayed a few minutes and talked. Daddy always came too and kissed her goodnight, sometimes so late that Kit barely knew he was there.

She started climbing the stairs. Tonight, for the first time in her life, she didn't want to go alone to her room.

Zenoa's room.

147

Three

Pam sat squeezed against Craig in the front seat of his Ford Mustang, nursing the ice in her drive-in Coke. They had parked in the driveway at home, the way they always did, and Craig's right arm lay almost too snugly around her neck, his fingers just missing her breast. They talked, sometimes at the same time. They never ran out of things to talk about.

Lately the conversation had been on engagements a lot. Craig was in his second year of college, studying business administration, and some of the couples he knew were getting engaged, even married. Pam wanted more than anything to marry Craig, but this wasn't the right time.

"Mom and Dad wouldn't like it," she said. "We just can't, yet."

"If not now, then when?"

Craig was three years older. His family lived on the same street, three blocks away, and Pam had known him all her life. But she hadn't paid much attention to him until she was about eleven, and then she noticed how good looking he was. She had developed a crush. But Craig seemed never to notice her. Then one day when she was fifteen he had caught up with her as she walked to school. He was a senior that year. They'd started talking. From then on they walked to school together, and finally, he'd asked her for a date.

In the two years since, they hadn't broken up once. She had never dated another boy, had never wanted to. Now she saw him only on weekends, from Friday to Sunday night. On Monday morning he drove back to the college town where he had a summer job, as well as additional studies. He was in a hurry to get his degree, his job, and get married. Their plans were tentatively made. She worked hard too, and saved all the money she could. It would help set them up in an apartment. Neither of them thought it was a good idea to live together before they were married. It would traumatize both families too much, and there was no advantage to it. They would announce their engagement at Christmas. Then, sometime next year, they would have a small wedding. Pam didn't want to cost her family thousands of dollars for something that could be just as lovely for hundreds. Weddings should be personal, they both agreed. Not public performances. For them it had to be that way. But the engagement had to wait until Christmas.

"What's wrong with Christmas? Like we agreed?" she asked.

"It just seems so far away. Why don't we run off and get married, so you can go with me? Tonight." He kissed her neck.

She giggled. "Don't be an idiot. Listen, I've been looking at patterns for a wedding dress. I haven't told Mom yet. She has in mind for me an education like her own, and I'm not sure how she'll feel about me getting mine after I'm married. She doesn't argue. Mom never argues. But the way she *looks* at you while she's listening, it's like somebody seeing right into your mind, you know?"

"Uh oh," Craig said.

"What?"

"The den lights went out. And now the hall lights. In a minute the porch light will be on, and that means trouble."

She laughed. "It means you have to leave and I have to go in."

"That's what I was afraid of," Craig said, as if it hadn't been happening every Sunday night for a couple of years.

Pam sighed. "Well, I do have to go to work early tomorrow morning, and so do you. Plus you have a two-hour drive. Love I hon?" she asked, the first line of a silly little verse that was part of their goodbyes.

"Co'se I do."

"Smack I vun?"

"Kindy onts to."

They laughed together, as always, then she turned to him for another round of kisses, before she whispered goodnight and ran to the house.

She turned out the porch light and went upstairs. Her parents' bedroom was at the front of the house, down a short balcony from the other bedrooms. She leaned over the railing two steps down from the top and called goodnight softly toward the open door. Her mother replied, and came now to close the door.

That door was never closed until all the kids were safely home. Pam saw her mother's smile. Her long hair was down. She was dressed in a satin robe tied at the waist. She was small and slender, with a figure as good as any of Pam's friends, and better, she thought sometimes, than her own. But she'd never been envious of her mother, only proud. Sometimes a little intimidated, maybe. There was a muffled sound of water running in their bathroom. Dad taking a shower.

Pam ran on up the stairs. The carpet muffled her steps, but still she quietly passed Nicky's darkened room. Beth's old room, across the hall from Nicky's, was now the guest room. Kit's room was at the back of the house across from Pam's. Its door stood halfway open. The room was dark, but the tiny night-light in the hall dimly outlined the white footboard and tall posts of Kit's new bed.

"Pam . . . is that you?"

It was a whisper as soft as an indrawn breath, barely heard as Pam reached the threshold of her room.

She stopped. Kit? Still awake at this time of night?

Pam went to the door of Kit's room and pushed the door farther back. Kit lay in the center of the new, large bed looking so small. It appeared to swallow her.

"Kit?" Pam whispered. "Did I wake you?"

Kit shook her head.

Pam went to the side of Kit's bed, leaned down and kissed her forehead. Kit's large eyes looked dark in the shadows of the room.

"Pam," Kit whispered, "something's been moving around in my room. Looking at things. Opening drawers, looking."

"Huh?" Pam almost laughed. But Kit's little face remained very serious.

"Something's been moving in my room."

Kit had a shy, quiet way about her. So different from the rest of the family. Her voice was always soft, but she continued now to speak in a whisper.

"I could hear it, all night. I heard it on the carpet, like something walking. It woke me up. I was afraid to move. I waited for you."

Pam reached toward the lamp on the small white table at the head of the bed.

"No!" Kit said quickly. "Don't turn it on!"

"Why? I was going to show you there's nobody in the room but us."

"But it'll see me if you turn it on."

"I can see you now. From the light in the hall."

"Well . . . okay."

Pam snapped on the light. It was a perfect room, so well coordinated. The decorator had fixed a room that a girl could feel good in all her life.

"What a pretty room," Pam said, in an attempt to draw Kit's attention away from her bad dreams. "Too pretty to have bad dreams in. Do you think you might have eaten too much ice cream and cake?"

"No. I wasn't dreaming."

Pam didn't know what to say. Never before in all Kit's life had she been afraid. Until tonight. Pam could see it in her eyes. She could feel it in the very atmosphere of the room.

"I don't see a single thing moving about. The desk is still against the wall, and the chair is in the corner, and—"

"It's gone!" Kit hissed, sitting up suddenly in bed, her covers clutched to her throat. She stared at the pink satin chair in the corner between the dresser and the window.

Pam looked at the chair. "What's gone?"

"The doll. It was in the chair."

"The doll . . . ? The one Gramma gave you?"

"I left it there."

Kit's whisper was frantic.

Pam walked around the foot of the bed, looking for the doll. She found it on the floor against the wall, just inches from the head of Kit's bed. It sat primly, the lacy skirt spread out across her legs like a vain little girl who had arranged it just so. Her head was tilted so that she looked up with that curious, questioning expression. It was an expression that held other possible interpretations. Flirtatious? Maybe even smug, self-satisfied. Weird, she thought, how much like a real child the doll looked, in the shadows cast by the bed. Pam picked it up and started to put it back into the chair.

"No! Not there!"

Pam turned and looked at Kit. She still sat with her covers against her chin, and her large eyes frightened and rounded.

"Where, then?"

Kit hesitated. "Put it in the closet."

Pam opened the door to the large closet and placed the doll carefully on the floor in a sitting position. Then she closed the door firmly and returned to the bedroom.

She eased Kit down into bed and sat down beside her. "There now, do you feel better?"

Kit whispered, "That was *her* I heard moving."

Shocked, Pam stared at Kit. "Are you serious?" Pam wished she could laugh it off as a joke, but she couldn't. "Kitten, you *know* that's not possible. Maybe in cartoons, but you know reality from fantasy. Now you go to sleep, and stop having such silly fantasies."

"Then how did she get against the wall? I left her in the chair."

"You must have forgotten."

Kit shook her head. Her pale hair moved on the pink pillow like spun silver.

"No."

"Then maybe Nicky came in to say goodnight, saw you were already asleep, and moved the doll."

"Why would he do that?"

"So he could sit in your new pink chair? While you were asleep? So you wouldn't know and laugh at him because he wanted to sit in a satin chair?" Of course Nicky wouldn't have done that, and Pam saw that Kit didn't for one moment believe it. But she smiled nevertheless, and that was what Pam was after.

Pam turned out the light, kissed Kit's forehead again, whispered goodnight and left the room.

She lay sleepless for a while, staring at the rectangle of her windows. She had a feeling of unease about Kit. No, it was more than that. It was a feeling that something was really wrong with Kit, and that terrified Pam.

Four

Comforted by Pam's presence across the hall, Kit slept. But her sleep was disturbed by the soft opening and closing of a door somewhere in her room. By movements so subtle they were like nightmares far beneath the surface of her mind. She turned restlessly in bed, and moaned in her sleep.

Bad dreams were as foreign to Kit as the unfamiliar sounds in her room. She sensed the whisper of clothing as someone came close to her bed. She felt the tug on her covers as if someone sat beside her. She struggled in her sleep away from the feeling that someone's face was closely above hers, staring down.

When she woke the sun was shining and the house was very quiet. She sat up and rubbed her eyes. Mama and Daddy and Pam would all be gone to work by now. Nicky would be outside playing. She could hear the faint pat, pat of the basketball as it hit the back of the garage where the hoop was hung.

Somewhere in the house Alice would be working, though, a comforting presence since Kit could remember. When Mama left, Alice came. It had always been that way. Sometimes they both were there. But still, she had been taught to clean her own room, make her own bed. Alice vacuumed her bedroom, and sometimes helped her with things that were hard to do. But Kit's mother believed that people should take care of themselves as much as possible. Pam and Nicky were big enough that they even vacuumed their own rooms sometimes. And Nicky had to keep his things picked up, everywhere. But then again sometimes he left his catcher's mitt on the hall table or the utility room cabinet, and nobody said anything.

Kit looked around at her room. The white woodwork, the white wallpaper with the pink and blue flowers, the lace curtain pulled back in folds at the window looked just the same as it had yesterday. There was no sign of the darkness of the night, and the fear that still hovered over her like a cloak, making her so aware that she was alone in the upstairs of the house.

Sunshine through the window and across the carpet began to make her feel better. She wasn't alone, she reminded herself. She could hear the pat, pat of the ball on the garage, and occasionally the bark of Gypsy as she chased the ball too. The night receded like a memory edged in black.

She slipped out of bed. As her feet touched the floor her eyes found the pink chair. The doll was there, sitting with her lacy dress arranged prettily across her legs, and her head turned so that she watched Kit.

Kit stood very still, looking at the doll. *Zenoa.* No, not Zenoa. Elizabeth. She had named the doll Elizabeth because Gramma Vee had told her she could. She saw the doll reading her thoughts. *Zenoa,* it replied through her mind. *My name is Zenoa. Go away, Kit, get out of my room. I don't like you.*

Kit returned the stare of the doll, and the night came back, smothering and dark and cold, and Kit was filled with a fear so strong she could not swallow. Her throat felt swollen with her need to swallow.

Kit could almost hear Pam saying, with a mixture of laughter and seriousness in her eyes, "Kitten, the doll doesn't care what name it has."

Yes she does.

"She isn't really watching you."

Yes she is. She doesn't like me.

"Her eyes are made of glass."

No. "Yes."

155

Pam was always right. Kit had always been able to listen to Pam. Anytime she had a problem, Pam helped her solve it. She helped just enough with her schoolwork to make Kit know she could do it herself. Pam knew everything.

Pam would say the doll wasn't angry because Kit had changed its name. And Pam knew.

In her head Kit knew, too. If she stopped looking at the doll, it would be all right.

She pulled her eyes away.

But, Kit wondered, who had brought the doll back into her room? Pam? Yes, Pam might have. Or Mama might have. Daddy wouldn't have, nor Nicky. They probably hadn't even come to her room. Well, Daddy might have come and kissed her goodbye, but he wouldn't have moved the doll.

Kit climbed across the bed and got out on the other side.

The closet door stood open a few inches, and Kit turned on the light before she entered.

She stopped, her hands going to her mouth. Then she stood staring at the closet floor.

Tiny doll clothes were strewn all over the floor, ripped, torn. A small Barbie doll lay naked among the clutter, its hair pulled out, its arms twisted, legs broken. The other Barbie doll lay back in the corner, partly dressed, but its clothing ripped and ragged.

Kit took several steps backwards. She bumped into something, then without looking to see what it was, turned and ran, tears filling her eyes. Worse even than finding her favorite dolls ruined was the terror that pushed her, something that was part of a nightmare world. From somewhere deep within that other world came the laughter, a high-pitched tinkling sound, as of glass breaking and falling.

Pam had been working an hour and a half when the manager came to her station and told her there was a message that she should call home. Puzzled, and worried, Pam closed off her lane. She had never received a call from home before. Alice must feel it was an emergency. Yet if it were, Alice would have called Mom and Dad. Pam finished checking out the customer, then hurried back to the lounge and a telephone.

She was relieved to hear Alice's voice, but disturbed by the urgency it held.

"Can you come home, Pam?"

"What's wrong, Alice?" Pam cried, adding in the same breath, "Of course. But, why?"

"Something has happened that has Kit very upset. I thought maybe you could talk to her. She doesn't want me to call her mother or father, she wants you. Nicky and I can't seem to do much. She wants you. She doesn't even want her parents to know about this."

Know about this? Rather than waste time on more questions, Pam said, "Sure. Be there in a few minutes."

She asked the manager for time off, then ran out to her small car and roared out of the parking lot. She lived close enough to the supermarket that she walked at times, but today she had the car, and was thankful she did. She drove with only half an eye on the speedometer. There was little traffic at midmorning on the streets she chose.

She whirled into the shaded driveway at home and shut off the engine. Gypsy met her at the back gate and accompanied her to the patio, tail wagging. Kit sat in a lounge with her elbow on the arm of the chair and her hand supporting her head. Her long blond hair had not been brushed. She was still wearing pajamas. Nicky and Alice both stood near. Pam had never seen either of them looking so helpless. Alice, in her early forties, wore her usual costume of blouse over slacks. She stood with her hands on her hips, gazing unhappily down at Kit.

The moment Pam reached the patio Kit slid out of the chair and came running to her. Clutching Pam tightly around the waist she hid her face.

Nicky had a bewildered, concerned expression. He said nothing. Alice started talking immediately, obviously relieved to see Pam.

"Kit came running downstairs with these big tears rolling down her cheeks. About nine-thirty. She didn't say a word. I asked her what was wrong, but it was like she couldn't talk. Then Nicky came in. He asked her. And finally she told us."

Nicky said, "Somebody tore up her dolls."

"*What?*" Pam thought of the beautiful antique doll. Torn up? "But why? Who?"

"That's what we don't know," Alice said and started toward the house. "Come see this."

Pam unclenched Kit's arms from around her waist and Kit went with her willingly. With Nicky trailing they entered the house and went upstairs. He began telling what a mess Kit's closet was, but it made no sense to Pam until she saw it.

The door was open, the light on, and the floor cluttered with torn Barbie doll clothes. Even the new ones Craig had given her. And in the center, in its way as shocking and gruesome as a real life murder scene on television, lay the torn and broken doll.

Pam was aware of her own gasp, and her blunt, spoken question. "How did this happen? Who did this?"

Her questions were followed by silence.

"Where's the new doll? Where's the big doll?" She had put it into the closet, but now, she saw when she backed out and looked around the room, it was in the chair in the corner.

Alice said, "There was no damage done to it, looks like."

"Only in the closet," Nicky added.

Pam got down on her knees and began picking up the torn clothing. She recognized tiny shoes that had come with the two dolls, and had been put on and taken off so many times they looked as worn as something from a dump. Even they had been torn. The little straps ripped off, the buttons hanging by threads. Pam swept it all up into a pile. The second doll was ruined too. There was silence in the room behind her, as there was a form of silence in Pam's mind.

158

No one would have come into Kit's room and done something like this. No one in the family.

"When did this happen? Do you know, Alice?" she asked when she came out of the closet. She had stuffed everything into the new pink wastebasket that stood in the closet, and she handed it to Nicky to get rid of.

"We don't know. She just came running downstairs at nine-thirty crying. That's all I know."

Pam looked at Kit. The little girl was no longer crying, but her eyes were larger than usual and looked moist, as if tears could erupt again at any moment.

Pam said, "It's okay, Alice, I'm glad you called me. Why don't you and Nicky go ahead with whatever you were doing, and I'll stay with Kit for awhile. Nick, would you mind emptying the basket?"

"Sure," he said. "After that, is it okay if I go down to Kevin's? We're going to try out the football."

"Just come back at lunch, I guess."

"Sure. I always do."

Nicky hurried away, the load off his shoulders. A moment, and he seemed back to normal. Alice, too, was obviously relieved to go back to her work. She offered both Kit and Pam an apologetic smile before she left.

Pam drew Kit toward the chair in the corner.

"Well, Miss—whatever her name is—Elizabeth?" Kit nodded.

"We need your chair."

Pam removed the doll from the chair and looked around for a place to put it. Forcing cheer into her voice she said, "Don't you think she'd look lovely on your bed?"

Without waiting for a confirmation from Kit, Pam arranged the lovely doll against the headboard.

"Look, she's even wearing a pink and white dress. Do you think Gramma Vee chose those colors on purpose to match your room?"

Kit's voice was so low Pam barely heard it. "I guess so."

"Wasn't it nice of Gramma to buy such a lovely doll?" Kit had lost her beloved Barbie dolls, and Pam sought to

159

draw her attention to the one doll she had left.

Kit didn't answer and Pam looked around. Kit's chin was puckered and trembling and her eyes ready to spill tears.

"Oh hey, don't cry."

Pam gathered her up with her in the pink chair. It was barely wide enough for both of them. Pam held her with both arms. Kit's head leaned against her shoulder.

"I didn't do it," Kit whispered.

Pam hugged her.

"Who do you think did?"

Pam felt Kit's slight shrug, a silent response that she didn't know who did it, or perhaps an attempt to dismiss the question entirely. Pam didn't know what to do. She wondered how their mother would handle this.

Then, as if Kit read Pam's thoughts, she whispered, "Pam?"

"Yes?"

"Don't tell Mama. Please."

"Why? Don't you want her to know?"

"She'll think I did it, just like Alice does. And Nicky. I wanted you to come home because I knew you wouldn't think I did it."

A guilty twinge made Pam feel almost ill. She had thought there was only one person in the house who was at all interested in the tiny doll clothes, and the two Barbie dolls. Only one answer to the destruction. But Kit had never in her life been destructive. She had never thrown a temper tantrum. She never even raised her voice at anyone except Nicky, and then, rarely, she'd yell at him to bug off.

Pam asked softly, "Why do you think Alice and Nicky think you did it?"

"Because . . . I don't know."

"Did they say so?"

"Well, Nicky said, 'What the devil have you done to your dolls?' and Alice said, 'Good gracious, Kit!' like she thought it was me."

"And did you tell them you didn't do it?"

"No. I wanted to tell you."

160

"When did it happen, Kit? I looked in on you before I went to work. I didn't see anything." Of course she hadn't looked into the closet, why should she? Kit had been sleeping soundly. She recalled now that she had noticed the big doll was back in the chair, but hadn't thought anything about it. So sometime during the night Kit had moved the doll again, she'd figured. And, it now seemed, had torn the doll clothes and destroyed her old dolls.

But Kit, who had never lied, said, "I don't know. It was like that when I woke up."

"So someone came in your room while you were sleeping and tore your doll clothes and ruined your dolls. Is that what you think?"

Kit shook her head. "No," she whispered.

"Then what do you think happened?" Pam asked, surprised at Kit's answer.

Kit pointed toward the bed. "*She* did it."

Pam threw an apprehensive glance in the direction of Kit's pointing finger. No one was there, of course. Only the doll, so lifelike, gazing steadily toward them.

"Kit, you don't mean—what do you mean, *she?* Who are you talking about?"

"Her. The doll. I heard her moving in my room."

Pam's chest and throat constricted. "Kit, baby. Remember, I put the doll . . ." *In the closet. Last night. In the closet where the destruction occurred.* "Kit, you had a bad dream . . ."

Bad dreams don't tear up dolls.

Pam tried again. "Kit, listen—"

She stopped. She had never felt so confused and helpless. Kit believed what she was saying. She was so sincere, and so frightened. Pam could almost believe it herself, knowing Kit. Yet she also knew, through her mother's work with ill children, that the mentally ill were convinced their hallucinations were reality.

Pam felt increasingly uneasy and concerned. She couldn't bear thinking that Kit might be having mental problems. Little Kit, her favorite child in the whole world. She had loved Kit the moment she was brought home from the hospital. For Pam, at age nine, it was like having a miracle happen. To make it even better, their mother had allowed Pam to do a lot of the caring for the baby. There was only one no-no. She could not carry the baby down the stairs.

Little Kit, so perfect and so pretty. Sweet and gentle. Had she been too passive, as their mother would say? Had Kit's passivity been covering a gathering storm? Pam wanted to hug Kit so closely against her it would destroy whatever was happening, push back into Kit's darkening mind the horror of whatever was wrong.

Pam said softly, "You're afraid of this new doll, aren't you?"

Kit nodded, looking down, as if she were embarrassed at her fears. As if she recognized the fears as unreasonable. Pam was heartened. Kit wasn't slipping away after all, not so far but that Pam might, had to, bring her back to reality.

"Look Kit, I hardly know what to say. But come here, let's examine this doll, okay? I'll show you, really, there's nothing to be afraid of."

They went to the bed and sat down. Pam pulled the doll over between them and carefully undressed it. She removed the frilly, lacy dress, and the white nylon slip beneath it. Then she removed the shoes, which were the size of a baby's first walking shoes. They had hard little soles. She removed the white stockings, and the lace trimmed panties. The doll lay on its back, naked, its eyes closed. The joints of the doll were revealed, and the myriad hairline cracks that covered the body and hadn't been repaired. Its age was there, beneath its clothing. The face was smooth, as if from a heavy layer of makeup, but the scratches on the cheeks were faintly visible beneath whatever the doll repair woman had used to make the doll pretty again.

"See, it was made of bisque porcelain, in Germany." She turned it over and found small markings, with the date in Roman numerals. "See, here's when it was made. A long time ago. Eighteen-sixty-eight. She's one hundred and one years old. Wow. She's old, right? Somebody made her, like Mama makes ceramics as a hobby. You can bend its arms and legs. But it can't bend them by itself. Right?"

Kit, leaning on her hand over the doll, shook her head.

"So she couldn't have torn up the dollies and their clothes, could she? Because she's just a doll, she can't move by herself. That's funny, right? To even think that she could." Pam tried to laugh, to get Kit to laugh. But she remained very serious.

After a hesitation in which Kit visually examined the doll, she whispered, "Then who did?"

Pam said, "I don't know, Kit."

She turned the doll over. The tiny cracks checkered the doll's back, stomach, arms, legs.

"Kit, do you ever wake up sometimes at night and find yourself out of bed?"

"You mean like walking in my sleep?" Kit asked unexpectedly.

"Yes."

"No. Not that I know of."

"Could it be maybe you get up and then go back to bed?"

"You mean and do things I don't remember?"

"Yes." Pam couldn't bring herself to look into Kit's eyes. It would reveal that Kit's faith in her had not been justified.

After a long moment Kit said in a lower voice, "That's why I didn't want Mama to know, because I know she'd think that. And now you think it too."

"No, I don't really think that." Yet she did, deep within. "I just don't see any other way it could have happened, Kit."

"I didn't do it!" Kit's mouth worked silently, then she added, "I don't think I did."

"It's okay baby. It doesn't matter. You had a lot of excitement yesterday, and sometimes changes in our lives, even good ones, make us anxious."

163

"Do you think that's what happened?" Kit whispered. She looked miserable, but she didn't look as scared as before.

"Whatever happened, it's over, and it's okay. We'll dress the doll again now. Do you want to dress her?"

At first it seemed Kit might, then she drew back and shook her head.

When the doll was dressed, Pam asked, "Do you still not want me to tell Mom?"

"No, I don't want you to."

"Where shall I put the big doll?"

"Not on the bed. Maybe in the chair."

Pam placed the doll in the chair. It looked at her from its incredibly deep glassy eyes, the unspoken word, or question, on its porcelain lips.

Pam took Kit's hand and they left the bedroom. Kit looked over her shoulder at the doll, and Pam glanced back also.

The doll actually looked smug and self-satisfied, as if she had accomplished something.

Of course it was only a trick of the light, Pam told herself, the filtered sunshine through the lace curtain.

Five

"I have an idea!" Pam said. "Let me run back into your closet and get your new shorts and blouse outfit and we'll go out to lunch, okay?"

Kit's face lit up, and the light entered Pam's heart.

"You run to the bathroom, brush your teeth, wash your face, brush your hair. I'll go get your clothes and be right back."

As she hurriedly gathered clothes for Kit, she thought of her savings. How much would it cost to replace the dolls and their clothes? She had been saving toward her life with Craig, toward college and the things she would need. But what the heck. This was an emergency. Kit's sanity, somehow it seemed, hung on the replacement of the things that had been destroyed.

She took the clothes to the bathroom and helped Kit dress. She brushed her silver-blond hair and tied it back with a ribbon at the nape of her neck.

"You're beautiful," she said, and kissed Kit's cheek. "Now let's go down and tell Alice what we're going to do."

"We've never gone out to lunch like this before," Kit said, and Pam was gratified to see that her face was no longer pinched with sorrow and fear, but filled with excitement.

"No, but maybe we'll just do this more often. Of course we'll have to do it on my day off after this. This is just a special occasion."

They went through the kitchen, and found Alice in the utility room starting a washing.

165

"I'll have her back sometime this afternoon, Alice. Maybe we can just forget everything that happened, okay? Don't say anything to Mom unless she asks."

Alice nodded. "Sure, I guess so."

Pam pushed open the screen door in the utility room and with Kit's hand in hers, went through the back gate and to her car. She settled Kit in the passenger seat and locked the door, then ran around to her side.

They were headed down the street when Kit asked, "Why would Mama ask, Pam?"

"Why would she ask . . . oh, you mean if she didn't know? Well, she might see that you have new dolls, or something like that."

"Am I going to get new dolls?"

"Sure you are, didn't you know?"

"You're going to buy me new dolls?"

"Why not?"

"Do you have the money?"

"Of course. I work, don't I? We'll just drive by the bank and get some money."

"Then what will we do?"

"Lots of things. We'll eat, we'll shop, we may even go to the zoo. We'll play around the whole day. But Kit . . ."

"What?"

"Tomorrow I have to go back to work. And the day after, every day. You know that?"

"Yes," Kit said. "It's okay, Pam."

Pam reached over and squeezed her hand.

She felt deceitful, as she never had before. She had to watch the time as the afternoon spun away, to be sure they arrived home before their parents.

At four-thirty she carried into the house and up to Kit's room the parcels that contained two new Barbie dolls, and clothing that Kit had spent hours choosing. They never had gotten to the zoo, or even to the park. Pam had forgotten how involved in shopping a child could become.

"Are you as tired as I am?" she asked Kit as they arranged the dolls and clothes on a shelf in the closet.

"Yes," Kit said.

"Then why don't you take a nap before dinner? I'll go down and help Alice."

"Aren't you going to take a nap too?"

"No, not yet. But I think you should."

Pam left Kit in her room, still in the closet looking at the new doll clothes. Her last glimpse of Kit had caught a sad expression on the little girl's face, as if a memory had crossed her mind of her other dolls, and the clothes she had so often dressed them in.

Kit didn't take a nap. She sat quietly in the closet, on the floor, until she heard the sound of cars arriving and the sound of the garage doors opening and closing, and voices downstairs. She hurried down, kissed and hugged both her parents. Though they worked in different places, Mama in the clinic, and Daddy at his office with all the other lawyers in his firm, they arrived home at the same time every day. It was a dependable in her life. What she thought of as a dependable, like Pam being her best friend, and Nicky her pesky brother. And Alice the person who was there and then who took her purse off the cabinet in the utility room and left after she'd cooked dinner and Mama had arrived home. If she listened carefully she could hear Alice's car start, and drift away.

The evening was like always. Kit sat in the den on the floor beside Nicky and watched television part of the time, and worked with her paints on the picture she was making of mountains and trees and houses with kids and dogs. In the window she drew the face of a doll. Then she added dark colors to the trees around the house so that it began to look like a witch's house in the dark woods. In the window the doll's face brightened, until it became the whole focus of her painting.

She hadn't intended it to be that way, and she put it away from her.

"Daddy," she asked, "how much does a canvas cost?"

"Hmm?" he said. Then, "It's after eight, Kitten, you'd better go to bed."

She got up, taking her canvas and her oils with her, and kissed her mother and her daddy goodnight. Pam was already gone, she saw, and remembered the phone had rung. She didn't kiss Nicky goodnight. When she did he wrinkled his face so much it made her laugh. And now he covered his face and rolled and groaned, pretending it would kill him if she kissed him goodnight too, until she laughed anyway. She felt like hugging him though when she remembered that he hadn't said a word to her mother about the doll clothes and her old Barbie dolls.

As she went up to her room she felt like crying. Those had been her favorite dolls. She loved her new dolls that Pam had bought her, but not in the same way she had loved her old ones. Pam had bought her the very same little suitcase of clothes that Craig had given her for her birthday. So now she had two little suitcases, even though she had only one set of clothes.

She went into the bathroom and took her bath. When she went down the hall she met Pam, on her way to the bathroom, and Pam turned back to tuck her into bed.

"Do you want a night-light tonight, Kit?"

Kit looked at the closed closet door, and at the big doll still sitting in the pink chair, its glassy brown eyes watching her.

"No," she said. But she didn't say why. Pam thought she was silly to be afraid of the big doll, to think that in the light the doll could see her, but in the dark it couldn't.

"Mom and Dad will be in to kiss you goodnight."

"I know. Goodnight Pam."

"Goodnight, Kit. I love you."

"I love you too." She watched Pam leave her room, and then called out, "Thanks, Pam." She almost added, for the dolls. But remembered and stopped. Mama might be coming up the stairs now.

After Pam was gone and her room silent Kit buried her face in her pillow. A knot had gathered in her stomach.

Every time she thought of her mother, and that in a way she had lied to her, the knot grew. She wanted to cry, but her face only puckered in her misery. She pulled the cover up over her head so the doll would not see any of her. Then she lay very, very still.

At eleven-thirty Fay went quietly into Kit's room. Les had gone to kiss Kit goodnight when he went up to bed at ten, and found her covered head to toe and perspiring. But when he tried to pull the cover back Kit had moaned in her sleep and pulled it up again. Fay hadn't known. She had brought some work home with her and had not gone up to bed for another hour. When she entered the bedroom Les drowsily asked her to check on Kit, and told her why. She was sweating, yet wouldn't let go of her cover.

Fay stood looking down at the slight figure beneath the down-filled quilt that was meant only to be a cover on the bed. The ruffled bed skirt hung to the floor in pink satin folds. It matched the fabric on the chair in the corner. The quilt was made in pink and white and trimmed in lace that matched the curtain on the window. It was much too heavy for this time of year.

Fay turned on the bedside lamp and pulled back the quilt. Kit, glistening with sweat, squirmed, cried out softly and reached for the cover. Fay took a tissue from the box in the drawer and gently wiped Kit's face.

"Shh," she whispered. "Shhh, it's all right. Mama's here."

She didn't want to wake Kit. Quickly, she pulled up the sheet and saw Kit grab it and turn, her face in her pillow. She pulled the sheet over her head.

Fay rolled the quilt safely against the footboard where Kit wouldn't be able to reach it. The room felt a bit stuffy and warm. She considered turning on the ceiling fan, but went to the window and opened it instead, and cool air flooded into the room, moving the curtains gently.

She turned out the light and looked back from the doorway. Kit was still, sleeping soundly as she always had. Kit

169

had always been, Fay thought as she softly closed the bedroom door and went down the hall to the master bedroom, the very best of her children. Absolutely no trouble at all. By the time she was two months old she was sleeping without interruption from six in the evening to six in the morning. In those early days her crib had been in the master bedroom.

When Kit was a year old they had moved her into the room where she was now. She had never even had a nightmare. She seemed a child perfectly content with the world.

Les stirred when Fay got into bed and asked sleepily, "She still roasting herself?"

"Yes, but I gave her the sheet instead. And opened the window. She didn't wake up. She'll be fine."

Les kissed her goodnight and turned over. His even breathing, deepening almost to snores, was a comfort to her tonight. She lay awake listening to the silence in the house.

She turned over, as Kit had done, and cushioned her cheek in the pillow, her left leg pulled up and her foot hanging off the bed. The sheet was smooth against her skin.

She slept, and woke, and lay listening. The hour was late. She sensed she had been sleeping a couple of hours or more, and she had awakened to an alertness that was unusual for her. A door had closed softly somewhere in the house, and it disturbed her sleep and disturbed her now. She asked herself why. There certainly was nothing unusual about a door closing. One of the kids had gone to the bathroom, probably.

She turned over and tried to go back to sleep.

Unable to rest, she finally slipped out of bed and went into the bedroom hall. The night-light was a tiny beacon plugged into an outlet across from the bathroom door. The bathroom door was open, and the bathroom dark.

She went down the hallway, her bare feet making only a whisper of sound on the carpet. Nicky and Pam's bedroom doors were partly open, and now so was Kit's,

170

though Fay had closed it earlier.

She crossed the threshold into Kit's room just far enough to see that Kit was still in bed, the sheet still covering her head.

Fay went back out into the hall, then checked on Pam and Nicky. Both were in their beds. She looked down the hall, puzzled. All the children were asleep. Then who had closed a door somewhere in the house?

She felt chills rise along the backs of her arms. She stood in her own hall, the place she had considered the safest in the world, and felt that someone had invaded their home.

Slowly, guided only by the dim night-light, she went down the stairs to the foyer. She stood in the dark, feeling uncomfortably that she was not alone down here, that an intruder stood watching her. With her skin tingling in fear she turned on the lights in the hall. No one. The hall was just as she had left it, and the front door locks were activated. She began a cautious check of the house.

The living room was neat, showing that it was rarely used. The den was the same old comfortable place. The dining room was neat and clean. So were the kitchen and utility room, and when she opened the back patio doors, their golden retriever came from the doghouse to greet her. She was a friendly dog, but had a loud voice and barked at strangers. Delighted to see her so calm, Fay sat for a moment on a patio chair with the dog's head on her knee. She caressed Gypsy's silky fur, then told her goodnight and went back into the house.

On her way back down the hall she checked the closets, on a whim. She opened the powder room door.

A small girl sat at the dressing table.

Fay stood in surprise, one hand gripping the door knob.

The child's face was only vaguely familiar, reflected in the mirror that covered the wall behind the vanity counter. She seemed totally unmoved that Fay had opened the door. *Why had she been sitting in the dark? Why was she here at all? Who was she?*

Then just as swiftly she saw it was not a child. In the

171

half-light from the hallway she recognized the large doll Virginia had given Kit for her birthday.

She wanted to laugh at herself, for being so startled, for even thinking that one of Kit's little friends had somehow come into the house. But she couldn't. She trembled, unnerved.

To be sure it was only the doll, that her eyes weren't deceiving her, she turned on the powder room light.

The doll had been placed in the tufted chair at the dressing table, facing the mirror. It appeared to be looking admiringly at its own reflection. Barely large enough to see over the counter, its head seemed disembodied in the long mirror that covered that part of the powder room wall. Reflected behind it Fay saw herself, wearing a pale blue nightgown. She saw the open door, the decorations hanging on the powder room wall. It was reality in reverse, and increased her feeling of being in a bad dream.

Someone had brought the doll down, placed her in the chair, and then softly closed the door. But the sound had awakened Fay. Then, she recalled, she had lain still, listening, and had heard nothing. When she checked on the kids all of them were sound asleep. Or seemed to be. Nicky hadn't been faking his deep breathing, she was sure, yet if she had chosen one of the children to have played this little trick, it would have been Nicky.

Fay picked up the doll. It seemed strangely heavy, almost like a child. The feeling of it in her arm was oddly repellant, and her instinct was to drop it and leave it there. But she forced herself to carry it with her. She turned out the lights and went back upstairs and into Kit's shadowy room.

She hesitated, wondering where Kit kept it. Perhaps in the closet with the rest of her dolls and toys. Fay opened the closet door, turned on the light and sat the doll down in the corner. She started to leave the room and paused, looking at the Barbie dolls standing on the shelf.

She recognized them instantly as being new.

Hastily she looked through the rest of the dolls and stuffed animals on higher shelves, but the old Barbies were gone. When had this happened? Also, the older clothes had been replaced by the new things Craig had given her. Then she saw the second suitcase. How very odd.

Fay turned out the closet light and closed the door. Kit was still snugly covered by her sheet, but the room was comfortably cool. Fay didn't disturb her.

When she left the bedroom she pulled the door shut.

In bed she wondered about the dolls and the doll clothes. Did it have anything to do with Kit's sudden desire to hide from the world?

Someone in the family had replaced Kit's old Barbie dolls for some reason, and that someone was probably Pamela. But Fay had no intention of questioning the girls about it, not yet at any rate. Give them time and they'd come to her. Surely.

She drifted uneasily back to sleep.

Six

Every morning when Kit woke the big doll was in a different place. The first morning it had been on the floor by her bed. The second morning it was in the closet, even though both times it had been in the pink chair, except the night Pam had moved it into the closet. And that night it had torn up the clothes and the dolls.

At least, that was what Kit had thought at first, until Pam showed her it hadn't happened. That it couldn't possibly have happened, because the doll was made of porcelain, and there was no way it could move by itself.

Her days were miserable, because she hadn't told her mother about what she had done to her dolls. When she tried to paint now her hands shook, and she spilled paint on her new white desk, and when she tried to clean it up it only smeared.

Finally, one night after being miserable for two whole days, she was awake when her mother came in to kiss her goodnight. She began to cry.

Mama turned on the small lamp at the bedside, and her face looked worried, and that made Kit cry only that much harder. She felt her mother's cool hand caressing her forehead and cheek, and heard her voice soft and low, and wished she were dead because she hadn't told her mother.

"Kit, precious, what is it?"

Kit tried to talk and couldn't.

Her mother gathered her into her arms and whispered, "Shhh, it's all right. You can tell Mama."

"I tore up all my doll clothes and my Barbie dolls, Mama."

Her mother was still a moment.

"Why did you do that?"

"I didn't know I was doing it. In my sleep I got up and did it, and in the morning I went to my closet, and saw what I had done. Only . . ."

"Yes?"

"Only I thought it was Zenoa — Elizabeth — who had done it."

"Elizabeth? Your new big doll?"

"Yes."

"Why did you think that, Kit?"

"Because . . . I couldn't remember."

Mama held her and murmured to her, and Kit told her of Pam replacing the dolls and clothes, and not telling Mama because Kit didn't want her to.

"Why didn't you want me to know?"

"Because . . . you would think I did it."

"But now you think that."

"Yes, because Pam showed me the doll can't move."

Her mother was quiet for a long time, and Kit looked up to see that she was staring at the wall, or the window, or somewhere far away. Her face was worried and sad, and Kit was sorry now that she had told.

"Don't be mad at Pam," Kit whispered.

Mama smiled down at her, though the sadness didn't leave her eyes. "Of course I won't be mad at Pam. She just proved herself to be your very best friend, didn't she?"

"Yes."

"I won't say anything to her at all. It can still be your and her secret, in a way, all right? Now, I want you to sleep. Just sleep, and dream sweet dreams."

After she was gone Kit lay in the soft darkness of her room feeling better. She even felt more brave. When later in the night she was awakened by the sounds of movement, by the sound of someone passing from her room to the hall, she had the courage to sit up and listen.

175

It had not been a dream. She had heard something.

The doll couldn't move. Pam had told her, and her mother the same as told her that also. She knew now the doll couldn't move. But the shadow of the doll was no longer in the chair.

Kit slipped out of bed and went slowly halfway between the bed and chair to look at the pink chair. Although it was dark in the corner, she could see the outlines of the chair and it looked empty. The darker shadow that had been the doll was no longer there. Was it? She wasn't sure. A pale light seeped through the window and as Kit stared at the chair it grew more visible. It was empty, she was sure. Growing braver, she went to it and with her hands felt that it really was empty.

When she went to bed Pam had asked her if she wanted the doll put in the closet or left in the chair, and Kit had chosen the chair. Now, she was gone.

Kit turned on the closet light and looked in. But the doll wasn't there either. She turned out the light and stood in the darkness while her eyes adjusted, and the window took shape again. The outlines of the pink chair became visible once more.

Since the doll couldn't move by itself, who had taken it from her room? And where was it now?

Kit left the bedroom and stood listening in the hall. This was the time of night when there was no sound. No one drove on the street. Even the dogs in the neighborhood had stopped barking and were asleep.

Kit went along the hallway and paused at the top of the stairs.

In the hall below a light fell across the carpet in a thin crack from the powder room.

Softly and slowly, her hand on the bannister, Kit went down the stairs.

In the lower hall she could see the powder room door stood about three inches open. The light across the hall carpet was like a wall that stopped her.

Familiar sounds came subtly from the room. The opening of drawers, the rattle of things within. A drawer closing. The opening of another, soft slidings, mouselike movements, tiny tinkles as when someone rummaged through things in a powder room drawer.

She edged closer to the door, until she could see through the crack into the lighted powder room.

The doll sat on the stool at the dressing table. She was looking into the mirror, and Kit could see her face. She looked large, as if she had grown suddenly and was now a teenage girl.

As Kit stared, her skin rippling coldly, tightening across her cheekbones and pulling her hair tight, she saw Zenoa's arms raise. There was a hair brush in her right hand, and as she looked at herself in the mirror she began to brush her hair.

Her lips widened into a smile as she gazed at her reflection.

Then suddenly her eyes lifted, finding Kit's face in the mirror, and the soft expression in the eyes turned blank and glassy. The doll leaped up with the swiftness of a snake striking, the hair brush raised in her hand. It hissed through the air as she struck at Kit's reflection. It struck the mirror just above the counter and lightning cracks spread from the point of impact.

Kit whirled and ran, pulled from her long moments of paralysis at last by the movement of the doll.

She found the stairs and climbed upward, coming into the dim light of the bedroom hallway. Breathless, terrified, she threw a glance over her shoulder. The doll hadn't followed.

Terror made her unable to think. The doll had tried to kill her. Kill her image in the mirror.

Kit looked behind her, but the hallway was still empty, and the top of the stairs lost in the shadows on the balcony.

She wanted to go tell Pamela, but Pam had said the doll couldn't possibly move. She had shown her it couldn't. Pam had thought maybe Kit was walking in her sleep. Was that what this was? Walking sleep? Had she only dreamed the part about the mirror?

She slipped into her room and closed the door, then she climbed into bed and pulled the sheet over her head.

For most of the night she was awake. She thought she was awake, but maybe this too was part of the dream. Still, she listened hard for the opening of her bedroom door. At times she thought she heard the doll moving about in her room, but she was afraid to look. Finally she slept, waking again, then sleeping more soundly. In her dreams she called for help, but it wasn't a doll that she ran from, it was a strange woman with the doll's face.

At times during the moments she knew she was awake, she longed desperately to go to Pam and tell her. She would take her by the hand and lead her down to the powder room and make her see for herself. If she hadn't been dreaming after all, walking in her sleep, the mirror would be cracked.

No. Pam hadn't believed her about the clothes and the dolls that Zenoa ruined. Kit had listened to her and had come to believe it was herself, and not Zenoa. But now she didn't know anymore.

Her breath indrawn made her body tremble. It jerked as it came from her lungs. Tears froze somewhere behind her eyelids, and found no escape. Finally, she slept again.

When she woke sunshine came in spots through her window, shadowed by the big tree on the east side of the house. A soft breeze blew her curtains in and out, like somebody breathing against them. Kit turned her head. Her bedroom door was open. She looked quickly toward the pink chair.

She was there. Sitting in the chair, skirt arranged prettily, head slightly tilted. There was nothing in her hands.

The night past was like a bad, bad dream. Something that had never happened. Kit slipped out of bed, her eyes not leaving the doll. But the doll stared with her glassy expression straight ahead, as if she were incapable of seeing Kit.

Kit ran on tiptoes down the hall. She heard someone in the bathroom, taking a shower. Her parents' door was open, which meant they had already gone to work. She hoped she didn't see anyone, not even Pam, or Alice.

At the powder room door she paused, then she stepped into the shadowed room.

Even with the light out she could see the cracks in the mirror, reaching upward from the small smashed hole like rays of light.

She hadn't been dreaming. She hadn't been walking in her sleep.

She closed the door and tiptoed back upstairs to her bedroom. The doll was still in the chair in the corner.

Nothing in her hands.

They lay on the full skirt of her pretty dress with fingers curled, looking as if they had never changed and moved and gripped the handle of a brush.

A doll? No, it wasn't a doll. Elizabeth wasn't its name. *Zenoa.* Zenoa was something scary, terrible, dangerous. From the beginning Kit had sensed it. She knew it. Why was it no one else could see what she had seen?

Keeping her eyes on Zenoa, afraid of the sudden changes she was capable of, Kit hurried into the closet, got her clothes and ran to the bathroom to dress.

Zenoa's room.

It was, now, Zenoa's room. Kit was afraid to be in there with her.

For everyone else the day was normal. Kit's mom and dad were gone to work. Pam was gone to work. Nicky ran in and out of the house. Alice worked. She even went upstairs and made Kit's bed, while Kit sat on the patio with her paints and canvas. But she only dabbed at it, and stared off into the trees at the back of the yard where the tall privacy hedges closed them off from the neighbors.

179

Alice came to her, put her hand on Kit's forehead as if feeling to see if she had a fever.

"What's wrong, Kit? You sick?"

"No."

"You didn't even make your bed. And you hadn't even put away your dolly clothes."

Kit sucked in her breath. Put away her dolly clothes?

From somewhere deep within her came an emotion new to her. Suddenly she was angry. The room was hers, not Zenoa's. The new dolls were hers, and the little clothes. What had Zenoa done now?

She went upstairs, alone, and into the room.

The big doll sat in the pink chair exactly where she had been when Kit woke up. Not even its hands had moved. Its head was still slightly tilted, and its eyes looked somewhere across the room in a glassy stare. The sunshine was no longer coming through the window, but the curtain still moved a little from the little puffs of air that entered.

Kit dared to go closer to the doll. In the bright light of day she could see where the cheek had been repaired. She could see the tiny cracks on the backs of the hands that Pam had shown her, the cracks that helped indicate how old the doll was. You don't repair all the cracks, Pam said, on any antique thing, or it loses its value. It was good that the doll had those tiny cracks that you could see only in good light.

Kit looked at the doll and thought of something. In the daytime it was only a doll. When the light made by the sun shined on it, even in a shadowed room, it was only a doll. But at night, when there was darkness, something happened.

Kit backed away and went into the closet. The floor was neat, everything put away. She didn't know what Alice had referred to, and she didn't want to ask. She didn't want to hear that the dolly clothes had not been in their suitcase on the shelf, but perhaps strewn on the floor.

She took the suitcase and the dolls and carried them with her back down to the patio. Carefully, she checked the items of clothing one by one. But none of them was torn.

Nicky came by and stopped.

"Hey, neat, you got new dolls?"

Kit looked up quickly. "Shhh, don't say it so loud."

"Why not?"

"Because," she looked over her shoulder. "Somebody might hear."

Nicky frowned. "You're getting weird."

He went on into the house, leaving Kit staring again at the privacy hedge. Getting weird? Something inside her turned heavy and still.

In the afternoon Danielle came over to play for an hour. She lived three doors down, and even though she was a year older than Kit, they waited for the school bus together, and sometimes played together at recess. But mostly Danielle had other friends, and Kit played with girls in her own class.

"Is this what you got for your birthday?" she asked, looking at the new dolls and the dolly clothes.

Kit hesitated, then murmured, "Yes." Adding, "Sort of," as if that would help excuse the lie.

"Where are your other dolls?"

Kit shrugged without answering, and behind her Alice said, "Why don't you take Danielle up and show her the beautiful antique doll your grandma gave you?"

Danielle looked eager to go. "Really? Antique?"

Kit got up and led the way upstairs to her room. She opened the door, always half expecting to see the pink chair empty. Danielle entered.

"Oh!" she breathed. "She's gorgeous."

The doll was still in the pink chair, and just for an instant Kit saw it through Danielle's eyes. It *was* beautiful.

Danielle ran to the chair, sat down on the footstool and reached for the doll. Then she paused, her hands on the doll beneath its arms.

"Can I hold it?"

"Yes," Kit said and stood watching.

Danielle caressed its hair, its face, picked at its lacy pink and white dress.

"Isn't it the most wonderful present. How old is it?"

"A hundred and one."

"Years?"

"Yes."

"Gosh! So *old*. But it looks just like new."

"It has a new dress, and shoes and things like that. All its clothes are new. I think it has new hair too. Part of it anyway. And Gramma Vee said its cheeks were fixed, like makeup being put on."

She stood while Danielle held the doll and exclaimed over her, then finally she said, "Let's go back downstairs."

"Can we take her?"

"I guess so."

Kit trailed behind as Danielle carried the doll downstairs and out onto the patio. She arranged the doll carefully in one of the chairs at the small round table, and during the rest of the hour Kit hardly noticed it. Alice brought out small muffins and glasses of lemonade. Then, too soon, Danielle's hour was up and she had to go home.

Kit walked with her to the driveway, then she saw her bike and decided to ride around the block. She rode around three times, and was joined by Eddie, a little boy who was still riding a training bike. Other kids joined them for awhile, then rode off toward the park three blocks away. Kit wasn't allowed to cross Vincent without Nicky or Pam, so she rode back toward home.

It was time for dinner, and everyone was home. Alice finished putting the food into bowls, the way she always did, leaving it on the cabinet, then she got her purse, said goodbye and left.

Kit washed her face and hands in the utility room sink and helped set the table. At dinner she listened to her mother tell about an incident at work that everyone laughed at, but which Kit didn't understand. Pam excused herself early because she had a letter from Craig. They called each other only twice a week, because they were saving their money, Pam had told Kit, and between times they wrote fat letters.

It was Kit and Nicky's night to do the dishes. They cleaned off the table, put the food away in plastic containers and put the dishes into the dishwasher. Tomorrow morning Alice would empty it, and put the dishes away.

Kit didn't think of the doll, and that it had been left on the patio, until it was time to go to bed.

Before going upstairs she ran out to the patio. In the corner patio lantern lights she saw Gypsy, curled on the lounge now that no people were there to tell her to get down. She wagged her tail. Kit rubbed her ears, then left her on the lounge. She had as much right on the lounge as anyone, Kit thought. The only thing was sometimes her feet were dirty, and the dirt rubbed off on the cushions. But she was part of the family too.

The chairs at the patio table were empty. The big doll was gone.

Someone else had moved it. Probably Alice.

Or, when dark came, it had changed.

Maybe it had gone away and would never be back.

Kit went back into the house and quietly passed the den door where she heard the sounds of television and occasionally the voices of Daddy, Mama, and Nicky.

She paused at the powder room and looked inside. The mirror on the opposite wall reflected her in the doorway. The room was empty.

She went on upstairs, through the dimly lighted hallway, and to her room. She turned on the overhead light.

The doll sat in the pink chair, exactly as it had before Danielle took it downstairs. There was only one difference. Instead of its head turned so that it looked at the wall, it was turned so that it gazed at Kit as she entered the room.

The look in its eyes was no longer glassy and vacant.

Seven

Kit didn't sleep. Pam came and kissed her goodnight. Nicky stuck his head in the door and said, "Sssst, hey, you're okay, kid," in a loud whisper. Kit knew what he meant. He was apologizing for calling her weird. But it didn't matter. She felt almost as if she and the doll, Zenoa, were in one world, and her family in the other, old world.

She was still awake, but pretended to be asleep, when her mother and daddy came and gently kissed her and pulled the sheet down off her head and folded it at her waist. Tonight they had come in together, the way they did sometimes, and they went away murmuring in a low voice to each other. Kit made no effort to hear what they were saying.

She left the sheet off her head. Mama and Daddy had left the door open, and light from the hallway made a pale path into her room. The bed was in darkness, but the very end of the light touched the pink chair, and the small figure that sat there. Kit stared at it, stared until everything blurred and became formless. Then she refocused her eyes and saw the curtain, moving in and out at the window so slowly like the fluttering wings of a large pale moth.

She tried to pick out from the shadows the figure of the doll, and realized it was no longer in the chair. It was standing. It looked so tall, almost as tall as a real girl.

Kit held her breath, terror icing her skin. She watched it move into the light, and the illusion of tallness faded. It moved with a peculiar sound, the brushing of small feet against the shag carpet, a whisper of sound that seemed to envelop Kit. A sound that could have been only imagined. All of this, Mama would say, was hallucination. Illusion. Delusions. None of this was happening, Mama would say, except in the mind of the sick child. Kit had heard her tell bits and pieces of things about some of the children she treated. Some of them were so seriously ill they had to be taken away from their families and placed in institutions.

Still, the powder room mirror was cracked.

Kit watched the doll go through the doorway and out into the hall. The night was very quiet. The time of night when darkness was the most frightening. This was the time when Kit always covered her head, now, these nights.

The doll turned right, and Kit could no longer see her. But she knew where Zenoa was going.

Kit slipped out of bed and ran on tiptoes to the doorway and peeked around. The doll had reached the top of the stairs and was going down.

Kit followed.

In the lower hall Kit paused in the dark at the bottom of the stairs. She waited. As she knew it would, the powder room light came on. Then the door moved, narrowing the light on the carpet and on the wall opposite the door. It remained a thin crack of light, as it had before, the first time Kit had found the doll in the powder room.

She crept closer, until she could see into the powder room. The doll's face in the mirror smiled at itself, smiled into the cracked lines. It was no longer just a doll. The lips curved more deeply into the cheeks as it looked with pleasure at itself. Then its lashes lowered as it looked down. A drawer slid open, and the lipsticks and combs and makeup clicked together as she rummaged.

The doll looked up at herself again and began to apply cream makeup to her face.

Kit drew back. She stood in the darkness behind the streak of light on the floor. Then she hurriedly climbed the stairs. This was her chance. Her chance to prove to Pam that she had not torn up her little Barbie dolls and their clothes. A chance to prove that she wasn't lying about the new doll, that she wasn't lying about anything. That she hadn't been walking in her sleep.

And if Pam saw too what she had just seen, it would prove that she wasn't having hallucinations, or delusions, and that she wasn't sick, and wouldn't have to be taken away and put in an institution.

Pam felt the touch on her cheek, and she almost jumped out of her skin. From a deep sleep, she had been brought savagely awake, her own brain unable to make the adjustment fast enough to keep her from the sudden, brief fit of terror. She heard her own muted cry as she jerked up in bed. Then, seeing Kit's small, pale face, like a mirage in the deep shadows of her room, she didn't know whether to laugh or cry.

She turned on the small reading lamp on the head of her bed.

"Kit! What time is it?"

Kit blinked in the light, and Pam pulled her up onto the bed and gave her a quick hug. But Kit slid away, and with her hand clutching Pam's wrist, tugged on her.

"Come and see, Pam," she whispered urgently. "Hurry. I want you to see."

"See what?"

"The doll. I watched her. She went out of my room and downstairs to the powder room where all the makeup is. She's there, now."

"What?"

"She's putting on makeup, Pam. I saw her. I want you to see too, so you'll know." Kit spoke so rapidly, so breathlessly, Pam had problems separating the words. "Last night she was there. I saw her there. She was sitting on the stool and brushing her hair. Then she saw me in the mirror, and she leaped up and threw the brush at me. At me in the mirror. My image. It hit the mirror, Pam. She was trying to kill me. But then I thought when I pulled the covers

186

over my head that maybe I'd been sleepwalking. Only this morning, the mirror was cracked. I wasn't sleepwalking. I'm not sleepwalking now. Hurry, come and see."

Still stunned by sleep and what Kit had told her, Pam followed Kit, pulled along with the small hand on her wrist. They went down the hallway in the muted night-light, then down the dark stairs. At the foot of the stairs Pam automatically reached out and turned on the light switch. The foyer lights came on, and hall lights leading to the back of the house, as well as a light over the stairway. Kit jerked to a stop and turned, alarm mixed with the fear on her face.

"Why did you do that?" she demanded in a hissing whisper. "Now she'll know we're coming!"

Pam blinked down at the face of her little sister, then she walked on to the powder room and pushed open the door.

She wasn't surprised to see the antique doll sitting on the vanity chair in front of the mirror. It was barely large enough that its face was reflected in the mirror. Strangely enough it had makeup smeared on one cheek.

Also, the mirror had been struck with something at the bottom, and thin cracks reached upward and outward, like half of a star Kit might have drawn.

"Good Lord, Kit, how'd you break the mirror? It'll cost a fortune to have that replaced. Have you told Mom?"

Kit was silent.

Pam turned and looked back at Kit. She stood at the foot of the stairs watching Pam, her face puckered as if she were ready to cry. Behind her was the grandfather clock, and the hands pointed at two-thirty-five.

"Never mind," Pam said. "They hardly ever come in here. Maybe they won't notice until—well. I guess every kid is entitled to one mirror, or one window. Remember when Nicky broke that big picture window in the living room? Wow."

Still Kit said nothing.

Pam entered the small powder room, took a tissue from the box on the vanity and wiped the makeup off the cheek

187

of the doll. She noticed that it was still damp and easily wiped away.

She didn't know what to do about Kit's fantasies. The playacting wouldn't be so bad if it hadn't happened in the middle of the night when she should be soundly asleep for hours.

She heard a sound and looked into the mirror. Kit stood in the door staring at the reflection of the doll. Horror was etched on her face, in the drooping lines of her open mouth, in the depths of her eyes.

Pam watched her, feeling the slow rise of horror in herself as she faced a new truth. Something was seriously wrong with Kit. The fear in her face was not playacting, nor was it normal in any way.

Pam turned away from the vanity. She had to get Kit away from the doll. There was something about the doll. Not the things Kit said, but something else, something that caused Kit to become so delusional.

Pam knew she should take this to their parents, especially to their mom. But she had to think first, to settle something in her own mind. She felt as confused as if she were facing a puzzle in a thousand little pieces waiting to be put together.

She pushed Kit out of the room, then turned out the powder room light and closed the door, leaving the doll in the chair. With her hand on Kit's shoulder she guided her to the stairs.

They climbed the stairs. She went with Kit to her room.

The story of the doll came to her mind, and suddenly Kit's actions of the past few days, since her birthday party and her possession of the doll, made more sense. She put Kit into bed and sat down beside her.

Kit's hand was limp in hers as she rubbed it gently. Kit's eyes now refused to meet hers. She looked everywhere in the room that she could without turning her head, avoiding Pam's eyes.

"Kit, I want to ask you something."

Kit gave a half nod of assent.

"Did Gramma Vee tell you the history of the doll?"

It explained everything. Pam didn't understand why it would affect Kit so much, but just knowing about the little girl who had died in the insane asylum had probably been too much for her.

But Kit looked at her now, obviously puzzled.

"History?" she whispered.

"History, yes. I mean, did she tell you about the little girl who owned the doll a hundred years ago?"

Kit's head shook back and forth on the pillow, and her eyes looked steadily into Pam's.

"What about her?" Kit asked.

Pam sighed. No, of course Gramma Vee hadn't told Kit. She hadn't even talked to Kit that Pam knew of since the birthday party, and Pam knew she hadn't told any of the doll's history that day. She wouldn't have told a nine-year-old girl about another little girl who'd been accused of stabbing her sister and aunt to death, and then had died in an insane asylum without ever speaking.

"You haven't even talked to Gramma Vee, have you?"

"No. Why?"

"I didn't think so."

Pam's eyes found the pink chair in the corner. It looked strangely empty and unfinished without the lovely antique doll.

The puzzle had shattered again, just as she had thought she'd found the first piece. She drew a long sigh. In just a few hours she had to be at work. Her boss would begin to think she was too immature to handle a job if she asked for another day off so soon.

"Kit," she said, without planning what she was going to say, "how would you feel if I told you I believe you? About the doll . . . taking on . . . umm . . . magical proportions at night, and—uh—moving on its own and everything?"

Kit's face brightened pathetically, and Pam felt sad and guilty just looking at her. Was she feeding the delusions of a sick child? She didn't know. She didn't understand why she had even said that, but part of her was glad she had.

189

Just the look of relief in Kit's eyes was enough to make up for whatever mistake she might have made.

"You do?"

"Yes. Now will you do me a favor?"

"What?"

"Go to sleep. Try real hard to go to sleep."

Kit's eyes moved away from hers and the fear came back. She whispered, "What if she comes back to my room?"

"She won't come back tonight."

"She thinks it's her room."

"Well," Pam said playfully, trying desperately to take the fear out of Kit's eyes again. "I don't know why she thinks that, because we know it's your room."

Pam wondered what their mother would say, knowing she was doing this to Kit? The longer she stayed here and tried to comfort Kit the more problems she created.

"No," said Kit thoughtfully, "the old room was mine. This one is hers. She'll be back."

Say no more, Pam warned herself. She had to talk to their mother first. She was the psychologist, not Pam. Don't mess with her mind, whispered a small warning in the back of Pam's own mind. *Don't mess with Kit's mind.*

"Go to sleep, okay?" Pam kissed Kit and tried to draw her hand away, but Kit clung to her.

"Pam . . ."

Pam saw Kit's chin tremble. She saw the same terror in her eyes that she had seen downstairs when Pam turned on the lights. The fear that seemed to be destroying the old Kit.

"Pam, what if—"

"Shhh. You promised me you'd go to sleep."

"But Pam, what if she comes back and kills me?"

"Kills you! Good Lord, Kit, whatever made you think of that?"

"Because she wants this room?"

"Hey, I promise you she isn't capable of doing such a terrible thing. And, why can't you share the room? I'll bet she just wants to share the room with you. But, Kit, if you

190

want to get rid of the doll, we'll do that, too."

"We will?"

The eagerness on Kit's face made Pam feel like crying again. She was disgusted with herself for becoming so emotional lately.

"Yes. First, let me talk to Gramma Vee, and see if she'll take it back, okay?"

Kit nodded. "Okay."

Pam turned out Kit's light as she left the room, and closed the door. She stood in the hall, listening to the silence. Then she went back to bed. Downstairs the clock struck three. In three hours she had to get up and get ready to go to work. She had to shower, wash her hair, dry it.

She lay in bed, unable to find a comfortable position. She had to talk to their mother about Kit. Or would it be better to just ask Gramma Vee if she'd take the doll back? For some strange reason the doll seemed to carry a . . . curse? Was it possible?

She turned and twisted, and sometimes dozed off only to wake abruptly again and lie listening. She was awakened once by a door closing somewhere, and she got up and looked across the hall and saw that Kit's door was still closed. She went back to bed thinking it must have been a dream.

She heard the clock downstairs strike five, then she slept and the next thing she heard was her own radio come on softly with music she had no heart for. She turned it off quickly.

Day was breaking, and a murky, ghostly light had entered her room. She put her robe on and went into the hall. Kit's door was still closed.

Just as she started to enter the bathroom, she turned away on sudden impulse and went downstairs. She opened the powder room door. She wasn't surprised to see the doll was gone.

She ran back up the stairs and down the hall to Kit's room.

191

Kit was sleeping soundly, half on her stomach, one arm flung over the side of the bed, her right leg bent. Her face looked as peaceful and content as an angel's, as if something had been resolved for her in sleep.

Back in the pink chair in the corner the doll sat, her skirt arranged carefully, her hands down at her sides, her head tilted a bit to the left and her brown eyes gazing toward the white lace curtains that moved in the breeze through the open window.

Kit had brought the doll back, sometime in the night.

Eight

Pam was so relieved that she almost fell asleep as she took her shower. She turned the water on cold to jolt herself awake, stepped out of the shower and toweled herself vigorously. She almost sang, she was so glad to see that Kit slept soundly after having gone down and brought the doll back up. That meant, it seemed to Pam, that she had decided to share her room with the doll. Perhaps to accept it, to stop imagining so many terrible things.

Yet beneath Pam's relief was the black edge of dread, pushed back but not forgotten.

In the hall she saw her dad, already on his way down to breakfast. He was dressed in a tan linen suit, no tie. Pam waved at him. She usually didn't see him until dinner.

"No court today?" she asked.

"No court. How'd you know?" Then he put his hand up to his collar. "Oh, no tie?" He pulled a folded tie out of his pocket and showed it to her. "Just in case something comes up. Aren't you a little late this morning?"

"Maybe you're the one who's late," Pam answered.

"Maybe. See you this evening, Pammy."

"Bye Daddy."

Her conversation with Dad hadn't disturbed Nicky. She saw through his open door the foot of his bed and his bare feet sticking out like two big white flags, toes up. They weren't moving.

Kit's door was still closed. Pam went into her own room and quickly dressed. Then, on her way out to go to work she dared to take one more peek at Kit.

She was awake this time. She lay in bed, looking toward the doll in the pink chair.

"Ssst, hi," Pam said as she went toward Kit's bed.

Kit turned her head and looked at Pam. There was no alertness on her face. Her eyes seemed almost blank, her face expressionless.

"How are you this morning?" Pam asked, sitting beside her. "I just have a minute, then I have to go. Are you going to be all right?"

Kit's eyes cast down, she said nothing.

Pam touched her face. "Is everything better now?"

Kit nodded.

Pam leaned down and kissed her. She didn't want to leave. She wondered if this was the way mothers felt when they sensed something going wrong with their child and still they had to go to work to support that child. There were two single mothers working at the market with whom she talked occasionally. Both were divorced and having problems with money, kids, ex-husbands. But their problems seemed distant and simple compared to what might be happening to Kit.

"Are you sure?"

"Pam . . ."

"Yes?"

"Don't tell Gramma Vee to take the doll back."

"Really? That's great, honey. You like her better, right?"

Kit looked up. "I'm afraid she'll scare Gramma. I'm afraid she'll kill her."

"Oh my God. Kit, stop this. I thought you had dealt with this. Damn it, Kit, it's only a stupid doll! I think I was wrong not to tell Mom, so when I get home this evening, we're going to tell her."

Tears sprang to Kit's eyes. She began shaking her head back and forth on the pillow. Her hands came up to her face, and Pam saw they were trembling, and Pam's heart broke. She gathered Kit up into her arms.

"Oh baby, what am I going to do with you? Why don't you want Mom to know how you feel about the doll?"

"I told her about the clothes, and my Barbie dolls."

"You did?"

"Yes."

"Well that's great, honey. So why don't we tell her about you not liking the big doll?"

"Because . . . she'll think I'm sick. And sick kids have to go to institutions. Away from home."

"Oh no. Mom would never do that to you." But the cold dread deep within Pam began to take shape. She thought of the little girl who died in an institution a hundred years ago.

"Listen, Kit, I have to go to work. Will you promise me something? I promise you I won't say anything to Mom yet. You can do that when you feel like it. I'll think of something else. I'll make it all okay."

"You will?"

"Yes. But you have to get up, go downstairs today, and play like you always did. Will you?"

"Y-yes."

"All right. Promise me you'll do all the things you would have done last week, before your birthday."

"I promise."

"All right. I'll see you this evening."

Kit watched Pam leave. She was dressed in a pretty cotton miniskirt and white blouse. Her legs were shapely and pretty in tights that matched the deep rose of one color in the skirt. Her dark hair hung past her shoulders and was tied back loosely with a ribbon. She waved goodbye at the door, and smiled. But the smile was only halfway.

The door was left open so Kit could see across the hall. A picture hung in the space Kit could see. It was of mountains and a stream, and Kit had looked at it lots of times.

She turned her head and looked in the other directions. She saw the corner of her room with its new wallpaper, and the two smaller framed scenes that hung there, above the pink chair. And in the chair was the doll, looking toward the window. But in the daytime, Kit had noticed, when the sun was bright, and you could see the tiny cracks in the porcelain of the doll, it

195

never moved. It was at night that it changed.

She got out of bed, gathered up her dolls and their suitcase, her oils and brushes and canvas, and her clothes. She carried it all to the bathroom where she brushed her teeth, her hair, and washed her face. She dressed, then she went downstairs carrying the things she was going to play with today. Maybe she would even play ball with Nicky for awhile if he wanted to. Or Chinese checkers. He liked that game. Maybe they would go to the park on their bikes.

She would keep her promise to Pam, and not think about the night. But tonight when she had to go to her room, the doll would be there. She'd begin to be something besides a doll, with scary, awful thoughts that were like whispers Kit couldn't quite hear. She didn't want the doll to go live with Gramma Vee. Because Gramma Vee was all alone. She didn't have someone like Pam to help her.

Pam had difficulty concentrating. As each customer came through her line she remembered to say, "Good morning, how are you?" Until one elderly gentleman who came in almost daily answered, "Afternoon, young lady. Where are you today?"

So she changed to wishing them good afternoon, thankful it was afternoon, which meant she didn't have much longer to work. Tonight, she had decided, she was going to tell Craig everything and get his opinion and advice. She wished it were Friday. He would be driving back from the university town where he was working and taking extra classes, and even though she wouldn't get to see him Friday night, she at least knew he would arrive in town before midnight.

She wished she had gone with him, taken a job there, enrolled in the university. Then immediately she knew she didn't wish that. What would Kit have done if she weren't here? Who, in the family, would Kit have turned to? Nicky? That was a laugh. Nicky had a basketball for a head, one might say. Though he did show quite a lot of heart at times, still he wouldn't have been able to handle this problem. But was she much better? She had thought it all would straighten out by itself. She must have thought that. She couldn't remember the confusing mess of her thoughts. First there had been the destruction in the closet, the dolls, the little clothes, and Kit blaming it on something inanimate.

Pam was suddenly struck by something she hadn't thought of before. All the destruction had been on the Barbie dolls and clothes. The other dolls, stuffed animals, things on the higher shelves, had not been touched.

Why had Kit torn up only her favorite dolls? The ones she played with?

Or was there another reason? Like, for instance, whoever, *whatever*, had ruined the dolls and their clothes, had ruined them only because they were on shelves it could reach?

Pam's fingers fumbled stiffly doling out change. She remembered to say, "Thank you, come again." But her voice sounded distant and unfamiliar. Smiling became a forced stretching of her lips.

She remembered closing the doll into the closet. Because there was something about it that disturbed Kit.

If Kit were right . . . *if she were right* . . . then the doll must have been enraged at finding herself closed into a small room in which she couldn't open the door. So she had turned her rage upon those things she could reach, Kit's favorite dolls. Perhaps it knew they were Kit's favorite dolls. If it had the eerie and frightening capabilities that Kit claimed it did, then one could assume it also might be able to read minds.

What am I thinking of?

"Excuse me, miss. Pamela?" The lady read Pam's small name tag. "Those aren't my things."

"Oh, sorry." She had just kept checking, going from one group of items to the next without noticing what she was doing. She had to correct the mistakes.

She took time to sneak a look at her watch. It was almost time to go home.

The next hour passed slowly. It came close to being the longest hour of her life. But finally it was over and she closed off her lane and went wearily back to the lounge. She took off

197

her checker's jacket and hung it up.

She didn't want to go home. Not right away.

She drove by a drive-in, got a Coke and sat in her car. She watched the other customers go to the window, place their orders. Kids on bikes got ice cream cones, truckers parked out on the gravel and went to the window for large orders of fries and burgers and milk shakes.

The Coke didn't help. She was still weary, no energy. She could almost hear Grandpa say, "What? At your age? Wait until you're sixty-seven."

She thought about her mother's parents. They had left this week on a trip. She recalled they had asked if Nicky and Kit could go along. They were just driving, heading north, maybe out to find some mountains somewhere and some cool mountain air. But they were traveling in a pickup with a camper on the back, and the kids would have had to ride in the back, and Mom had simply laughed and replied, "You're not serious. Those two riding all day in that small space?"

Pam thought now they should have taken Kit, anyway. Especially Kit. But Kit hadn't shown any interest in leaving home, even to go with Grandma and Grandpa Elkins, who were a lot of fun to be with. Kit was a little homebody. She never even wanted to spend the night away from home with a friend. Pam had thought she just wasn't old enough yet. But maybe Kit was . . . and Pam hated even thinking it . . . but maybe Kit had always been too introverted.

Pam didn't want to start thinking again, so she started her car, pulled out onto the street and drove slowly toward home. The closer she came to her own street the less traffic she found. The houses were on large lots with trees and hedges providing privacy. She could remember when her parents had bought this house. They all had loved it. Large, dark brick, with white framing beneath the porches, it was one of the older houses in an old, established neighborhood that was quiet and safe. Kids rode their bikes wherever they wanted to. She had, and still did on occasion. Sometimes when Craig was home he came over and they rode miles around the streets nearby and through Vincent Park. But those happy days seemed to belong to someone else. Even though she picked them up in memory, there seemed now to be a dark curtain between herself and her feelings.

She arrived home and parked her car beneath the big shade tree at the edge of the driveway. She had a spot in the three car garage but left her car out most of the time, where it would be handy to hop into and visit a friend or go to the drive-in and hang out. That carefree girl seemed almost like a stranger now.

All the bikes were in their racks at the end of the garage. Gypsy came to the gate wagging her tail. She never barked at family members except for an occasional distinctive *woo-woo* that sounded as if she were saying hello.

Pam paused to pet her, enjoying the feel of silky fur, the gentle, loving eyes, the friendly and happy grin. She followed Pam around to the patio. Kit was at her favorite table working on the canvas.

"Look Pam," she said. "I added a girl."

Pam looked. It was a picture of a house with trees, a mountain background, a brown road. And now a little girl. Every line was exquisitely drawn, in proportion, with depth and perception.

"Hey, that's good."

Kit smiled. She looked almost normal, and Pam allowed herself to hope.

She went upstairs and changed to a comfortable pair of shorts, and stretched out a few minutes on her bed. Then she got up and went downstairs to help with dinner so that Alice could go home.

All evening Pam watched the clock. As soon as dinner was over and the kitchen cleaned, she went upstairs. Mom, Dad, Kit, and Nicky were in the den doing the things they did every evening. Mom, on the couch with her feet up, always had something to read. Dad in his big, comfortable chair, had the newspaper, and sometimes, Kit on his lap. This evening Kit sat on the floor with Nicky. The television was on.

"Goodnight," Pam said at the door. "I'm going up to call Craig, okay?"

Her parents exchanged glances, each of them waiting for the other to give assent. Finally both of them nodded.

Pam hurried to her room, closed the door and stretched out across the bed. She dialed long distance, hoping Craig's roommate didn't answer.

When she heard Craig's voice she almost wept she was so relieved. For a couple of minutes they talked of casual things. What he had done today, what she had done.

"I spent the day making mistakes," she said. "I was doing all kinds of crazy things." She told him a couple.

"So next you're going to tell me you were half asleep on your feet because you were out with some guy last night and didn't get home till dawn."

He was joking, but she said, "I do have something I want to talk to you about, Craig. Really."

She heard a pause. She could almost see his brain making all sorts of connections, none of them correct. Hurriedly she said, "It's Kit. Something really weird is going on with her, and I don't know what to do."

"What?"

She asked him if he remembered seeing the doll Gramma Vee had given Kit.

"Yeah, sure. Unusual looking doll. Antique."

"Well, Kit was almost instantly afraid of it, and—and strange things have started happening."

She told him about the destruction of the Barbie dolls and the suitcase of new clothes he had given her. She told him about the doll being down in the powder room with cream makeup smeared on one cheek, and Kit coming after her to go look at the doll. She talked quickly, in a low voice, hugging the phone between her cheek and the pillow, her eyes on the closed door. She had an increasingly eerie feeling that someone was on the other side of the door listening, and she lowered her voice even further.

"Pam—Pam—I can't hear you."

"I don't know what to do, Craig."

"You sound scared, Pam. You don't believe her, do you? It's crazy. I mean, she's just a little kid. She's pretending. That's all. Kids like to pretend. They do it all the time, you know that."

"Craig, this doll has an unusual background. It's over a hundred years old, and it belonged to a little girl who killed her sister and her aunt, and then was never able to speak. She died in an insane asylum."

There was a pause, then Craig asked, "Kit was told about this stuff that happened a hundred years ago?" He sounded incredulous, bordering on angry.

"No! That's the weird part, Craig. She wasn't told. But it's almost as if she were, somehow . . . aware of it."

There was a hesitation. The line hummed faintly. Craig said, "You sound like you believe Kit's got reason to be afraid."

"No! But this is so extreme, Craig." She felt hot tears at the back of her eyes. Craig wasn't giving to her whatever she needed. She wasn't sure what she needed, or what she had expected of him.

"Christ o'mighty, Pam. Your mom is a child psychologist. Why the hell don't you tell her if you really believe Kit's got problems?"

"Kit asked me not to."

There came another long pause. She heard him sigh. She could almost hear his thoughts. *I've got studying to do. Class tomorrow night.* Pam felt cold and deserted. A thought she didn't like came to mind. *Craig can't handle problems. He doesn't want to be bothered with problems beyond his own.* Immediately she was ashamed she had even thought that. She felt disloyal.

But then he said softly, "I love you, Pam. I'll come home early Friday night and we'll talk, okay? Between now and then remember I love you, and I'll be working on this thing. We'll figure it out."

Nine

After Nicky and Kit had finished with the bathroom Pam locked herself in, ran the tub full of water as hot as she could stand it, poured in a couple of capfuls of bubble bath and slid in for a long soak. With her hair pinned high on the top of her head she buried her chin in hot water. Then she stared at the wall until the fish floating there in their own permanent bubble bath became colored spots before her eyes.

She wished she could just forget the past three nights, look forward to Friday night, and think of nothing else. But Kit's problems hadn't gone away, as she had thought they would the first night. Craig had said talk to her mom, but Pam wanted to avoid that. Mom had problems enough with the little kids who were her clients, and even worse problems sometimes with their parents or guardians. But Kit didn't have a broken home. She had always been secure, loved, treated gently. She'd never been homeless. She'd never been abused in any way, even the most subtle of abuses like some of Mom's clients. The kind of hidden abuses that weren't revealed until after months of therapy brought it out. The little kids were always so afraid of being taken away from their families, which was all they knew. Even the abuse was better than being alone among strangers, with no one to care at all.

It hurt Pam to think that Kit had even thought she might be put somewhere like that if she talked to Mom and Dad about her imaginings.

There was one person Pam could talk to, and who might help her understand what was happening to Kit. Gramma Vee. It was she after all, who had heard the weird history of the doll.

Pam dried herself, dressed in a nightgown, and went to her

bedroom. She closed the door so that her voice wouldn't disturb Nicky or Kit, and dialed Gramma Vee's number.

"Did I wake you?" Pam asked when Virginia answered after a half dozen rings. "I didn't realize it was so late. I was just going to hang up and try again tomorrow."

"Pam! No, you didn't wake me. Even if you had it's a delight hearing from you. Nothing's wrong, is there?"

"Well, Gramma, yes, sort of. Nothing really serious, I hope. I'd like to come over and talk to you after work tomorrow if I may."

"You can come over anytime you like. How about making it dinner, too? We'll cook something light, or go out, whichever you prefer."

"Good. That sounds good."

"How are your mom and dad?"

"They're fine. How're you, Gramma?"

"I'm enjoying my retirement. I've never been so busy in my life."

Virginia laughed, and Pam smiled, enjoying her laughter, that sound of normalcy.

"And Nicky and Kit?" Virginia asked. "How are they? And Beth and the baby, and Ross? I haven't heard from anyone since Sunday, which isn't very long, of course."

"I guess Beth and Ross and Tresa are okay. Nicky's like always. But Kit . . . it's Kit that I want to talk to you about, Gram. She's been acting really weird since her birthday party. I haven't told Mom. I didn't want to tell her yet. I just kept hoping Kit would get over this thing and be okay. But I thought you and I might talk, but I'd rather do it there than on the phone, because someone else might pick up one of the extensions. I'd feel more comfortable there."

"I don't understand. Is Kit not well?"

"It's not that exactly . . ."

"I'm sure you'd tell your parents if you thought she was sick. In fact, they should be told, no matter what it is, if you think it might be serious."

"I don't know. Gram . . . what was that history of the doll?"

"The history . . . ? Oh. Zenoa, the antique doll. Didn't I tell you?"

"Yes, but — I'd like to hear it again."

"It belonged to a little girl who was found in the house alone with her aunt, with whom she and her sister had been living. The sister had died a few days before, and it was considered a natural death. But a neighbor found the surviving child, who was just six years old, alone in the house with her aunt, who had been stabbed to death with an ice pick. The aunt had been writing a letter to the effect that the child had stabbed her sister, and the aunt felt she must institutionalize the little girl."

"So the little girl killed the aunt?"

"That seems to have been what some people thought, but the murder was never solved."

Pam paused, feeling cold even though she had just taken a hot soak. She pulled a blanket up. "Maybe a neighbor did it," she suggested.

"Sounds more logical, doesn't it? They said the house was locked. I went back over to the antique shop yesterday to see what else I could find, and the owner asked me if I had given the doll to my granddaughter yet. Then he went into a long, detailed story of the family who had owned the doll. They were a good, solid family in the community for the most part, and he seemed to know a lot about them because the story was so unique, I guess. It was passed along from grandfather to grandson."

"The doll was never owned by anyone else?"

"No, not until now. Is Kit enjoying her?"

"Gram, Kit is afraid of her."

"Afraid! But why? Does the doll's history frighten her?"

"She doesn't even know the history. I didn't tell her. I haven't told anyone but Craig. You didn't tell her, did you?"

"Oh no, I'd never tell that to Kit, not until she's older. I told only you."

"Well . . . that's what I want to talk to you about. At first I thought maybe you'd just take the doll back?"

"Of course I'll take it back if Kit doesn't like it Then we can go shopping and pick out whatever she likes."

"Well, but then Kit said she didn't want you to take it back."

"Oh?"

"She's afraid . . . the doll will hurt you."

204

Pam could visualize the concentrated frown on Gramma Vee's face. It would be the same kind of frown she'd been feeling on her own face as she tried so hard to make sense of Kit's fear. There seemed to be a connection to the doll's history. And that was too weird to believe. Especially since Kit knew nothing about it. Maybe it was just because the doll was old.

"I'll talk to you about everything tomorrow, Gram," Pam said. "Now I'd better hang up."

"All right, dear. Why don't you just bring the doll on over when you come? This is all so strange . . . but if she's actually afraid of it, there's just nothing to do but get it out of the house. So bring it back to me when you come, will you? I'll send Kit a new doll, and get her mind off this."

"Thanks, Gramma."

She felt so relieved she could have cried when she hung up. She snuggled down into bed, feeling as if Gramma Vee had just smoothed her troubles away. Why hadn't she called Gramma Vee that very first day, when she came home from work to find the dolls and their clothes destroyed? It would have saved Kit's further descent into her own private little hell.

Just one more night, that's all Kit had to deal with. Then, after the doll was out of the house, if anything else happened to Kit, she'd just have to tell Mom and Dad.

She was so tired suddenly. Having Gramma Vee take the load off her shoulders was like being six years old again herself, and being tucked safely into bed by someone she loved and trusted.

But, she thought as she drifted to sleep, she was certain of something. That little six-year-old child who lived a hundred years ago had not stabbed her sister or her aunt. She didn't believe it for one minute. It was probably the neighbor.

Or . . .

Kit stood in the shadowed hallway, in the silence. The door to her parents' room was visible across the balcony. It was dark wood, and closed.

She paused near Nicky's door, heard him snoring a little and knew he was asleep.

The door to Beth's old room was closed. So was Pam's door.

Kit moved silently back toward her own pink bedroom. She had never felt so alone. She wanted to go crawl into bed with someone. With her mama and daddy, with Pam, with Nicky even. She didn't want to go back into the room that was the doll's room now, not hers. She had lain in bed a long time, staring at the doll sitting so still in the chair, and listened to the sounds of everyone going to bed. Nicky had taken his bath. He always made a lot of noise, no matter what he was doing. But tonight Kit had listened to his every move, because it meant she wasn't so alone. Not just her and the doll. "Elizabeth," she whispered as she stared toward the dim outlines of the doll in the pink chair. "Elizabeth." In saying the name she'd given the doll, she tried to make it *her* doll, *her* friend, but it didn't work. Elizabeth wasn't the doll's name. As if it spoke to her the name came in silence. *Zenoa.*

Then Kit realized the house had grown quiet. Nicky was in bed. Pam, Mama, and Daddy were in their rooms.

The curtains at the window had made tiny rustling sounds as they moved in the breeze. The pale light coming in from the hall made things in the room, even the doll in the shadowed corner, just barely visible. If Kit could see the outlines of the doll, its blond hair, its pink and white dress, the ghostly round face, couldn't it see her also?

She had gotten out of bed to shut the door, so the room would be dark, but she stood with her hand on the door, unable to shut herself into the room with the doll. It was as if the doll were saying to her, *This is my room. Go away, go away, go.*

Kit stood in the hall.

She could go into Beth's room. The guest room now. But she had seen Alice remove the sheets, even the pillowcases, from the bed after the last overnight guest. There was only the bedspread over the mattress cover. She couldn't sleep there.

She moved in silence along the hall, slowly, going back to the pink room. As she started to enter she saw the figure standing in the space between the foot of the bed and the dresser. As before, it looked as large as a real girl. She saw the outline of the hair, the part in the middle, the two ribbons that held up small sections of hair on each side. She saw the flare of the lacy dress. The doll was standing in profile, as if it stretched tall to look

206

into the mirror.

Kit backed silently away. She stared at the door. As if her stare caused the door to move, it began to open wider. Kit pushed back, until she was wedged into the corner.

She watched it come out of the room. It stood surprisingly tall, its head turning. Kit tried to make herself part of the wood of the house, part of the wallpaper in the darkness of the corner.

The doll moved, turning, going toward the stairway. The night-light shone for a moment softly on the white stockings it wore as it passed the tiny bulb that burned at the electrical outlet. A shadow, large and long, fell across the opposite wall. Kit heard above the difficult pounding of her heart the whisper of movement the doll made as it passed Nicky's room and went on to the balcony.

It paused again and turned. The movements weren't quite like a human. There was an awkwardness, a turning of the whole body, as if it were manipulated. It was, Kit thought suddenly, like someone unseen was moving a puppet about. Then it would move again and begin walking, and become more flexible. It was as if it was part puppet and part something else that was like a real girl.

It looked at the closed door where Kit's mama and daddy slept, and a terrible fear entered Kit. One she hadn't thought of before.

What if it went to their room? *What if it hurt them?*

But then the doll was moving again, down the stairs. And Kit knew where it was going.

She waited until it was out of sight, then she slipped silently to the balcony and looked over. Yes, the thin streak of light lay across the hall and up the wall opposite to the powder room. The doll had entered there, and, as if she couldn't quite close the door, she had pulled it almost closed.

Kit turned hurriedly back into the hall.

The touch brought Pam out of a vague dream in which a girl and a doll had become interchangeable, and at the touch she almost screamed as reality mixed with dream. The hand was small, a doll's hand, or the girl in the dream that was at times a doll. But the hand was warm, and the hissing whisper belonged

207

to Kit.

Pam sat up.

"Pam, it's there, it's down there again, Pam. I didn't put it there. Please come and see for yourself, Pam, please."

Pam snapped on her reading light, and Kit put up an arm between her eyes and the light as if she could no longer bear light.

"Pam, come and see," she pleaded. "I stood in the hall a long time, and I watched her come out and go downstairs."

This is the end, Pam thought to herself, anger rising. This is the goddamned end. She shoved her covers back and threw her legs out of bed.

"I'm going to finish this thing once and for all, Kit. We can't go on every night with you awake and scared half the night. That damned doll is not going to do anything to hurt you, understand? Where is it?"

"In the powder room," Kit whispered, standing back, looking shy and terrified and lost. Pam's heart caved in. She reached out. Kit came to her and Pam gave her a warm hug.

It hurt even more when Kit whispered, "You're mad at me."

"No, I'm not mad at you, sweetheart. I promise. But I promise you too, there's not going to be any more of you being afraid of the doll."

She stood up and started out of the room, Kit coming closely behind.

"What are you going to do?" Alarm was in Kit's voice.

"I'm going to lock that damned doll in the attic, okay? Then we'll come back down here and sleep."

Pam walked down the hall with no attempt at silence, with Kit coming hurriedly behind. They went down the stairs and Pam shoved open the powder room door. Bright light poured out into the hall from the fluorescent tube over the long mirror. Kit remained in the hall, away from the light.

The doll sat in the chair, just as it had last night, primly, peeking over the vanity table at its reflection in the mirror. The half-smile on its face was almost like a pleased, awed look, as if it couldn't believe its beauty. This time there was not only a smear of makeup on its cheek, but a touch of lipstick on the upper lip.

208

Pam picked up the doll and tucked it under her left arm like a sack of potatoes she had to carry back to the produce department. Why this fascination with the powder room? What was here that drew Kit? What difference did it make that Kit had brought the doll down, obviously, and then put a small amount of makeup on it before she decided to get scared and come running to her? What kind of game was she playing? Or, did something in her brain click, and turn in another direction, blocking out all memories of her actions so that she thought the doll was doing it all?

Well, with the doll locked in the attic tonight, and taken away in the morning to go back to Gramma Vee's, Kit's problem would gradually be revealed as something triggered by the doll, or something that just coincided with the arrival of the doll. If Kit continued to imagine things, then Mom and Dad had to know. No more secrets.

Kit followed closely beside Pam as they went up the front stairs, down the hall, and to the attic door. Pam paused and looked back at Kit.

"You stay here. I'll take the doll up and put her somewhere."

"Up *there?* You're going up there, too?" Kit whispered frantically.

"Yes. You can stay here."

Pam opened the door and heard a dreary squeak, the door was so seldom opened. The enclosed stairway, barely wide enough to haul up unwanted items from the house below, rose like a black tunnel. At the bottom of the stairs was a small square area where Pam hesitated, looking up into the darkness.

Kit pleaded, "Just leave it here, Pam. At the bottom. Can't you just leave it here?"

"No, I'll take it up. You stay here."

"Pam . . . don't go up."

"Shhh. Stay there. I'll be right back."

Pam began to climb. There was a railing on the right wall. With the doll under her left arm Pam held to the railing and climbed.

She had never liked the attic. It had only one window, so that even in the daytime it was a gloomy place. One bulb hung on a long cord at the top of the stairs. Pam crept up in the dark, where the only light came from the shadowed hall below. She should have turned on the hall lights. She thought of calling down to Kit to turn them on. But instead she went on up and felt awkwardly about in the air for the string that hung from the light. She found it, turned it on. The light barely reached the steps.

She looked around. Boxes stood scattered on the bare wood floor. She knew from memory that some of the boards were loose and squeaked when walked on. Over in the corner stood the things that had come out of the rooms as kids grew older. A couple of cribs, with mattresses, an old chest with cartoon figures painted on the front, some little lamps in the shapes of Mickey Mouse and Donald Duck.

She saw old chairs and a broken end table. But the best place to put the doll was in one of the cribs. Or, a drawer in the big chest that stood in the center of the attic.

At first the feeling of movement was like a transfer of weight, as if the doll had shifted beneath her arm the way a sack of potatoes often did. She paused to adjust it. The doll shifted again, and this time she knew it was not that she had let it slip.

She jerked away from it, letting it fall. It struck the floor and sprang back at her, and in utter shock she felt herself falling. She fought for balance. The doll launched itself at her again, rising up against her with hands out. Pam fell helplessly toward the tall chest of drawers.

She was part of a dark fantasy. None of this was real. It was the nether world, ruled by fear and darkness and peopled by things seen only in night terrors, then forgotten on awakening, too horrible to accept. The gloom of her surroundings, the dust, the webs that hung from the ceiling, the old pieces of furniture that stood spotted here and there on the attic floor were like eerie peaks in a dead landscape. Moving within it was the doll.

The sharp pain in her head obliterated consciousness, and she slid to the floor.

Ten

Kit had been listening to Pam's soft steps. Barefoot, Pam made almost no sound at all, except when she stepped on a squeaky board. Kit listened, heard her walk away from the top of the stairwell. She could no longer see her. She was lost in the dark. Then a dim faraway light came on. For a long time, there was silence. Kit wanted to call out to her, but if she did others might hear, too. She waited. *Please, Pam, lay it down and come back.*

Then suddenly Kit heard the sound of a heavy thud, as if . . . as if . . . Pam had dropped the doll. No, it was more than that. It was as if Pam herself had fallen.

Kit disobeyed Pam's instructions to stay in the hall and stepped into the stairwell. She started up, then stopped. "Pam, Pam?" she cried out softly, tearfully. *"Pam?"*

A board squeaked faintly, and Kit held her breath, looking up. Then silence again.

"Pam?"

She started to climb the stairs. When she was halfway up she heard the squeak of another board in the attic, and she stopped, staring upward.

A head came in view, silhouetted against the light behind it. Light shined through the hair. There was a dark halo, but it wasn't Pam's hair. The hair was golden. The smirking face of the doll gazed down at Kit for a heartbeat, then suddenly it was running down the stairs. Its right arm was lifted over its head as if it were going to strike. It was holding something. In a rush of terror she saw it was the old ice pick Pam had told her and Nicky they couldn't play with.

211

Kit whirled away. She fell to the bottom of the stairwell, feeling none of the pain of the fall. She pushed herself to her feet and ran through the door, her hand instinctively reaching back to shove the door shut. She started down the hallway, running, reaching for Daddy and Mama. Then she felt the touch on her back. Something sharp and stinging hit her between the shoulder blades. Her breath gushed out of her and the outlines of the hallway faded. She fell, face down, far, far away from her daddy's door.

Nicky got up, half asleep. Someone had been running in the hall, and then they had fallen. Now there was an ominous silence. A weird sound of nothing. Blinking, he took a few steps toward the door. Then he stopped, staring into the hall where the nightlight glowed softly down upon Kit, sprawled face down. But there was something on her back . . . blood spreading over the material of her pajamas, and something else, stabbing, stabbing . . . He could see the hand holding something long and dull and rusty and thin and round . . .

With a cry he rushed forward and then stopped, stunned, shocked to silence and inaction.

The small girl rose from Kit and came toward him. She looked up at him with large, round, dark eyes. A girl . . . no not a girl . . . something wrong . . . wrong . . .

He stared, unable to move, as the girl who was all wrong somehow rushed at him with surprising speed. He tried to make himself come alive and fight her, but he only stood because he was beginning to see her face better, even in the darkness of his room, and he recognized that face.

Fay woke and sat up, listening. The house was quiet. Almost too quiet. In the wide bed beside her Les slept, but his deep, steady breathing hardly ever deepened into a snore. He hadn't been disturbed. But she had a sensation of something having fallen somewhere in the house, and she felt that she had heard in her sleep the running of bare feet. Then another fall, and the sound of a scuffle, somewhere. Yet now, listening, fully awake, she heard nothing.

She started to get out of bed when the bedroom door, pushed almost shut but never latched against the children at night, began slowly to open.

Fay sat still, watching. There was no inside light in the room, but a street light, mixed with the light of a full moon, spread broad paths from the windows, and the outlines of the furniture were only masked in an overlay of shadows. As the door continued to slowly ease inward, a strange sense of dread entered Fay.

This was not one of her children opening the door. Nicky would have pushed it open as he pushed open all doors, sometimes banging them against the wall with the fervor of his entry. Nicky, always running to play ball, or go biking, or even to go watch a certain TV show. Nor was it Kit, gentle little Kit. And Pam would have knocked first.

Though she had an urge to crawl back into bed and snuggle safely against Les, she put her feet to the floor and stood up, staring at the door as it continued to ease inward. It was as if someone were sneaking in.

Her mind ran swiftly over the closing of the house at bedtime. She had seen to it herself that all downstairs windows and door were closed and locked. Whoever came in the door had to be part of the household.

"Kit?" she said softly. Kit, the quiet, shy child, the introvert, who had confessed to her the ruining of her dolls? Kit, who might be having periods of somnambulism.

"Kit?" she said again, going around to the foot of the bed.

She heard Les wake, his deep breathing ending with a soft gasp. The bedding rustled when he sat up. Then his voice came like a warning.

"Good God!"

As if the image hadn't reached her brain until Les spoke, Fay saw the small child who had entered the room. A little girl dressed in a fluffy, lacy dress that flared out around her knees, standing out like a parasol. Yet the significance of his cry, the horror in his voice, remained a mystery for several heartbeats. The child was a stranger, but only a child. Then suddenly she was seeing the small face more clearly, and she knew at last that it wasn't a child at all.

Pam's consciousness returned to a dreamlike state of mind. She didn't know where she was. Reality was altered, and she was vaguely aware of it in the depths of her mind, yet couldn't rise above the dreams. She saw in her mind the large wedding picture of her mother and father. Fay, young and beautiful in white, the veil tossed back from her face, laughing at the camera as, her hand in Les's, she hurried toward the car that was decorated with banners announcing they were newlyweds. Les in his tux coming behind her. They complemented each other so well, that spring day years ago. For a moment Pam drifted with them in the car as they drove, and clearly saw Fay leaning over against Les's shoulder in a teasing and flirtatious way, and his glances toward her as if he couldn't keep his eyes away.

Then the scene changed. She was one of the party that went to see the older house in the well-established neighborhood where old trees had been left standing. Nine years old, she stood with her parents, sister Beth and four-year-old Nicky in the driveway and looked up at the white-trimmed, two-story brick house. Then suddenly she was in the house and running excitedly with Nicky through the rooms. Their voices echoed in the empty house as they ran upstairs and pounded down the back hall choosing bedrooms. "Here's mine," she yelled, going into the bedroom with the double windows, and behind her Nicky yelled, "Here's mine, here's mine!" in all the rooms.

Then she was older, and climbing the long, narrow stairs that led up into the attic . . . she was carrying something . . .

She sat up. The pain in her head throbbed, and she put a hand up and felt her hair gummy with something almost gluelike. She pulled her hand down and looked at her fingers. Red. *Blood.*

What was she doing here?

She looked around, twisting on the dusty wood floor. The

pale bulb hung still on its long cord not far away, leaving a pool of light beneath it and gathering shadows all around. Yet it was no longer night. Birds sang outside the window. Daylight blended with the light from the bulb.

She was sitting beside the old chest that was part of the furniture that had been in the house when they bought it. She clearly remembered her mom saying, "Oh, let's save it. I might want to refinish it someday and put it somewhere." So Les and the man who was helping them move carried it piece by piece upstairs. She had tried to carry one of the drawers, but it was too heavy to get it all the way. The man had come to the stairs grinning and taken it from her and with one hand carried it up.

What am I doing here?

Using the chest for support, she pulled herself up. She must have fallen, though she couldn't remember it.

What was she doing here, in the attic? Her last memory was of going to bed. Why had she come into the attic? How long had she been unconscious?

Her head hurt. The pain burst anew with each beat of her heart.

She turned slowly to look at the steep, dark drop of stairs. They were like a hole in the attic, with no protection, no railings. She started toward it, her head held sideways. Her hand, reaching automatically to the wound, hesitated. She couldn't bear the thought of touching that drying, sticky blood.

The bathroom . . . she had to go down to the bathroom and wash the wound. She felt it gingerly with her fingers. Not a large wound, as it felt inside, but just a big bump, with a small cut. How could it ooze so much blood?

The house was so quiet. Too quiet. The silence surrounded her, an icy warning. With the ice burrowing into her heart, her limbs stiff, she went to the top of the stairs and looked down. In the dim light that seeped into the stairwell she saw the door was shut.

She had a sudden, vague memory of leaving Kit standing in the square space at the foot of the stairs, the door open behind her. It had been dark then. Why had she gone into the attic, leaving Kit behind watching?

In growing fear she hurried down the steps.

With her hand on the doorknob she hesitated. The silence beyond the door was like a black wall. She felt if she opened that door she would be opening a door into a black wall of hell, a darkness that dropped off into a kind of space where no light ever glowed.

But her family was there. Her life was there. She opened the door.

At first glance the small figure sprawled on the hallway floor looked unfamiliar. But it was only a flash before recognition. Kit! Face down. The back of her pajamas shredded and torn, and darkened with something . . . with . . . with blood.

Pam ran down the hall and fell to her knees beside Kit. Groaning abjectly she picked her little sister up and felt the complete limpness of her body. Her head fell back over Pam's arm, her face as white as if all blood had drained from it, yet with strange, puddled dark blotches like bruises on her cheekbones and chin and one side of her forehead. Her eyes looked blankly up, staring with complete vacuity at nothing. Her flesh was beginning to hold a terrible coldness.

The sounds, soft, low, sobbing, reached Pam's awareness. She heard herself crying over and over, "Oh my God, oh my God . . ."

What had happened here? Where were Nicky, and Mom, and Dad? Daylight seeped into the night shadows of the house, pushing them farther back. Sunshine came weakly from the distant horizon, touching the floor of Pam's room with a color different from a night-light, and spread weakly into the hall from the open bedroom door. The blood in the hall looked black and alien, an eerie and terrible greeting to this early morning.

She wanted to scream for help, but the silence in the house stopped her. She had to get help. Now. Where were Mom and Dad? Where was Nicky?

She laid Kit gently back onto the floor. She had a brief thought of taking her into the bedroom and placing her on the bed, but she had to hurry instead and get help. Someone

216

might save Kit's life, if she hurried.

So she left her lying on the hall floor. She had to find the others. Nicky. Mom and Dad.

She turned on the hall lights, then wished she hadn't. Blood had been splattered over the wall near where Kit lay. It didn't even enter Pam's mind how Kit must have been injured. She saw the blood, and it was there, and nothing helped. Nothing stopped that terrible fact.

She ran past the blood-soaked area where Kit lay and went to Nicky's room. He was facedown on the floor, halfway between his bed and the door. Pale sunlight came through the window, slanting from the east. She had a glimpse of the sun, a huge, red ball edging slowly above the earth, shining through the trees near the house. There was even more blood here than in the hall. She stooped and touched his cheek, but knew before she touched him that his skin would hold the same chill that Kit's did.

She backed out and ran across the balcony to the master bedroom door screaming, "Mom! Dad! Oh God, please, help!"

The door stood open. Her cry became a soft scream that throbbed in her head. The walls of the master bedroom were splattered with blood. Blood seemed to be everywhere, surrounding her mother, her father. They lay still, as still as Kit and Nicky. She backed slowly out of the room, unable to tear her eyes away. How could this have happened to her parents? Her dad, large, healthy, strong. He too was on the floor, like Nicky, like Kit, like Mom. Sprawled helplessly themselves. Blood soaking their clothes. Wounds invisible. For just an instant she wondered how this had happened, how there was so much blood, so much destruction and death.

Who did this?

Then she was running. She had to have help. Ambulances, doctors, nurses, paramedics. Her family might be saved, if she hurried.

She ran downstairs. Daylight came in at the door, through the oval glass. She fumbled with the locks, and finally got the door open. She flung it back, and it struck the wall, then she

217

glanced over her shoulder into the foyer, and stopped.

An object lay on the floor between the front door and the foot of the stairs. It was covered in blood, all except a portion of the wooden handle. Mesmerized, she stooped and picked it up.

She recognized the old ice pick. It had a long blade with a sharp point. She remembered it being among some other old junk that had been in the attic, a box of items her mother had said were interesting. So it had stayed there. Stayed, waiting for the night when someone would pick it up.

She noticed then the door to the powder room was slightly open.

She stood up, walked forward, and pushed the door open.

The antique doll sat at the dressing table, looking with admiration at her reflection in the mirror. She turned slowly, and looked at Pam.

In a flash of memory Pam saw herself taking the doll up into the attic. Leaving Kit at the bottom of the stairs she had climbed into the dim, dusty attic and stood looking for a place to put the doll. She had started to take it over to one of the old cribs. Then she had felt something in the doll. Almost a sensation of squirming.

The icy fear she'd felt then returned to her like a shock wave. She recalled pulling out the top drawer, on a sudden urge to put the doll in there. *Where it couldn't get out.*

The doll had twisted, then, as if it knew what she had in mind. She had dropped it, repelled, frightened. She had felt it come alive and push her, shove her so hard she had fallen, her head striking the corner of the chest.

She stood almost lifeless now as the doll slid off the seat of the vanity and came toward her. Specks of blood covered its face, its dress, its white stockings. Droplets of blood clung to its bright hair like dark, terrible stars in a distant universe. It came into the hall, its round brown eyes holding her with an icy gaze of death. It came into the hall, and the light of day. Pam backed into the wall, afraid to turn her eyes.

A ray of dimly reflected sunshine touched it. Abruptly, within inches of Pam's feet, it toppled sideways.

It lay, its eyes closing, its arms stiffly upright. Whatever had powered it gone with the night.

Pam found herself outside. She was running. Running and screaming. She was in a yard somewhere, going toward a house, but on the street a pickup truck stopped and a man called to her.

"Hey! Hey, what's wrong?"

She turned and ran toward him. He got out of his truck and started to meet her, then stopped, staring at her hand. At something she gripped in her hand. She looked down, and saw the bloody ice pick. She dropped it, then put her hands to her cheeks and stood screaming.

People came from everywhere. Doors opened and slammed, and people ran toward her. She collapsed onto the grass sobbing, her hands covering her face. She was aware of movement around her, of cars stopping, people running. Then came calls of neighbors and strangers from her own house. Splatters of calls, like the blood on the walls, on the bodies of her loved ones.

"Good God! Get the police!"

"She's killed them!"

"She's stabbed her whole goddamned family to death!"

No. *No, no, no.*

She was in an ambulance, and the siren wailed like a lost soul. No, she hadn't killed her family, no. But no one heard her.

She was alone in the body of the ambulance. Paramedics had looked at her head, and then helped her into the ambulance, all the while ignoring her cries. "Help *them.* Go help my family, please, I'm all right. I'm all right! Go help them."

"Let's just get you to the hospital first," the paramedic said in a strange calmness.

So she rode through the streets, and the memories flashed back, like a rerun of her life.

Kit had come to her, telling her the doll was in the powder room. Again. Pam had gone downstairs with her, half-angry that this game of Kit's had gone so far. Tomorrow she was taking the goddamned doll back to Gramma Vee, and Gram could do whatever the hell with it she wanted, but tonight she had to shut Kit up and put the damned doll someplace where Kit wouldn't worry about it.

Oh Kit, Kit baby.

Who else could have torn up the doll clothes, and the dolls, but Kit? Not Nicky, and not — not what Kit thought.

"She did it."

Kit's words, shy, frightened, trusting Pam. And Pam had let her down.

Why had she been so sure that Kit was having mental problems? If she'd gone directly to her mother with the whole truth, her mother would have determined that it wasn't Kit who was aberrant. Not Kit, after all.

An inanimate object, such as a toy or a doll, can't move without being powered from some source! Yet it had. It had been moving, in the deep hours of the night, ever since it had entered the house. Kit had known it. Her young, accepting mind had seen it. Pam had denied it.

What kind of horror lay within the antique doll Gramma Vee had inadvertently brought into the family?

The history of the doll came to her mind. The little girl who had been accused of killing her sister, then the aunt. The little girl had known the truth. She had lived her life mute, because she knew what had killed her sister and aunt, and she knew no one would believe her.

No one would believe her.

As now, no one would believe Pam if she told the truth.

Eleven

"The injury isn't serious, she can be released. Take aspirin or acetaminophen for pain."

Her pain was mental. She wanted to go home desperately to see if any of her family lived, yet cringed from reentering the house. A nurse accompanied her from the emergency room cubicle out into the emergency room lobby. Beth was there. Her face was as pale as the blouse she wore, and her lips so tight they were thin, white lines. She was carrying a robe, and held it for Pam to put on. Pam saw with horror that her pajamas were stained with blood. Her hands were creased with dried blood.

A nurse saw her looking at her hands, and guided her toward a bathroom. Beth went with her, but said nothing as Pam washed her hands.

As soon as Pam arrived at the hospital she had been asked about next of kin, and she had given them Beth's name. Beth lived nearby. Gramma Vee lived on the other side of the city. And Grandma and Grandpa Elkins were on a trip. Next of kin. *Mom, Dad* . . .

It seemed hours Pam had waited in the emergency room, the cubicle created by curtains. A nurse looked in, reassured her that a doctor would be with her soon. She had felt like screaming the whole time, until finally the doctor came, and cleaned the wound on her head.

Now she was free to go. Go where?

Tiny freckles stood out on Beth's pale face. Pam saw them, and was surprised she even noticed. Yet everything seemed oddly distinct. The lobby was painted off-white and the furniture upholstered in deep rose. A counter created an entry almost like a hallway, and behind it were two nurses. She was aware of nurses, of people waiting to see people, and the tall man in a casual suit who waited in the lobby watching. He obviously was from the police though he wore no uniform. A man with him got up from one of the chairs.

Pam hugged Beth tightly. She didn't want to let her go. Beth did not return the hug. Pam started toward the door, and Beth said something that struck Pam as oddly inappropriate.

"I gave them your name, but I didn't have any insurance information. I told them to just send us a bill."

Hadn't Beth been told about the deaths? That anyone would be concerned about money at this time seemed unbearably callous to Pam, yet it also seemed to enter a note of reality that was welcome. The other reality, the blood, the still bodies, was one she couldn't accept. Suddenly she was desperate to go home and *see*. Perhaps it had been a horrible nightmare. Or, hallucinations caused by the wound on her head, and by her period of unconsciousness.

She clutched Beth's wrist.

"I want to go home, Beth. I need to see if they're all right."

Beth didn't look at her. For the first time Pam noticed that Beth hadn't once met her eyes. Her pale face turned away, and her lower lip quivered. She tightened it, puckering her chin to keep her mouth steady. She blinked rapidly against tears that welled up but didn't spill.

The two men came toward them, and one of the men spoke gently.

"I'm Detective Jefferson and this is Detective Hart." They both held out identification for her to see, but she only glanced at them. "We need to ask you some questions, Miss. We'd like you to come down to the station with us."

Pam looked at Beth. Beth said to the detective, "What about her clothes? She needs something to wear." Her voice was weak and thin.

The detectives looked at each other, and looked at the bloodied pajamas beneath the short robe. They seemed at a loss.

222

"No one is allowed back into the house at this time, ma'am. Could you lend her something?" Detective Jefferson said.

Beth nodded. It didn't matter that Beth was larger. Anything would do.

"We'll bring her by your house."

"Why can't she just go with me?"

The two men exchanged a glance, and Detective Jefferson nodded. "We'll follow you."

Beth turned quickly and almost ran to her car, parked out in the emergency room parking lot. Pam hurried behind her, vaguely aware of the sound of birds in the trees that lined the street not far away, of traffic, of people's voices. Such normal sounds while within her such a storm raged.

She huddled in the car, her arms hugging her waist. She had begun to shake. Beth drove almost recklessly it seemed, pulling the small car in quick turns and exits and gunning the engine when she reached the street. Pam caught a glimpse of the detectives' sedan in the rearview mirror.

"My God, Pam," Beth cried, *"What happened?"* She began to sob. Her shoulders jerked, her hands clutched the wheel. "They told me everyone's *dead.* Mom, Dad, Nicky, Kit. *What happened?"*

Pam's mouth worked wordlessly. It was true then. After all. She stared at the road. Did she dare tell Beth the truth?

"Beth," she finally said. "I have to tell you something. Do you remember the antique doll Gramma Vee gave Kit for her birthday?"

"Yes, of course I do. What the hell does that have to do with what happened? Where were you? How did it happen — that that *you* escaped the killer? Pam, *when did this happen?"*

"It — in the night. Kit came to me, and told me the doll had gone down to the powder room again —"

"What?" Beth screamed, throwing Pam a tear-drenched look. She jerked her stare back to the street and whirled the car around another corner. Her house was the second on the block. She whirled the car into the driveway and slammed to a stop.

Pam said nothing more. She got out of the car and hurried

223

up the walk toward the front door. Beth ran ahead of her, and opened the door. A woman got up from the couch, unspoken questions on her face as she looked from Beth to Pam and then out the large picture window at the brown sedan that had pulled into the end of the driveway and parked behind Beth's car.

"Martha, do you mind staying longer with Tresa?" Beth asked. "There's been a real tragedy, and I have to go with my sister. I'll explain later."

The middle-aged woman nodded. Beth hurried Pam into the hallway toward the bathroom.

"You take a shower. I'll bring you something to wear."

Pam stepped into the shower gratefully, and for a blessed, thoughtless moment closed her eyes and let hot water, as hot as she could stand it, gush down over the back of her neck. The wound on her forehead throbbed. She avoided wetting the bandage as she turned beneath the shower.

She left the shower stall to find Beth holding a shirt and a pair of shorts. The bathroom door was closed.

"Beth, I have to tell you. I can't tell them because they won't believe me. But I want you to know the truth."

Beth nodded. She had stopped crying, and seemed resigned to the kind of hopelessness that Pam felt, but she didn't know the horror yet, would never know the real horror.

Beth said nothing as Pam hastily told her about Kit's fears concerning the doll. As Pam dressed in shorts that were loose and baggy, and a shirt that hung so long it almost covered them, she glanced occasionally at Beth, and saw once again that Beth was not meeting her eyes. She nodded a couple of times as Pam told her about Kit, about her fears.

But when Pam told her the rest, Beth's eyes lifted and she stared into Pam's eyes.

The words rushed from Pam. "I carried it up into the attic. I was going to lock it there until morning, and then I was going to take it with me to work. And after work I was going to take it over to Gram's. And leave it. And . . . I felt it move, Beth, in my arm. I felt—as if I held something—awful. I dropped it."

224

Beth stared hard at her, eyes steady, unblinking, her lips slowly parting until her chin dropped. She continued to stare in silence.

"It jumped, and shoved me. It hit me hard. I fell and hit my head on the old chest there, in the attic. When I came to it was dawn. The house was so quiet. For awhile I didn't even remember what I'd been doing in the attic. I went downstairs . . . and—and I found them. I didn't know what had happened. Then, when I was running for help, I saw the doll in the powder room again. There was blood spotted all over her. She came toward me. Walking. Just like a kid would, like Kit said she did. Then when she reached some sunlight she fell. And was a doll again."

"My God in heaven! What's wrong with you, Pam? What's happened to you?" Beth added in a furious hiss, *"They said you were holding the ice pick, Pam!"*

"It was in the foyer. I picked it up. I—"

Beth had started crying again. With her eyes closed, her face tipped toward the ceiling, she wept. Pam reached out.

"Beth, have you called Ross?" Pam pleaded, thinking of Beth, and that she needed help. "Let me call Ross for you, Beth."

"They're waiting," Beth said shortly, "We have to go, Pam."

She grabbed a handful of tissues and pressed them against her face, then led the way out of the bathroom. Martha was still standing in the living room. As Pam followed Beth to the door she heard Tresa start crying. Beth didn't turn back, and Martha hurried down the hall toward the baby's room.

Detective Hart got out of the sedan and opened the back door for Pam. She got in and sat down. When she looked back Beth was getting into her car again, and as they drove away, Beth followed.

Pam didn't see Beth again at the station even though she had checked behind often, and saw Beth following. At the station Beth drove into the parking lot at the front, while the detectives drove to a lot reserved for police.

They escorted Pam into the building and asked if she minded if they took her fingerprints. She shook her head no. She was trembling so hard the woman in uniform had to hold her wrist to steady it as she rolled each of her fingers and thumbs across the ink pad and then onto paper.

The detectives accompanied her into a room where there was a table and chairs. Pam sat down and clutched her hands together on the table. She stared down at the ring Craig had given her. Not an engagement ring, not really, even though they had whispered that to each other. It had a tiny diamond, with tiny rubies surrounding it. Rubies, as red as blood. She turned the ring around so that the stones were cupped in her hand.

"Could you tell us what happened, please, Pamela?"

She shook her head. "I don't know. I—lost consciousness. When I came to, I found them. I don't know what happened."

"What caused the loss of consciousness?"

Pam looked at the wall. It was grey. A horrible, depressing grey. She couldn't tell these men the truth. They would no more believe it than she had believed Kit. They would only stare at her incredulously, that she had even thought they might believe.

Exactly the way Beth had stared at her.

She could tell them she was struck while in her bed, that she didn't know who had struck her or why. But they would know that no one had broken into the house.

She said, "I don't know. I—felt the pain. I lost consciousness."

"Were you struck?"

"I—"

She had never lied. She was not comfortable even with the thought of lying, now that it entered her mind briefly.

"I was in the attic," she finally said. "I—sort of fell, and hit my head against a chest there. That's all I know. When I came to it was daylight. I went downstairs and found them."

"What about the ice pick you were holding when you ran for help?"

"I found it in the foyer. I just picked it up, that's all."

They kept questioning her, about time, about why she was in the attic. She told them it was perhaps three o'clock in the morning when she'd gone up into the attic.

"Why did you go up?"

"I went up to—to take a doll."

"At three o'clock in the night?"

She hesitated, her lips parted, her head beginning to hurt again. She put her hands up. "Please," she said, "can I have an aspirin? My heads hurts."

"Yes, of course."

They both left. After a few minutes a woman in uniform came in with a glass of water and two aspirins. Then she too left and Pam put her head down on the table. Darkness swirled through her mind. Darkness mixed with the visions of Kit, of Nicky, of her mother and father, and blood. Visions of the doll sliding off the vanity and walking toward her, blood on her face, in her hair, on her clothes. She—it—came toward Pam, walking as gracefully and smoothly as a little girl, her lovely half-smile, and her dark eyes. She walked into the foyer into the light of day, and had changed. In the blink of an eye, the beat of a heart, she had changed. In front of Pam she fell, and lay stiffly, eyes closing, blood drying on her porcelain skin, in her golden hair.

She lay still, within feet of where she had dropped the bloody ice pick.

Twelve

For hours she sat in the interrogation room, sometimes alone, sometimes being questioned by the two detectives and various others. They brought her lunch, which she couldn't eat. They brought her Cokes, which she drank, the cool liquid tingling in her mouth and throat.

"Can I see my grandmother, please?" she asked. "May I go home with my grandmother?"

"What is your grandmother's name?"

She gave them the name. Virginia Armand. She gave them the names of her mother's parents. They left and came back again, and said nothing about her grandmother or sister.

Then as she put her head down on the table in exhaustion they came back and Detective Hart told her, "We'd like to read you your rights, Miss. You're under arrest for the murder of your family."

She stood up, and swayed. The world faded away, briefly, mercifully. During all the questions, during all the hours of trying to truthfully answer questions without telling them the absolute truth about the antique doll, it had not occurred to her that anyone would think she had killed her loved ones.

Someone helped her back into the chair and asked her if she were all right. She nodded as the mental withdrawal passed and reality became hard and real again. She stood up and heard a voice telling her she could call her attorney.

"I want to see my grandmother. Please. Someone let me see Virginia Armand." She had to warn her against the doll.

* * *

Virginia stood with Beth and Ross waiting. She had never been inside the doors of a police station before in her life, and was surprised there was so much activity and noise. Like other family groups, she stood in a close circle with Beth and Ross. Beth was trembling so hard she appeared to have chills. Virginia felt numb. She had been told that Pam had been arrested for the murders of Fay, Les, Nicky, and Kit. She didn't believe it.

Someone from the station had called her, and told her. She thought it must be a horrible nuisance call, and she had immediately phoned the house. The phone had rung six times with no answer, and she knew something was wrong. Alice would have answered on the second or third ring. Then she called Beth's house, and a lady answered and said Beth was gone. "Gone where?" Virginia cried, her manners gone. "What is going on?" The woman told her, "There has been a terrible tragedy. I think Beth is at the police station." So Virginia called the police, and the deaths were verified.

Her son was dead. So was her daughter-in-law, her only grandson, and her youngest granddaughter. She got into her car and drove over to the quiet suburb where her son and his family lived, and saw the street blocked with police cars. She turned around and drove to the police station, making several wrong turns, and finally having to stop and ask directions.

She found Beth and Ross waiting among all the other people, the pedestrian traffic in and out. Beth looked so large-eyed and pale that Virginia was instantly worried about her. The baby was only two months old. Maybe she couldn't handle this. But Ross was with her, at times touching her reassuringly.

"What happened, Beth?" she asked in a hushed voice. She couldn't accept what she had heard. It wasn't true.

Beth almost collapsed into her arms. Virginia hugged her, and looked over her shoulder at Ross.

He shrugged. "We don't know what happened. Maybe an intruder. We don't know. Pamela couldn't have done that. Did you go out to the house?"

Fay and Les's house, he meant, Virginia knew. She nodded.

"But I didn't stop. I just saw the police cars and turned around."

Ross shook his head. "It's horrible. You don't want to go there."

But eventually they would have to, Virginia knew.

They waited to see Pamela, and finally they were taken into the back of the jail, down a flight of steps and into an area of barred doors and cells. The sound of televisions on in individual cells struck Virginia as oddly incongruous.

Pamela looked so pitiful in the small cell, like a frightened animal in a cage. One wall of the cell was made of bars, the door of bars opening outward. The police matron who had accompanied them unlocked the door.

Pamela fell into Virginia's arms weeping.

Virginia held her. She felt so small and vulnerable, hardly larger than Kit, it seemed. Eighteen years old, entering college in the fall, her life ahead of her. Nothing must interrupt that. None of this was real. What had happened?

She didn't ask. She said instead, "We'll get you out of here as soon as we can, sweetheart."

Pamela pushed back and looked at Virginia with reddened eyes that continued to spill tears.

"Gram," she said in an urgent, low whisper. "I didn't do it."

"I know you didn't. Of course you didn't. We'll see a lawyer as soon as we leave."

Beth asked in a surprisingly calm voice, "Do you need clothes, Pam? What can I bring you?"

"I don't know. I don't know what they'll let me have."

She was dressed in a shirt and shorts that were too large, and on her feet a pair of flip-flops that protruded at least an inch beyond her heels. Virginia knew they were Beth's things. Beth had told her all she knew. She had gone to the house. She had seen Pam with blood on her hands and on her pajamas. She had seen the house. She had identified the bodies. Then she had gone to the hospital and taken Pam and dressed her, then followed her to the police station, but this was the first time she'd had a chance to talk to her since.

Still, knowing this, something blocked it from Virginia's

230

mind. She had to be the strength of the family. What was left of it. They needed her.

Les had worked with four other lawyers, but none of them was experienced in criminal law. He had been a tax lawyer, with only occasional court appearances. Still, they turned to his partners. Late in the afternoon they sat in the office of Clint Manning. He was a calm, white-haired man who listened to the little they could tell him. He sat leaning back in his chair with his hands folded across his stomach as Beth told briefly what had happened to Pamela.

Clint Manning sat forward abruptly and reached for the telephone. He punched a button and said to the secretary who answered, "Get me Gerald Amos."

Then with his hands together on the desk, he said, "Don't worry about it. Gerald is the best defense lawyer I know of, and he'll do what he can to get Pamela out. You all look exhausted. I suggest you go home and get some rest. These things can drag out into days, and you can't wait around at the police station for her to be released. You won't be doing her any good that way."

They returned by cab to the parking lot at the police station where they had left their cars, and stood together again near Virginia's sedan. Night was falling, lights blinking on. They had gone back into the station to see if they could talk to Pamela again, and found she had been moved to the county jail.

"Where the hell is that? What did you take her there for?" Beth screamed, leaning over the counter toward the policeman in uniform as if she could strangle him. Ross put his arm around her and drew her back.

It was the only time Virginia had seen Beth lose control.

In the parking lot Beth said, "Come with us, Gram. You can't stay by yourself."

"There's no one to feed the animals," Virginia said. "I have to stay alone sometime. I'll be all right, don't worry about me."

"Call me when you get there."

"Yes, I will."

She drove home with the same numbness, the same sense of being only half alive, only half aware. She remembered this was the way she had been after Ted died. For a month she went around the house with the image of Ted being in another room in the house, or out in his shop, or working in the yard. He was there with her. Nothing had changed. At times she even heard his voice calling her, and she would stop and listen. The real pain didn't start until one evening she went into the bedroom and saw his bed so empty.

The pain was like a bursting heart. It spilled out into her, seeping into every nerve of her body. Gradually it eased away, but never, for months to come, did it leave entirely.

So she knew the pain would come.

As she had before, she found comfort in the company of the dogs and cats. They enjoyed their food, just as always. They knew nothing of the world beyond their yard fence. She rubbed their heads and backs and found herself relaxing. She hadn't seen the house, as Beth had. She hadn't seen the bodies of her son, of Fay and the children. It helped not to have seen them. If only, when she closed her eyes at night, her imagination did not fill in the details.

She got up and took one of the sleeping pills her doctor had given her after Ted's death, when the pain had struck so hard.

Beth lay in Ross's arms. She had sat for almost an hour rocking Tresa, and had found comfort in the tiny warm body. Tresa had gone to sleep, and Beth sat looking down at her infant's face. Ross had come into the room, put his hand on her shoulder in silence. After a few moments Beth rose and put Tresa into her crib for the night.

She bathed in a tub of hot water, her eyes closed. Then, hoping she could sleep, she crawled into bed beside Ross. And everything within her broke loose. Ross held her as she cried and talked.

"She told me the craziest story, Ross. I don't even know how she could have made up such a crazy thing! She said . . . do you know what she said?"

She lifted her head from Ross's shoulder and looked into his eyes. She leaned on her elbow above him. Ross's blue eyes were filled with sorrow as he looked at her.

"She said it was the doll. The *doll*. Can you imagine that? She said Kit had been afraid of it since Gram gave it to her on her birthday, and Pam had taken it up into the attic. And it knocked her down. She fell against the chest. She said . . . Oh God."

Beth lay her head down again, weeping, wishing she could scream. Ross patted her back and held her, saying nothing.

"Why is it so hard for me to see that something horrible has happened to Pamela? She doesn't *act* insane, Ross, but why would she tell me such a crazy story? It was just as if she expected me to *believe* it."

Ross finally said quietly, "I think you have to accept the fact that she did murder the family, Beth."

"But why? *Why?*"

"No one knows that. Pam was never . . . she never showed any indications of . . . she just . . ."

Beth understood his difficulty in putting anything about Pam and what had happened into words. There were no words that would explain what Pam had done. Yet Beth did accept it, in a way. She knew, in the part of her mind that still thought rationally, there was a reason Pam had been the sole survivor. Her fingerprints were on the ice pick. She'd been seen carrying it. But in another part of her mind she couldn't believe Pam was the killer. Not the Pam she knew. How many layers are in a person that are never seen, she wondered.

"Why didn't she just say that someone came in, broke in to rob the house, and hit her on the head? And when she regained consciousness she found them. Like that."

"What did she tell the police?"

"She said she didn't know what happened. But she also told them she'd fallen against the chest in the attic. I think they might have thought she'd been struck, but she told them she fell."

Her tears gradually dried, and she lay still, her head cushioned on Ross's shoulder. They were quiet. The house was

233

still, and silence filled the neighborhood. The small light on the table glowed softly, touching the curtains, the pictures on the wall, the mirror on the dresser.

Beth said, "There's something else, Ross."

"What?" he asked softly.

"The weapon was an old ice pick. It was in a box of stuff the former owners had left in the attic. I can remember us kids looking through that box. We found that rusty old thing, and Mom told us what it was. We'd never seen one before. She told us to leave it alone, and we put it back into the box."

Ross said nothing.

Beth said, "An intruder would never have found that old ice pick."

For the first time Beth knew positively Pamela had to be the killer.

Virginia woke, feeling heavy and tired. She got up and let the dogs out into the backyard. She considered calling Beth, then looked at the time. Not quite eight.

She went instead to take a shower and dress. She had barely stepped out of the shower when the telephone rang. Virginia answered and heard Pam's voice, sounding so young, so much like a little girl.

"Gram, can you come and see me?" she pleaded. It was like a cry of anguish out of the night.

For the first time tears rushed into Virginia's eyes, and the pain raged like fire in her chest. "Of course I can dear. I'll be there as soon as I can."

"There are only certain times I can have company. They have visiting hours here."

"Are you all right, Pam?"

"I need to talk to you."

"I'll be there, at the first visiting hour."

"I have to go now. Bye Gram. I love you."

Virginia was weeping uncontrollably when she hung up the phone, then told herself that wouldn't do. She began making phone calls. She found out she could go see Pam at ten o'clock.

Then she called Beth's home. Ross answered and told Virginia Beth was sleeping.

"She didn't go to sleep until daylight. She's really torn up about this, of course. The police haven't been able to find the Elkins yet. I'm going to stay with Beth today."

The hours drifted on, in a strange sense of finality. The clock ticked, and Virginia looked at it and thought, it's ticking our lives away. So many of her family gone, and she hadn't even had a chance to say goodbye.

Then suddenly, as she was driving over to the county jail, a thought struck her. Someone had killed all of Les's family except Pamela. *Who?*

For the first time there came the crush of reality. She knew the police thought Pam had done it. But Virginia could not accept that. She would never accept that. Hadn't Pamela herself been injured? Whoever the killer was had hurt her too. Perhaps he had thought she too was dead.

She clutched the wheel tightly and made up her mind to talk to the police, and to Pamela's lawyer.

Thirteen

Virginia listened closely to Pamela. The room in which they sat at one end of a table had other visitors talking to other inmates, and Pam had kept her voice so low that Virginia at times wondered if she were hearing correctly. But she had. There was no doubt in her mind.

Intermingling in Virginia's mind with Pam's terrible story was the history of the doll and the story the man had told. Virginia couldn't forget Pam had heard that story.

She had been holding Pamela's hands from the moment they sat down. They felt thin and cold when she squeezed them, trying to convey the understanding she had no voice for. Tears did not reach Virginia's eyes. They clogged the veins of her heart instead.

"Do—do you want me to take the dog?" Virginia asked. "I don't think Beth has a fenced yard."

She felt Pamela pull back. She slipped her hands away and said, "You don't believe me either. Gramma, didn't you hear a word I said?"

Virginia nodded. It was the most incredible story she'd ever heard. Why hadn't Pam just made up a story about a stranger coming into the house? Why had she told something so crazy as the thing about the doll?

"Who all knows this story, Pam?"

"Nobody, just you and Beth." Pam looked down at her hands. "Beth didn't believe me either. And the thing is, I understand. I didn't believe Kit. So why should I expect you to believe me?"

Virginia wanted to say, I believe you. But she couldn't. She

236

said instead, "I'll take it. The doll. I'll put it away."

"No!" Pam leaned forward and clutched Virginia's arm. "No, leave it where it is!" Then she appeared to think about something and added, "What is Beth going to do with the house? Gramma, don't let Beth go in there alone. Please. See to it she doesn't. Tell Ross not to let her go in there alone. Especially at night. Please?"

A police matron came at that moment and touched Pam's shoulder. Both Pam and Virginia looked up, surprised at the intrusion. Although the room had several other people, Virginia had felt for a moment that they were alone.

"I'm sorry," the matron said. "Your time is up."

Virginia stood up when Pam did, and hugged her. Against her hair she heard Pam's whispered, "Please, Gram?"

Virginia nodded. In her mind she saw Pam going back into a small cell, such as the one they had seen her in back in the county jail, though at the beginning of her visit Pam had told her it was different here. Here, she was in a larger room with several bunks, and several women. But this too, Virginia understood, was temporary. If Pam were convicted, she'd be sent on to the women's prison upstate.

Convicted. Her precious Pamela, her little girl who had always been so gentle with creatures, with dogs, cats, birds. Pamela who cringed if she had to get rid of a cockroach.

As Virginia went back out to her car she recalled once when Pamela was visiting her for the weekend. Ten years old, she was filled with talk, from waking to sleeping. They had found a spider in the kitchen. Pamela had cried out, "Don't kill it, Gram!" even though Virginia had not intended to. Pamela grabbed a paper napkin. She caught the spider gently and took it outside, opened the napkin and watched it scurry away. Then she turned to Virginia and said softly, "Did you see? It was scared too, Gramma. Just like it knew that I could kill it. I didn't want to hurt it. It just wants to live like everybody else. It can't help being what it is."

Virginia knew suddenly and without a doubt that her granddaughter had not murdered anyone.

* * *

Pam sat on her bunk leaning forward, her arms holding her stomach. She felt sick. She hoped she wouldn't vomit. There was only one toilet, and one wash bowl for the dozen women in the cell, and neither was private. She had waited until night to use the toilet. She had cringed even from using the wash bowl, with its brown stains and the dirt that looked so old and ground in it would never come off. She had never been used to this lack of privacy, even for being sick.

Her mind flashed back. Home. Mom and Dad. Nicky. Kit. She had never realized, then, how safe she had felt. How loved. How surrounded by loving and caring people. At times now she lay down on her bunk and closed her eyes and pretended she was back again. That everything was the way it was . . . then, last week, the week before last week. The week before the birthday. The day before the gift.

Gramma Vee hadn't believed her either. She had told the two people with whom she knew she stood a chance, and neither of them had believed her. Grandma and Grandpa Elkins had been found by the police as they were driving into Canada, and told what had happened at home. They were on their way back. And they would come to see her, she knew. But she would never tell them the truth about what had happened. She loved them dearly, but she had never been as close to them as she was to Gramma Vee.

But now, her last chance was gone. There was no one left to tell. Craig? Maybe. He hadn't been to see her, but they had talked on the phone. All they'd done was cry. "Pam, what happened?" he had pleaded over and over, and she couldn't tell him.

"I'll come to see you, Pam, as soon as I can."

But, he hadn't come yet.

They had talked on the phone twice more, and Pamela told herself she hadn't told Craig the truth because she wanted to tell him face to face. In her heart she knew the real reason was she didn't want to lose him.

"Pamela Armand," a voice said.

Pam looked up. A police matron stood on the other side of

the bars. The voices of the other women hushed. Here, everyone saw what was happening to everyone else. She stood up.

"Your lawyers are here to talk to you."

"Hey, kid," a prisoner said as Pam walked past, "maybe they're here to get you out of this hole."

The matron unlocked the door. The sound of metal against metal was something that Pam would hear for the rest of her life, she knew, even if the woman was right and her lawyers were here to get her out and she never saw bars again. She'd remember them, always, the sound of a door made of bars closing against a wall made of bars. As she followed the matron down the corridor she wondered where she would go if she were released. Gramma Vee's? Would Virginia even want to take in a granddaughter she believed had murdered her family? Pamela felt she couldn't even ask her. She had to go home. Where there would be no one but herself, and the blood . . . and the doll . . . yet she had to go back, find the doll . . . find it . . . do to it what it had done to her loved ones . . . destroy it, *kill it*.

She had met Gerald Amos and Valerie Stevens twice before. The first time, in a crowded room, they had told her they would be working on her bond, trying to get her released. But the second time, at the hearing, she had learned there would be no release. Still, each of them had patted her shoulder and smiled and told her they'd be working on it.

Valerie Stevens reminded Pam of Beth. She wasn't much older than Beth. She was taller than Pam, heavier, and wore a calf-length skirt with a long jacket that fell past her hips. When she stood up the jacket, a soft, thin material, clung to her hips. She put out a soft hand to greet Pam.

Gerald Amos was a middle-aged man with a paunch and a bald head. He too had a soft hand, warm, smooth. But it cuddled hers in a way that reminded her of her dad.

This time they were alone. The room was not large. There was a table and chairs. The attorneys sat on one side of the table and she sat on the other.

"How're you doing?" Gerald Amos asked. In front of him

239

was a black folder filled with papers.

Pamela said, "Okay."

Valerie smiled gently at her. "Of course, what can you answer to a question like that?"

"We're here to talk about your defense. You have said no one entered the house. That you fell, you weren't struck."

Pamela nodded.

"We're wondering if you remember correctly. Could you have been struck, although you didn't see the intruder? The wound you sustained is proof that it could have happened that way."

Pamela looked at them. From Amos's serious face to the gentle smile on Valerie's. She looked from face to face.

"But . . . then they'd be looking for someone else."

"We would have a stronger defense."

"But that's wrong." Pamela bit her tongue. Too much said. "I don't know." *Do what they say.* Craig had told her that. And so had Mr. Manning from Dad's office. Do what they say.

"It would be better if you told us the absolute truth about what happened," Valerie said. "We would be able to handle your defense better, to try to figure avenues. Maybe even make a deal with the prosecution to plead guilty on a second degree charge."

"But I didn't do it. I'm not guilty." She had said that so often that she could no longer put anger or disbelief behind her words, no longer anything but exhaustion. She looked down. "The house was locked. No one came in. The police know that no one broke in. They can see that. I didn't kill them. My mother and daddy? Kit? Nicky? I didn't kill them."

But if she told these logical, realistically thinking people the truth, what would they do? Walk away from her? Refuse to handle her case? Or . . . enter a plea of insanity defense?

She shook her head. "I don't know what happened. All I know is I didn't do it." That was what she had told the police, and that was all she could say to anyone. Other than the two people she had trusted to believe her.

240

Fourteen

Detective Jefferson was off duty when he drove into the driveway of the house on Dresden Lane, the most inexplicable and gruesome scene of murder he had ever investigated. The yellow police line was still attached to the yard fence and stretched across the doors. But the area was no longer under police protection. The house keys had been given back to the daughter, Beth, except for copies needed by the police for continuing investigation. In the backyard the dog barked then howled forlornly.

Lights were on in neighboring houses. Street lights glowed through the old trees like something searching in the darkness. Jefferson walked into the backyard where a yard light burned, revealing a generous area of grass, some large trees, shrubs, and a patio of furniture that looked comfortable and homey. The dog came quietly and slid her nose into Jefferson's hand. A sliding glass door joined the patio to a long room that was part kitchen and part dining room. Jefferson stood on the patio for awhile in the quiet of the summer evening.

It was hard to believe that such a tragedy had taken place here, in a solid two-story house on a quiet street. And even worse, that a daughter of the family had committed the murders.

That was Jefferson's problem. He didn't believe she had done it. There was no motive. The family was picture perfect. A happy, intact family. Everyone who'd been questioned confirmed that. There were no dark secrets hidden beneath the surface that he or any of the other investigators had been able

241

to uncover. But he had carefully checked every door and window, and no one had entered, of that he was certain also. Not unless they entered with a key. But even more puzzling, the daughter herself said no one had entered. She had gone up into the attic, fallen, and struck her head. When she regained consciousness she was still in the attic. She went downstairs, and found the stabbed bodies of all her family who still lived at home.

Then, she had run outside with the bloody ice pick in her hand.

All of the investigators believed she was guilty. Except Jefferson.

"Your elevator's not going all the way to the top, man," his partner had said, for the first time in their four years together. "It's plain as your nose, and man, that's plain. She's guilty."

"Maybe. But if so, she doesn't remember." Jefferson believed that.

He had a daughter a few years younger than Pamela. He hadn't lived with Jenny since she was seven years old, but she came to spend one weekend a month, and two weeks in the summer. He would spend more time with her if her mother hadn't remarried and moved three states away.

Maybe he identified Pamela with Jenny, who was thirteen now. Or his own young sister. Maybe that was all there was that made him feel the girl wasn't the one who stabbed those kids and their parents. That was one of the reasons he had come back tonight, alone. He wanted to understand better what might have happened.

He used his key and entered by the back door. He turned on the lights. This was a quite large washroom, or utility room. It was clean and white, with a pastel wall paper that had vines climbing toward the ceiling and flowers similar to morning glories. There was a deep laundry tub, white washer and dryer, an ironing board, with an iron standing on end. A clothes rack held a couple of shirts and a little girl's ironed dresses. No one had taken them down. There was also a small adjoining bathroom, barely large enough to serve its purpose. Beside it was a coat closet, filled with coats, jackets, boots. A space cluttered with the things a family of four or five would need.

Windows in two walls made the room almost a sunroom. Tonight, the windows reflected Jefferson as he looked around. In the other wall was the open door into the kitchen.

Jefferson went into the kitchen and dining room, turning on all the lights. The kitchen was sparkling clean, its white cabinets untainted by the blood he knew was upstairs.

Whoever had killed the family had not entered this area at all.

He went into the hall, turning on lights and leaving them on. There was a formal dining room with a polished oak table and matching hutch. Decorative plates hung on the walls. A chandelier hung over the table. The carpet was clean, with no sign of blood. This was a room where a family gathered on special occasions.

The den was across the hall, a warm, lived-in space of sofas and chairs and a television set. The newspaper, dated the day of the murder, was still on the arm of one of the recliners. Here too there was no blood.

The living room was small and formal. The picture window looked out onto the front yard.

The blood, one small spot, began in the foyer. Something small had lain there. The ice pick. Pamela had said she found it there, on the floor, and she had picked it up. Just after she unlocked the door, just before she ran out into the yard screaming for help. She had turned back and picked it up.

Everything Jefferson saw proved that. There was very little blood on the deadbolt lock she'd had to unlock, and none on the door knob.

There was one other room in the downstairs. A powder-room. The only light switch was just inside the door. Before it was touched he had shone a flashlight on it and seen blood. It was dusted for prints, and a sample of the blood was taken before they used the switch to light the room. Jefferson turned on the switch now. The light was a long fluorescent tube over the mirror that covered the wall above the full-length vanity. It brightened the room totally.

The mirror had been struck with something at its lower edge, and hairline cracks sprayed upward from it.

The wallpaper was a pale flocked flower that resembled a lily

243

pad. The toilet, in a cubicle without a door, received its light from above the mirror. The thing that had puzzled him was that there was a blood smear low on the door, as if a small hand had touched it and pushed it open. But there were no finger-prints or handprints.

There also was blood on the vanity stool. Just smears, on the edge mostly. But it definitely had been touched by a bloodied object.

He turned out the powder room light and closed the door. Then, his eyes searching as he walked, hoping to find some-thing he had missed the other times he had been in the house, he went upstairs, slowly, walking to one side of the generous stairway that went to the second floor.

Here the clues were obvious, especially at the top of the stairs. There was a very plain footstep, and it belonged to Pa-mela. She had been running, and she'd left prints of one bare foot. Three bloody steps that came down the stairs, fading as they progressed. By the time she reached the foyer there were no more indications of exactly where she had stood. She had said she went over and picked up the bloody ice pick, because she didn't know what it was until she held it in her hand. She said she did not go into the powder room.

Jefferson believed her.

But who left the bloody marks in the powder room? That, he thought, was the answer. Whatever that was. He never felt so frustrated as when he thought of that room, of those marks, and who had put them there.

The only prints on the locks on the front door belonged to Pam. Her bloody fingers clearly left prints and clearly indi-cated how she had nervously struggled to open the door.

There was only one other explanation that he could see. Pa-mela had gone upstairs, to put a doll away, she had said, and her fall had done something to her brain. She had come down-stairs, committed the murders, then regained consciousness and remembered nothing. But she said she came to while still in the attic. If that were so, why was there no blood in the attic?

His partner had said, "You're assuming she's telling the truth, Jeff, and obviously she's not going to." When the partner called him Jeff, he was serious.

Her trail was as clear as if it had been laid out in new snow. She had first approached her young sister, Kit, lying in the hall. Footsteps touched with blood went from there to the bedroom where Nicky lay, and from there, running, to the master bedroom. They stopped at the doorway. She hadn't gone in. She had only looked in. And that was exactly as she had said she'd done. Then, running, she'd gone down the stairs and to the door, but her steps had faded and no longer were a record of her passage from the house. She had picked up the murder weapon, and gone again to the front door. The blood on her hands had come from touching Kit, she'd said. She had not touched the others.

Beneath the lights, and with the aid of his flashlight, he looked again at other bloody spots that had puzzled him. The other investigators had looked too, and finally shrugged it off as one of those unaccountable mysteries that plagued some murders. But Jefferson's thoughts kept going back, picking them up, rolling them around, trying to make sense of them.

They were small spots almost like the footsteps of an animal, except the steps were perfectly aligned. A two-footed animal? No toes, but a curve at the back that suggested a small heel. They showed up in the upper hall, and twice on the stairway.

Chunks of carpet had been cut out where Pamela had walked, or run, but the small spots, now turned a dull brownish red, were still there. As was the chalked areas where the bodies had lain, and the soaked carpet. Blood had splattered on the wall of the hallway near where Kit had fallen. But the walls of the bedrooms were clear.

The master bedroom, with its private bath, was at the front of the house. It was a large room with several windows, and two large walk-in closets that joined both the bedroom and the bathroom. The beds still had their covers tossed back. Nothing had been touched. Clothes still hung in closets. Drawers were filled. Jefferson felt sorry for Beth. She was the one who would have to deal with all this.

The motive, the investigators had established, must have been money. Everyone in the family was insured, with trusts set up for survivors. Pamela and Beth were the survivors in this case, and both would be well cared for financially. That is, the trust paid out enough money to keep them out of poverty. Even though Pamela might spend the rest of her life in prison, the money would go into an account for her.

But Jefferson didn't believe that she had killed for money. He knew her, through knowing his own daughter, sisters, cousins. Jubilant, filled with life, in love with a young man, looking forward to college, working full time. Money meant something different to an eighteen-year-old. It meant having enough in your pocket for a Coke, or a new outfit, or keeping your car up and running. That's all it meant. Kill your family just for their money. No. Never.

Yet some do. But their backgrounds were different. They were different inside, somehow. Even the psychiatrists hadn't been able to decipher that difference.

There were four bedrooms other than the large master bedroom. Nicky had slept in the first room down the hall on the right. Jefferson turned on the light, but didn't enter. He'd gone over the room and the closet, again and again. Tonight he was after something else. He wasn't sure what. He just felt if he came here, near the hour when the murders had happened, he'd get a different feeling. A hunch, something more. Somewhere in this house, he was sure, was the answer.

Was Pamela covering for someone? Craig, he at first thought. But he had talked to Craig, and Craig was one of those all-American types, blond, good-looking. Besides, Craig had the best alibi in the world. He'd been snoring away in his bunk while a roommate had been snoring away in the other. Of course, no one had determined just how soundly the roommate slept, and whether Craig had slipped out during the night then back in. But if he had, and driven the distance, that would have taken four hours just for the trip. It hadn't happened.

The bedroom across the hall was a guest room. It had belonged to Beth, but most of her personal things were gone. A few of her old clothes still hung in the closet, that was all. The room was clean and untainted by blood.

Down the hall were the other two bedrooms. Neither of them was blood stained. The stabbing of the little girl had taken place in the hall. She might have been running. Perhaps to her parents.

It was here the small, oval spots began. They moved irregularly down the hall to Nicky's room, then to the master bedroom, sometimes disappearing for yards at a time.

Pamela's room was neat and clean. The covers had been tossed back, indicating that she had told the truth when she'd said she got up in the middle of the night. There was nothing else in the room that so much as whispered an answer to the mystery.

Across the hall was the little girl's room. It was the brightest room in the house as to color. Pink and white, a little girl's dreamroom.

He turned on the light.

He stopped and stared.

In the pink chair over in the corner sat the large doll. Its clothes were splattered with those terrible brownish stains of blood, just as Kit's had been. Who had put the doll back into the untainted chair?

He had noticed it once before, but then it was downstairs in the foyer, lying on the floor against the wall, as if someone had nudged it out of the way. The blood on the doll indicated that it had been with the little girl when she was stabbed. She must have been holding it in her arms.

Jefferson stepped back out into the hall and tried to imagine what might have happened that night.

Pamela had gone upstairs to put the doll away, she had said. When she fell, Kit must have taken the doll and run downstairs. She was stabbed, repeatedly. She must have turned, tried to fight her attacker, because the wounds ranged from back to front.

That indicated that the killer had been following her. Perhaps from the attic, where Pam was unconscious. If she had the doll in her arms, that would explain the blood on it. Then, someone had moved the doll down into the foyer.

The doll appeared to be in the center of this. His thoughts kept coming back to it. He had asked Pamela to explain, again and again, exactly what had taken her up into the attic at two or three in the dead of night, and it was always the same.

"I went to take the doll up."

"Why?"

247

"Kit wanted me to take it up."

"Why?"

"She — she was afraid of it."

"Afraid? Why was she afraid?"

"I don't know. It's antique. I don't know. I don't know, please, leave me alone, I don't know anything."

He had wanted to take her into his arms and hold her and pat her back reassuringly, the way he would have done his own daughter. But the facts remained, she had taken the doll up, she said. But Kit must have brought it back down again when her sister fell.

"Did Kit go up with you?"

"No. I — I don't think so."

She couldn't be sure.

He thought he understood how the night was a nightmare of confusion. How could she remember each step she'd taken?

His partner had asked Pamela, "Did it make you angry that your little sister woke up late in the night and asked you to take the doll upstairs?"

"Not really. Not a lot. I never got really angry with my baby sister. I adored her. Loved her with all my heart."

"See," the partner said to Jefferson later. "She hesitated. It affected her in some way that she didn't want to talk about. I vote for angry. She became so furious that she not only murdered her little sister, she turned in, and killed them all."

That was the consensus of the prosecutors, and Jefferson hadn't been able to show them any facts that proved differently. But he knew he would never enjoy another full night of sleep if that girl was convicted of murder.

He opened the attic door, climbed steep steps to the top, and pulled the light cord. The light was hardly brighter than a firefly, high in the peak of the ceiling above. He used his flashlight, turning his beam into every edge of the stairway. Dust, undisturbed, still coated the edges. Only the center of the steps were somewhat dust free.

Upstairs was the usual clutter. Boxes of things packed away and kept for some reason known only to the owners. Some held tablecloths and napkins, and other old kitchen items that looked as if they were older than the house. There were a few pieces of furniture that didn't match anything, and needed to be refinished. And almost in the center of the room was the chest of drawers, a large, old solid wood piece. It was here she said she had struck her head, and actually they had found a very slight trace of blood to prove her right.

Jefferson moved slowly and quietly around the attic. He shined the flashlight on two cribs with their mattresses upended. Nearby were boxes of saved baby clothes.

He was standing quietly when he heard a door close softly somewhere in the house. A strange tingling went up the back of his neck, that old warning that danger was right behind him.

He turned, sweeping the beam of the flashlight toward the open fall of the stairwell. He stood very still, listening.

Nothing. Then, another door closed. Softly, muffled.

Feeling suddenly as if he moved through a house alive with a kind of evil he had never faced before, he went quietly to the top of the stairs.

He pointed the flashlight beam down into the shadowed hole of the stairwell. It struck the solid surface of the door.

Closed.

He had left it standing open, as he'd left all the doors in the house open except for the powder-room door.

He went down the stairs and turned the knob, noticing the only lock was on the outside. A metal slide fastener, that crossed the door, could not be opened from the attic side. Whoever had closed the door could have locked him in the attic.

But the door was not locked. He eased it open and looked out into the lighted hall.

The first thing he noticed was the door of the little girl's pink and white room was also closed.

He stood in the hallway looking at the door, listening, every nerve in his body strung as tight as piano wires. There was no draft. The attic door, standing partway open, did not swing in either direction. It was perfectly balanced.

He heard no sound. There was no footstep, not even a barefoot movement. He would have heard it. Nothing creaked. Outside, all traffic had ended. The bugs that sang, whistled, sawed in the early part of the night, had grown silent.

He walked quietly to the bedroom door and put his hand on

the knob. Then quickly he opened the door and pushed it back. His flashlight beam picked up the doll in the chair, her head tilted slightly to one side, her dark eyes looking toward him in a way that was eerily human. No one had moved her.

He shined the flashlight everywhere in the room, then into the closet. He checked the door again, watching it a moment. Like the attic door it was perfectly balanced. It stood still, half open.

There was no way either of the doors could have closed without being pushed.

Fifteen

He looked around the pink room once again, even shining his light beneath the bed, which didn't even allow space beneath for hiding. He shined his flashlight into shadowy places the overhead light didn't seem to penetrate well. He looked up at the rose globe of the light. None of those things ever held more than a sixty-watt bulb.

At the door he flashed the beam once again around the room. It struck the doll. Then moved on. He turned it back to the doll and steadied it.

The light beam centered on the soles of the doll's shoes. He crossed the room to the pink footstool that was the same height as the seat of the chair. The doll's feet barely reached the stool, the soles of the small shoes pointing outward.

He knelt by the footstool and shined the light on the soles. They were stained with a brownish substance that looked like dried blood. He estimated the size to be that of an infant's first hard-soled shoes, with a defined heel. They were white, laced.

He looked at them a moment longer, then untied both little shoes and slipped them off the doll's feet.

When he went into the hall he turned out the bedroom light and closed the door.

He walked a few steps over to the place where the strange little spots began, where they were clearly spaced between the dried blood of the little girl and the place in the bedroom where the boy had died. He went down on one knee and carefully placed the doll shoe over one of the spots. The fit was perfect.

He sat back, one arm resting on his bent knee. His gaze followed the fading tracks. They went straight out onto the balcony and disappeared.

He got up and slowly tracked the footprints of the doll, because now he was certain that was what it was. He went to the master bedroom, shining the flashlight down, searching for something to which no one had paid any attention.

He found them again in the master bedroom. Clearly the spots left the area where the carpet had been soaked with the blood of Fay and Lester Armand. The spots trailed back toward the door, then to the stairway and down. Now they showed up only occasionally, and only in part.

Each step, he saw, was separated from the other by about six or seven inches. Exactly as if someone had held the doll and had walked it along.

A memory flashed into his mind. His daughter, bending over one of her dolls, moving it as if it were walking, holding it so that each leg swung forward. It would have made prints similar to these, even though it was a smaller doll than the one in the bedroom.

He turned out all the lights in the house, went out the back door and locked it behind him. When he reached his car he took a plastic bag from the glove compartment and slipped the doll shoes into the bag.

He sat, his hands on the steering wheel, looking up at the house. It was an older home, as most were along this street, with ancient trees and plenty of space. The house had a peaked roofline with dormers and porches below. But looking at the house did not answer his question. How had those doll footprints gotten from one bloody body to the next? Who had 'walked' it, and why?

He had questions to ask Pamela, though he had a feeling she would give him the same answer. "I don't know."

It seemed she had barely gone to sleep when the clanging began in the corridor and the matron was calling out that it was time to get up. Sleep had not been coming easily to Pamela. At times she felt if she couldn't get out of this terrible place she would go mad. She woke wanting to scream, every morning.

She covered her face and her ears, but only for a moment. She had to get up, do what she could to clean up, and stand in line for breakfast.

She had no appetite. And when she folded her arms around her, as she did often, hugging herself across the stomach, she could feel her ribs. She recalled vaguely, as if it came from a distant world she had once glimpsed, that she used to envy the skinny girls. "It takes a skinny girl to look good in a bikini," she remembered saying to Craig. He had looked at her. "Skinny? What's the matter with you? You'd better not be getting skinny around me. I like girls, not boys."

Craig wouldn't like her now. But Craig had been to see her only once, while he was home on the weekend. And he had looked stunned, unable to talk, unable to see her clearly. They hadn't been able to touch, except to hold hands. Among the other people in the visiting room they couldn't kiss, though there were some who did. She wanted him to hold her, but he had only held her hands.

When she thought of home, of Kit, Nicky, Mom, and Dad, she burst into tears. Lately, all she could do was cry. Her lawyers were getting disgusted with her because she didn't seem interested in her own defense. They wanted her to lie. They had even suggested that her family was abusive. That it might work as a defense *No, no, never,* she had told them. They wanted her to say that someone had come in, struck her, and then killed the family. But she couldn't let some innocent drifter be accused of something he hadn't done.

They questioned and questioned her, and finally Valerie had said softly, in that way she had of speaking and smiling at the same time while her eyes were serious and penetrating, "Pamela, you're not telling us everything you know. I don't think you're telling us the truth at all."

She hugged herself, bowed her head, and wanted to cry, even as she followed along in line for breakfast.

If she told them, they would only stare blankly at her, as Beth had done, as Gramma Vee had done.

There was no one she could tell. She had even decided she could never tell Craig.

* * *

253

It was almost noon when Virginia drove into the driveway of the lovely old home that had belonged to Fay and Les. It had always looked so solid and safe. In a good neighborhood, it seemed secure from danger. Now they were all gone, even Pam. Only Beth's car stood in the driveway.

Beth had called an hour or more ago and asked Virginia if she'd meet her there. "They've given me back the keys, Gram. But I don't want to go into the house alone."

Beth came to meet her. She looked much thinner, her face tapered where it had been rounded, her freckles standing out against a complexion that was washed of blood.

Virginia returned her hug, and felt Beth clinging to her. When Beth drew away there were tears in her eyes.

"It will never end, will it, Gramma? It will always be this way. They're gone. And Pam's gone too. It would have been better if it had been done by a stranger and Pamela had been killed too."

Virginia couldn't believe what she had just heard. "Oh no, Beth. Pamela is alive. You can't want her dead too."

Beth didn't meet Virginia's eyes. She fumbled with the ring of house and garage keys. "At times I wish she'd never been born, Gram. If she hadn't, Mom and Dad would still be alive. So would Nicky and Kit."

"Beth, Pamela didn't kill them."

Beth gave her a quick glance. "If she didn't, who did?"

Virginia had no answer for her. Slowly, they went toward the front door, walking side by side up the curved, brick path. Beth inserted the keys into the locks.

"No one else even knew that rusty old ice pick was in the box in the attic, Gram. No one but us, the members of the family."

"What old ice pick are you talking about?"

"It was in a box of stuff that was left in the house by former owners, Gram. You probably never saw it. Us kids went through that box. It had old kitchen tools in it. An ice cream scoop, some tableware, knives, forks, spoons. And the ice pick. We didn't know what it was. We were told to never touch it. Nicky was so young then he probably wouldn't remember it . . . I mean, wouldn't have."

A fresh burst of tears flowed down her cheeks. She pressed

them away with a tissue.

She opened the door.

The odor was overpowering. A sweetish, rancid smell rushed out of the house to meet them like something physical. The house was strangely warm, as if the heater had accidentally been turned on. Beth started in, then turned back.

"I can't do this, Gram. I just can't."

Virginia stood still, just inside the door. She finally said, "I think I should check the thermostat. Where is it, Beth?" She understood Beth's reluctance to enter the house, even to gather clothes to take to Pamela. The feeling of death was here, and the horrible smell, mingling with memories, almost a ghostly sensation of sound, of voices, Kit, soft, gentle, Nicky, yelling on his way out to play. Les, the son who was her life. Only her determination to help get Pamela out of jail, and her desire to take some of the burden off of Beth, seemed to be keeping her from giving up.

Beth pointed. "Just down the hall."

Beth stood on the small entry porch, her head bowed.

Virginia checked the thermostat and saw that it had indeed been on heat, eighty degrees. She turned it off. She went back to the doorway near Beth.

"It must have been touched accidentally. I'll go up and get Pam's clothes, Beth. You stay here."

Beth nodded. She tried to speak, Virginia saw, but then she swallowed as if she were ill. Virginia paused and touched Beth on the shoulder.

"Do you want a glass of water?"

She shook her head vehemently. "Not out of there. I could never touch anything in that house again."

Virginia waited a moment, until Beth told her she was all right, then she went back into the house.

The upstairs was even more stuffy and warm than the downstairs. The dark stain was instantly visible in the center of the hallway when she entered the back bedroom section. She had to step around it to go into Pamela's room. The chalked outline of where Kit's small body had lain was like surrealistic art, or some terrible graffiti. She had difficulty pulling her eyes from it.

255

Yet in a way the deaths still had almost no reality for her. She knew from having lost loved ones before that the disbelief, the shock, the numbness that protected her from raw grief, would come. It would come, perhaps, with the funerals. But the bodies hadn't been released yet from the medical examiner's office, and she had been told it might be another few days.

Beth's other grandparents were helping with the funeral arrangements. Plots were purchased and ready for the four of them. Matching coffins had been chosen.

Pamela's room was clean and neat, just as Pamela herself was. There was a robe hanging over the foot of the bed, and slippers neatly side by side beneath the edge of the bed. When Pam had gotten up that night she hadn't bothered to reach for her robe.

Kit woke me. She was scared. She said the doll had gone again to the powder room.

Virginia hadn't talked about this to Beth. She doubted if she ever would. The history of the doll kept intermingling with the terrible things that had happened here. Somehow they seemed tied together, but Virginia could not unravel the myriad thoughts and make sense of them. A little girl had been accused of murdering her sister and aunt with an ice pick. She had died in an insane asylum, without ever saying what had happened.

Now Pamela was telling Virginia the doll had come to life . . . no, that was a wrong description. Very wrong. The doll had become animated, somehow, and had knocked her against the chest. Then when she woke everyone in the family had been stabbed with an ice pick. And the doll was down in the powder room.

There was a terrible kind of sense there, somewhere, but Virginia, like Beth, couldn't handle it. It was as if her mind closed against anything that had to do with the horror of what had happened in this house.

In Pamela's closet she found a suitcase. She pulled it down from the shelf and began putting clothes in it. Her good dress, a nice suit and three blouses. Something she would need for court appearances. From the drawers in the chest she took underwear, socks, pajamas. Back in the closet again she chose a robe. Not the one over the foot of the bed. She left it untouched. She put in a pair of dress shoes, and a pair of loafers. The weather could turn cold one of these days . . .

No, no, she admonished herself. Pam wouldn't still be there when cold weather came.

She closed the suitcase. She put in a small amount of costume jewelry. There was other jewelry in a box in the dresser, gold rings and necklaces. But she left it all there. Nothing valuable was to be taken into the jail. Prison. It was like a prison, with solid walls and towers with armed guards. Large, wide, barred gates let people in and out, even to the front office. They called it a county jail, but it was a prison. What did the women's prison upstate look like? That was where Pamela would go if she were convicted.

Virginia could not allow that to happen. She had already offered Pamela's lawyers all the money she had, as well as the sale of her home, if they could get her out. They had told her they were doing the best they could, and Pamela's trust was paying them.

Why were so many criminals let out on bail, or bond, or whatever it was, she had asked, while my granddaughter, who is innocent of any crime, is kept in jail? Because, she was told, the judge felt there was enough proof to hold Pamela without bond. He felt she was too dangerous to release.

Virginia started to leave, then stopped.

The doll. She should take the doll out of the house. Perhaps take it back to the antique dealer and tell him it carried some kind of terrible curse. She didn't want it. She wished she'd never seen it, and wished to God she'd never given it to Kit.

Why hadn't Pamela told her sooner that Kit was afraid of the doll?

She crossed the hall, the suitcase in her left hand. She tried not to look at the white chalk on the carpet in the center of the spread of brown stain.

She opened Kit's door.

Here too the bed was unmade, but the room was neat. Some of Kit's books lay on the desk, amid her drawing paper and colored pencils. The box of oils was to the side, and the canvas she'd been working on propped against the wall.

Virginia opened the closet door and looked in. The doll was

257

not there. She glanced around the room once more. If anyone had removed the doll she hadn't heard. Where else would it be? Not in the attic. Pamela had said . . . the powder room. She had found it down in the powder room.

Virginia went downstairs. The powder room door was closed but not latched. She opened it to see the lights were on over the mirror, and the doll was in the chair, its head barely above the vanity so that it appeared to be smiling coyly at itself in the mirror.

Virginia picked it up by one arm. She noticed it was spotted with the brown spots like a blight. Parts of the front of its dress were almost solid brown. The flecks of brown were everywhere except on its back. They were in the bright hair. On the face. The hands were stained, as were the long white stockings. Oddly, the doll wore no shoes.

She looked on the floor for the small shoes, but they were gone. She pulled a towel from a drawer and wrapped it around the doll.

Virginia went out onto the porch. "We can go now."

Beth began working with the keys, choosing the two that would lock both the ordinary lock and the double bolt. As she pulled the door shut and began the process of locking, she began to talk.

"I was planning to clean the house up. Get rid of everything personal, and sell it. Sell the furniture, the house, everything, the cars, bicycles, even Nicky's footballs. But while you were in the house, Gram, I decided I can't. I don't want to go in there. Ever again. I don't want to hire anyone to come and clean. What I'm going to do is keep the place locked just as it is. This is it. I'll keep the keys for Pam. She can have it all. I don't want it. I don't want anything to do with any of it. I just want to go home, live with my husband and our daughter. Live the best life we can."

Virginia carried the suitcase and doll to her car and put them in. She stood by the open door, waiting. Beth had followed her, still talking.

"I can't stand the memory of any of it. I'll never drive by here again." She glanced back. "Of course I'll have to have someone mow the grass. But — maybe Ross will take care of that."

She started toward her own car, then turned back once more. "I'll never be going to the jail anymore either, Gram. I'm sorry. Tell Pam I'm sorry, but this is it."

She got into her car and started it. There was barely room in the driveway for her to back out and away. She didn't look again at Virginia or the house. She drove down the street, her dark head held firmly forward.

From the backyard came a mournful howl.

Virginia sagged against the car. The numbness that had helped her get through the house cracked, and the pain rushed in, not only for Pamela now, but Beth.

And for the lonely animal that knew only by instinct what had happened to her people.

Virginia made her way to the backyard gate. Gypsy greeted her lavishly, whining, licking her face when Virginia bent to take her collar.

"Come on, girl. You're going home with me."

Sixteen

Virginia sat in the waiting room of the office of the attorneys who were defending Pamela. She had taken the suitcase to the county jail, and waited while everything in it was checked. The clothes had been taken away by a matron, and finally Virginia had been allowed to see Pam. But the visit was brief and Virginia tried to keep it cheerful. She hadn't told Pamela about the visit yesterday to the house, or that she had brought the doll out. It was still in her car. She hadn't decided yet what to do with it.

Pam had seemed even more depressed than usual, and it frightened Virginia. She had simply clung to Virginia, saying little. The visit was over too soon. Virginia had assured her the dog was fine, getting along in her yard with her own dogs and cats. It was all Pamela had asked about. She hadn't asked about Beth, or Craig, or friends who had called.

The secretary motioned Virginia to go on into the conference room. Virginia entered to find Gerald Amos and Valerie Stevens at the table with folders open in front of them. Amos got up, shook hands with Virginia and pulled out a chair for her. Valerie looked up and spoke.

"I have something I want to tell you," Virginia said. "I want to know if Pamela told you about the doll."

"The doll?" Valerie said.

Amos's face took on a look as blank as Valerie's, and Virginia knew her hunch was right. Pamela had not told anyone but herself and Beth about the doll, because she knew it would not be believed. Virginia was desperate.

260

"I want to know, first, what kind of chance does she have of being acquitted?"

They glanced at each other.

Amos took in a long breath that expanded his rounded front. He looked at the papers in front of him.

"The prosecution's case is very strong. Pamela isn't helping much. If she'd said she found the front door open — if she'd said she heard a noise and went out into the hall — and was struck. If we could convince her to just change her story, and say she was confused, she might have a chance. But frankly it's terrible."

"She seems to have no interest in her own defense," Valerie said.

"None at all. She insists that wasn't the way it happened, but when we try to find out what did, she claims she just doesn't know."

Valerie said, "I remember mention of a doll. Don't you remember, Gerald?"

He shuffled papers, stopped and read briefly. "She said she carried a doll up into the attic. In the middle of the night. She doesn't give much of a reason. Said her little sister was scared of it and so she just thought she'd get rid of it. And that's why she was up in the attic."

Virginia asked, "Is that all she told you?"

"Yes — um — that's all I see."

They both looked at her. Virginia glanced from one to the other, watching their expressions.

"The doll she's referring to is a large antique doll I bought for my little granddaughter for her birthday, which was just a few weeks ago. I found it in a small room at the back of an antique shop, and the owner told me it had been in the shop since eighteen-seventy. The doll had a terrible history. It had belonged to two little girls. One child, the aunt had written in a note, had stabbed the other to death with an ice pick. But then the aunt was stabbed also, and the child was found alone with the murdered aunt. She was put into an asylum and left there until she died. She never spoke a word the rest of her life."

They stared at her. A slight frown etched slowly between Amos's eyebrows. "Ice pick? Strange coincidence."

Virginia continued, "When I found the doll it needed repairs. Its hair had to be redone. Its face was badly scratched and I had that repaired also. One eye was bad. But still, it had been a beautiful doll. When the repairs were finished it was a very pretty doll. I thought my granddaughter would love it."

Valerie nodded, but there was a strange, tense expression on her face. She didn't fidget or glance away.

"I didn't know there were problems with the doll until the night before the murders. Pam called me, told me Kit had been having mental problems. She was scared of the doll. Later, Pam told me she'd thought it was Kit who had torn up her favorite old Barbie dolls and all their clothes, even though she told Pam the doll had done it. Kit claimed the doll moved about on its own at night, that it kept going down to the powder room where it sat on the vanity stool and admired itself in the mirror. It even applied makeup, so Kit told Pam."

Virginia paused, expecting looks of disbelief, perhaps even smiles. But the two faces were as deadly serious as Virginia's voice. She felt some of the tension go out of her body. Her back had begun to ache, she was holding herself so stiffly.

"Pam was getting . . . well, disgusted, she said later. She just told me, then, that she wanted to come over the next day after work and bring the doll. I told her of course. I'd be watching for her." She swallowed, remembering. "The next morning I received the phone call about the deaths. And that Pamela had been taken into custody."

She paused, but neither lawyer spoke.

Virginia continued, "When I had a chance to talk to Pamela she told me a story I don't think she's told anyone else, except Beth."

"What story?" Valerie asked softly, leaning forward against the table.

"She said Kit woke her again, at two or three in the morning, perhaps earlier. She didn't look at the time. Kit told her the doll had gone again to the powder room. So Pamela got up and told Kit she was taking the damned doll upstairs to the attic. She went down to the powder room, in the first floor, and got the doll. Kit went with her to the attic stairs. She told Kit to stay at the foot of the stairs, and she took the doll up. She was going to put it in one of the drawers in the chest, when suddenly it lunged in her arms and threw her against the chest. She struck her head. When she came to she found everyone dead. She ran downstairs, and saw the ice pick on the floor. She picked it up. Then she saw the powder-room light was on and looked in. The doll was there. It came toward her, but when it reached the light of day it fell. Whatever was causing it to move about was destroyed by the sunlight."

Virginia took a deep breath, then added softly, "The doll, Pamela said, did it. I have to tell you, Pamela knew the history of the doll. Kit didn't. Pam . . . did." She looked down at her hands, finally, trembling in her lap. There. She had done it. She had no way of knowing if Kit had ever been afraid of the doll. She had only Pam's word. She waited.

Still they said nothing. Finally she looked up again.

"Isn't that," she asked, "something you can base an insanity defense on?"

They looked at each other, then Amos said, as if speaking for both of them, "You feel her knowing the history of the doll caused her to repeat that history?"

"Yes. Perhaps. I do know this, with all my heart. Pamela did not commit those murders, as far as she knows. I've thought of this repeatedly, and that history ties in. It's too much of a coincidence. Pamela was the only one I told the history to. Maybe she told Kit — she said she hadn't. Maybe there's such a thing as a curse. But Pamela didn't kill her family. Not that she remembers."

"I think we should talk to her about that possibility," Valerie said.

"We've been waiting for psychiatric examinations," Amos said. "We'll see what comes up. However, you understand don't you that being innocent because of insanity can keep a person behind bars forever? It's no guarantee of freedom. It can be just the opposite. We'll talk this over. It could be we'd be much better off if she'd just change her story."

Virginia rose. "She'll never do it. Pamela will stick as close to the truth as she understands the truth to be."

Doubts plagued Virginia on the drive home, and through the evening. What had she done? She fed the pets, and made sure the back gate was securely locked so that Pamela's dog

263

wouldn't try to get out and find her way home. She seemed almost as unsettled as Pamela. Last night she had howled until Virginia brought her into the house. Tonight, at least, she was quiet.

Virginia was getting ready for bed when she remembered the doll. Though it had hardly been off her mind, she had forgotten to bring it into the house. It was so much a part of her other thoughts this afternoon since her visit with the lawyers in her feeble attempt to find some way to get Pamela free. If she could only bring Pam home and keep her, safe from everyone, safe from anyone who wanted to make her pay for something she hadn't done.

Virginia went out into the garage, turned the light on, and took the doll out of the car. She hesitated. Perhaps she should just leave it here and take it back tomorrow to the antique dealer. No, it might be needed, in some way, for evidence.

She closed the car door, turned out the light, and went into the house.

She sat down at the kitchen table, the doll across her lap. Then, as if her eyes had focused belatedly, she saw the brown flecks on the doll's face, hair, clothes. She covered the doll with the towel and took it upstairs to the bathroom. With a damp washcloth she carefully cleaned the blood flecks off the face. She thought of undressing the doll and washing its clothes, but she was tired. So tired. She rewrapped the doll mummylike in the towel and left it on the bathroom counter. Tomorrow she'd take it back to the antique store.

After a hot bath she went to bed, and didn't remember that she hadn't eaten until she was in bed. But she wasn't hungry. When she had forced herself to eat her throat rebelled against it, so that at times it took her several efforts to swallow. She wondered if it were that way with Pam and Beth, both of whom were getting so thin.

Even baby Tresa seemed affected. Virginia had been to Beth's house twice since the deaths, and both times the baby was fussing. Yet when she was picked up she still seemed unhappy.

Virginia could understand Beth's desire to try to put it behind her, try to live now for her small family. Making a new life, after half of it is ripped away. How was it possible?

What was there for Virginia?

Pam, try to stay well for Pam.

Her legs ached with tension, and she turned, and turned, trying to find a comfortable position. Bedclothes rustled, and the bed made its own little sounds as she moved. The other sound seemed at first a part of it. Then she heard it again, as she lay still. It was as subtle as a whisper beneath the wind. A sound of sliding. A snakelike movement, out in the hall, or across the hall.

She got up, turning on the bedside lamp. Its soft glow made a cone of light beneath the shade. The hallway was gloomy, the bathroom door across the hall a dark rectangle within the shadows.

She crossed to the bathroom and turned on the overhead light. At first she saw nothing different, then she remembered she had wrapped the doll in a towel. It was uncovered, the end of the towel hung over the side of the vanity counter.

The doll's eyes were closed, but the curious little half-smile was on its lips, and its pale eyebrows raised in that questioning expression that had so intrigued her. She carefully put the towel back up, her eyes on the doll's face. Oddly, she felt not alone. She was aware of the doll in a way she never had been before, as if it were aware of her.

She covered the doll again with the towel and started back to bed. Then on impulse, she opened the medicine cabinet, and removed the bottle of sleeping pills. She took the last two, and left the bottle on the counter near the wash basin.

When she went back to bed she left her bedroom lamp on. She had never been able to sleep with a light, but she didn't feel comfortable suddenly with the dark.

She lay looking at the ceiling fan. It spread on the ceiling like a large insect with five wings.

What had Pamela said about seeing the doll move? Suddenly she couldn't remember. Pam had come downstairs, running to get help, and had seen the weapon, the ice pick, on the floor. When she went to pick it up she had seen the doll in the powder room.

Yes, it had moved. *It came toward me, like a real girl, but the*

265

moment it came into the light of day it collapsed, whatever that was alive in it destroyed by daylight.

Had Pam been so distraught by the blood and the sight of the bodies on the floor that she had imagined that? There was no other answer. No satisfactory answer.

Her eyelids were growing heavy. She could feel the effect of the pills on her brain, as if the brain waves were on a monitor in front of her eyes. They were slowing, growing heavy and long, and she was beginning to feel very heavy, as if moving were impossible now.

She tried frantically to rouse, as if her life depended on it. She wished, fervently, for one moment, that she hadn't taken the pills.

Then her eyes closed.

Strange, her thoughts wavered slowly, like her brain waves, so strange that the same kind of weapon had been used. Now, as one hundred years ago.

Somewhere within her, where she was still alert, she heard the thump, as if something in the bathroom had fallen. Then she heard the scrape of the vanity chair on the tile floor. She heard the opening of the vanity drawer and the rattle of makeup, soft, quiet noises, mouselike noises.

She tried to sit up. She pulled her eyes open with effort as her heart began to thud in terror. It was as if she were divided into two parts, her brain which was growing slower with each heart beat, and her heart, which was racing in a mixture of fear and excitement.

If she could see the doll, see that it actually did become animated. If she could see . . . she could set Pam free. She could take the doll, show the world that all things are not what they seem, and . . . Pam . . . would . . . go . . . free.

She tried to stand, and fell to her knees.

It stood in the doorway, looking taller, larger, as if in becoming something other than a doll made of bisque, glass, wires, it had grown.

It watched her, its head tipped to one side, the curve of its lips almost smiling.

It took a step toward her. It came slowly, as if it knew she was helpless, that she was heavy with drugs and couldn't even rise

266

from the floor.

The light shined on something in the doll's right hand.

The distance between them narrowed suddenly, as if it had decided it was tired of playing the game. As it approached, she saw it was holding the straight-edge razor Ted had kept, another antique that had belonged to his grandfather.

Virginia slid to the floor. The face that came close above hers only resembled a doll's face. If she could have reached up Virginia knew she would have touched soft skin, and silky hair.

She tried to scream, to draw the attention of neighbors. She had to leave a message, somehow, to warn others.

She barely felt the sting on the inside of her wrists.

She struggled up. It was gone. She was alone in her bedroom.

In aching slowness she pulled herself to the bedside table and reached for the drawer. It fell out, spilling her diary, pens, notepaper.

She picked up a pen, steadied her hand on the floor and tried to write. Blood gushed from her wrist and she knew finally what it had done. There would be no obvious murders this time. It had learned. This time they would call it suicide.

There was an intelligence at work there that was terrifying.

She wrote one word agonizingly. Blood covered the paper, flowing over the blue ink.

With a long sigh she put her head down and the pen dropped from her fingers.

Zenoa.

267

Seventeen

Detective Jefferson was driving to the station when he heard on the police radio a familiar address. He had been there a couple of times to talk to Virginia Armand, grandmother of the girl accused of killing her family. Something was wrong at her house. Neighbors requested investigation.

He made a U turn in the street and drove through the dreary heart of the old city to the area where Virginia lived, using the siren as he needed to travel the narrow old streets and cross the intersections. He had a bad feeling about this, but hoped it was only because of the coincidence of relations.

At the house, a pleasant two-story white frame, there were already an ambulance and two city police cars. A small knot of people stood in the yard. In the fenced yard Jefferson heard a soft howl, and the barking of a smaller dog. Beyond the slats in the picket fence he saw the same dog, a golden retriever, that had been at the house in the suburb, and beside her, jumping at the slats, a small terrier with a whiskery face.

Two men were carrying a stretcher from the house with a covered body. The uniformed police milled about, going from the open front door to the cars, to the knot of people waiting.

Jefferson showed his identification to the medics. "Mind if I take a look?"

"Sure. But she's already been identified. She lived alone here. A widow. In her sixties."

Jefferson uncovered her face briefly, and nodded. "What happened?" He thought of Pamela, of all she'd had to suffer in the past two weeks, and now one of her grandmothers dead.

268

The one, he had noticed, that she called on most often.

"Suicide. Slit wrists."

They slid the stretcher into the back of the ambulance, and Jefferson walked toward the two officers who were standing in the hallway just beyond the open door.

"I'd like to look around," he said.

The officer who nodded permission was one Jefferson knew vaguely. Like most of the city police who gathered at one time or another at the restaurant near the station, Gus Spencer had been among them. Jefferson had never worked with him. Spencer was younger, and hadn't shown up until recently. Jefferson didn't know his background, how long he'd been in police work. He barely knew his name.

He went ahead of Jefferson up the stairs, explaining. "This Virginia, which I guess you know, was the mother of that tax lawyer who was murdered, along with his wife, son, and youngest daughter. One of the neighbor ladies had been coming over to check on her each morning since then, and this morning she came to check on her as usual, and got no answer. So she called the station, and my partner and I came out. We found her car in the garage, so the neighbor gave us a key she had. This neighbor, Clara Smith, hadn't wanted to go in alone. She's older, in her eighties at least. So we went in."

They had reached the upper hall and Spencer motioned toward the bedroom. Jefferson paused in the doorway. Blood had ruined the rug at the side of the bed. The bed, unmade, revealed nothing. The body was gone. There was no chalk mark. This was a suicide, not a murder. The investigation had probably already ended.

"We found her there, on the floor, at the side of the bed. On the floor beside her was one of these old straight-edge razors, the kind that was used years ago. It looked like she had sat on the side of the bed, cut her wrists, and then fell onto the floor."

Jefferson walked into the room. He had no doubt that Virginia had killed herself, yet it seemed oddly incongruous with the woman he had met. She had seemed more concerned about Pamela than about herself.

"No chance of something else happening here?"

"No. The doors were locked. Windows downstairs locked.

The only unlocked window in the house was this bedroom window. It was open about two inches. Why would you think anything else had happened?"

"It just seems like something she wouldn't have done, that's all."

"You knew her?"

Jefferson shook his head. "Not really. Met her, talked to her once after the murders of her family. Was the room just the way it is now?"

"Except for that small drawer in the night table, there by the bed. It was lying on the floor, its contents spilled."

"Who put it back?"

"I think Jim did. One of the guys."

So if there had been any finger prints on the drawer besides Virginia's, they were smudged beyond recognition, probably. Still, Jefferson took out his handkerchief and used it to pull the drawer open again.

"There was a piece of note paper she started to write something on," Spencer said as Jefferson looked into the drawer without touching anything. Blood stained part of a small note pad, and the outside of what looked like a diary.

"What did the note say?"

"Nothing, that made sense. Here, you can take a look."

He drew from his pocket a plastic envelope and opened it. With his fingers touching one corner of the note, he pulled it out.

Barely legible beneath the bloodstains was one unevenly scrawled word.

He read aloud, "Zenoa?"

"Probably doesn't mean anything."

Jefferson looked at it a while longer. Taking it from Spencer he turned it over. But the only word was the one nearly obliterated in blood.

Jefferson said as he gave it back, "Just keep it in the file. Mind if I take a look around the house?"

Spencer shrugged. "Just lock up when you leave. We're through here as far as I know. Someone has to tell the family, whatever family she has left. The neighbor lady says she has two granddaughters, one of them in custody."

270

"Pamela Armand. I'm not sure she's guilty."

"It does seem a little odd that she could have killed both her parents, with a six- or seven-inch ice pick, while the other didn't try to stop her. She would've had to have supernatural powers, it seems to me. And if she did, she wouldn't be in jail. Would she?"

"I think you're right," Jefferson answered, although he knew the officer was only half serious. It was a mystery that puzzled everyone who knew the facts. He said, "The other sister is Beth Larson. I'll drive over and tell her."

"Thanks. That's a job I can do without."

Spencer left. Jefferson heard him run down the stairs, leaving a hollow echo behind. A door closed, outdoor sounds became muted.

Alone in the house, Jefferson looked through the bedroom closet. The clothes were neatly arranged. Shoes were placed side by side on the floor beneath the clothes.

He went out into the hall. The floors were hardwood, with occasional rugs. The rug where she had fallen was soaked with blood, and blood had oozed out onto the hardwood floor. He thought of Beth. Another house she would have to be responsible for. She was all that was left of the family, except for Pamela. It didn't seem reasonable that Virginia would have added this burden to anyone, especially her granddaughter, a young woman with an infant child.

He looked into the other bedrooms, then into the bathroom. A large towel lay on the tile floor. He moved it only to check that it covered nothing. The house was so neat, everything in place. The towel on the floor seemed as out of place as the fact that Virginia had killed herself.

He went downstairs and out through a neat kitchen to the backyard. The two dogs came to him. He stooped, petting them, looking around. There was a sitting area, with an umbrella table and chairs. They were dusty, as if they hadn't been used in quite a while. There was another lounging chair, over near the house, sheltered by shrubs, with a small table at its side. A large yellow cat eyed him from the chair. That, he knew instantly, was where Virginia sat when she came out to be with her pets.

On the small porch were the feeding dishes of three animals. As he approached them the cat decided to be friendly, and came to its dish meowing, its long tail curling hopefully around Jefferson's ankle.

"Sure," he said. "As soon as I can find it."

He went into the kitchen and began opening cabinet doors. He found the food on a lower shelf, right next to the door. A can opener sat on the cabinet above. He brought out dry feed for the dogs, and opened three cans of food, one for the cat. The cat's dish was slightly apart from the dogs', and Jefferson roamed the yard, watching, to make sure there was no confiscation taking place. But the dogs ate without even so much as a glance at the slower cat. They were in too much of a hurry to join him as he wandered the yard. The golden retriever kept looking up at him with a question in its eyes that cried out its perplexity. What had happened to her people? Her home?

He found the watering can. It was under a hydrant at the back of the house, and almost full. He filled it up.

When he went back into the house the terrier whined to go in too. When he apologized and pushed it back, the dog scratched on the door frantically, and outside in the yard, a fitting accompaniment to a silent house, the golden retriever emitted its soft and eerie howl.

He rinsed the spoon he had used, and laid it on the counter. He rinsed the cans and dropped them into the wastebasket. Outside, the animals seemed to have settled down some. The small dog had stopped scratching on the door.

He was on his way to let himself out the front door when he glimpsed a movement in the hall above. He turned. The hall light was out, and the area half dark. He knew the ambulance and police were gone. He had assumed he was alone in the house now, but perhaps one of the neighbors had come in. Or someone who had been passing by. At any rate, he had to get them out. It was his responsibility to lock the house.

"Hello?" he called.

There was an eerie silence. Whoever was there, hadn't intended to be seen.

He climbed the stairs.

The bedroom doors were still open, and quick glances into

those rooms and their closets revealed no one. He kept a close eye on the hall, and no one tried to slip by.

He stood in the hall near the door to the one bathroom. It was not quite closed. Whoever was here had to be in the bathroom.

"Excuse me?" he said, and tapped lightly on the door. No one answered.

He pushed the door inward.

The blind was pulled on the window, and the room almost as dark as a closet.

He turned on the light and stepped into the room, puzzled. He could have sworn he had seen someone dart out of sight in the shadows of the upper hall, but no one was here.

The light over the vanity mirror illuminated every corner of the small room. A robe hung on a hook on the back of the door. He moved the door, and noticed something on the floor between the door and the wall.

At first glance it was like finding a child hiding. But it was only the doll. The same doll he had seen in the murdered child's bedroom and removed the bloodied shoes from. It sat, as if someone had pushed it there out of sight. Its large, round, curiously brilliant brown eyes gazed past him.

He paused, taking a closer look. Its face had been cleaned of the blood specks he had seen on it in the other house.

He started to leave, then paused again, squatting on one leg. Curiously, the bottom of the doll's stockings were soiled.

After a quick and thorough search of the upstairs, he attributed the movement in the upper hall to one of those unexplainables that happen. He left the house, locking the door carefully. Then he drove toward the suburb on the other side of the city where Beth lived.

As he drove he thought of the tracks made in blood in the murder house. Small tracks that he had proved beyond a doubt belonged to the doll shoes still in his possession. But he couldn't connect those tracks to anything plausible. A doll walks by someone holding its arms and swinging its legs forward. And someone had to have done that very thing in order to make the tracks. And that was where his thoughts stopped. It was as if his mind came to the end of a road that was blocked by a solid wall everywhere he looked.

Now, just seeing in his mind again those small white stockings with the stained feet, brought the wall even closer. Did that mean that Virginia herself had been the one who 'walked' the doll?

Did Virginia have something to do with the murders?

He flinched at the images that swept through his mind. Virginia, in the murder house, walking that doll through the blood? Then, going back several days later to take it home with her. She must have noticed the shoes were missing. But then, something had soiled its white stockings. Its feet had looked exactly like the feet of a child who has run through the house, hitting every dusty spot.

Suddenly he saw something he hadn't really seen. The doll's stockings. Blood. Blood on one of the stockings.

He took the first turn to the right, drove around the block and headed back to Virginia's house.

He parked in the driveway. Beyond the picket fence gates the dogs barked at him as if he were an old friend. But this time he ran to the front door, let himself in and bounded up the stairs.

He found the doll in the bathroom. Beneath the bright mirror light he examined the stockings.

The old flecks of blood on the stockings above the shoe line were now dried brownish red. But on the edge of the stocking foot was fresh, damp, red blood.

He looked around, carefully, using his flashlight to better illuminate the shadowed areas in the bathroom. But he found no further sign of blood. He carefully checked each side of the towel, and found it clean.

He stood up, and looked again at the doll. Then on sudden impulse he crossed the hall to the bedroom, shining the flashlight on the hall floor. Nothing, no sign of blood visible to the naked eye.

In Virginia's bedroom though, he found it, as he had suspected he would. Inches away from the blood-soaked throw rug where she had lain dying, was a small smear of blood. It was half an inch long and half that wide. Almost precisely the size of the bloodstain on the doll's stocking.

He sat in a crouch frowning at the spot, shining his light in search of other such blood spots. He finally found one, less visible, closer to the door to the hall, and the bathroom. There were no drips of blood that might have indicated Virginia began the slitting of her wrists, then seeing the doll, not wanting to ruin it further with bloodstains, carried it to the bathroom where it would be safe. Then returned to her bedroom to finish the job.

It made no sense that Virginia had moved the doll. But someone had.

Probably one of the medics, or one of the city police. Put it in the bathroom out of the way. Why not on the dresser, or back in the corner of the bedroom? Nor did it explain why there were so many prints between the murdered victims back in Pamela's house.

Someone had deliberately walked that doll through the blood. There was no other explanation he could come up with. He had mentioned it to his partner once and got the question, "Who the hell would want to do that? Makes no sense."

Then, after looking for himself, said, "Must have been made by something else. Some of the people going through. We get too many damned tracks in cases like this. Too many people looking for clues and shitting up the whole thing. Face it, Jeff, we have our killer. There's nobody else."

Certainly all evidence pointed to Pam as the killer. But he had thoroughly investigated her background, and found no problems. Her teachers, her friends, everyone said she'd always been a happy outgoing person, intelligent, with college and career plans. Also, it seemed, marriage plans. Craig Wilson, son of a local pharmacist, had sworn Pamela didn't do drugs, even an occasional drink or cigarette. She was the ideal next-door girl, helpful, cheerful.

Nor were there any hidden secrets in the family that he could find. Both parents were educated professionals. Perhaps the mother hadn't spent as much time bringing up her children as might have been preferred, but a good caretaker, Alice, had been working for them since Kit was only a few months old.

There just was no damned reason for Pamela to have killed her family. And so brutally? There was something inscrutable behind those vicious stabbings, which in Kit had been counted

275

by the M.E. to be more than twenty. Also, the stabber had been strong. The ice pick had been buried in the bodies, even in the body of the man who, Jefferson would have thought, could have defended himself. The first stab wounds to both adults, the M.E. had said, were to their eyes. It was one way the killer had of debilitating and weakening them. They would have staggered, probably with their hands to their faces, and so the killer attacked the vulnerable and unprotected areas, aiming then for the heart.

Did that sound like a young girl eighteen years old, who was happy in her relationships?

No. He would never believe Pam was guilty.

Her memories of that night ran through his mind dozens of times a day, and at night when he was trying to sleep, it continued. As if somewhere in his brain a connection was trying to form, one that would answer the unanswered questions.

"I don't remember," she said, a hundred times, to him or other investigators. In such a patient, soft, tired voice she went on and on. "I don't remember. I went upstairs. To the attic. It was about two or three in the night. The morning. The light is dim there. I stumbled, I guess. I fell against the chest and hurt my head. When I came to it was daylight. I went downstairs and there was Kit . . . in the hall. And then, Nicky, Mama, Daddy. I ran downstairs to get help. I saw something in the foyer and I picked it up. It was an ice pick. Bloody. I screamed and ran outside. I had trouble opening the deadbolt on the door because I was so scared."

Since no one else had entered the house, there was only one possibility. She actually didn't remember, but when she struck her head and blacked out, she committed the murders. Only Jefferson didn't believe that, either.

Asked why she had gone upstairs, she had said, "I took the doll up."

Why had she taken the doll upstairs? Her answer puzzled him. "Because—because Kit was afraid of it."

Yet he had seen the doll in the pink bedroom, so obviously someone had brought it back down.

One thing, it moved around too damned much. It was always there, with blood on its clothes.

There were times in this case when Jefferson felt as if some terrible supernatural evil were at work, one that blended into the darkness of night and remained there, a part of the blood, the deaths.

He was alone in his continued efforts to understand these deaths, which now included Pam's grandmother. She was already dismissed as a suicide. But . . .

Maybe he should change his occupation. He had been in police work since he got out of college when he was twenty-two. He was now thirty-six. He had always been interested in growing things, the freshness of green leaves, and the intricate beauty of flowers. His dad owned a nursery in a small town about thirty miles east. Maybe it was time for him to see about joining the business. But if he did, he would lose contact with Pamela, who he felt in his heart was innocent. He was the only one who felt that, so he was the only one who might be able to help her.

Jefferson started toward the stairs, then turned back abruptly to the bathroom. He picked up the doll. She looked as if her face had been partly cleaned, and with her long sleeves and long stockings, there probably would be no fingerprints. But he took it with him, holding it carefully by the back of the dress, its legs and arms dangling, face down.

The driveway was clear. Three people stood in the neighboring yard, but shrubs between the two yards gave him only a shattered view of them. He opened the car trunk and carefully laid the doll inside. It was going to forensics for testing.

Eighteen

Beth sat with her baby, rocking, holding the bottle against her breast to simulate breast feeding. She had been one of those mothers who wanted desperately to breast feed, but it just hadn't worked. Tresa hadn't thrived. She'd had too many colicky spells, too many sleepless nights for both of them, and Ross too. So for the baby's sake they had worked with the doctor until she had found a formula that agreed with sensitive baby Tresa. Now she was a plump twelve pounder, incredibly warm and cuddly. Beth at times sat with her lately, gazing down into Tresa's smoky blue eyes, in an attempt to lose herself in the innocence she saw there.

Even then, flitting images of her mother came to her mind. Her mother, face down, halfway between the bed and the door, the back of her nightgown soaked in blood. And images of Dad. Closer to the bed, as if he were getting up, but had fallen there. Crumpled on his side. His neck had looked as if it had been chewed by something tiny and very evil, the stab marks were so close. Blood soaked the shoulder of his pajamas and made a puddle in front of him, turning the blue carpet to a terrible dark, evil color shadowed from window light by the bed.

Tresa . . . in her arms . . .

. . . Kit . . . in the hall.

Nicky.

Nicky.

Beth had loved all her siblings. But she'd never felt as close to Kit as she had to Nicky. Nicky grew up beneath her guidance,

278

in a way. Ten years old when he was born, she had carried him around, played with him, fed him. As Pamela and Kit had been close, in that same way of big sister fondness and love, so had Beth and Nicky.

Pamela, four years younger than Beth, had been more of a nuisance than a pleasure, at times. It was Pam who wanted to experiment with Beth's makeup. It was Pam who had wanted to wear Beth's clothes.

Tresa . . . innocent, precious, baby.

Beth watched her eyes close. Her mouth drooped away from the nipple. Drops of milk were white against the pink of her inner lip. She drew a long sigh in Beth's arms. It was time to put her down for her morning nap.

She was just starting to rise when the doorbell rang. The baby jerked nervously, her hands fluttering in the air, but she didn't open her eyes. "Damn the doorbell," Beth whispered. She sat still watching Tresa, hoping that whoever had rung the bell would go away. She understood the feeling of intrusion. Her own heart had leaped and speeded at the sound of the doorbell. *Just go away, please, and leave us alone. Let us live in peace again as we were, before you came along. Whoever you are.*

Tresa relaxed again without waking, and Beth carried her to the crib and made her comfortable. Not on her stomach. She was so terrified of losing her now, after all the deaths, that she wouldn't even put her down on her stomach for fear she'd smother. She made sure the blanket was pulled down beneath her arms.

The doorbell rang again, but this time the baby didn't stir. Beth closed the nursery door softly, and went down the hall.

She stopped, her first glimpse of the detective bringing back the shock of the police coming to her door that first time. Through the glass she saw him, and every nerve in her body began to tingle. With her jaws tightened, she opened the door. He held out the folder that contained his identification, but she didn't even glance at it. She didn't remember his name, but she knew the face. Strong, high cheekbones, skin stretched tight over a bony frame. He was tall with square shoulders. His age could have been twenty-five or forty. He was the type that would look much the same at eighty as he looked now. But who-

279

ever he was, whatever he stood for, she didn't want to see him. *Go away. World, go away.*

"Jefferson, Ma'am. I'm one of the investigators in the—"

"I know," she said. She stood in the open door and didn't invite him in.

He looked at her, and she detected a flicker of sympathy in his eyes. They were a deep blue with flecks of grey and brown. She found herself looking away. *Don't feel sorry for me, just leave me alone.*

"I'm afraid I have more bad news for you, Mrs. Larson. Would you like to sit down?"

Her gaze leaped back to him. "Pam? *Pamela?*" A sudden and horrible vision of Pam, hanged in her cell, came like a picture in the back of her mind.

"No, not Pamela."

His hand cupped her elbow and without invitation he guided her into the living room and to a chair. She sat down. If not Pamela, then who? *Not Ross.* Dear God not Ross. She looked at him helplessly, waiting, as he sat on the edge of a chair not far from her.

He shook his head. "Not your husband," he said as if he'd read her mind. She slumped, her heart pounding heavily. She could face almost anything except losing Ross. Losing Ross, losing Tresa, those were beyond her ability to bear.

"It's your grandmother, Virginia Armand."

Beth lifted her head. "Gram! What . . ."

"She was found by a neighbor this morning. She's dead. It's believed she slit her wrists."

She stared incredulously at him, seeing instead the face of Gramma Vee. A blush of makeup, a pleasant smile, calm natured, like Daddy. She had always seemed so capable.

"Oh Lord. Poor Gram. Why didn't she call me? I mean, I didn't know she—she was so despondent. What I mean is, she was more concerned about Pam than she was about herself. She chose Pam's clothes, I couldn't. She said she'd take care of the dog. She didn't seen—she didn't seem—I had no idea. Gram has always been so strong, you know. After Grandpa died she never asked for help. Pam used to go over and stay

280

with her some, but the rest of us — I guess we just went on with our own lives."

She put her head down again. It was so hard to believe, about Virginia. If it had been Grandma Elkins, who was so dependent on Grandpa Elkins, it would have been understandable. Both of them had nearly collapsed altogether on hearing of the murders. Their only daughter gone, their granddaughter charged with the murders.

Beth, in her own losses, had not realized how hopeless it all must have seemed to Virginia. She raised her head.

"Nothing's happened to Pam, has there? I mean that would cause Virginia to do this?"

"No. I haven't seem Pamela this morning, but I'm going from here. Do you have someone who can come and stay with you?"

"I'm all right," she said. She thought of Tresa, asleep, a human angel in her crib. She pushed the reality of Virginia's death from her mind. She thought of Gramma Vee in her house, in her flower garden, sitting in the backyard with the dogs and cat. She was there, at home. She would always be there at home in Beth's mind. It had to be that way.

He held his hand out and she heard a metallic rattle. He put a couple of rings of keys in her hand.

"These are Virginia's house and car keys. Since you're her closest relative and probably the only heir, other than Pam, they're yours. I'm afraid all the unpleasantness is yours too, just as it is with your parents' home. Someone always has to dispose of the belongings, arrange the house for sale, or whatever."

She nodded. She didn't tell him that she hoped never to enter her parents' house again. It would wait, as it was, for Pamela. She was the one who had caused it to be the way it was, empty, haunted. She could have it. Gramma Vee's house was another matter, but she didn't even want to think about it.

"If you feel up to it I have a couple of questions I'd like to ask you."

She nodded again.

"There was a large doll in your parents' house. On the morn-

281

ing after the deaths. Evidently your little sister's doll. I found it in her room."

Not the doll again. She didn't want to hear about the doll. She could feel the sharpening of her senses, the narrowing of her eyes as she stared at him. Did he know the crazy story Pam had told her and Virginia? Perhaps even Craig? Had she told anyone else?

"That same doll was in your grandmother's house this morning. I was wondering what significance it has in your family."

She wasn't sure what he meant by that. His questions were headed somewhere, but were different from what she'd expected, though she wasn't sure what she had expected.

"Gramma took it home with her," she said. "She went with me into the house, at home, my old home, and took a suitcase of clothes for Pam. She carried the doll out in a towel. It has no significance. Just a doll."

"Why would she have taken it?"

"She gave it to Kit for her birthday, in June. It's an antique doll. I suppose she took it on impulse, no reason."

I don't want to talk about the goddamned doll!

Jefferson tapped his fingers on his knees, his gaze on her face as he hesitated. Then he said, "Who played most with the doll?"

Beth frowned. What a strange question to ask. "I have no idea," she responded quickly. "I suppose if anyone played with it, it was Kit. It was her doll, after all. I don't know why Gram took it home, unless she wanted to keep it, or something. I don't know anything about the doll, I don't see what—" Her voice had been rising. She was on the verge of hysteria, and she bit her lower lip. Not the goddamned doll again!

Jefferson sat back a little. "There's something strange about it, Mrs. Larson. I removed its shoes in your parents' house because their soles are stained with blood. Someone, it seems, stood the doll—"

She jumped to her feet and put her hands over her ears. "No! No! Please. Just—no more about the doll. What has the doll got to do with *anything?*"

He stood up, and she felt his hands on her shoulders. "I'm sorry. I didn't mean to upset you."

For just an instant she leaned against him. His pat on her back was paternal and tender, then she pulled away.

"Did you — have you —" she hesitated. "Have you talked to Pam about — about the doll?"

"No. Why?"

She shook her head. Thank God for that. She wasn't sure why, yet, that she felt Pamela would be better off without people knowing that insane story. Maybe someday it would straighten out in her mind, and she would understand her own feelings.

"One more thing, if you don't mind, Mrs. Larson. Does the word 'Zenoa' mean anything to you?"

A soft cry came from the closed nursery. Suddenly more than anything in the world she wanted to go hold her baby.

"Zenoa? No. Thank you for coming to tell me. Thanks for — the keys. My baby's awake. She needs me."

She held the door open until he was off the steps, then she closed it and hurried back to the nursery. For several minutes she stood by the crib with Tresa in her arms. Crooning softly she rocked the baby in her arms until she relaxed again in her sleep. Tresa had been sleeping an hour in the mornings and an hour in the afternoons. Her morning nap was only half over.

Beth laid her carefully back into the crib, then went back to the front room. She thought of dialing her grandparents to come over and sit with Tresa, but that would take time, and she wanted to get this over as quickly as possible.

She ran out of the house and across the yard to her neighbor. Lucy Cawley was herself a grandmother, and a widow. Her children lived hundreds of miles away and she seldom saw them, so she had appointed herself Beth's guardian. Lately, she had been one of the most comforting influences in Beth's life.

Before Beth reached her comfortable, old-fashioned porch with the swing and the flowers in pots, Lucy was coming down the steps.

Just the sight of her started the tears flowing. For the first time, Beth wept for her grandmother. Lucy put her arms out.

"Not something else. Not more that you have to contend with."

Beth told her about Virginia.

"I saw the police at your door again," Lucy said. "After a while a person gets to recognize them even without uniforms and without marked cars. Do you want me to stay with Tresa while you go there?"

"Would you? I have to go make funeral arrangements. I have — so many things I have to do."

"Of course. You go right on. If there's anything else I can do —"

"I don't know. I don't know what I'm doing, Lucy. If Ross calls, tell him — I don't know what to tell him."

Pamela's obsession had reached her, so that as she drove the streets toward Gramma Vee's house, she had only one determination. She was going to get rid of that doll. Someway. Somehow. Like an evil omen death followed it, wherever it went, it seemed, and she wanted no more to do with it.

She drove into the driveway and parked. The street was quiet. Next door neighbors appeared to be gone. There was no sign now of the activity that must have occurred here this morning.

As she got out of the car the dogs barked, and beyond the closed gate at the back of the house the golden retriever stood with its front feet on the gate. Gram had said she'd take care of Gypsy. Now here were not only her folks' dog, but also Gram's. The responsibility of pets was more urgent than the responsibility of the house, but now, at the moment, the house, the doll, came first. Ross would take care of the dogs. She would suggest that they get someone to feed and water them until fences could be built around their own backyard. Or something.

She hurried up the front walk, unlocked the door, and entered the deadly quiet house.

Where was it? Detective Jefferson hadn't said where he'd found it, or if he had taken it with him, which was a possibility.

She paused in the small foyer, thinking. Where would Gram have put it? Upstairs, probably.

She ran up the stairs, and down the hall to Gram's room. After Grandpa's death, Virginia had moved into another bedroom. That was the one thing she had told Beth. "I thought I'd feel closer to him in the room we'd shared. But it only made me more aware that he was gone. So it's better for me in the other

284

room."

Beth stopped short on the threshold. The bright light of day spilled through a window and onto the ragged circle of blood on the throw rug at the side of the bed. Beth turned away.

She felt suddenly so sick to her stomach that she didn't think she'd make it across the hall to the bathroom. Yet what was there in her stomach to vomit. She hadn't eaten breakfast. Not even a glass of water.

She stood over the toilet until the sensation of brutal nausea passed away. When she turned, she saw the towel on the floor. She recognized it instantly as being part of a new set Mama had bought for the powder room. It was the towel Gramma Vee had wrapped around the doll.

She looked in every room, every closet, every place Gramma might have put the doll.

It was nowhere in the house.

She heard a soft and eerily mournful howl, and something as old as time within her heart responded. As if she had reverted to her animal ancestry she ached with sorrow, and the inability to shed tears to relieve that sorrow.

She went to the back door and out. Gypsy came to her, and nuzzled against her. The small terrier stood looking at her with questions in his eyes. The cat sat alone in the shade of the lawn table, but he too watched her.

She left, the dogs following to the gate. She saw their eyes watching her through the slats as she walked away.

"As soon as we can get a fence in," she said, and hoped they understood. Even they were lost, their lives changed forever by the terrible deaths.

Zenoa? What had Jefferson meant by that? The word was a name, obviously. She wasn't sure she'd ever heard it before, even though somewhere in the back of her mind a faint warning throbbed.

Nineteen

Pamela saw the few remaining members of her family at the funeral, a closed casket service for her mother, father, brother and sister, and her grandmother Virginia. Five identical coffins arranged among the overpowering silence and fragrance of flowers. Beth, with Ross, and Grandma and Grandpa Elkins, sat on the front bench in a secluded area away from the main congregation. Behind them sat other family members who considered themselves close. Aunts, uncles, cousins. Hardly any of them even turned when Pamela, with Detective Jefferson at her side, came quietly in at the last moment and sat alone at the back. A few faces glanced back at their silent entrance, and one face took a second look, a severe stare that spoke without words her shock and disapproval that Pam had been allowed to come.

Never before, in her days in jail, had Pamela felt so abandoned by her family. Halfway through the service Jefferson reached over and covered her clenched hands with his in a sympathetic touch. Tears rolled out from under her closed lids.

As the service ended and people rose, Beth, weeping, was taken by Ross and Grandpa Elkins over to the row of white caskets. Grandma Elkins turned, at the whisper of one of the cousins, and looked at Pamela. Beth moved a few steps toward Pamela, then in sudden convulsive weeping she covered her face and turned away, and a distant family member put his arm around her and led her beyond reach of Pamela.

"Perhaps we'd better leave now," Detective Jefferson said.

"I'm sorry, Pamela. Maybe it would have been better if I hadn't brought you."

But she had to come. To cling as closely to her loved ones as she could, as long as she could.

She looked for Craig, but did not see him.

When she had heard that Gramma Vee was also dead, that she had killed herself, she had thought she'd go mad. Gramma Vee was her lifeline. It was Gram to whom she planned to go when she got out. Gram was the only one she could count on. On the telephone Beth had cried out at her, "It's your fault, Pamela! How dare you tell me you can't stand this! If it hadn't been for what you did, she'd still be alive! Because of you she killed herself! She couldn't stand it either, Pam! She'd lost everything when she lost Daddy! Don't you see that?"

"Beth!" Pam had screamed into the phone, sensing that Beth was going to hang up. "Beth, I have to know! Was the doll—"

Beth hung up.

Was the doll with Gram when she died?

Telephone privileges were carefully rationed. She had used up her ration on the one call. She had to wait until the next day to call Beth again, and Beth's neighbor took the call, then after a hesitation said Beth was not home. It was so obvious. Beth didn't want to talk to her.

On the morning of the funerals Detective Jefferson had shown up at the jail. Until then she hadn't known that she would be allowed to go.

Driving now away from the funeral home and back to the county jail, Pamela sat in silence, staring out the window at a blur of green. The road was a two-lane blacktop that curled through an area of alfalfa and clover meadows. Hay had been cut and rolled into large bales. Trees lined the winding road. Against a backdrop of woods the jail looked like a prison, with high fences made of cement blocks painted grey.

Although she had left the jail with handcuffs on, Jefferson had removed them while they were still in the car. She sat now with her wrists free. Once she glanced down to see if the door had a handle she could open. A fantasy flitted through her mind of opening the door, rolling out into the green grass in the ditch, then running, running forever into the freedom of the land, toward the forest to the north where the trees rose like a sanctuary beyond the prison walls.

Her body sat still. Only her soul escaped into the cool, shadowed protection of the wild.

Her mind went back to the service and the people there. Hundreds of people, it had seemed, and as she had left the funeral home and went with Jefferson into the large parking lot, those people were leaving through the double doors that were open at the front, and they all stared at her. There were people who looked at Pam as if they felt it was a disgrace she had been allowed to come. That she should have had the decency to stay away. Pamela could see in their faces their belief that she was guilty. She couldn't look at them, beyond the most brief glances. Their belief in her guilt made her guilty. She felt weighed down with it.

Among them were the neighbors she had known much of her life, the ones who had run out of their houses in answer to her cry for help. That day . . . so long ago, yet still happening . . . so many hours ago . . . so many heartbeats that were filled with pain for all that was lost. Her family. Each member. Nicky, who seemed never to have a serious thought in his head. His games, his dog. Mama, Daddy, the cornerstones of her life. Gramma Vee. Security. Love. Kit, lovely little Kit who had been so good, and at last, so frightened. In front of the accusing stares of the people who knew her she bowed her head because she was beginning to feel she was guilty.

When Jefferson came to the jail earlier that morning and told her she could go to the memorials she had looked at him in disbelief.

"I can?" she whispered.

"Yes, of course. Get your prettiest dress on."

The matron brought her a dress. "Blue," she told the matron. "I'd like the blue, with the wide white collar." But the shoes the matron brought were not the ones Pamela would have chosen. The few clothes Gramma Vee had brought were being kept in lockers. She was allowed to keep very few personal items with her. She couldn't even keep a pen and writing paper. In order to write, she had to request permission. "Don't you see," the matron said gently, "A pen or a pencil can be used to gouge eyes

288

out, and that sort of thing. One of the tough gals could take it away from you so fast you'd wonder if you ever had it to start with."

Perhaps some of the inmates might be considered tough, but Pam saw them only as other figures in this strange world she now inhabited. She was close to them in one sense, but in another as isolated as if she were lost in dark space.

Jefferson didn't take her to the cemetery, and she was glad. Beth would not want her there. In Beth's eyes, briefly, Pam had seen the message. *You caused this. Why are you here?*

She looked for Craig among the congregation and didn't see him. He had come to see her twice since she had been in the county jail, and had difficulty looking at her. On the second visit she'd thought of telling him the truth. Anything to close the terrible void that was growing between them. "Craig," she'd whispered, pleading with her eyes, her hands on his, to believe in her. "I didn't do it, Craig. You know I wouldn't."

"I didn't think you did," he said, but he didn't meet her eyes. "I never thought you would. I never thought—anything like that would ever happen."

"Craig . . ." She stopped. She could see in his attitude toward her that he would never believe the truth. Was there no one in the world who would believe the truth? She knew when he kissed her goodbye that day, the quick touch of his lips as if he were kissing a sister, that he would never be back. Craig, with all their plans, their dreams of a future together, was gone. She stood and watched him go. Later she asked for pen and paper, and thought she would write the truth, but she put nothing down on paper.

Protect yourself, came the whisper as if from a voice just behind her. *Protect yourself. Tell no one. They'll begin to think you're insane, and you'll spend the rest of your life in an asylum. Just like the little girl who owned the doll a hundred years ago.*

She had told Gramma Vee and Beth, and now Gram was dead.

But where was the doll now? She had to know where the doll was. She had to find out in a way that wouldn't make anyone think she was insane.

Was it in the house with Gramma Vee the night she died?

289

Would Beth now take it home with her?

Oh God no, no, no.

Pam turned to Jefferson, "Was she alone when she died? My grandmother."

"Yes, as far as anyone knows."

"What — what time of day — did it happen?"

"Sometime during the night," he said. He glanced toward her. He was driving very slowly, no more than twenty miles an hour. The road was clear of traffic. It wound like a lane between the rows of trees, between the meadows, but the walls of the prison were beyond a grove of trees not a half mile away. Even so slowly they were approaching it much too fast.

He said, "She was found early the next morning. Her neighbor, who was always used to Virginia coming out of her house at least by sunrise, became alarmed and called the police. They went in and found her. She'd been dead, the coroner said, since about midnight." He paused, then said, "I wasn't going to upset you with details, especially today. But since you're able to talk about it, would 'Zenoa' mean anything —"

"Zenoa!"

"Yes." He glanced sharply at her. "It's a name?"

"Who told you?" she whispered, and bit her lip. Had Gramma Vee, or Beth, told him what she'd said about the doll?

He said, "It appeared that your grandmother tried to write a note as she was dying. She wrote one word. There was nothing else. I asked Beth, and she didn't know what it meant. What does it mean to you?"

She was unable to answer. Scenes of Gramma Vee writing in blood came to her mind. She squeezed her eyes shut against the vision.

"What could it have meant to your grandmother?"

A nerve jerked in Pamela's cheek. Nerves in her cheeks and at the corners of her mouth had begun jerking lately, at times uncontrollably. She could stop the nervous tics only by putting her face in her hands and forcing silence to her mind.

"Zenoa," she said, her voice breaking, "is the name of the doll Gramma Virginia gave my sister, Kit, for her birthday last month. It's antique — uh — probably valuable. I was wondering — did she take it home with her? Was it in the house the

290

night she died?"

"Yes, it was."

"And—Gram wrote a note . . ."

"Only the one word. Zenoa."

The doll was in the house. Dear God. Gramma Vee hadn't believed her. She had gone after the doll after all, and now she was dead.

Then another thought burst through, like a bubble softly opening, allowing some of the guilt Pamela had suffered to escape. *Gram hadn't killed herself.*

"Where — where —" she said when her voice could work, "Where is it now? The doll — where is it now?" Locked safely in Gram's house, where no one lived anymore?

"I took it to forensic to see if there are any prints on it, and a few other tests."

"Will it be locked up?"

"Only temporarily. When they're finished with it of course it will be given back to whomever owns it."

"Not Beth!" she cried. "You aren't going to give it to Beth!"

He looked at her. "Why don't you want your sister to have it?"

She couldn't explain her reasons for not wanting it in Beth's house. She looked out the window. She had to talk to Beth again. She must. Even though she knew Beth hated hearing about the doll. For a hundred years it had been closed into a room in an antique shop, but now it was out, and anyone could get it. And no one must have it.

"Because." She hesitated. "Could you just—destroy it?"

"Instead of giving it to your sister?"

There was a strange look on his face. Was he thinking Pam didn't want Beth to have it just for selfish reasons? She said helplessly, "It was Kit's doll. It should have been buried with her." For some reason she didn't want him to think badly of her, not like this, not over something that to him would seem childish.

He drove to the side of the road and parked, leaving the engine idling. "There's something I want to ask you about the doll, Pamela." He reached over to the glove compartment and removed a small plastic wrapped package.

He gave it to her. She opened it, and shock washed over her

291

as she saw the doll's shoes. Originally white, dark spots had ruined them. Though it was now dried and darkened, Pamela knew it was blood. She dropped them, jerking her fingers away instinctively.

"The doll's shoes!"

"Yes. Those little shoes have blood on the soles. Not just a few spots. They've been soaked in blood."

She forced herself to pick up the shoes. She looked at the soles, caked brown, with dried blood in the sewn area where the tops joined the soles.

He said, "I noticed when I was in the house, your house, strange little spots made on the carpet. They were about six inches apart, and regularly spaced. Almost like footsteps. Then I noticed the doll's shoes had blood on the soles. I don't know what this means, Pam, do you?"

Here's your chance, something whispered urgently in Pam's mind. Then the other voice whispered forcefully, *Don't be a fool. You were a fool to tell Beth, or Gram. Protect yourself. You don't want to die in an insane asylum, like the girl a hundred years ago.*

She said nothing. She stared in horror at the ruined white shoes. In her mind she could see the doll walking, taking its small steps, from one victim to the next. Attacking with incredible, demonical strength. She had felt its strength. Why had it let her live? Why hadn't it stabbed her? It must have thought, as she lay still, that she was already dead.

Jefferson said softly, "Can you think of any reason why someone would have been playing with the doll after the murders were committed?" When still she said nothing, he continued, "This reminds me of my kid sister. She had a bunch of dolls, one of them big. She could walk that doll along as if it were another child, and its legs would swing forward. As if it were walking. That's the only explanation I can see for the doll's footprints in the blood."

She shook her head.

She shoved the shoes back down into the plastic bag, opened the glove compartment, and put it all out of sight. She was trembling so hard she was afraid he'd notice.

"There's something very strange, though," he said, almost as if he were speaking to himself as he pulled the car back onto the road. "There are no other footprints. Whoever played with the doll, was very careful not to step in the blood."

Beth sat in the visitor's room, at the corner of one of the two long tables. Pam had pleaded with Beth to come see her, she had to talk to her, but days had passed. Now finally she was here, but Pam could see how she hated being here, and Pam understood. She didn't want to be here either.

All around them were the voices of other prisoners and their visitors. Not far away a woman and her boyfriend kissed, a long connection that dismissed everyone else from their world. But Pam knew that the guards would allow it to go on only so long, then the couple would be tapped on the shoulders, and if that didn't stop it, they would be separated and the prisoner taken back to the cell, and the visitor shown to the iron gates.

"I have to talk to you, Beth. There's something I have to know," Pam said urgently in a low voice, leaning as near to Beth as Beth allowed without pulling away. She and Beth had never been as close as some sisters, they had never taken problems to each other, and now Pam felt that distance.

Beth looked at her watch. "I don't have much time. Tresa needs me."

"Okay, but, Beth, please listen. I know the doll was in the house with Gramma Vee when she was killed. Detective Jefferson told me he took it for some tests, but he's going to give it to you. Do you have it yet?"

She had tried to ask Beth that question, that important question, over the phone, and Beth had made excuses to hang up. Tresa needed her. She'd come to see Pamela soon, she promised, but days had gone by and Beth hadn't come, until today.

Beth's face was pinched when she turned it toward Pam. She looked as if she were going to burst into tears. "Pam, why do you have such a horrible fascination with that damned old doll?"

"Beth—"

"Listen to me, goddamnit! I don't know where that damned doll is! I went over to Gram's to get the crazy thing, and it wasn't there! It's gone. Someone took it. Pamela, please forget

293

the doll."

"I told you, Beth, Detective Jefferson took it! But only for a while. He said he was going to give it back to you. Beth, you can't allow that to happen. You don't have it, do you?"

"No, I don't! Now please, let's just forget this crazy stuff, Pam, please, *please?*"

Pam felt some of the tension go out of her. At least the doll was not in Beth's home, where baby Tresa lay helpless in her crib, where Beth and Ross would sleep unsuspecting in their beds.

Beth added, "We did bring the dogs over, and Gram's cat. To keep the cat from running away and trying to go home again we're keeping it in the house. Tresa thinks it's a fantastic addition. You should see her wave her arms and croon. She loves the cat. And the cat kind of likes her too, I think. It likes to cuddle up against her. So far, thank goodness, Tresa isn't allergic to cat dander! Maybe something good will happen, and Tresa will grow up to be an animal lover and do something good for the poor plight of animals. Something good has to come from this somehow."

"Beth, listen!" Pam gripped Beth's arm, and held tight even as she felt Beth try to draw away. "If Detective Jefferson brings the doll to you, have it destroyed. Don't take it in your house. Especially at night!"

Beth glared at her. Pam could almost feel the intensity of her disgust, of her wish to put all this behind her, including Pamela. Her lips pressed tight. She said nothing.

"Beth," Pamela pleaded in a last whisper, as Beth stood up and prepared to leave. "Beth, put the doll in the trash, so that it can be destroyed."

"I've talked to your lawyers," Beth said. "They were considering an insanity defense, but felt you might have a better chance going along with an unknown person having come into the house, by some method they haven't figured out yet. My impression was, all you have to do would be to lie, and they might get you off with a lighter sentence. Maybe even get a not guilty verdict."

Pam too stood up. "Lie?" she said. "And say someone hit me?"

"Something like that."

"Beth — I don't lie. Even about the doll, Beth, I didn't lie. And I'm not crazy. I'm scared to death, Beth. You're all I have left, you and Tresa. The only family I have, except Grandpa and Grandma, and they haven't been to see me but once. I've lost Mom and Daddy and Kit and Nicky, and now Gramma Vee. Even Craig is gone. It's like he's scared of me now, as if he doesn't know me anymore. I don't want to lose you, Beth."

Beth took a deep breath and turned away. "I have to go, Pam."

Pamela followed her as far as she could. One more time she tried, "Beth. Please? Destroy it."

Beth left without looking back.

Twenty

There were times when Beth could work in a certain mind-lessness, as if all her energies were concentrated in one direction. In her kitchen, with all the lights burning, she cleaned up after dinner. Her hands moved, wiping the counter, taking the throw rugs out into the backyard that now contained two dogs. She could almost smile as both dogs danced about as if she were playing a game with them when she shook the small rugs.

She paused in the backyard to look up. The sky was a mixture of rose and blue and in the east a couple of bright stars were dimly visible. One of them was Mars. Or was it Venus? She always had trouble remembering. She had asked Nicky at least a dozen times, and he had told her. He was the space freak. He was into planets and constellations and whatever all those things were called. She was into earth. The simple things. Life, love, and growing things. Flowers. Babies.

She went back into the kitchen, put down the rugs, locked the door. She washed out her dishcloth, wrung it out, and hung it on the rack in the pantry.

From the front room came the muted voices of newscasters. Ross was there, his feet up, watching the news. Tresa was in bed. She'd been going to sleep at six in the evening and waking at precisely six in the morning since she was a month old. At that point she had decided she wanted a two o'clock feeding only if she weren't feeling very well. The past few nights she'd been sleeping soundly.

Beth tensed when she heard the doorbell. Police. She knew it instinctively. In the backyard the dogs barked.

She stood still, listening. Ross turned down the television and opened the front door. Beth heard the deep tones of Detective Jefferson, and Ross answering. She didn't want to face another policeman as long as she lived. In the pantry she stood as if she were hiding.

Then she heard the front door close. After a brief silence Ross's footsteps crossed the occasional rug in the hallway and then came into the kitchen.

"Hon?"

She stepped out of the pantry. Ross was carrying a bulky object in a brown plastic bag. He stopped, looking at her critically as he'd been doing lately. Especially since they suspected she was pregnant again, and Tresa less than five months old. But so what, they had decided. It wasn't planned, that was for certain, but they hadn't wanted to rear Tresa alone anyway, and if Beth's health could stand it, another baby might be just what they all needed. Two children, growing up together. Two girls, maybe. Almost twins.

"You okay, hon?"

Beth's eyes were on the plastic bag. She could make out the shape of the thing within. A rounded head, arms, feet. The doll.

Like a nightmare, it kept recurring.

"What is that?" she asked. "Was that Detective Jefferson?"

"Yes." He held out the bag toward her. "It's the antique doll, he said. Seems they'd been doing some tests on it of some kind. What kind of tests would they have wanted to do on a doll do you suppose?"

"Why didn't you ask him?"

"Never thought of it. What do you want to do with it?"

Beth went toward the sink and drew a glass of water though she wasn't thirsty. She wanted nothing to do with the doll.

"Put it in the pantry," she said.

"Everything goes in the pantry. Is there room?"

Beth shrugged. "Just put it on the floor."

For three hours Beth sat on the couch with her legs up, soft cushions supporting her back and head. She could see Ross, in his favorite chair in the corner, his feet on the ottoman. She watched him as much as she watched television. At times she tried to get interested in an article in the magazine she had chosen at the supermarket counter. Sometimes she thought of how they would handle the bedroom arrangement after the new baby came. For a few years both babies could use the same bedroom. But after they got older, each child would deserve a room of its own. Having her own room at home when she was growing up was so important to her. Before they had moved into the big house they had lived in a two bedroom house. She had shared one room with both Pamela and Nicky. The baby, Kit, had slept in a crib in their parents' room. So she could well remember what it was like not to have her own room.

The magazine had pictures of houses, and of one house being remodeled. She examined the remodeling pictures carefully. It looked so easy.

"Do you suppose," she said, "we could build on an extra room later on? Maybe build a really nice master bedroom, so we can use our old bedroom for a guest room."

Ross said, "Have you thought about moving to your folks' house?"

"*What?*" Images of blood came like ink blots before her eyes as she looked up in a blur of shock.

Ross didn't seem to notice. "Well, it's a big house. And it's yours."

"It's not mine! I don't want it!"

He caught the panic in her voice and came over to her, squeezing in to sit beside her on the couch. It was a close, tight fit, but his body against hers, his arm around her shoulders, were warm and comforting. He kissed her, several times, on the cheek and forehead.

"I'm sorry, sweetheart. I know, I wasn't in the house. You were. You saw it. I just wasn't thinking. We'll remodel however you want to. Or buy a new one." He stood up and pulled gently on her hand. "Come on, let's go to bed."

He turned off the living room lights and the television, and holding her hand, walked with her to the bedroom. She went into the bathroom and soaked in a tub of hot water until it had cooled. She dressed in a soft nylon nightgown. When she went into the bedroom, Ross was sleeping soundly.

Beth entered the hall and went to the room next door. A

night-light in the shape of a lamb with a garland of white daisies around its neck, gave the room a soft twilight. Tresa, in her shadowed crib, slept soundly. She seemed entirely silent, her breathing so soft. Beth put her hand on the baby's chest to make sure she was breathing. She felt the gentle rise and fall of the tiny chest, and something tight within Beth relaxed.

Now she could go to bed. She could sleep. She had trained herself not to think of the murder scenes. Yet when she closed her eyes, just as she was trying her hardest to fall asleep, they began flashing through her mind. Walls splattered. Carpets spongy and red. Bodies sprawled, legs and arms askew. Familiar faces in horrible, unfamiliar death.

She turned in bed, and put her arm across Ross. In his sleep he reached for her and slipped his arm under her head. Her eyes stared at the outline of the door that led out into the hallway. The night-light from Tresa's room lighted the hall also, in a dim, shadowy light that tonight seemed eerie. Filled with moving figures, shadows that shifted, pale lights that danced, as if the light were thrown by a distant candle.

And somewhere in the house she heard a sound. Movements. Soft disturbances. Something in a closet, moving about.

She listened, alerted. She heard only the quiet, then, as if the sounds of movements were only in her mind. She snuggled closer to Ross and closed her eyes.

Pam walked through a dark, silent tunnel. It sloped downward, and she began to fall. In her dream she reached out her arms, her hands searching for a hold on something, anything, that would keep her from dropping into the horror she knew lay below her.

A dim light appeared and as if she were swimming, she went toward it. She came to a stop in a large room. The walls had psychedelic paintings in red. Then she saw the red was liquid, and was slowly running, in fat round drops down the wall.

She whirled. There was one doorway, and coming through the door was a tall young woman.

The young woman came closer. She walked oddly, stiffly, as

299

if her legs were not jointed at the knees. Then Pam saw her face, with the slight overbite, and the large, round, dark eyes.

Not a young woman, but a large doll, the size of a grown girl.

The antique doll.

Pam tried to move, tried to scream. The huge doll came closer, closer. She carried something in her hand. A thin, pointed metal object, rusty and old, coated with blood.

Pam screamed.

"Christ alive, girl, wake up!"

Someone shook her, and Pam moved from the dream nightmare to the nightmare of reality. One of the inmates was over her, a wrinkled face with stringy grey hair falling on each side of her face. Pamela recognized the oldest of her cell mates. In other bunks she could hear moans and the rustle of bedding as disturbed sleepers tried to get comfortable again.

"Every goddamned night," someone muttered.

Clara, the one who had awakened Pam, straightened and said, "What you need, girl, is one of them shrinks."

Another voice said, "Could you let us get one good night's sleep? I wonder when the hell my lawyer is going to get me out of this dump?" Her voice dwindled away, muttering her complaints to herself.

A bright light shined in Pamela's face. It came from beyond the bars, the guard behind it only a silhouette in shadow outline. Up and down the corridor voices rose, swearing, one laughed briefly.

The flashlight beam remained full on Pamela for a moment before it flashed briefly over the other inmates. It withdrew, and the guard moved on, ignoring the calls from women asking that Pamela be taken somewhere else.

The light in the ceiling was always on, but it was a sixty-watt bulb, and the shadows in the corner on the bunk where Pamela lay were like the shadows in her nightmares. Thick and stifling, and filled with horrors.

Still, she slunk into it. With her arm over her face she pushed against the cool wall. Every night the nightmares came. Always different except for the size of the doll and the fall down the dark tunnel. Pamela had figured out the tunnel. It was the stairway out of the attic.

The hugeness of the doll was something she didn't understand.

Midnight. Beth got up and went to see about the baby. Once again she laid her hand on Tresa's chest to see if she were breathing. She considered sitting down in the rocking chair and resting. She was so tired. But to sit in the chair without the baby in her arms wouldn't seem right. She would feel so empty. And the baby was sleeping too well to be disturbed.

Beth went back to the other bedroom, pausing in the hall to listen. She still, occasionally, heard a faint rustling sound. It was somewhat like a mouse nosing about somewhere in the house, but there were no mice, no holes for mice to enter.

She drew a glass of water and drank it. She hadn't turned a light on, anywhere. Only the night-light in the baby's room filtered into the hallway and even, like the last dying rays of moonlight, into the kitchen. But through the windows, filtered by a tree in full leaf, the street light on the corner shone. She could have walked through the house in total darkness, though. She knew the location of every chair, every table, every doorway.

She listened, but like a mouse the rustling had stopped as she moved about, as if it heard and grew quiet, itself listening.

Maybe, she considered, it was the dogs. Somehow. Both dog houses were against the back of the exterior wall of the kitchen, and Ross had put some old throw rugs in each house. Perhaps the dogs were as restless as she.

Beth went back to bed.

One o'clock.

She got up again. She hadn't gone to sleep, yet it seemed she had dreamed. Scenes of Kit in the hallway mingled with Pamela behind bars. Beth shifted and turned in bed, and tried to put the bloody scenes out of her mind, but every time she closed her eyes they were there again. Her mother, lying with so many stab wounds they were even on her face, peppered horribly. For as long as Beth lived she'd see her mother's face staring up with dead eyes at the ceiling. Dead, yet strangely horrified even in death. And Daddy, face down. Thank God, face down. His back like her mother's face.

How could Pam have done that? All of that. Such hatred. Rage unbounded. That was not like Pam. What had happened to her? Beth could so easily have believed that a stranger, a madman, broke into the house, if Pam hadn't told her the story about the doll.

Why had she chosen such a ridiculous story? Why?

Pam had continued to be so concerned about the doll. Where was it, she kept wanting to know. Did Gramma Vee have it in her house when she died?

Even now Beth felt the same sense of shock and uneasiness, the anger, too, the fury she couldn't get rid of. Every time she heard Pam mention the damned doll. Yet it had been there. How strange that Gramma Vee had taken it home and chosen that night to kill herself.

She heard the rustling again, this time sharper, more precise and final. In the silence of the night more defined.

Beth got up and stood at the side of the bed, and with her movement the rustling stopped.

She moved swiftly and scarcely without thought, toward the kitchen. She turned on the bright overhead light and stood with her bare feet on the cool linoleum. She'd had restless nights before, but not like tonight. Was it because the doll was in the house and Pam had gotten through to her in some way so that she couldn't sleep when the old doll was around?

She went to the pantry and looked in. In the shadows of the pantry the doll gazed at her through half open eyes, its head and arms fully emerged from the plastic bag.

A strange tingling went through her body. She stared back at the doll, feeling as if she were being observed by a fully intelligent mind.

She backed up and pulled the door shut. Then she opened it again, went in and picked up the plastic bag. The top had come open, that was all. When Ross put the doll down into the pantry he had let it slip, somehow untied it.

Beth pulled the heavy bag fully over the doll. The bag, she noticed, was a type she had never seen before, with a tie attached a few inches from the top. She pulled it tightly and tied it again. Then she stood the doll, completely secured in the bag,

302

against the wall.

She stood in the kitchen a moment looking at the bag. The bulge of the doll's head against the top of the bag seemed larger, the doll taller Her first impression of the doll, on Kit's birthday, was that it was perhaps twenty or twenty-five inches tall. But the doll was several inches taller than that.

Kit was afraid of the doll.

Pamela had told her that. The look on Pamela's face was wild and desperate, yet secretive. She hadn't told anyone but Gramma and herself, Beth thought.

Beth went to the bedroom, leaving the kitchen light on. Enough of the light shined into the bedroom so that she could see how to dress. Swiftly she pulled on jeans and a shirt. She looked down at Ross. His face was in shadow, but his breathing was even. Besides, if she woke him to tell him she was taking the doll home, back to her parents' house, he would argue her out of it. She could almost hear him saying, "That's foolish, Beth. Wait until morning, and I'll take it. You shouldn't go alone into that house. At least not until it's been cleaned."

She left the bedroom, and in the kitchen took a notepad and pen from the drawer. She wrote a brief note, in case Ross woke and came into the lighted kitchen looking for her.

Then, her car keys in her hand, hoping she could slip away without waking Ross, she took the doll and went into the adjoining garage.

She opened the garage door. Thank God, she thought as she started the car, the bedrooms were on the other side of the house.

The streets were quiet. Shadows of trees fell beneath street lights on corners. An occasional porch light gleamed out onto a walk. No one moved about, not even a cat.

Within minutes she turned into the driveway of the house she still called home. Home, both places, her own small house, and this large house where she had spent her teenage years.

She parked in the wide driveway and turned off the engine. A street light reflected into the second floor windows at the front, the master bedroom.

The thought of entering the house chilled her. But she had to put the doll away, tonight. Get it out of her own house, her life,

303

the lives of her remaining loved ones.

She got out of the car, closing the door softly. The plastic of the bag that contained the doll rustled softly. *The same sound she had heard in her house.*

With that awareness in her mind, she hurried toward the door. She set the plastic bag down just long enough to unlock the door and turn on the foyer light.

The house seemed huge, empty, haunted, a cavernous place filled with shadows and memories, and sounds that were now silent. She had thought to leave it here, in the foyer. Just put it down, back out of the house and go home. But she found herself climbing the stairs, running upward, turning on lights as she went, like the child in the woods leaving grains of corn to mark the way back. With her eyes straight ahead she went toward the attic door. She slid against the wall when she came to the area that was stained with Kit's blood, but she didn't look down.

She opened the attic door. As she climbed the steps into darkness she told herself she'd have to do something about the house utilities, make a decision, finally, and at least have them turned off. She kept her mind carefully away from the deaths, deliberately phasing them out, yet snatches, images, flashed through her mind like shattered pieces in a kaleidoscope, and invisible hands of fear tugged at the backs of her arms and neck.

At the top of the attic steps she pulled the light cord. Her eyes fell on the tall chest, where Pamela said she'd been planning to put the doll in a drawer. Where the doll supposedly had shoved her so that she fell and struck her head.

Beth started toward the chest, aware of far-reaching darknesses in the corner of the attic, of shapes not clearly defined as furniture or boxes.

She heard the rustling of the bag, and it seemed the doll turned. She felt the weight shift against her. She dropped it quickly onto the floor, and here in the shadows of the large attic she could almost believe the story Pam had told.

Without looking back she turned and ran, down the steps,

into the hall.

She slid the lock shut, fastening the door securely. Then she hurried down the hall, turning out lights behind her.

She locked the front door securely. Then remembered.

She had not turned off the attic light. When she went to the driveway she looked up. Above the back porch, and up the slope of the roof above the back bedrooms, the dim light glowed through the single attic window.

Now, at least, perhaps that would propel her to have the utilities turned off. She was not going back into the house to turn off the light. Anything but that.

As she turned away she saw a movement in the attic window. For just a glimpse she saw a face. The outline of a head. But when she looked back again sharply, her eyes squinting, nothing was there.

"You have a visitor, Pamela," the matron said. The large ring of keys jingled as she unlocked the door again.

Several of the inmates had remained in the cell because visiting hour had brought them no visitors. Like the others, Pam sat on her bunk. Unlike the others, she never talked, never attempted to carry on a conversation. A few had tried to talk to her, but they always asked why she was in, and Pam had nothing to say. Also, she was alone in being long term. Weeks had passed, others came, and left. But Pam remained.

She stood up. Her attorneys usually came in the mornings, or later in the evenings, not at this time of day. Pam had lost hope that Craig would come. Maybe, she thought, it was Grandpa. He seemed to be the only remaining member of her family that could stand the sight of her. When he came to visit he talked of what Grandma was doing, or Beth, and he talked about the baby. At those times his face brightened. Pam was reminded of Kit, every time, and the way her face brightened when she unwrapped her antique doll at her birthday party. Brightened, and then, within days, had gone pale and terrified.

Without asking who her visitor was, Pam followed the matron.

They passed through two gates of bars, then went through

305

the door into the visitor's room.

The room buzzed with voices. There was even a touch of laughter now and then. Pam looked for a face that was familiar. Then she saw Beth.

Today, for the first time since before the deaths, Beth looked as if she were surviving. There was even a touch of color in her skin, and she had applied a pale lipstick.

She sat at the corner of a table where there was an extra chair. Pamela hurried toward her eagerly. She wanted to touch her, hug her, hold her. But Beth did not rise to meet her, though she smiled faintly as Pam sat down.

"How are you?" Beth asked.

Pamela nodded. She couldn't say fine, she couldn't tell the truth, either. No one wanted to hear how hopeless hopelessness could be.

"Are you okay?" Pam asked. "And Tresa?"

"We're okay. I can't stay but a minute, Pam," Beth looked down, avoiding Pam's eyes. "I just came by to tell you that I took the doll back to the house. I took it upstairs, and put it in the attic. Then I locked all the doors."

Pamela closed her eyes, tightly, briefly in relief. She'd been so afraid, not knowing where it was. So afraid it would somehow wind up in Beth's home.

"Detective Jefferson brought it to the house last night, in a brown plastic bag. So I just took it back. It's yours, Pam. The doll, the house, everything. I had the utilities turned off today. I locked the house last night. I'll keep the keys for you. That's all. When you get out, you can do what you want with everything, the house, the furniture, the doll. Everything. I don't want it, I don't want the responsibility, I don't want the house. Okay?"

The doll was secured. It was locked in the attic. That was all that mattered. Beth was safe. And Tresa . . .

"Okay," Pamela said.

Nothing else mattered.

Twenty-one

The trial was not a long one. For less than two weeks Pamela was taken each day to the courthouse where she sat and listened to the evidence against her. On the bench behind her sat her grandfather, but only once did her grandmother come, and then she sobbed into her hands, and Grandpa had to lead her away.

I didn't do it, Pam wanted to tell her, *please believe that I would never hurt them, or anyone,* but she sat with her head bowed and in silence.

Sometimes Ross came, and he told her Beth was in her ninth month of pregnancy, and not able to come. The emotional strain would be too much.

Pictures of the victims were shown. Pam turned her face away from the screen so that she wouldn't see those images she saw in her mind every day, every night. Tiny Kit, with the back of her pajamas stabbed so many times it looked as if the material had been pulverized.

Kit, so afraid, coming to her for help. She hadn't gone to anyone else, not Mom, not Daddy. She should have. But Pam knew Kit was afraid no one would believe her and she would be taken away, and put in a place away from home and family. How much better that she could have been.

Pam heard the prosecution say that she had gone up into the attic and retrieved from a collection of old kitchen tools in a box, that had been left by former owners, a rusty ice pick with a six-inch blade. Then she had gone downstairs. Kit, her little

307

sister had heard her in the hall, and come there to meet her death. Then Pamela Armand had gone to her brother Nicky's room and stabbed him, twenty-nine times. Some of the stab wounds had been perpetrated possibly after he had died from a fatal stab wound in his heart. After that she had gone to the room of her parents and killed them. She had killed her mother first, as her father was waking, then had gone to him.

Some of the wounds in the little girl, Kit, had completely penetrated the body.

Pam tried to shut out the sound of the voices of the prosecution, yet she understood their side. After killing everyone, she had run outside calling for help. In an effort to pretend she hadn't done it. Yet she had admitted that she had unlocked the door. There were bloody fingerprints on the front door locks, and all the rest of the downstairs was locked. She admitted she saw no intruder, that she fell and struck her head, no one attacked her.

Not once did she speak aloud or use her voice. Her attorneys talked for her.

She was surprised at her defense, and she lifted her head and listened. Gerald Amos's voice was deep and resonant, and sure of his theme.

"This young girl did not kill her family. It's true the doors were locked, and no one entered. The downstairs windows were locked. No one entered through them. But there was one window that was not locked. And it was there the intruder entered, and when Pamela went into the attic at three o'clock in the morning, he was waiting for her."

They had not told her they were going to say an intruder was there, although she didn't see him. If they had told her, she hadn't been listening.

The well-dressed, chubby attorney continued, "Doesn't it seem strange that Pamela did not have blood on her clothes? Wouldn't the killer have blood at least sprinkled on his clothing? Yes, of course." Amos pounded one fist into the palm of the other hand and his voice rose like a fundamentalist preacher's. "She thinks she fell and struck her head on the chest of drawers, but I say she was struck by an object! An intruder climbed through the attic window, which was not locked, which does not in fact even possess a lock, and was raised a couple of inches for ventilation. The attic window is accessible from the ground by climbing a trellis at the end of the porch. The roof above one of the second-floor windows rises to a few feet beneath the attic window. I don't know why he was there, but he was there. Perhaps he only intended to rob, or perhaps he was a madman, someone who has killed in other areas and now has passed through. But all this happened while Pamela was unconscious.

"She regained consciousness at daybreak. She went down-stairs, found her family, ran down the stairs to the foyer, going for help, and found the ice pick. Stunned, in shock through what had happened to her, she paused and picked it up. The prosecution has admitted there was blood only on her right hand, the hand that held the ice pick. She ran out for help, screaming."

Pamela thought of home. The house had been locked for eight months now. The doll was safely put away in the attic, the door bolted shut. Was it true that the attic window had no lock? She had never known.

The prosecution didn't challenge Amos, and Pamela knew he was telling the truth about the window.

He had said to her once months ago, "Your grandmother, Virginia Armand, came to us and told us the story about the doll, Pamela." His eyes didn't meet hers, nor did Valerie's. She managed to be very busy with the growing stack of papers in the folder in front of her. Amos continued, "We decided it was better not to go for insanity. We'd rather not have you declared insane, because being not guilty because of insanity can have very far-reaching effects. We're planning to get you off, on at least a lesser term."

Now, today, the trial was over, and the wait for the jury's decision began.

Pam was taken back to her cell.

She was alone now, her nightmares a continuing distur-bance. She had seen two psychiatrists, and several psycholo-gists. She had taken tests, answered questions. She had seen the puzzled gazes of the professionals, but no one had told her the results of any of the tests. One of the psychiatrists had prescribed tiny white pills to be taken at bedtime, but they hadn't stopped the nightmares.

She thought of Beth, often, and Tresa. How big Tresa must be getting. She was probably walking now. Maybe even trying to talk.

Think of something pleasant, she had told herself often.

But the other never went away.

Someday, she would be out of here. Then she would go home, and she would go in the daylight into the attic with a hatchet, and axe, and she would destroy the doll.

After only one day of deliberation the jury was ready. Pam was taken back into the courthouse. It was filled, as it had been every day of the trial. Pam didn't look for familiar faces. Not this time. She stood with her head bowed as the verdict was read.

"We find the defendant, Pamela Armand, guilty of murder on all counts . . ."

Faces blurred. The world blurred. Pamela was lost, reaching out and finding no one. There was another wait, filled with the close walls of her cell, of the narrow spaces of corridors, of feeling that she couldn't breathe. Yet she wasn't surprised at the verdict. Had she expected they would set her free?

Then again, for the last time, she was to enter the courthouse. She heard the judge set the sentence.

"Thirty years to life."

She was moved to the state prison for women in the northern part of the state. But she found she had something to live for after all.

She lived to go home, to destroy the doll.

BOOK THREE
1993
Zenoa

One

At the last, the prison guard seemed one of her few friends. A matron, Pamela had known her for ten years. Silvia was the one who helped Pamela dress the day she was to walk out of the prison gates, a free woman. She had served twenty-four years, and now it was over.

They gave her a blue suit. The skirt came to mid-calf, with a slit in the back. The blouse was a plain white polyester-cotton, smooth and soft to the touch. Pamela trembled so hard Silvia had to button the small cloth-covered buttons.

"There, there," she said in her motherly manner, "You'll do fine."

The waistband of the skirt had elastic at the back, which Pamela didn't need. It hung loosely on her. Her shoes were low-heeled black with a couple of tiny buttons for decoration. She was even given a handbag. The prison was dressing her for her release like a parent dressing its child for the first day of school. Silvia had helped Pam with her hair. All these years she'd drawn it back into a braid or ponytail, but Silvia had brought her some curlers, and helped her put them in. Today her hair curled softly to her shoulders.

"You look like a girl, Pamela," Silvia said. She hugged her. "Now don't look so scared. You're free! You're not so old but that you could still marry and maybe even raise a family."

No, that wouldn't be possible now. Not one of her own genes, at least. The prison physician had said it was the stress of the incarceration that had plunged her into an early menopause, several years ago. But what did it matter? Her vision of life had

313

altered so much that she walked out of the prison a person only distantly related to the girl who'd gone in twenty-four years ago.

She said goodbye to people who had become friends. Some of them cried when they hugged her. She had worked for fifteen years in the library, and knew many of the inmates, though very few closely. In her single cell she had learned to like solitude. In the library during the day she catalogued books as they arrived, checked them out to the inmates, and read every minute she could, everything from novels to science to pseudo-sciences. She had read the bibles, all of them, searching for a belief of her own. On television she had seen the nature shows, her only touch with life outside the prison, her only feel of a green leaf. To her surprise, though, she had found that cats were allowed in the prison, on a limited basis, so one of them became hers. A warm body to curl with her at night, and to sleep on her desk during the day in the library.

The cat, whom she had called Susie, grew old and died one night as she lay beside Pam. Three months ago. Afterward Pam had spent intense hours trying to decipher the meanings of life and death, as so many far greater minds had before her, and would after, and nothing she had read during her years in the prison library, nothing she had ever concluded, was satisfactory.

She was not even free to bury her cat. Susie was taken away in a plastic bag with the trash.

Nature herself cared so little for life, and yet she sought to replace it constantly, with too much, too quickly.

Pamela was scared, she realized, as she walked into the prison yard, into the bright sunshine. She got into the prison bus that was taking her, and several others, to the local bus station. People would stare, she was told. Even though they were used to the prison bringing parolees to the bus station in town where they would scatter to various parts of the country, still there were people unused to them who stared. But once on the commercial bus, the passengers wouldn't recognize her as being an ex-convict.

With the small crowd she rode from the prison, through the streets toward the bus station. Others of the prison looked both excited and scared. Like herself they were all a slightly sickly color, with very little makeup if any at all, and like herself none of them had family who had come to get them. Most of them were not as fortunate as Pamela, and she wondered what they would do now. With no money, no family, little chance of getting work, what would they do?

In her case the trust had continued to accumulate, and her attorney had told her the income would take care of her, if she didn't expect to become a jetsetter.

Once a year during her years in prison she had received a letter from Beth. At Christmas the package came from Beth, and dutifully signed also by Ross, Tresa, and Justin. They sent a lovely nightgown, every year, a couple of pairs of pajamas and house slippers and robe. But the part that Pamela read and looked at until she knew them by heart were the letters and pictures. Tresa began writing to her, off and on, during her early teens. In pictures she had seen Tresa and Justin grow up. She had pictures of Justin in his baseball cap, holding a bat, when he was ten years old. She had a picture of him in his graduation gown. She had pictures of Tresa growing into a lovely young woman who looked nothing at all like her mother, nor her father either, but must have received the genes that created her outward appearance from so many different and distant ancestors that she was a creation in her own right. In the pictures she had lovely dark brown hair that hung past her shoulders. The hair, Pamela thought, was something like her own had been then, and still was, though now it was touched with a few grey strands. But Tresa had grown up taller than Beth, and Pamela judged, taller than herself. She had a nice smile and kind eyes. In her earlier years she seemed always to be holding two or three pets. Dogs, cats. Pamela had come to know the animals as well as she knew the people. For years her own dog had been one of the happy animals Tresa held, and Gramma Vee's little dog. Also Gramma Vee's cat had been in the picture. Beth never mentioned animals in her yearly letter, but the pictures told the story. One by one the older animals disappeared and young ones took their places. Then those too disappeared. Finally, the snapshots of Tresa and Justin no longer included pets.

The last two years the pictures had been very formal, a handsome young man that always made Pam think of Nicky, as if Nicky had been reincarnated to live again, and Tresa, serious and lovely in her studio picture.

Several years ago Grandma and Grandpa Elkins had died, a year apart. But the announcement came almost formally, like the Christmas packages. Pamela hadn't been allowed to go to the funerals. She suspected the family requested that she not be included.

Through the years she had thought of one thing. One thing that never left her. A goal that was all she had lived for.

She was going home, and she was going to destroy the doll.

The prison bus had stopped without her even being aware that it had completed its short journey. She had ridden through streets without seeing them, she had stared at trees without being aware of them. She had been seeing in her mind the faces of her niece and nephew, and little more. She had reread again in her mind the letters that had come over the years.

The bus was emptying. Pamela got up, put her shoulder bag in place against her side, the strap over her shoulder, and followed the others from the bus.

She looked around. It was a small town setting, with stores across the street that were no more than two stories tall. Cars drove slowly, not many, some of the drivers taking a second look at the women going into the bus station. She would not be culture shocked as prisoners must have been fifty years ago. Television had taken care of that. She saw very little that looked different from 1969.

She was the last to go up the walk into the bus station. It was small, with a few benches, and only a couple of customers waiting, suitcases at their feet. They hardly glanced at the ten women who lined up quietly to buy their tickets to freedom.

Pamela spoke her only word when she told the clerk the name of her city. He gave her the ticket, said, "Thanks," when she paid him, and then, "Have a nice trip."

She moved over to the window and looked at the green grass of the small front lawn. There was a tree, too, and its shade fell across the walk in a way that reminded her of the big oak tree at home. Was it still there, she wondered, after twenty-four years? Beth had never mentioned the house, not once. But Pamela had talked herself into being encouraged by those omissions. If Beth never mentioned the house, it must mean that nothing had changed. It was still there, still the prison of the doll.

They both had been imprisoned, she and the real killer of her family.

Over the years, every night, as she lay staring into the shadows of the corner of her small cell, she had gone over ways of destroying the doll. It would have to be during the day, because sunlight had caused it to fall, to become harmless. Or so, at least, it had seemed.

She would dare not approach it at night, because its strength must have been formidable. If she were to destroy it, it would have to be during the day. And if she tore it literally limb from limb . . . would that be enough?

Always, with the thought of the doll, came the thoughts of Jefferson. He had kept in touch with her, to her surprise. He was the only visitor she'd had during her years in prison. Every three or four months he came to the prison and for a few minutes they talked. The conversation was casual. He always asked her how she was getting along, and if she needed anything.

At times he told her he was working to get her released, and perhaps it was his efforts that had helped to finally get her out. She didn't know. She had seen the touches of grey come into his hair, and the lines in his face, but that only made him more handsome. She looked forward to his visits. Finally she came to know that she loved him, even though he treated her only with a paternal kindness. Still, there were times, the way she caught him looking at her, that she thought he might feel the same way toward her. She expected nothing of him though, even now that she was free. She hadn't called him, or told him the date she was being released. She had only one purpose: to accomplish her mission of destroying the antique doll.

She thought of Craig, still, and wondered what had happened in his life. Beth had not mentioned him in her letters.

A long bus drove in, and people began to rise. Pamela adjusted her shoulder bag and went to the door. A cool wind had risen, and in the west a storm cloud was gathering. She would arrive in her home town at three-thirty in the afternoon. She would go to Beth's in a cab, and get the keys to the house.

Then she would go home, and walk into the memories that were still fresh, as fresh as blood spilled minutes ago.

Two

The bus pulled into the larger station at exactly 3:30. Along with passengers who had been picked up during the four-hour ride, Pamela passed through the bus doors and into the station. There was more activity here, but still it was nothing like the bus stations of her youth. As if the people who once rode buses had joined the exodus to something far more wonderful, the old station languished. A few homeless men and women had come in out of the rainstorm that had passed over. A few more people, far better dressed, more alert, carried suitcases toward the doors.

Pamela looked around once more, the last time she would ever be here she felt. Every experience she'd been having today held that same conviction. *I am doing something I will never do again.* It was a strange feeling. It was almost as if she were facing a total unknown, and that she would never pass this way again.

She found a row of telephones and put her coin in. It took a quarter now, she found, not a nickel. She smiled at her slight sense of surprise. Of course she had known that. Again from television, but she had known it distantly. She had not experienced it.

She dialed Beth's number.

"Hello," the voice said softly on the fourth ring. It was an unfamiliar voice, and Pamela thought it might be Tresa. Or had she forgotten the sound of Beth's voice? She started to speak, then her eagerness was slammed to disappointment. "You have reached the Ross Larson residence. If you will leave your name and number at the beep, we will return your call."

The beep sounded in Pam's ear and then the line hummed softly waiting for her voice. She hung up.

She turned. A damned answering machine, and she had no way of reaching Beth, of seeing if she were home, of anything. She hadn't planned to go to Beth's house without being asked. She had even thought that perhaps Beth would prefer to meet her somewhere away from home and give her the keys to the house. Now she had no choice. She had to have the house keys. Too bad they hadn't made an arrangement. Now, Pam thought, belatedly, she could have had Beth rent a box at the bank and leave them there. But of course she'd had to have a key to get into the bank box, so that wouldn't have worked either. Perhaps they could have arranged a hiding place at home for the keys.

Pam went outside to a taxi and gave him Beth's home address. She then settled back in the seat and stared out the window. This was her first car ride since the day she had gone with Jefferson to the funerals of her family. She had been transported in a van from the county jail to prison. Long ago. Yet it seemed the ride to the funerals happened only days ago.

The city hadn't changed much so far as she could see. Market Street still had the same old buildings, though now and then she saw fresh paint. Nor was the traffic much heavier than it used to be. This was the same traffic, though the cars were sleeker, that had worried Gramma Vee so much. The access to the freeway hadn't changed. The traffic there was still a lane to lane row of cars and trucks speeding east and west and around the city. But Pamela found herself trying to shrink away from them, and she saw the difference in being forty-two and eighteen as she had never thought of it. She hadn't expected a culture shock in returning to an outside life. She wasn't used to the noise and the speed, and she cringed from it.

Then the taxi was off the freeway and dropping into residential areas that were everywhere now. She rode through unfamiliar places to Beth's home. Years ago, when the children were still small, Beth and Ross had done the same thing Pam and Beth's parents had done. They had left a small house for one that would accommodate their family. Beth had sent pictures of the new house. It was in a development not far from

320

their first home, still in the same school district. Which meant it was within walking distance of Pam's house. Home.

Pam remembered the streets well enough to know they were getting closer and closer to Beth's house. Her heart began to beat faster. Nervousness made her mouth dry. She hadn't wanted to walk unexpectedly into Beth's life. Now she realized she should have called from the prison and left a message. *I'm being released. I'll be coming by for the house keys.* She had no intention of intruding on Beth's life, but how would Beth know that?

She hadn't warned Beth of her possible release, because she hadn't known of it herself. She'd had one day to prepare herself. One day of eager anticipation and black fear and depression. For twenty-four years she had lived with one goal: go home, destroy the doll. In her mind her life had ended there. She had made no plans beyond that. The release seemed in a distant future, and she was comforted only by knowing the doll was confined in the attic of the house.

Then suddenly she was free. Out of prison. Going home.

The cab pulled up in front of a house that was familiar only in pictures Beth had sent. Pam got out, picked up her small suitcase and adjusted her shoulder bag. She crossed a strip of grass to the sidewalk, then walked along it to the front gate.

She paused, looking at the house. It was easy to picture Beth here. A white picket fence enclosed a small front lawn. The flagstone walk looked polished, it was so neat. It was spring now, and flowers were beginning to bloom in the boxes that lined the small porch. The front door had a glass insert, and glass panels rose the length of the door on each side. Beyond the house the tall tree in the backyard was like a protector. Shrubs neatly lined the driveway. Beth had worked a few years after her children were old enough to be left alone, but two Christmases ago she had mentioned in her letter that she had quit work, that both she and Ross liked it better when she worked only at home. She enjoyed yard work, she told Pamela, she enjoyed cooking and cleaning her house. The letter was filled with such small facts self-consciously, as if it were an effort to write to Pam. She never said, tell me what your life is like.

Beth's house was picture perfect. Beth's life was simple,

321

homey, uncomplicated. Perhaps to make up for the tragedies she had made it picture perfect too.

As Pam walked toward the front door she began to tremble. Her heart pounded. She paused again, and thought of just running away. She had the money to live in another city, another country. She should go and leave Beth with her life.

Then she thought of the doll. If she disappeared, Beth would sell the house. That meant she might also go into the attic and bring the doll down. Perhaps history would repeat itself and she would give it to a small granddaughter someday, the way Gramma Vee had given it to Kit.

Pam set down her suitcase on the walk, and continued to the front door. As she pressed the doorbell she thought perhaps no one was home. If so, what would she do then? Sit down and wait?

She heard no footstep, only the turning of the doorknob. Suddenly the door was moving smoothly inward, and Pamela was looking at Beth.

. Her face had lined, but her hair was carefully done and without grey. She had grown round of figure, as plump as Grandma Elkins had been. And, Pam saw, she resembled Grandma Elkins, with the soft, gentle features.

"Pam!" she cried softly, an outward gushing of breath.

They stared at each other. Pam caught a glimpse of her reflection in the glass of the door, and saw a thin figure, almost paperlike in its lack of substance. Her grey-streaked hair was parted in the center and hung to her shoulders. She reached up with one hand and pushed the left side behind her ear. Why had she let Silvia talk her into letting it hang loose?

"Hello, Beth," she said softly. Behind Beth was a small foyer. A stairway rose, dark wood, polished to a sheen. The carpet was pale beige. A patterned rug lay just inside the door.

Beth glanced behind nervously. Her body blocked the entrance, but beyond, as the door drifted wider open, Pam saw a doorway into a bright area that had a linoleum floor. When Beth looked again at Pam she had gained composure, and she smiled.

"Pam! I — when did you get out? I wasn't expecting to see you — I thought it was probably a salesman."

"I was released today. I called, but got the answering machine. I'm sorry to shock you like this, Beth. I just came to get the keys."

Beth's eyes passed Pamela and lingered a moment on the suitcase, out on the path. She opened the door wider. Then, as if she were still undecided, she suddenly reached out her arms and Pam found herself being hugged. Beth's embrace was soft and warm, and again Pam thought of Grandma Elkins. When Beth drew back her eyes were moist and she drew a tissue from a pocket and wiped her eyes.

"You must think I'm horrible, Pam, letting you stand there like a stranger. Come on in. Bring your suitcase, if you want to."

"No, Beth. I didn't come here to mess you up. I just came for the keys."

"You're not going over there to stay tonight!"

"Yes, why not? You said it's mine, didn't you? I mean, you can change your mind, that's your privilege."

"Oh no. I had the house put in your name years ago. I've been paying the taxes for you, and a mowing service mows the grass, but otherwise no one has been in it since — since —" She drew a long breath and turned away. "At least come on in while I get the keys." Beth went to a door to the left of the stairway and disappeared into a room.

Pam crossed the threshold. To the right was the living room, separated from the foyer only by a polished railing. The furniture was floral and colorful, in tones of burgundy and mauve. The draperies were mauve, against paler walls of the same color. Standing self-consciously on the rug just inside the door, Pam looked at the lovely room. Not until now did she realize how much she had missed color, how terribly grim her surroundings had been. It had not seemed one of those things that would have been important, yet now, drinking color as if it were liquid, she felt her loss.

Beth returned, and handed the keys to Pam. Pam slipped them into her shoulder bag. A silence hung between them.

It was time to leave. In a way she was glad Beth had not invited her to stay. Pam felt uncomfortable here, in this loveliness.

"You have a beautiful home, Beth."

"Thank you," Beth answered, pleased, but showing signs of agitation she tried to hide. She glanced around, then back at Pam. "I'll—I'll have to show you all of it, sometime."

"Well, Beth, thanks for taking care of the house. Thanks for—the house, too."

Beth shrugged. "I didn't want it," she said. "I could never bear to enter it."

Pam looked down. She had acquired a strange sense of guilt, knowing she was found guilty not only by the jury so long ago, but also Beth, and all the family. The visions of that last night in the house, of finding them lying in their own blood, froze in her mind.

"Pam," Beth said suddenly, her words quick and breathless as if she wanted to hurry and speak before she changed her mind. "Why don't you sell the house? You should get a good price. The market is very strong, and real estate has risen a lot since you went away. Sell it, take the money, and leave. Change your name. Start a new life."

Pam shook her head. "I don't know. Maybe I will. I hadn't thought that far ahead. Right now, I just have to go home."

Beth offered her palms to the sky. "It's not that we—that I don't want you here . . . I just thought . . . it would be easier for you . . ."

Pam stepped out onto the porch, gave Beth a quick goodbye smile, and went down the steps. She heard Beth running behind her as she stooped to pick up the suitcase.

"Pam! I'll drive you . . ."

It was almost a question. Pam straightened. The suitcase was light. It contained underwear, house slippers, a robe, pajamas, soap, shampoo, two pairs of slacks and three blouses. She hadn't needed clothes for a long time.

"It's only a few blocks over to Maple, isn't it? Where you used to live?"

"Yes."

"Then it's only about a mile home. I'll walk, Beth, thanks anyway."

"It might rain again."

"It doesn't matter. Thanks again, Beth."

* * *

Beth stood still, her hands nervously clutched together. The shock of finding Pam, older, a ghost of the girl she had been, standing outside her door, still quavered within her. Of all people, she hadn't thought of Pamela. All these years she had tried, she knew in her heart, to forget Pamela. Now she felt as if her heart were bleeding.

She wanted to call her back. Please Pam, come back. I didn't mean to push you away. But she stood still, and watched her sister disappear beyond the shrubs at the corner.

Slowly she went back into the house and closed the door. But there was one thing she could do. She hurried into the den and looked up the numbers of the utilities, and called them one by one. Turn on the electricity, the gas, the telephone. Each of the utilities seemed to be run by empty-headed girls who didn't know the location of anything. Beth patiently waited as she was passed from one department to another in order to make her request, and then was told it would probably be three or four days before it could be done.

Pam would have no light, no heat, no way to call for help . . .

Help? Why had that word come to mind, she wondered. What was there to harm Pam? The house had been closed twenty-four years, and was no doubt dusty, maybe even webby, but certainly safe enough.

Beth thought of Tresa and Justin. And good Lord, Justin's wedding date, only a few days away! Had he ever told his fiancée about Pamela? Had Tresa told Blake? They would have to meet Pam. They would have to know, sometime, that Pamela was now out of prison.

She had never mentioned Pamela to anyone other than her kids and husband. She had made a point of never mentioning the past. The old picture albums were on a shelf in the storage room. In her efforts to forget what her sister had done, she had even tried to forget her parents.

But the pain was still acute. As if it had been covered by a scab, scraped away by the unexpected appearance of Pam on the doorstep, it was bleeding again. But her heart was grieving too for Pam. Now, it seemed even more impossible that Pam had ever been responsible for the murders.

She went to the kitchen and family room in the back of the house, unable to settle down. It was time to start dinner, but she couldn't make herself concentrate on something so ordinary.

The wedding! Dear Lord, how could they go through with Justin's wedding without asking Pamela? Now that she was home, she would have to be included. And the date so close. A small wedding, they had demanded. In the backyard, with only closest family and friends. Beth and Ross had willingly complied. Tresa too was engaged, but she and Blake were getting married in the fall, in church, a larger affair.

Justin's plans had come so quickly it had been almost a shock. First, he had dropped his old girlfriend with whom he had practically lived since he developed a crush on her years ago, then suddenly he had brought the new girl home and a week later had told them they were getting married. Period. In three weeks. That meant they had known each other one month, or would, at the time of the wedding, so far as Beth had been able to determine. She had almost said, "Why don't you just live together for a while?" But living together before marriage was not as popular as it was a few years ago. Nor, of course, had she asked. But she and Ross had discussed the speedy decision, and both of them were puzzled even though the girl was lovely. "Do you suppose she's pregnant, Ross?" He had answered, "I wonder."

Nevertheless, now that Pam was home it would be impossible to leave her out. Nor, Beth decided, as she began to grow calmer, did she want to.

She wished Ross would come home from work. But it was another hour before she could expect him. As a hospital administrator it was more likely he would be needed there for something or other, and be late rather than early.

As she began dinner she also began to plan the way she would tell about her sister. "Ross, you'll never guess who came to the door today —" No, too much of a surprise, as it had been for her. Rather, she would say, "Ross, Pamela has been released from prison." Simple and quick.

326

Then, to her children. "Tresa — Justin — I have something to tell you. Your Aunt Pamela . . . is out of prison." No, not like that. "Tresa, Justin, we need to talk. Alone."

With a long sigh she went to the telephone and left identical messages on the answering machines at the apartments of both Tresa and Justin. "Can you come to supper tonight? I have something important to tell you. We need to talk, make plans. Come alone, please."

She might as well get it over, as soon as possible. As she continued to stand by the telephone she began to plan a dinner for some night before the wedding. She would ask Pam to come, to meet the kids, and the young man and woman they would soon marry.

Three

Had the trees ever been so large? The street so quiet? Pam's footsteps sounded hollow and ringing to her ears, as if she were walking over an empty grave. She felt as if the reflecting windows of the larger homes she was passing were staring at her. There was the house where Carol used to live. They had walked to the corner to wait for the school bus together. Did her parents still live there?

She slowed as she crossed the street and came to her block. The house on the corner still had the hedge around its large yard. The house still looked the same, with a porch that ran the length of the front and partway down one side. Only the porch furniture was different.

The next house was home. She stood on the sidewalk looking toward the tall, Victorian house. It was almost hidden among trees, but still she saw the ruin. The paint had peeled, so that the once white porches and trim looked scabby and ancient. Weeds grew in cracks of the driveway. Shrubs had grown tall, the trees enormous. They were all still living, thank God, hiding the house from the neighbors, from the street. She wondered if complaints had been issued. A crumbling house in a neat, upper-class neighborhood. Why hadn't Beth had it painted?

But why was she expecting Beth to see that it was done? It was enough that Beth had seen to it the grass was cut and the taxes paid.

She walked up the driveway and paused. The three-car garage was now visible, and she wondered if the cars were still there. Her mom and dad's cars, and her own, a 1966 VW her dad had helped her buy. He had co-signed a loan for her at the bank, but of course she had known if she couldn't make the payments, he'd make them for her. It was her first step toward independence. She remembered vividly the day they went to the bank, and how excited she was when he drove her back to the dealer's to get her new-used car. Afterwards they'd had lunch together at Alfred's, the only time in her life she'd had lunch alone with her daddy.

How could Beth think she would have stabbed to death, only weeks later, the person who meant love and security to her? It hurt more that Beth thought her guilty. It was Beth who mattered. Long ago it had also been Craig.

She rarely thought of Craig now, but she thought of him as she passed beneath the tree where they used to park and talk.

She went to the small door in the enclosed breezeway that joined the garage to the house, and unlocked the door. She looked into the gloomy darkness of the long garage, and reached for the light switch at the side of the door. The garage remained dark. With lightning-bolt surprise she realized she'd expected lights at the touch of a switch. Of course the utilities weren't on, and wouldn't be, probably, for several days.

She stepped into the silence of the garage, her eyes adjusting to the muted light. The cars were still there. The smell in the garage was cavelike, damp and earthy. On a wall hung the old garden tools, dark shapes in the shadows. Leaning against the wall, where it had always stood, was the axe. It was one of the weapons she had long planned to take with her into the attic. In prison she had lain night after night, year after year, planning every step. The doll would never leave the attic. Pam would carry with her the axe, and the pruners with the sharp pincers. She would chop the doll to bits, there in the attic. She would use the pruners to sever fingers, even, to make sure that nothing of it could ever regenerate. In her nightmares she had seen the hacked pieces of the doll moving back together, like a video running backwards. It must never happen. She would carry it from the attic in pieces, and scatter them through the city, putting an arm in one dump, the pieces of a leg in another.

She gathered the tools, the axe, the pruners, then, pausing, she also took a smaller hatchet. With the selection securely in her arms she left the garage.

She walked through the old breezeway, to the door into the utility room of the house. It too was locked. She searched until she found the right key.

There was more light in the utility room. Surprisingly, it looked as clean and neat as Alice always kept it. On a second glance the layer of dust was so uniform it seemed only part of the overall design, a slight dimming of colors. In the corners of the ceiling, though, spiders had built homes. They didn't worry her.

On the rack hung ironed shirts and a couple of small dresses. The ironing board was still standing with the iron tipped up. It was plugged into a socket that was woven in cobwebs.

Kit's dresses. She remembered them so well. One, a floral print on a white background, had a tiered skirt. Kit had looked like a doll in it.

Pam went on into the kitchen. It was less occupied than the utility room. Only one web in a ceiling corner. Strangely, the spiders seemed more like companions than something to fear. She was not so alone in the house.

She had to find lighting before dark fell. It had taken her an hour to walk from Beth's, and twilight bathed the backyard in mauve. The house was growing darker by the moment.

She put down her shoulder bag and suitcase and began to look through drawers for a flashlight. But she would need more than that. She needed a lamp. Was there a lamp anywhere? She didn't recall there being any lamps for emergency power outage in this house. Gramma Vee had always kept a couple of lamps, she recalled. One of them sat on the mantel.

She finally went into the dining room for candles. They were still in the drawer, along with the box of matches.

There, too, was a flashlight. She tested it, and found to her surprise that the batteries still had some power. They seemed almost as good as new, though they could fade away at any moment. She would have to hurry, before the light was gone.

Carrying the axe, hatchet, and flashlight, she went through murky halls, pausing briefly at the powder-room door. It was still standing open, but the room was dark, the vanity chair a skeletal outline. She didn't waste light on it. She closed the door then hurried on up the stairs. Without turning on the flashlight she saw the stain on the carpet where Kit had lain. It was like a black hole, and seemed to cover the middle of the hall. The wall was stained with dark blotches where moist red blood had clung the last time she had passed along this hall.

She stepped carefully across the stained carpet and went on to the attic door. The bolt was still in place. It shrieked as she slid it back, slicing through her nerves like a shock wave. The house, afterwards, throbbed with the silence.

She pulled the door open cautiously. She had known the stairway would be dark, and she turned on the flashlight as the door revealed the slanting tunnellike access to the attic. The doll could have been at the foot of the stairs, waiting. But the stairs were empty, only the dust was there, and more webs. There were no footsteps in the dust, no small tracks such as the ones that had puzzled Jefferson and which Pam could never talk to him about.

She climbed the steps, making a conscious effort to move in silence, on tiptoes. Slowly she advanced, the light beam preceding her. Beth had said she brought the doll into the attic. Where had she left it? Pam had never asked.

She came to the top of the steps. The attic received a dying light through the window. Pamela stood still. The silence was broken by faint creaks of wood, somewhere. They could have been caused by a natural settling of the house as the outside air cooled. Or by something that moved, walking across old boards.

She stooped and laid down the awkward load as quietly as she could. Her gaze moved intently across the floor, watching for movement. She kept the hatchet. She could handle it and the flashlight at the same time, and it would at least give her something with which to protect herself.

She straightened. Every movement now was filled with a tense caution, and fear began to eat at her, icing her skin, pulling her hair tight.

It was here, somewhere. As an animal picks up odors, she sensed the presence of the doll.

Pam shined the flashlight across the floor. The round dimming beam touched upon boxes, the old cribs with the mattresses on edge, and the chest of drawers.

Puzzled, she walked to the end of the attic, looking. She opened the drawers of the chest, but they were either empty or contained old clothes, tablecloths, even a couple of pairs of curtains. She looked into the cribs and beneath them. As darkness replaced the mauve twilight at the attic window, she continued to search. The small alcoves were empty except for more webs, more spiders that had found a place where they had been long undisturbed. She looked again, moving more quickly, going from chest to cribs, and even to boxes. The flashlight was fading. She felt as if she were going gradually blind, that she couldn't see what was so plainly in front of her. Where was the doll? Finally, she lifted the light to the attic window. It was closed.

She went to it. The floor was roughened and warped in an area of at least three feet, in a semi-circle, as if rain had swept in undeterred many times over the years, ruining the wood. The window had been open, sometime, far more than the two inches Pam remembered her attorneys talking about.

With the flashlight tucked under her arm, with darkness hugging her back, with the creaks continuing like soft cries through the house, Pam put her hands on the closed window.

She pushed upward, and to her surprise the window moved easily, quietly, as if it were often used.

She pushed it up, opened it as far as it would go. There was no screen. She leaned forward, looking out. The roof sloped directly below the window, and there at the corner, in the glow of her flashlight, was the trellis. Also, there was a lower roof, the one that joined the house to the garage. And, she knew, another trellis.

An exit. Not difficult at all. Her attorneys had carefully researched that before they had used it as a defense.

An exit that *it* must have found.

Pam pulled back and slowly, thoughtfully closed the window. Where was it now? The doll, that strange creature made somewhere, long ago, by the hands of a man, or a woman. Or perhaps not. Perhaps its creator was part of the horrors of an unknown that was not accessible to the human mind.

She reached up to lock the window.

There was no lock.

She remembered the defense. Her attorney had found the attic window had no lock. Something she had never known, and which she had nearly forgotten.

Four

Pamela went back to the top of the attic stairs, her eyes continuing a desperate sweep of the attic. Large patches of shadows loomed like black caves dropping into the earth through the walls and floors, moving as her light moved. She directed the flashlight against the darkness, leaving other darknesses. They followed always behind her, edging against her like mute beings from hell. She had a feeling the doll was still here, within the moving darkness, waiting for her. Or had been here only recently. Her senses could not be that wrong. As if it had known she was coming, as if it had known what she had planned for it all these years, it was prepared to meet her in a setting in which it had waited and thrived. But although she felt its presence, she could not see it.

She started to leave, then carefully checked the attic again, looking into drawers, into the cribs, into every hiding place. She threw glances behind her at every move, hearing sounds so subtle they must have come from inside her own head, or from deep within the wood between the floors.

She finally had to accept the truth. The doll was not in the attic.

She went to the stairwell, cautiously carrying with her the hatchet. Unnerved, perplexed, she went down the stairs. The doll had been taken away by someone. She thought of Beth. Would Beth have come back and taken it? Or . . . it could simply have been stolen. Someone could have climbed into the window. Perhaps years ago at the trial that idea had been given to someone who came and took the doll. Only the doll. Nothing else seemed to be missing from the attic.

There was no other exit. The attic door had still been securely bolted from the other side.

A sudden and terrifying thought occurred to her. The doll had gone out of the window on its own, and entered the house somewhere below. A second floor window. Like a fly it had scaled walls, and found a way in, and was now waiting for her.

In the dark, the macrocosm in which it animated, it waited.

Pam had to have light. It was a matter of life, or death. She needed full light, everywhere in the house, something more powerful than a flashlight with weakening batteries.

She paused to carefully bolt the attic door, then hurried through the dark halls. Downstairs she checked the front door, but the deadbolts were still activated. No one, nothing, had entered here. She had the keys in her pocket. She half-ran through the house to the door out of the kitchen. It too was locked.

Still carrying the hatchet and the flashlight, she went to the garage and got into her old VW. Dark shadows followed her every step, scattering away like demons when she whirled the flashlight's weakening yellowish beam upon them. With immense relief she closed and locked the doors of her old car. Instead of feeling safe, she felt trapped. Like a frightened rat in a tin can.

After all this time would the car even start?

The key was still in the switch. The house seemed oddly free from burglaries. Only the doll was missing. Perhaps it was the haunted atmosphere, it filled the darknesses everywhere around her. That haunted feeling that someone was there, watching. Some aspect of the dead, mutated from the living persons they had been, unable to leave, waiting for something or someone to set them free from the shadows. Perhaps that very ambience protected the house from burglary.

Though she had a sense of being surrounded, of being haunted, she had no feeling that her loved ones were near. In spirit she had released them long ago, to all the mysteries that lie beyond.

Now, she was desperate only to save herself from the darkness. That darkness in which she knew Zenoa lived.

335

Holding her breath, she turned the switch and pressed the starter button.

The engine ground slowly a couple of times, almost stopped, then speeded. It started and settled to a purr. She answered with a half-uttered prayer, a mixed groan and part laughter. If the tires weren't rotten with standing in one place for so long, she at least had transportation.

She pulled the lights on. They still worked too, filling this end of the garage with light. Leaving the engine running, she got out and opened the garage door. Aware of darkness around the corner, of darkness beneath the trees and behind every un-trimmed shrub, even beneath the cars, she ran back to the safety of the interior of the car where again she locked the door.

Her hands trembled as she backed out. Could she remember how to drive after so long? What if she were stopped by a policeman? No driver's license, a license plate dated 1969.

She backed around in the cracked, weedy driveway and turned, heading toward the street, praying the old supermarket was still there, blocks away.

The car moved down the street with only a slight deviation from a straight line. Her hands clutched the wheel tightly. She tried to relax. When she met another car she pulled as near to the curb as she could and when one came up behind her she prayed it wasn't a cop.

The supermarket was not only still in the shopping center, it was brightly lighted. It had expanded into something called Super Store, open twenty-four hours a day. The parking lot was about half full, and she was careful to take the first spot she came to. Better to walk across the entire lot than try to go up and park where she might in her nervousness scrape the shining fender of another car.

She entered the store feeling as if all eyes were turned toward her. But as she paused and looked carefully about, she saw that no one watched her. *Don't be paranoid,* she warned herself.

Tonight she needed only a lamp and batteries. But after she found the flashlight batteries, the lamp and a bottle of oil to fuel it, she remembered she'd had no food since she'd left prison. She wasn't hungry, but she might not be leaving the house for several days. Not until she located what she had come home for. She hurriedly gathered oranges, apples, a carton of milk, and a loaf of bread. During her years in prison she had finally arrived at thinking not only of her family, and herself, but other creatures. By the time she had lived in something that resembled animal pens she began to feel as they surely felt. An animal yearns too, toward the wide open spaces for which it was intended. Freedom to live its own life, as nature intended. Nature gone awry. Trapped in her own cage she had stopped eating meat. Those creatures, abused and exploited, as if they were on earth only for the use of mankind, came to be kindred souls.

For protein she chose a can of beans and a jar of peanut butter, and the bread for grain. She needed nothing beyond that.

Tomorrow, or when she was free and could move on, then she would stop for other food. Fresh vegetables. Potatoes. Milk. Eggs. She had nothing against using products that did not destroy or abuse animals. But she shuddered as she passed the packaged meats. She thought of the billions of live animals killed each day, and she felt removed from the kind of society that could still live and eat without really thinking of what it was doing, or managed to justify it by one wrong way of thinking after the other.

It was time intelligent humans were controlled by genetics, not murder.

She went to the checkout stand and stood in line. The magazines on the newsracks weren't new to her. They came into the prison daily. The news media, television, books, magazines, had kept the outside world no stranger to her.

She paid for her purchases and left. Sitting in her car, in the brightly lighted parking lot, she watched the shoppers enter the store and leave. She could go to a motel, and perhaps she should. It would be better than facing the dark house with only her feeble lamp. But her suitcase was at home.

She remembered suddenly there would be no water in the house, except in the bathroom tanks. She returned to the store and bought four bottles of water, all she felt she could carry in one trip. She returned to her car and drove away without waiting to analyze her situation further, or to allow herself to give in to her fears of going back into the house.

337

Home, now, was only a word, a location, a house with no heart. It was a place of horror. A place she remembered with tortured feelings. As she drove slowly through the streets she was torn by her mixed feelings. The memories of a great life with her family was overlaid by her last view of them, and of the house.

At times, over the years, she had begun to wonder if perhaps the prosecution was right, and in falling and striking her head she had risen a different person Perhaps it was she who had actually killed. Then, after the stabbing of Kit, Nicky, Mom, and Daddy, she had gone back upstairs in a daze, and suddenly regained consciousness. Consciousness with no memory.

What did she actually know of the doll? Had she seen it move but that one time? Had that been part of the deranged reality of her mind? Was it she who was dangerous, rather than an old doll onto which she had foisted her own crimes?

No. She knew what she had seen.

She had to find the doll and destroy it. It must be done.

Junie, who had murdered her abusive husband and was serving a life sentence, had told Pam when she was released, "Go and forget it. Don't ever think about it. That's what I've done. It's the only way I can live without losing my mind."

That was all Pam had ever heard Junie say about the tragedy that had put her behind bars. She too had been alienated from her family, just as Pam was.

She had left the garage door open. She shouldn't have, she now thought, because the door from the garage to the house was unlocked. For twenty-four years she had been used to having doors locked for her. She would have to be more careful.

She drove into the garage. The car lights outlined rusty old garden tools hanging on the walls, and opened up the dark corner. From the corner of her eye she saw a movement, dark and shadowy, small, off to the right. It seemed to dart beyond the station wagon in the next space.

Pam sat still, her hands frozen to the steering wheel. She stared into the dark end of the garage, beyond the two cars, the closed doors. Nothing. Nothing more.

It could have been a cat, or a neighbor's dog. Or it could have been the doll. It was that size, small and quick.

Her throat tight and dry with fear, she sat, lights shining on the wall ahead, and in the corner. Then it seemed she noticed a dimming. The battery was old, and running down.

She had to revive her courage. She turned off the lights. The darkness in the garage at first seemed so intense that strange, dark figures from the nether world of darkness were almost visible. Spots in her eyes, she reminded herself. Not something made of darkness, of worlds not visible to the light-oriented humans. In prison as she lay with her mind wandering on those long nights when she couldn't sleep, she had allowed herself to wonder how many worlds were entwined, the world of light unable to see the worlds of darkness. Had the doll risen somehow from that other world, and taken on the half-soul of some human to whom it had belonged? A creature with no conscious, who had no compunctions against doing whatever it had to do to get what it wanted?

"It wants my room," Kit had said. "She wants my room."

Perhaps she had wanted everything in the house. Perhaps she had wanted it for herself, as Kit had said. Hadn't the doll always gone down to the powder room? Why? To admire her beauty, to enhance her face by applying makeup. As someone to whom she had belonged once did. The doll, made of that other world of darkness, and now thrust into the world of light, possessor of something from someone . . .

Pam moved. When thoughts of the doll, of other worlds not visible to the human eye, and only partly visible to the human psyche, possessed her, she sat and stared. In the library where she had worked for so many years, Junie would say something to bring her out of her intense mental world and back to reality. Junie never touched her. Not once in their twelve years of working together had Junie reached out to her. Like Pam, she had lived in her own world. Perhaps she too had seen those worlds beyond darkness, the nether world. Perhaps only the killers of the world of light knew for certain of the existence of those terrible worlds so easy to step into and so difficult to rise from.

She reached for the flashlight and turned it on. Its light too was dying, but it had to last until she got into the house.

She got out of the car and shined it toward the other end of the garage. She thought she heard something move, but couldn't be sure. Wind had started to blow, as if another storm were coming up, and the movement of tree limbs obliterated softer sounds. She had to take a chance nothing was there, and close the garage door.

She went to the door. Light from a street lamp half a block away barely touched the driveway in patches no larger than her hands. They too moved, like light flashes in the eyes, as the tree limbs swayed in the wind. She felt reluctant to close herself into the dark garage. Looking over her shoulder, seeing movements in shadows as her flashlight beam touched feebly upon one thing or another, she decided to leave the door open. If a cat or dog had slipped in, it would leave later. She could lock the door into the house.

She quickly gathered her packages from the car and went through the breezeway to the house. She closed the door, put her purchases down, and locked the door. Then she paused to look at the doorknob. It was a new experience, locking a door. She felt she should have some kind of emotion about it, a sense of being in control of her own life, or something, but she felt nothing. She didn't even feel safe. The door had been unlocked during the time she'd been gone.

She went on into the kitchen, put the lamp in the middle of the kitchen table. She placed the flashlight so that its pale yellow beam touched the lamp. Behind her, around her, darkness moved closer, like the clouds that were bringing the wind.

On a dark and stormy night . . .

The thought came to her mind unexpectedly, and she giggled. But she was frightened. More afraid than she'd been in the years in prison. She wanted to look behind her, but she hurried instead and filled the lamp. She fumbled with the little box of matches, spilling, gathering up again, and finally getting one lit. She touched its flame to the lamp wick and sighed in relief as the flame swelled. She put the globe on.

It made a soft, yellow light, but it reached from corner to corner in the kitchen. She looked around, saw the old desk in the corner that still had a writing pad and pen waiting for a grocery list to be made. On the wall above the desk was the wood hanger that held incoming and outgoing mail. Letters were in both. Strange, she thought, that no one had ever taken them out.

She put fresh batteries in the flashlight, then she sat down, aware at last that her legs were trembling with exhaustion. The flashlight's beam was a piercing white, and cut through the dimmer lamp light like a laser.

Trying to ignore dark rooms off the hallway, hatchet tucked under her arm, she carried the lamp, flashlight, and suitcase up the stairway to the second floor hall. She paused, listening. Wind rattled a window somewhere on the other side of the house. Something loose tapped softly, a shingle, perhaps a tree limb grown over to touch the house. The trees had changed in twenty-four years, hovering much larger and closer to the house as if to enwrap it and protect it.

She used her shoulder to push open her half-closed bedroom door, and stopped almost in shock.

Pink sheets on her bed. She had almost forgotten. Pink sheets and a thin white blanket. She had tossed them back when Kit entered her room that night, and had not returned to the room until now. The bed was just as she had left it. Dust darkened the folds. Light had faded the colors. But otherwise it was as she had left it.

The walls were still holding the two old posters she'd put up behind her bed, though the thumb tack had come out of the corner of one, letting it fold down limply, hiding faces whose names she was no longer sure of.

She placed the lamp on the dresser, next to the little ceramic dish with the lid that once held earrings. Slowly she lifted the lid. They were still there. One pair, shaped like a flower, in delicate purple stones with a pink crystal in the middle, had been her favorites. Craig had given them to her.

Where was he now? She hadn't heard of him since the trial. He was probably married, with children. Living with someone else the dream he'd had with her. "Three kids," he'd said. "One for you, one for me, and one to kick around." She remembered well how she had giggled. "Oh Craig, you idiot." Yet their dreams were serious, she had thought then, even if they did have a few gross jokes now and then.

She had forgotten to bring up a jug of water. She felt grimy and dusty, and in need of a bath, even if it were only out of a jug. But she couldn't face leaving her room. With the door closed, the hatchet always within reach, she felt safer than she had in so many, many years, as if in being here she had subconsciously reverted to the girl she had been.

She looked into the closet.

It was empty. All her clothes had been removed. Puzzled, she stood looking at the empty shelves where her shoes had been, and the rod where even the hangers had been taken away. Hadn't Beth said she had touched nothing? That she'd left the house exactly as it was? She remembered Gramma Vee had brought her some things from her room, but she hadn't brought it all, certainly.

She left the closet and returned to the bedroom.

She began going through the drawers in the dresser and chest. The drawer that contained sheets was still neat, everything as it had been. But the drawer that held her nightgowns and pajamas was in disarray. She stood staring, puzzled.

Unlike the drawers of bedding, this one had been rummaged through. Clothing had been removed and thrown back. There was nothing neat about the drawer.

Hastily she pulled out drawers that had contained underwear, stockings, delicate night things she had liked when she was young. Empty, all of them, except the underwear drawer contained one pair of panties.

She picked up the lamp and hatchet, and went cautiously out into the hall. Her eyes were drawn immediately to the dark stain on the carpet, and the dark teardroplike stains on the walls. She pulled her stare away and faced the door across the hall.

It was closed, as if the last person to enter the room had tried to shut it off from the rest of the house. Pam wondered, had all of Kit's clothes been taken out too? While downstairs in the utility room some had been left hanging?

She touched the door knob. For a moment it seemed she could hear Kit, humming as she sat at her desk drawing, or painting with water colors or the oils Nicky had given her for her last birthday. Yet she hadn't hummed after that birthday. Not after the doll had entered their lives.

Pam turned the knob and pushed the door open. It swung inward silently, unlike the other doors she had opened in the house. As if its hinges had stayed young while the others grew old.

She entered the room.

It seemed not to have changed. Except . . . someone had made the bed again, pulled the bedspread up neatly, and arranged the pillow shams. Kit would have left it unmade that night she died.

Pam opened the closet door and felt a jolt of dismay. Kit's clothes had been taken down and thrown into a heap on the floor, pushed back into the corner. Her own clothes hung on the racks, and her shoes were neatly arranged on the shelves.

Miniskirts. Short dresses, small, made for a petite, girlish figure. Sweaters, jeans, a couple of robes. *Hers.* In Kit's closet. Why? Who had put them here?

She backed away without touching them, as if they were venomous.

Who had done this? Beth had not entered the house after the deaths but twice, briefly, she'd said. She had first run in to see them, to see for herself. She couldn't believe they were dead. She had disobeyed the warnings of the police, and entered the house anyway, but she had gone only as far as the hall before she ran out again. She had not entered the house since except to leave the doll. Pamela believed her. "It's been closed. Waiting for you. It's yours, Pam, I don't want it. I'll never go in that house again."

Gramma Vee had gone in only to pack a suitcase for Pam. She wouldn't have done this.

Pam slowly closed the closet door. Someone had been here. Someone other than Gramma Vee and Beth. They would never have done this strange and somehow horrible thing, moving Pam's clothes into Kit's closet, throwing Kit's clothes on the floor.

Pam doubted the detectives who had gone through the house would have done such a thing.

But someone had.

Why make something of nothing, she asked herself. It was probably something the police had done, after all. Maybe they'd removed her things and looked them over then forgotten where they belonged.

Anyway, she had to stop being spooked by everything. Every sound, every shadow, every item moved from where she'd left it became a source of worry. So shut up and go to bed.

She returned to her room, closing the door firmly.

From the suitcase she took a pair of cotton pajamas and put them on. She'd rather go to bed with an unwashed body and face then go back out into that dark, haunted hall.

Quickly she remade the bed with old, musty sheets from a drawer.

She turned the lamp wick low and got into bed. She sighed, closed her eyes, and let herself sink into the soft, old bed.

Oh God. If only she could wipe away the past twenty-five years and again be a seventeen-year-old with a little sister and brother and mom and dad, and a married sister who was expecting her first baby.

If only.

Five

Beth checked the table. Even for an impromptu supper everything had to be right. She had always loved feeding her kids. It had hurt when they each decided to move out before they were married, even though she knew in part of her heart how important it was for them to grow up, grow away, become fully independent. Knowing logically, and feeling instinctively were like trying to be two different people. It was easier for Ross, she thought. He hadn't stayed at home with them while they were growing up.

Justin came in through the kitchen door, said, "Hi, Mom, what's up?" gave her a kiss on the cheek, asked, "Where's Dad?" even though he knew Dad was always in the den watching the news on television at this time of day. Then he went on through the kitchen and toward the den, and Beth heard their voices though not their words. She knew Ross would say nothing about Pamela. That was up to her.

They were going to eat in the kitchen, her favorite place. It was a long, double-duty kitchen, with a dinette in one end. The round, oak table sat in front of double windows that looked out on her flower gardens in the backyard. Priscilla curtains were folded back. Potted plants sat on a low, narrow table in front of the window. She had opened the windows. The day had been lovely, between showers. The overhang of the roof protected the windows from rain, should it happen again. Beth could see it threatening in the west, thin streaks of lightning darting through black clouds, and she thought of Pamela. Surely she would go to a motel tonight, and not to that terrible place where there was not even any electricity.

When she told Ross that Pamela had unexpectedly shown up on the doorstep he had asked, "Where is she now?" And she told him, with guilt edging into her like bitter gall, "She went home. She wanted to go home." But she remembered that she hadn't offered her own home, this night, the first night Pam was out of prison.

As she cooked supper she had carried on an internal dialogue with that illogical part of herself that she didn't understand very well. *You should have asked her to stay. No, never, no, no, no. You're being selfish, Beth. She's your sister. Yes, but . . . she murdered my family. Our family. No, she didn't. Yes, she did, no one else could have.*

With Justin in the den with Ross, and Tresa on her way over, Beth began to feel better. Perhaps she had clung to her kids more than she otherwise would have. Maybe if Pamela hadn't destroyed most of what made up her world, she wouldn't be the nervous, clinging mother that she was. She tried very hard to accept the young man and woman Tresa and Justin had chosen to marry, but she had doubts. Doubts she didn't even share with Ross. She found herself wishing at times that living together before marriage was still in vogue, but she didn't really want it that way either. Yet often as she lay awake at night she wondered. Was Blake all that he seemed to be? Of course he was. He and Tresa had met in college. He had grown up in a suburb on the north side of the city. His family was well established in the area, and had brought him up with a good, solid religious background. He had received his business degree this spring, and now had a good job just minutes from the house they were having built. He was such a solid young man that wildness in youth seemed not to apply to him at all. Who, Blake? Ross had said with a laugh when Beth had once wondered what kind of things he might have done in his teenage years. How many unprotected sexual encounters, in this time of sex being so dangerous. Ross had laughed outright. Blake? He's probably a virgin. God, Beth hoped so. Beth hadn't asked Tresa. She wouldn't presume to be *that* nosy.

But . . . had he been tested for AIDS?

Tresa and Blake had dated for a year before they came home

one evening and announced they were getting married. "But we don't want a large wedding, Mom, Dad," Tresa said, almost apologetically. "Just the family. In the fall. When the leaves are their most colorful. We want to furnish our house instead of spending money on a honeymoon, or wedding, or anything like that." Then they began to talk eagerly of the house they were going to have built.

As if it were a disease and very contagious, Justin had brought the lovely girl he'd met recently and said they too were getting married. Nor did they want anyone but family. In this case it would be only Justin's family because Zenoa had none.

She was a beautiful girl with long reddish blond hair, large brown eyes, a slight overbite that was charming rather than unattractive. She was so soft spoken one had to listen carefully to understand her. Justin was madly in love with her, watching her every move as if he couldn't believe that she was real. Beth felt she had seen Zenoa before. Her name . . . but no, if she had ever met Zenoa, she wouldn't have forgotten. She was so — so — Ladylike? Delicate? Old-fashioned, perhaps. The way one thought of the nineteenth-century girls. Except *girl* was not the right word. Not for Zenoa. Woman? No, not that either. Young lady. Yes.

After meeting Justin's girlfriend and hearing of their wedding plans, so soon, Ross said, "If you're going to worry about anyone, Beth, maybe you should worry about that girl."

"Zenoa?" She was surprised. Ross, who never criticized anyone or worried about the people the kids dated, wondered about that lovely person? "Why?"

He stood that night looking at the wall, his pajama top half pulled on, his smooth chest bare. "Something about her," he said. "Where's she from? Why doesn't she have a family? Everybody has a family."

"Maybe she grew up in an orphanage." Beth was surprised further by finding herself on the defensive. A lovely girl like Zenoa was just what she wanted for Justin. She worried about him so much. He had dated so many girls, starting when he was fifteen, and some of them had been absolute horrors, it seemed to her. Calling him at all hours, clinging to him in front of everyone. That he had finally found one who didn't hang on

347

to him so much was probably why he had fallen so hard.

She quizzed Justin a little when they had lunch together a few days later. "Where did you meet her?"

"Oh, just around, Mom. At a club where I hang out sometimes. Isn't she great, Mom?" His eyes glowed. She wondered if Ross had ever looked at her like that. For just a heartbeat she knew fear, and dread. What if Ross were right and Zenoa was not as good as her first impression had been? What if she didn't love Justin as much as he loved her?

"Where's she from, Justin?"

"She's lived all over, Mom. Her dad was in the service. They lived in Hawaii, but her dad died of cancer and her mother died a few months later. It left Zenoa alone."

"What on earth is she doing here, so far from home?"

"It wasn't really her home, Mom. As I said, she's lived all over."

She cut the questions off, seeing irritation on his face. Their wedding now was only a week away. She would leave it up to Justin whether or not his Aunt Pamela should be invited.

Tresa came in from the front hall just as Beth put the last glass of ice water on the table.

"Hi, Mom."

"Hello, sweetheart."

They kissed cheeks while Tresa eyed the table. "Looks good. I'm starving."

Beth laughed. "Don't you ever cook for yourself?"

"Sure I do. I made pizzas and salad last night for Blake and me."

"Frozen pizza."

"Sure. What else? Why are we having dinner tonight? And why couldn't I bring Blake along?"

"It's not dinner, it's supper. And I needed to talk to you and Justin. Alone."

"Isn't Dad going to eat?"

"I mean alone without Blake and Zenoa."

"What on earth about?"

"If you'll get the guys in here, I'll tell you."

"All this mystery!"

She went back toward the hall. Beth watched her go. She was

348

dressed in clothing she had worn to work, a loose, thin jacket over a mid-calf skirt with a slit up the back that allowed glimpses of her nicely shaped legs halfway up her thighs. Beth shrugged. Back in the sixties she had worn flower-child clothes, long, full skirts, casual blouses. But what difference did it make? The sexual mores of the sixties had been much more lenient than they were now. At least she assumed, and hoped, they had been. Sex was too dangerous now. Mother nature at work, no matter how people tried to deny it. Nature had a way of cleaning up after itself, balancing carefully, keeping things under control even if her way seemed horribly cruel. It didn't keep Beth from worrying about her kids. She wanted them healthy and happy.

She took the hot buns out of the oven and turned them out onto a plate. She brushed butter on the browned tops. The fragrance of hot, fresh bread filled the kitchen.

They came in, and both Tresa and Justin moaned in delight, sniffing the air.

"Fresh baked bread," Justin said. "Why did I ever leave home?"

"And baked it herself too, I'll bet," Tresa said. "Mom would never buy that frozen stuff, ready to bake."

Beth smiled. Actually, she had. After she'd called both kids and insisted they come for supper, she'd run down to the store and bought frozen bread and a couple of other things. Even the meat had come out of the freezer and been thawed in the microwave. There were some things the kids just didn't have to know.

They sat down in their old places. Justin with his back to the windows, and Tresa facing him. They ate the way they had since they developed appetites at age thirteen or so. Especially Justin. Tresa, having grown figure-conscious in her teen years didn't shovel it in quite as vigorously as did Justin. Beth paused in her own eating just to watch her son. It filled her heart with an indescribable joy to watch him eat. He had grown up into a broad-shouldered, flat-bellied man, and she thought he was very handsome. Far more handsome than Blake. Blake was nice, but he was the kind of guy who blended in with the crowd, someone most people would never look at twice.

"Mom, I wish you'd teach Zen how to cook," Justin said unexpectedly, "If you don't, we'll have to come home and eat."

"Don't tell her that," Tresa said, "or she certainly won't teach Zenoa how to cook."

"Can't Zenoa cook?" Ross asked, as if he had no sense of humor. Where Zenoa was concerned, it seemed he didn't. Beth threw him an irritated look.

Tresa said, "I'm surprised they've even gotten that far from bed." There was a bitter edge to her voice that brought Beth's attention to her. What was wrong?

Justin bristled. He sat back in his chair and glared at Tresa. "Hey! Zenoa's not that kind of girl. She insists on waiting until we're married. No kidding." He grinned. "Why do you think we're getting married so fast?"

Tresa let out a breath that was more snort than sigh. "Honestly, Justin," she hissed, in her former way of scolding him when he'd done or said something that disgusted her. "We're at the table with Mom and Dad."

Beth said, "It isn't as though we've never heard of sex before."

"Well," Tresa said.

Justin asked, "What's this gathering for, anyway? I was going to take Zenoa to the movies tonight. If I hurry, maybe I can take her later."

Beth glanced at Ross, but he was giving her no help. Of course she hadn't expected him to. If she had listened to him in the past, the kids would have kept in closer touch with Pamela. They would even have gone to the prison to see her, at least once a year. Her name would have been mentioned more freely. Zenoa and Blake would have been told about her. By Beth.

She said, "Do Blake and Zenoa know what happened to my parents and brother and sisters?"

Both Justin and Tresa gave her their sober, silent attention. For several seconds neither answered, then Justin asked, "Why?"

"Because Pamela came home today."

Tresa cried, "She did?"

Beth nodded. "I didn't know she was being released. She came to the door, rang the bell. I was shocked, of course. At first I hardly recognized her. Not that she's changed that much, but I just wasn't expecting to see her."

"God no," Justin said. "A murderer right on the doorstep."

"That's rather blunt, Justin," Ross said.

"What did you do?" Tresa asked. "I mean, why isn't she here?"

"Here!" Justin demanded. "Are you crazy? I seem to remember that Aunt Pam killed a bunch of people. Mom would be out of her mind to ask her to come in, wouldn't she?"

Ross started to say something again, but stopped.

Beth said, "It's not that I'm afraid of her, Justin. It's — well — I don't know. She's my sister. She's — well, perhaps I am afraid of her. Certainly I can never forget what she's done. She destroyed our family. Even our grandmother Virginia committed suicide over those murders."

"What caused her to go off the wall like that?" Justin asked. "Was she isolated from the family? Angry? Had something happened?"

"No. Pam was outgoing, friendly, happy. It was a complete shock." She toyed with the proper arrangement of flatware beside her plate, placing her glass just so, unaware of the actions of her hands. She'd never told the kids much about Pam at all. Only that she was in prison for killing four members of the family.

Tresa said, "I read the transcripts of her trial just recently. I'm not sure she's guilty."

"What?" Justin cried. "This is the first I've heard of that."

Tresa said nothing. Beth was relieved when Ross spoke up.

"It couldn't have been anyone else, Tresa."

Beth patted the back of Tresa's hand. "I know you would like to think her innocent."

Justin asked, "Why do you think she's innocent, Tres?"

After a pause, Tresa said, "She was in the attic, and she fell and struck her head on a chest of drawers. She blacked out, for a couple of hours. When she came to, she went downstairs and found them. It just has the ring of truth."

"Maybe," Justin said, "she really doesn't remember. Or recognizes it as a good excuse, anyway."

351

Tresa shook her head. "There's more that hasn't been told. I just have a feeling."

"The issue is," Ross said, "your mother was concerned about Blake and Zenoa, and whether Pamela having come home would cause any problems."

"It's a hell of a time for her to show up," Justin said. "It would have been better if she'd waited until after my wedding. But Zenoa accepts everyone. She loves everybody. I don't anticipate any problems. I never really told her about Aunt Pam, except there's this crazy lady who's my aunt. We were looking at the old house. Zenoa likes it. I told her it belongs to my aunt, who's in prison. But I didn't tell her it was for stabbing the family with an ice pick — in that house."

Beth said, "She came to my door, unexpectedly. I had no idea she'd been released. I guess I should have asked her to stay. But I couldn't, I just couldn't."

"So what happened?" Tresa asked. "She must have wanted to see you, or she wouldn't have come."

"She only wanted the keys to the house, that was all."

"You mean she went back *there?*" Justin asked.

"Yes."

"Of course you know you have to meet her," Ross said. "And so do Zenoa and Blake."

Justin tipped his chair onto its back legs. Five years ago Beth would have told him to sit down, but she had given up. He would always tip his chair.

"So my bride has to meet my crazy aunt, right? Right on the eve of my wedding, so to speak."

Beth asked, "When would you suggest? We can have her over to dinner, or wait until Sunday and the wedding."

Tresa said, "Probably the dinner first would be better."

Justin shrugged and stood up.

"Whenever," he said.

Though his words were light, there was still a strangely intense look on his face. With his thumbs hooked in his back pockets he looked out at the birdbath where a bright red cardinal was taking a vigorous bath. But he seemed not to be seeing the birds or the flowers.

Beth wished fervently that Pamela had not come home. Why

hadn't she just gone away, and started a new life somewhere no one would be hurt? She didn't like the look on Justin's face. She wondered if he were more worried about Zenoa's reaction to Pam than he had let on.

Then Justin said something totally unexpected.

"I'd been thinking about trying to rent the house, because Zenoa likes it so well. But if she's back, there no chance of that."

Six

Justin drove through the streets toward the old apartment house where Zenoa lived. He had tried to get her to move in with him. At least he had a decent place. But she had insisted in staying in that old dump that looked as if it probably had rats running up and down the steep stairs at night. She lived somewhere on the fifth floor, he thought, but he wasn't sure, because she would never let him take her up to her apartment. Tonight though, he was going up there whether she liked it or not. This business of not having a phone where he could reach her made it too damned hard to get in touch with her. "I'll call you," she had said, from the beginning, with that incredibly sweet smile, and that soft voice. Just the memory sent thrills of a million shades through him. He adored the girl. He worshipped her.

When he met her, that night hardly more than a month ago, he thought he had seen everything and felt everything, but he was wrong. He was twenty-three-years-old and had been dating girls since he was fourteen. Earlier than his folks knew. He used to meet them in the mall, take them to a movie, and hold hands. Thrill, thrill. He began to sneak kisses, and they were just as willing as he.

Later he began going to their houses when the folks were away. After school for thirty minutes of hot kissing and messing around. Then he'd graduated to a car. Finally out of high school and into college the girls had slid in and out of his life so fast he'd had several so-called steadies at one time now and then.

He received his college degree, had no interest in going fur-

354

ther, and nailed down a fairly good job with a company that was going places. It was not the kind of job that took his attention away from women. He'd even had one fairly serious relationship that lasted a year. She had wanted to get married, but he didn't. He was too young for that stuff. Besides, there was a possibility his company would transfer him anytime, and he wanted to be free to go without encumbrances.

Then he'd gone to the club alone one night. He was standing at the bar with a drink in his hand, talking to a stunning brunette when a soft voice spoke at his shoulder. At first it was almost like hearing a voice in his mind, a memory evoked from a dream "Hello Justin," the voice said. Then he noticed the brunette, whose name he didn't know, was staring oddly past him. Her eyes were cast slightly lower, as if whoever had spoken was several inches shorter than her own statuesque height.

He turned.

She stood smiling up at him, a petite girl with long golden blond curls, highlights of red like flecks of fire. She had large, round dark eyes, as dark as night, with pale eyebrows that lifted above the bridge of her nose as if she were questioning life. She had a slight overbite, just enough to make her face oddly different and exquisite in its beauty. She was curved just right, with a tiny waist. She was wearing a short, tight skirt that looked like leather, and a loose, short overblouse with a deep V that gave just a glimpse of breasts.

For the first time in his life he was tongue-tied. Then when he could speak he said the dumbest thing he'd ever said to a girl.

"Do I k-know you?"

He had even stammered.

Her half-smile deepened, and dimples appeared at the corners of her mouth. She laughed, a sound as soft as her voice.

"No. But I know you. That's enough, isn't it?"

He forgot the brunette. The rest of the evening was a blur. They danced. Her body was electrifying in its movements. Her eyes, he saw under a brighter light, were a soft brown. Her hair, he was sure, was natural. The colors were too varied to have been created in a salon. The reddish cast, the almost-brown, the childlike blond all blended in those odd little girl curls that hung past her shoulders. It was even a little girl style, parted in the center, a fringe of bangs hanging down on her ivory forehead. Two little ribbons held narrow ropes of hair on each side of the center part.

"How old are you?" he finally asked, when he was better able to talk to her. She had a woman's body, but her hair style, and her face were so childlike.

"Don't worry," she said. "You won't get arrested for buying me a drink."

"I don't even know your name," he said. "You have the advantage, you knew mine."

"Zenoa," she said.

"Zenoa? You're certainly an original, even to your name. I've never heard it before."

She smiled up at him. "Once is enough."

He drew her close in a slow dance. Her small body curved in against his and set him on fire. His voice dropped to a deep bass. "Zenoa what?"

"Just Zenoa," she answered.

He wanted to take her home, but she wouldn't let him. He wanted her phone number so he could call her. He then heard the first of the "I'll call yous."

He had to have her. He hung around the club every evening waiting for her to find him. They met for dinner, for dancing. He took her to his apartment and tried to make love to her, and it was then she told him, "No." The first of the nos.

Finally, after they'd known each other a week, she told him, "Not until I'm married, Justin. I have promised myself that." Then she looked up at him with that sweet, strange smile. "So, you see, you have to marry me, don't you?"

"You mean you would?" he asked, startled. Marriage was a new thought, but he liked it. Zenoa forever? Yes.

She nodded, her eyes looking up into his with that wide innocent expression, that curious expression that sometimes made him feel she was far more sophisticated than she looked, than her tender age should allow. Sometimes her expression made him feel that somewhere deep within her she knew something he didn't, and she was laughing at his naivete. But he was aware mainly of his own feelings, of his desire for her. She was

356

driving him mad with plain lust. He had to have her.

"When?" He visualized her in his bed, every night, all night long. Zenoa in his bed when he woke. Zenoa.

To his disbelief she had set the date. He had taken her to meet his parents once. What would they think? For one moment he was granted a cold-minded rationality. *This is crazy, man,* an inner voice said. But it disappeared beneath her kisses. She had a way of nibbling at his mouth, of not letting him really get to her for a long, deep kiss, that set him wild. Then, just as it seemed she would never give him more than little childish kisses, she let him burrow into her.

Only so far.

No actual sex. No penetration. Not even much fondling.

Nor would she let him take her up to her apartment. She allowed him as far as the door, just into the cramped little vestibule where he could see the flights of stairs winding up, up. "You don't want to go up there," she said, wrinkling her nose to show her distaste.

"I don't *mind,*" he said again. "Do you understand? So you're probably the worst housekeeper in the world. I don't care. But why do you live in this dump?"

"Have you ever heard of money?" she asked in a sweetly innocent way, as if she were serious.

At first he was almost knocked over. Then he laughed. He knew she worked as a receptionist. Somewhere. He'd never been at her place of work. They always met at various places in the evening.

He tried to give her money, but she wouldn't accept it. After they set the wedding date he took out life insurance with her as beneficiary, and in the evenings under the stars, or in the artificial lights of a restaurant or bar he told her all the things he would do for her. A house, made to order for her. And she wouldn't ever have to work if she didn't want to. The way she gazed at him with those large eyes and that half-smile made him feel almost like a god. Little Zenoa, so alone in the world. But now she had him.

Would she still want him, though, when he told her he had an aunt who had murdered her parents and two younger siblings?

357

He found a place to park on the narrow, trashy street near her apartment building. Trash cans sat in a clutter near the entrance to another building, and part of their contents had spilled out and not been picked up. The street on both sides was lined with old cars. Leaving his shiny red Jeep there where it was apt to be stripped by the time he got back to it made him edgy, but he had to talk to Zenoa. Tonight.

With long, fast strides he cleared the steps into her building and entered. A man and woman were just coming down the stairs, and he had to stand to one side in the tiny vestibule. They glanced at him and went on by talking to each other.

He checked the mail slots, but half the names were torn away. He didn't find Zenoa's.

The stairs were dimly lighted, and squeaked as he climbed. He heard a woman screaming swear words at somebody. Her kids, he thought, since she referred to someone as, "You dumb little sonofabitch." God. What miserable lives some children lead, he thought. The adults too, he supposed, otherwise why would they behave the way they did? Making life so damned hard for others? Why did Zenoa have to be so stubborn about staying here? He felt like picking her up and carrying her out and keeping her. He hadn't realized just how bad the area was before now.

He passed the door on the landing where the woman was still swearing at someone and heard a muffled crying within. Their voices faded as he climbed the next flight of stairs. Other voices filled the stale air. Televisions, radios, stereos. Music. Laughter. More swearing. People hating people.

On the third flight he paused. He didn't even know which flight she lived on. She had simply pointed up and said, "Up there," when he persisted in knowing where she lived. But she had not let him beyond the entrance door downstairs.

He looked on the doors on the landing and down the hall and saw only numbers. He came back to the one by the landing, where he heard a muted television, and knocked. After a couple of minutes the door opened cautiously a couple of inches. He saw a pair of eyes set in wrinkles. White hair was like a nightcap on the woman's head.

"I'm sorry to bother you," he said with his most reassuring

smile. "I'm looking for Zenoa—uh—" Her last name almost escaped him. Norris? No. "Morris," he said. "Zenoa Morris."

The woman shook her head. "Sorry. Don't know her."

"She's a lovely girl, about this tall . . ." He put his hand to his chest, but the woman was shaking her head again. "My fiancée. She lives alone . . . she's . . ." He paused.

The woman looked behind her, and then stepped back, and a man took her place at the door. He released the chain and widened the space.

"Zenoa Morris?" the man said. He was younger than the woman. Probably her son. "She doesn't live on this floor. Might try down below."

Justin glanced up at the continuing flights that rose dimly, and the man shook his head.

"If there was a girl up there I'd a seen her. Families, no young, single woman. Some older people alone. No young women."

Justin thanked him and stepped back. The door closed. The manager, he thought. He should have stopped down there. He was running around looking for Zenoa as if he knew exactly where she lived. He hadn't realized there were so many apartments in this building.

He went back down the flights to the vestibule and the door that had a small metal sign: *Manager*. He rang the doorbell. It was the only door he'd seen with a bell button.

He waited. Upstairs another door opened and someone came out. But they didn't come on down the stairs.

The manager's door opened suddenly and Justin faced a man who looked as if he had decided about a week ago to grow a beard. He was taller than Justin's five-ten, and looked as if he worked out in a gym every day. He also looked as if he could handle any problem that came up in the building or on the street outside. Yet when he spoke he had a surprisingly pleasant voice.

"Yes sir!" he said, "What can I do for you?"

"I'm looking for Zenoa Morris. She lives in this building, but I don't know her apartment number."

The man's gaze became a stare of concentration. "Who?"

"Zenoa Morris. She lives alone. About twenty . . ."

The manager shook his head. "Sorry. You got the wrong building. Nobody here by that name."

He didn't have the wrong building, of that he was sure. He had noted the number on the outside every time he brought her home. He had escorted her up the steps and into the door. This entrance door, not the other doors along the street.

He tried again with the description, and a broad smile grew on the man's face.

"Look, buddy," he said. "I think the little lady slipped you a wrong address. I can guarantee you she don't live here. This is a house mostly of families. The only women who live alone here are widows. Old ladies. Sorry. Maybe next door. These places look pretty much alike. You might try some of the others."

The door closed. The man wanted to get back to his television and his beer and chips.

Justin walked out onto the street where he could see the house number again. No. This was the one. But just to be sure he tried a couple more down the street. At one there was no manager at all, and the only person he found who lived in the building looked too blank to be wrong. No. No Zenoa Morris or any young woman who fit the description.

He found his Jeep still intact, climbed in and leaned back. Tapping his fingers on the steering wheel he gazed down the sidewalk. "Aren't you rushing this?" his dad had said when he told them he was marrying Zenoa. His mother had said only, "She's a lovely girl."

Later, when he was alone with his dad, Ross said, "Justin, think about this. What do you know about this girl? Where did she come from? She has no family. Why? Most people have a family somewhere."

"Her family's dead, Dad." Justin hated being put on the defensive. It made him feel like a kid again, too young and inexperienced to know his own mind. And it also made him more determined to marry Zenoa. "Things like that happen. She never had any brothers or sisters, and her parents are dead now."

"But what about aunts, uncles, cousins?"

"They were a service family, traveling all over the world. I

360

suppose she just never knew any of her cousins. What the hell is this, anyway?"

"I just think you're rushing into this. There's something about her, Justin, that makes me a little uneasy."

"Hey! What the hell? I love this girl! How the hell is she making you uneasy? What do you mean about that?"

"Maybe that was a poor choice of words."

"You're goddamned right it was!"

They hadn't mentioned their near collision again, and Dad had treated Zenoa with the same respect as he'd always treated all of Justin's girlfriends And Justin had put it out of his mind. Why did he have to think of it now?

He drove slowly away from the street where he had thought she lived. In a few days she'd be his bride, and she'd be moving to his apartment where they would live until they found a house. But for tonight he didn't know what to do except go to their favorite bar and wait.

Maybe she'd show up.

Seven

Pam faced a long, narrow tunnel that led toward an endless darkness. Though she felt blinded by the dark, still she saw Kit, running, running toward her, arms out, mouth open in a soundless scream. Behind her came the doll, larger than Kit, grown to enormous size. The doll's arm lifted and plunged. As they came closer Pamela saw blood spraying from Kit. She saw the ice pick in the doll's hand. The blade was long, thin, sharp, and glowed as if lighted. Their footsteps echoed . . . echoed . . .

Pam jerked awake, breathing fast, her heart pounding. It was a variation of the same awful dream she'd had so many times, through her years in prison. Gradually the dreams had eased away, and for a long time now she'd had none. But tonight, again . . .

As her mind cleared she realized where she was. Her old room at home. Not her cell in prison. Her heart gave a sudden rise, a leap of fear as her gaze swept the dimly lighted room. The lamp burned low on the dresser, the way she'd left it. Her door was closed. Her clothes hung over the foot of the bed, just as she'd left them. But she had a feeling something was different.

Then she heard a sound, and knew she'd heard it in her sleep. It had probably triggered the dream. With her muscles tense, she listened.

A door had closed? Softly. Downstairs. Or a window had been pulled down. Something.

Then she heard the footsteps. They were running lightly up the stairs.

Someone had entered the house. Yet how could they have? She'd locked the doors. A window?

She slipped quickly out of bed, ran on tiptoes to the lamp and blew it out. Then she huddled into the corner and pressed against the wall in the darkness.

The footsteps came down the hall, hesitated, then went into the room across the hall. Kit's room.

They were the steps of a child, or a woman perhaps. Too light for a man.

Whoever it was remained in the room across the hall for several minutes, moving about occasionally. Pam remained hunched in the corner too frightened to reveal herself, to see who had entered the house. She had no idea what time it was, yet felt she had been asleep only a short time. Just long enough to fall into the nightmare.

Gradually her heart slowed and her tight muscles relaxed a bit. She could breathe easier and more calmly debate her situation. It was not she, she reminded herself, who was the intruder, but the other person. Probably some kid in the neighborhood who had used the vacant house as a playhouse. It was probably that kid who had taken Pam's clothes from her closet and put them into Kit's room.

Pamela stood up, moved to the door and put her ear against it. She heard sounds of movement more clearly. A footstep taken. The squeak of bedsprings, now grown rusty, as whoever it was sat down. Were they going to bed there? Was this a homeless person who had taken up residence and thought herself alone?

But the bed made a sound again, and then there were more footsteps. The door opened and closed. The steps came out into the hall and went toward the stairs.

Pamela eased her door open. The hall was dark except for light that came through the open door and unshaded window of Beth's old room, and the same street light shining in the entry door downstairs. Barely enough light for Pam to see the silhouette of a young woman as she walked confidently through the darkness toward the stairs.

Pam stepped silently into the hall, curiosity pulling her. On bare feet she ran, following. The young woman did not turn, or act as if she were aware of Pam's presence. Pam hurried to the end of the hall just in time to see the woman reach the bottom of the stairs and turn. The woman passed briefly through the thin glow of the street light shining through the glass of the door. It highlighted her hair, so that Pam could see it was light, long, and curly.

Then she was gone, toward the back of the house.

Pam stood still. A door closed. The house was quiet.

Pam listened. There was no sound of a car starting, no sound of the door opening again. No footsteps. Whoever had come so confidently into the house was gone.

Pam turned back toward her room, and relighted the lamp. Carrying it, she went across the hall.

Clothing had been thrown across the bed. A pair of jeans, and a knit top. Pam picked up the jeans. Size five. She dropped them again on the bed where their owner had left them. She went to the closet and looked in.

A skirt was missing. Blue suede. Her own old skirt, size five. The same size as the young woman who evidently had taken up residence here. Someone who had a key?

She remembered to check her wristwatch for the time. Twenty after eleven. She had fallen into bed exhausted an hour and a half ago, and gone almost immediately to sleep. Awakened then by the sound of the door closing.

She went downstairs carrying the lamp. The front door was still locked. The powder-room door stood open, and she distinctly remembered shutting it. She went past the doors into the living room and dining room and cautiously went on into the kitchen. Why had she expected to find a light? The girl had moved through the house in darkness, as if she were used to it, as if she knew exactly where she was going and needed no light.

The kitchen was lighter than the hallway. The windows let in wan light from the sky, from street lamps beyond trees. Pam was aware of windows unshaded as she placed the lamp on the table. She checked the doors into the garage and to the backyard. Both were locked.

She tipped kitchen chairs beneath the knobs of both doors to make sure they couldn't be opened. Then she hurried back upstairs and dressed. Carrying her suitcase, she went down to her car, started it and backed out of the garage. She left the car to close the garage doors, then drove off in search of a motel.

It had been a mistake, trying to stay in the house before the lights were turned on. She was a coward, she decided as she drove. She couldn't even face down an intruder who was no larger than she herself had been twenty-four years ago, two sizes ago. Someone who had helped herself to Pam's old clothes, and Kit's pink bedroom.

She hoped she would simply scare the stranger away with lights on, and doors more firmly secured, after the utilities were turned on. She doubted it would take more than that. She didn't even plan to report it to the police. She had a dread of police, though she knew they were necessary and did their best. Still, she felt reluctant to call and report a break-in, and bring attention again to the house on Dresden Lane. The media would not fail to miss that address, even though it had been twenty-four years since it was on the front page of the daily news.

Tomorrow she would go home, again.

A thought occurred to her. Was it the intruder who had found and removed the doll from the house? She would have to call Beth and ask her if she knew where the doll was, if she knew who might have a key to the house.

Justin sipped on his second drink, staring out over the crowd toward the door. Laughter, voices, music, swelled around him, at times making him want to rush out the door into the night. Friends and acquaintances came up to talk occasionally, but found him watching so closely for Zenoa that they soon moved away. None of them had seen her tonight.

He was thinking about leaving and going to another place they sometimes went to when they wanted to be alone when suddenly she was there, coming through the doorway. The dark cloud lifted from Justin. The music sounded great, fantastic, music from heaven, the raucous voices became angels singing. His world had changed by her presence. He shoved his glass aside and went to meet her.

The same sweet, innocent smile. The upward glance from her dark eyes, so flirtatious, yet so guileless. She was wearing a short skirt that fit her rounded hips to perfection, and made her legs look long and curvy. A sloppy sweater hung casually, almost too large, it seemed, the rounded neckline showing much of her shoulders and the upper parts of her breasts; He adjusted it so it would be less revealing. He could feel other guys ogling her.

"Where've you been?" he demanded, tempering his question with a smile.

"Where have *you* been?" she retorted, tilting her head sideways like a mischievous, flirtatious child.

But this time he wasn't going to let her put him off with questions of her own that distracted him.

"I tried to find you," he started to say, "at your—"

"And I've been looking for you. Everywhere we go. I didn't think it would take so long for you to eat. Without me."

She pouted prettily, yet her eyes contained that same, unreadable expression. The one that sometimes made him feel she was taunting him, laughing at him. What made him mad as hell was she'd look at Tresa's guy the same way, and it was noticeable that Blake was beginning to gaze puppy-eyed at her. He just hoped to God Tresa hadn't noticed.

"I didn't want to eat without you but—" Here he was letting her put him on the defensive again. He took her by the arm and propelled her toward the door. They went out toward the parking lot where a few couples like themselves stood leaning against cars. The lights scattered across the area left shadows behind cars. He had parked near the front, and they stopped by the car.

"Listen," he said, getting new wind, a breath of fresh air. "I went to find you—"

She lifted her pale eyebrows, which gave her round eyes a questioning innocence. "To take me with you to eat with your parents after all?"

"Listen, hon. I have to talk to you about that. Mom wanted to talk alone to Tresa and me because we have a problem in the family."

366

"A problem!" She looked more sympathetic, less incensed that she was left out of the family gathering. "*Your* family has a problem?"

"It happened a long time ago. Before I was born. My mother had two sisters, Pamela was eighteen, and Kit was nine. She had a brother, too, who was twelve. Well, Pamela murdered them."

He paused. He hadn't thought it would be difficult to put into words, but it was. It made his mouth dry, and did something odd to his chest. He wasn't used to being so unaccountably uncomfortable.

"*Murdered*," she whispered. "That's terrible. But—not your mother? I mean, this sister killed everyone but your mother, obviously."

"Well Mom and Dad were already married. It happened in nineteen-sixty-nine, when Tresa was just a few months old."

"How terrible. So your mother went over to the old house and found her parents and brother and sister dead, and her other sister . . . arrested?"

"Yes, something like that."

"And this sister, Pamela? Was she put to death?"

"No. Actually, she's just been released from prison."

The expression on her face changed, before his eyes, instantly, and became oddly blank. Doll-like she gazed up at him, her eyes rounded, her lips slightly parted and curved into that expression that was not quite a smile. So often he caught her looking like that. As if for a moment, or two, something happened and she froze.

"It's okay," he assured her. "I haven't even met Aunt Pam myself. But the thing is, Mom wants you and Blake to meet her."

"Oh yes," she said, with no change in her expression. "Of course we must meet her. When?"

"Mom is having us all for dinner on Friday night."

"Just two days before our wedding."

"Yes," he said, wishing she'd smile, wishing his touch would bring her out of that strange, set look. "It'll be all right, I promise. We don't have to be around her much at all. Just an occasional dinner."

"But she'll be at our wedding."

"Isn't that all right?"

Instead of answering that question, she asked, "Where is your Aunt Pam staying?"

"She went home. Where she lived when she murdered the family. You know, the old house. The one you like."

He expected to see a frown of disgust that anyone would move into the old house before it was cleaned. When they had walked around it, more than once, he'd told her it belonged to the family, that it hadn't been lived in for a long time, that it hadn't been cleaned. But her set look remained. Although her eyes were turned toward him, he felt as if she didn't see him at all. She was looking through him, the way she did when she went into that . . . trance?

Suddenly she tugged at his arm. "Justin, will you take me back to the apartment now?"

"Sure, sweetheart." He opened the car door for her.

As he drove he kept glancing her way, but she stared straight ahead.

"This isn't going to change anything between us, is it?" he pleaded.

"Why should it?"

"You seem — distant."

"No. Just tired."

She never said she was tired.

"You mean you're shocked. That I have something like that in my family. You're afraid it might be in our family genes and might affect our children?"

"Of course not. You can't help what your aunt did."

"I've never even met her," he said, as if that would help distance him from what had happened. "I used to write her a note occasionally at Christmas. When I was a kid. Frankly . . ." He reached for her hand. It was soft, and boneless. He squeezed it, but not very hard. She seemed so tiny and fragile. "I was hoping she'd just fade away, like stay there forever, I guess."

She looked straight down the street. He found a parking spot within feet of the steps that led up to her apartment. When she started to get out of the car he hurried to help her. She didn't object to having her door opened. But she was already halfway around the car and he walked beside her.

At the foot of the steps up to the entrance door he held on to her arm.

"I came here earlier," he said. "I tried to find you. The manager said you don't even live here."

She laughed. She was his Zenoa again. The strange, blank look was gone.

"That funny guy. He's like that. He's protecting me. No strange men, you know. Of course I live here!"

"Well, I'm coming up."

"No, not tonight."

"Why?"

"I'll see you tomorrow night." She started to turn away, then paused and said, "I might move in with you until the wedding, would that be all right?"

"What?" He didn't believe it. He had begged, practically on his knees, dozens of times.

"Yes. It's only a few more days, and my rent is almost up. Go away now and let me get organized."

She entered the building and closed the door in his face.

He ran down the steps with the bounce of a teenager. Zenoa in his apartment, at last. When? Tomorrow? He should have asked. He wished he had teased her a little. "Now I'll get to see how you look in the morning when you wake up. Without makeup."

Kissable. Like a dream. Like a doll.

He drove away in a buzz of happiness. Not even the murderess Aunt Pam was going to spoil things for him.

A couple of thoughts popped into his mind after he parked his car in his allotted spot at his own apartment complex. He hadn't told Zenoa that Pam had killed her parents too. She had only, and instantly, deduced it.

But of course it would be something that anyone would deduce.

And . . . her explanation of why the manager wouldn't give him her apartment number seemed odd. If he knew her that well, why hadn't she told him she was engaged to be married? Why hadn't she given her manager the name of her fiancé, in case he came asking for her?

Ross had gone to bed. The reading light was still on, the television turned off. He lay with his arms under his head yawning. Beth looked at him with love, a motherly love such as she felt for her children. He was such a darling, her Ross. He had the same little habits every night. He went to bed with a book, yet read hardly more than a page or two as he also listened to a bit of late news. Then he'd turn off the television with the remote control, and lay it and the book on the bedside table. Then the arms would go under his head. He'd yawn, look at the ceiling, stretch, and relax. Then he'd grin at her as she came toward the bed, and his right arm would stretch out across her pillow so that she'd have to use it when she lay down. Then he'd curl the arm up, around her neck. One kiss, usually, then he'd pull his arm away, turn onto his side and start snoring. Immediately. But softly.

Many, many nights since the night of the murders the sound of his snoring comforted her. Ross had no idea how much comfort his ability to rest had given her. It was almost as if when he rested, part of her rested too.

She was just getting ready to lie down when the phone buzzed.

She jumped, inwardly and outwardly, terror racing into her soul. The phone had rung early one morning twenty-four years ago, at an unexpected time, and since then the sound of the phone between the hours of nine in the evening and nine in the morning sent terror into her heart.

She reached for it, trembling all through her body. Her eyes found the digital clock. 11:48.

Something had happened to one of her kids! Visions ran rapidly through her mind. *Justin, his car wrecked, his crumpled body bleeding. The cherry red Jeep lay on a hilly drop among trees. A mountainside. It had gone over a cliff. Darkness swirled around him like fog, his eyes stared in death.*

"Oh my God," she murmured, her hand going to her throat.

But the voice on the phone was not a stranger's. It was familiar, in a distant way she didn't at first recognize.

"Beth? I'm so sorry to call you at this hour, but it's very important. Can you talk a minute?"

Oh! "Pam!"

Beth sat down on the bed, too weak to stand up. The strange vision of Justin dead on a mountainside stayed with her. Where . . . why . . . had she imagined him on a mountainside? There were no mountains within a hundred miles.

"I'm in a motel, Beth. I was at home. Someone broke into the house."

"Broke in? When?" She saw the house in her mind, a window broken, the interior vandalized.

"No, I don't really mean they broke in. I mean, it looks as if someone has been living there. They're wearing my old clothes. Someone who must have a key."

Beth's emotions took an eighty-degree turn. She felt herself smiling with relief. Thank God, that was all. "Really?" she said, and almost laughed. It was probably a nervous reaction, she thought, but difficult to control. The giggle stayed beneath the surface, thank God, for Pamela sounded almost frantic.

"You didn't — give someone a key by any chance? A girl, who had no other place to live?"

"Good Lord no, why would you think that?"

"I didn't really, it just occurred to me. It would have been an explanation that would be easy to handle. So you don't know who it is who is living there?"

"I had no idea anyone had ever entered the house. Are no windows broken?"

"No, none. Whoever it is went through a door."

"A girl, you said?"

"I didn't get a good look at her, but I'd say yes, a girl. She wears my old clothes. They were size five mostly."

"So you didn't actually have a run-in with her? I mean you didn't exactly meet in the hall?"

Beth was almost giggling hysterically again, visualizing that situation. Surprise! On the part of both women.

"No. I was asleep in my room, when I heard a noise. She came upstairs, went into Kit's room, stayed a while and left. I slipped out into the hall and saw her going down the stairs. The only light came through the glass panels on the front door. She had light-colored hair, long and curly. She was obviously female. Later, I noticed she had changed clothes. She left a pair of jeans on the bed. Size five."

Something about this that Pam was telling began to seem odd to Beth. If it were the truth, and Beth was no longer sure of anything concerning Pam, then all this had taken place in the dark.

"You mean the girl changed clothes and everything in the dark?"

"Yes. I'd gone to the old store where I used to work and bought a lamp. But it was in my room, and turned very low. When I heard footsteps I blew it out."

"Strange. Did you call the police?"

"No. I knew if the media got hold of it, everything . . . would be brought back again."

"Yes, you're right. Well, when she realizes the house is no longer vacant she'll probably leave. Did you say you've gone now to a motel?"

"Yes."

"One thing, Pam, I called the utility companies. They'll all be there tomorrow, and you'll have lights. The girl probably won't show up again."

She waited, wanting to say goodnight. Ross's warm, safe arm was waiting for her as he listened intently to her side of the conversation.

"By the way, Pam," she said, "can you come over to dinner Friday night? I want you to meet the kids, all of them. The soon to be in-laws, too, okay?"

"Friday?"

"Yes, about seven."

"All right."

Pamela sounded suddenly distant, and shy. For a moment Beth felt sorry for her.

Pam said suddenly, "There's something else, Beth. I have to know. Did you put the old doll in the attic?"

Not the damned doll again! Would her obsession never end?

"Yes, years ago."

"It isn't there."

A picture of the attic came into Beth's mind. She could see the exact spot where she had laid the doll.

"I put it on the floor, just at the top of the stairs, Pam. It was in a large, brown plastic bag."

"It's gone."

There was a silence. Beth found herself frowning, trying to come up with explanations. Then it hit her.

"The girl! The one who has made herself at home there. She must have taken it, Pam. Perhaps she's gradually been selling things out of the house in order to have money. Have you checked to see if anything else is missing?"

"No, I haven't. I was concerned . . . about the doll."

"I wish," Beth said softly, "I would never again, as long as I live, have to hear that word. I'll see you Friday, Pam."

She hung up, and sat with her head bowed.

Behind her Ross said, "Still thinking about it, huh?"

"I was hoping, *praying,* that Pam would come out of prison and be the sister I used to know. Before that cursed doll came into our lives But it's hopeless, Ross. She'll never forget."

Eight

Why did I do that? Pam squeezed her arms as if she were cold as she put the phone down. Why had she bothered Beth, as if Beth could make things right? She had vowed to herself she would never mention the doll to Beth again, because she had vivid memories of how Beth had thought she was insane. She could see now how right her lawyers were. If she had said that someone struck her, and when she regained consciousness she found herself the only survivor in her family, everyone would have been sympathetic and she probably would never have been sent to prison. But she had stubbornly stuck to a story of falling and striking her head. And worse, she had told Beth the truth. She had told Gramma Vee. Of course neither of them had believed her.

There were times when she herself doubted. What had she really seen? What had she felt? Her memory had not failed. She had definitely felt the doll shove hard against her as it pushed away. She could still feel the movements of something against her, of a superhuman push, and a lurch.

Then, in the birth of a new day, the sun risen, she had seen their bodies. And downstairs, she had seen the doll. It had moved from the vanity chair in the powder room as easily as a child might have, and it had walked out into the hallway. A nightmare of the unreal, then and now. A twisted reality. Again she felt the horror of seeing it coming toward her, until it reached the light in the hall. Daylight. Created by the sun.

Was it possible that by then she was only hallucinating? There were times in later years when she had begun to wonder.

She lay down and closed her eyes and eventually found she was growing drowsy.

She slept uneasily until it was almost time to get up and then fell into a heavy sleep so that when she did wake it was later than she had intended. She got up hurriedly, saw it was past nine, and quickly showered and dressed. Then in her faithful old car drove back home.

A utility truck was just coming out of the driveway. She rolled down her window. The uniformed man stopped the truck long enough to ask her if she were the owner, then assured her the electricity was now on.

Pam drove on into the garage and took her suitcase out of the car. The garage light worked. She wrote a note when she reached the kitchen. Light bulbs, lots of them, along with the groceries she would need.

At the foot of the stairs she paused and looked up, the suitcase growing heavy in her hands. The house seemed filled with a living, breathing presence. Dangerous. Threatening. Evil.

How could she go back up there, where the carpet was stained dark, and the wall discolored? Where the vision of Kit, of Nicky, Mom, and Dad, were still vivid in her mind?

She had to. She had a job to finish. She was going to find the doll. Only in her own belief, struggling now against her doubts, was she sure of the killer. It had to be destroyed.

For the rest of the week she worked hard. She was unable to get a carpet layer immediately, and chose to clean the hall carpet the best she could. She tried to hire a painter and was unable to get one on such short notice, so she purchased paint and a roller brush and painted the hallway herself. She closed the doors of Nicky's room and the master bedroom, to wait for a professional painter and carpet layers. She worked, cleaning until she was exhausted, dusting, vacuuming, knocking down spider webs that filled corners and were woven even beneath the kitchen table.

Whoever the girl was who had helped herself to Kit's bedroom and Pam's clothes had not eaten in the house. There were no signs of food. The food left twenty-four years ago in the refrigerator had dried to hard knobs. Small round objects that once had layers of leaves she guessed were lettuce and cabbage. The refrigerator had long ago lost any odor of rotted food. Now it was simply strange items that were slightly sticky, or covered with old mold and dried to nothing. She raked it all out into a garbage can and tried to restore the refrigerator. She put paper towels down to lay her fresh vegetables on and shut the door. The fridge hummed and grew cold, turned on for the first time in so many years.

At night she was so tired she heard nothing. She carefully locked the doors, waiting too for a locksmith to have time to put new locks on. To insure that the intruder did not enter the house, she propped kitchen chairs under the knobs of the kitchen- and utility-room doors. Then she carried a chair up to her bedroom to use beneath that knob.

Exhausted she slept.

Still, on the third night she woke, to lie listening in the deep of night, sensing more than hearing movements. Someone — or something — had come into the house after all. She sensed a presence that was dangerous.

She sat up, her breath held in sudden understanding.

It knew Pam was there, and meant to destroy her before she could destroy it.

The doll.

It was somewhere in the house. It was not the intruder, a mere homeless girl, who moved about the house. It was the doll. In the dark of night, when the outside world was hushed and still, when things inanimate and insentient rise and respond to some evil command deep within them.

She did not leave her room.

In the light of the next day, she began to search again.

She looked again into the powder room, the first room that came to her mind. She had closed the door and not opened it since. She turned on the light, and saw that the long tube of bulbs above the vanity were like snaggled teeth, partly lighted, filled with shadows where bulbs had burned out. She had not yet cleaned the room, but it was strangely free from the dust, the webs that had been in other rooms.

It was empty, of course. It had been empty when she closed

the door. Still she looked, into the corners in the alcove where the toilet was, into the shadows beneath the vanity. She touched the vanity chair. There was no visible dust on the cushion. She pulled open the drawer. Old makeup had not been removed. Lipstick, still in the drawer. Pressed powder, and a couple of boxes of loose powder, as well as tubes of cream makeup. There were hairbrushes and combs.

She lifted one hairbrush that lay in the front of the drawer, and stared at it. Blond strands, golden, catching the light with a reddish tint. She dropped the hairbrush back into the drawer and closed it. But she felt as if she had touched death.

The only rooms she hadn't at least partly cleaned were the bedrooms upstairs. The only rooms she hadn't checked carefully, where the doll might be lurking during the day was Nicky's bedroom or the master bedroom.

She climbed the stairs and stood afraid outside the door of the master bedroom. How could she bear to go into those closets where the clothing of her mother and dad probably still hung?

She opened the bedroom door. The silence seemed overwhelming. She paused, listening to it, her eyes going from the ruined carpet to the bed to the walls. Old blood stains were touches of darkness that a stranger who didn't know what had happened here might think was wine splashed at some careless time. She had not touched the bed, leaving the bedding crumpled and thrown. Later she would strip the bed, remove the satin spread, the sheets, and take them to the cleaners with instructions to have them given to the homeless shelters. She would do the same with Nicky's things, and Kit's, along with her own old clothes.

She forced herself to enter the large closet. It seemed that as she stood in the center of the section her mother had used that she could still smell her favorite perfume. For just a moment she stood still, looking at the neat suits her mother used to wear. Then she hurriedly began to search, behind the clothes, in the corners. Nothing, no sign of disarray.

In her dad's section of the double closet she saw trousers hanging over the back of the chair where he sat to put on shoes and socks, and a pair of socks had been tossed in the direction of the hamper. They were on the floor. A thin layer of dust greyed the color.

The bathroom had a towel hanging over the side of the tub, as if it had been put there to dry. She closed doors behind her, and when she at last stood in the hall again she faced the closed door of Nicky's room.

She searched thoroughly and quickly. Nicky's room, like the master bedroom, seemed to be as he had left it. There was no doll, even in the clutter of his closet.

She moved on to the guest room, the room where Beth had lived for several years before she married Ross. The closet was empty. The space beneath the bed was empty.

The only room left was Kit's.

When Pam last had closed the door to Kit's room a pair of her old jeans had been on the bed. She had left them untouched.

The first thing she saw when she opened the door was the smooth, uncluttered bedspread. The jeans were gone.

She stood staring, thinking back rapidly She had closed the door. Then she had gone to a motel. When she returned the next day she had not opened the door again. Not until now had she opened the door. She had assumed that the intruder had not come back into the house. But the jeans had been moved.

She crossed hurriedly to the closet door, opened it, and turned on the closet light.

All her clothes, all those that had been moved from her room and into Kit's closet, were gone.

She was puzzled, but oddly relieved. That meant, it seemed to her, that the intruder had known she was here and had come back and taken the clothes away. She could have returned that first night, after Pam had gone to the motel.

Pam closed the closet door and stood looking at the pink bedroom. There was no dust in this room, no spider webs clogged the corners.

Pam went downstairs and fixed a glass of iced tea. She sat at the table with it, trying to think of somewhere in the house that she had not searched.

The doll was gone, after all. Those movements she had

heard in the night were like the nightmares. Touched by truth, twisted by her fears.

The phone rang, and she almost leaped out of her chair. She had forgotten it was now connected to the rest of the world. Who would be calling her?

It hung on the wall beside the door into the utility room, an old black dial phone. Beneath it, in the wooden wall rack, was a phone directory for the year 1969 as well as a new one. She had used the phone only to try to locate a painter to redo the bedrooms.

Beth's voice said, "Pam?"

"Oh. Hello Beth."

"Why on earth haven't you called?" She sounded irritated.

"I — I've been so busy, I didn't even think of it."

"I thought when you got the phone hooked up, you'd call and give me your number. I had to call information to find out if you'd been hooked up yet."

"I'm sorry. I just didn't think. I've been cleaning house. I've been very busy. Is something wrong?"

"Wrong? Oh no." Her voice softened, calmed. "I just wanted to know how you're getting along over there."

"Oh, okay."

"And to remind you of tonight."

"Tonight?"

"Yes, dinner. You know, to meet the kids."

Oh Lord, she'd forgotten. She put her hand to her cheek. "Of course. Tonight at seven? This is Friday, isn't it?" She looked around at the walls. A calendar hanging above the desk was turned to August, 1969. That was something she must remember to buy.

"Well . . . you can come as early as you like. The kids are supposed to be here at seven." She hesitated, then said, "Maybe you'd like to come on over and help me with the salad or something. We haven't really talked, for a long time. You haven't told me about these past years. What it was like for you."

Pam recognized what Beth was trying to do. She was trying to regain something of their lost relationship. Pam felt almost tearful as she listened to Beth's voice, with its hesitations, its pauses, its changes of timbre. Poor Beth. Pam saw their experiences from Beth's point of view, and Pam knew if it were reversed, and she was positive that her sister had murdered her parents and brother and sister, she would have a lot of difficulty accepting her back into the family. She would, indeed, be terrified of her.

She wouldn't want that sister around her children, even after they were adults.

"Thanks Beth," she said. She was going to leave, she decided suddenly. As soon as she finished what she had come home for. She was going to get out of Beth's life forever. She wanted to assure Beth of that. In person, over such homey things as lettuce and tomatoes. "Thank you. I'll be there."

Nine

"Are Justin and Zenoa going to be there?" Blake asked, as Tresa settled into the passenger seat and Blake started the car.

The evening was instantly ruined. Blake thought he was being cool, keeping his feelings hidden. Didn't he know his voice softened, as if strained, every time he mentioned her name? Tresa turned her head and looked out the window. What was in her that stopped her from screaming at him, telling him he was making a fool of both himself and her? She had never known such bitter defeat, such feelings of helplessness. Everything had been so perfect until Zenoa entered their lives.

"Yes," she said.

His attitude changed instantly. It was something she sensed, something he tried to hide. Where tenseness and strain was in his voice as he waited for her answer, now suddenly he was relaxed and talkative. Excited. He began telling her of his day at work, of complications that evidently had not concerned him much because now he was able to laugh at them. She could hear in his voice his eagerness to see Zenoa again.

Oh God, what am I going to do?

The wedding date was set. Unlike Justin's, it was going to be in church. Not a large crowd, only relatives and friends, but a hundred invitations had gone out. October, when the leaves were turning. Their house was being built. Everything had been great, until the day Justin had so proudly brought Zenoa home.

The moment Blake looked at her, Tresa felt the change. But

later she had thought she was only being insecure, for some reason. She had never been an insecure person before. What was there about Zenoa? She was beautiful, but so were a lot of her friends. Blake hadn't held his breath when he met them.

She tried to dismiss her feelings. Then she began to notice Zenoa's attitude toward Blake. She touched him, on the shoulder, on the arm. She looked up at him from those large, dark eyes in that so guilty-innocent way she had, that naughty little girl way, and Blake's voice began to change when he mentioned her name to Tresa. He always wanted to know if Zenoa was going to be at a family gathering. Of course. He wanted to know other things about her, but those were questions Tresa couldn't answer.

Perhaps his attraction to her would end with her marriage to Justin. But probably it wouldn't.

A sick feeling centered somewhere between her heart and stomach. Did she really want to live like this? No. But did she want to mess up her plans for her future with Blake? She loved him. He had loved her, up until a month ago. He still said he loved her, but she had noticed that he wasn't really there anymore when he kissed her.

"I have to talk to you, Blake," she said suddenly. "Park somewhere. It won't matter if we're a few minutes late."

He glanced at her, actually saw her. She sensed an alarm ringing in him. This was a Blake she had never known.

"Want a Coke?"

They were approaching a drive-in where they had stopped for drinks before. She said yes. He swerved in and parked. A voice came over the mike asking for their order. "Two Cokes," he told her. Tresa sat still, staring at the trees in the vacant lot beyond the parking area. A couple of vacant lots left in the old home suburb, like oases. Ever since she had learned to drive she had come here, alone, with friends, finally with Blake, and always parked so she could see the trees.

There was something magical about a forest of trees, even a tiny one like the lot. When she and Blake had set out to find a lot to build on they had gone north of the city to one of the newer developments where Victorian-styled houses were being built on large lots that kept as many trees as were possible.

382

Their new house, half finished now, had two large trees in the front yard and three in the back. She had a sudden premonition she would never live in that house. Those dreams of sitting under one of those trees with her children, of attaching a swing to one of the limbs as she had seen in nostalgia magazines, would never come true. She felt like crying. Blake had never seen her cry. What would he do if suddenly she burst into tears?

"It's almost time," he said. "Just two more days. Where are they going on their honeymoon?"

She opened her mouth, then closed it. The teenage boy who served the section where they were parked came out with the Cokes and Blake paid him and handed one of the paper cups to Tresa. Of course his mind would be on their wedding, wouldn't it? On Zenoa. She felt like throwing her Coke in his face. She almost laughed, visualizing his reaction, Coke dripping off his chin. Was he apt to get violent in situations like that? She'd known him two years, and had never seen him react violently, but she'd never seen a drink in his face either.

"What's wrong?" he asked.

"You noticed?" Sarcasm wasn't natural for her. Those two words made her feel cheapened. He didn't answer. She could see from the corner of her eye that he was staring at her. Once he would have reached over and put his hand on the back of her neck. A touch, any touch.

She said, "I'm not feeling very good about things, Blake."

"What do you mean?"

"I've noticed your attraction to Zenoa. I'm afraid everyone has noticed, especially Zenoa."

"What?" He let out a sound of short laughter, a snort of disbelief. "Hey," he said suddenly, turning it back on her. "You're jealous!"

She took a deep breath. A demon had entered her heaven. She had some serious thinking to do, yet knew all she wanted to hear from Blake was reassurance.

He leaned toward her, pulled her to him, and kissed the corner of her mouth. The teenage boy going by with a tray loaded for someone else glanced at them, and looked again. Tresa edged away. They weren't exactly into public displays, even one so innocent.

383

"I love *you*," he said, and she heard what she wanted so desperately in his voice.

She looked into his eyes, and saw the tenderness she had been missing so terribly lately. Tears rushed to the surface, a release that had been held back, growing toward the explosive point within her. Maybe her dreams would come true after all. Zenoa *was* getting married. After the weddings they really wouldn't have to see each other very often. Just at family gatherings.

"Do you, Blake?" she whispered.

"Yes."

His lips were soft. Their kiss gentle. His eyes told her it was all right. She believed it, she had to.

Then she remembered why they were going for dinner at Mom and Dad's.

"You might not even want to marry me after you meet my aunt. She's out of prison. She'll be at Mom's tonight."

"Aunt Pam?"

She had told him briefly one time early in their relationship, when it looked as though the relationship was going to get serious, that her mother's sister was in prison for murder. "No kidding," he had said then. She had explained that she had never met this Aunt Pam, but she felt sorry for her. He had said, "Every family has its problems."

"Yes," she said now. "Aunt Pamela. Mom's having this dinner specifically because she wants to introduce Aunt Pam before the wedding. She didn't want to just ignore her, you know, leave her out of everything."

"Hmmm." Blake massaged the back of her hand.

"The thing is, I didn't tell you who she killed." He said nothing. It was difficult for her. Never, in all her life, had she told this to anyone, not even her best friend. "They said she murdered the whole family, those in the house that night. Mom's parents, her brother, and little sister. Pamela was only eighteen."

"How old is she now?"

"Uh—well, she served twenty-four years."

Blake said, "So she's forty-two."

Tresa smiled. "That's the difference in being an accountant

384

and a secretary."

"So what's the problem with Aunt Pam? She's not exactly going to live with us, is she?"

"Not exactly. But she is part of the family."

"Doesn't sound like she deserves that honor."

Tresa looked down. In a strange way Pam had been a large part of her life. She had recently read the transcripts of the trial, and had felt more puzzled than ever. In her heart she had felt that eighteen-year-old girl was innocent. Still, she had never lost the feeling that Pamela knew something that would shed a new light on the old story.

"She showed up unexpectedly on Mom's doorstep," Tresa said. "What could she do?"

"I don't know. Not let her in?"

"I don't think she did, and then she got to feeling guilty and decided she had to invite her to Justin's wedding."

"She'll be at ours, too, then."

"Does it matter?"

He shrugged. "Where is she staying?"

"At her home. At Mom's old home. Where the murders took place. I never showed it to you, but it's within walking distance of home. Mom just kept the keys for her, because she didn't want anything to do with it. She gave her share to Pam. Pam had come for the keys, that's all. She didn't intend to interfere in Mom's life."

Blake kissed her cheek. "We'd better go, right? After all, I have this aunt to meet."

"It's okay, then?"

"I don't see what your aunt has to do with you. If you mean do I think our kids might turn out to be like her, well, I hope not." He laughed. "I'd hate to be afraid to shut my eyes at night. I can see me, putting the kid to bed and then staring into the dark all night long."

It wasn't funny to Tresa. "Blake, please."

He started the car. "Just kidding. Who knows what her problems were? How'd she do these killings?"

"With an ice pick."

"Good God. All four of them? They must have been asleep.""

"I think she was innocent."

"Oh yeah?"

"Yes, I do."

"Well, I guess she knows, doesn't she?"

That was the reason Tresa had considered going up north to the prison two years ago, close to the time she had met Blake. Yes, she was sure, Pamela knew. She had pleaded innocent. Although she hadn't taken the stand in defense of herself, her lawyers had claimed she was unconscious during the time of the murders.

Tresa wanted to know exactly what had caused her to fall and strike her head.

For the moment her torment concerning Zenoa and the changes she had made in Tresa's life were put aside.

Ten

Ross rose from his chair and shook hands with Pamela, the newspaper still in his left hand.

"You haven't changed much," he said, but Pamela only smiled. She felt she had, but perhaps outwardly she hadn't. After all, your skin doesn't get much sunshine when you're in prison.

"How are you, Ross?" she asked simply. She would have known him anywhere. He was heavier, with thinner hair, but he had the same pleasant face, smooth except for lines at the corners of his eyes and mouth, as if he smiled a lot.

Beth acted as nervous as Pamela felt. Once again she wished she had begged off. A dozen times while she was getting ready to go, and on her way over, she had berated herself for simply not telling Beth that she didn't have to try to include her in the family.

Yet she wanted to see Tresa, especially. Justin, too of course. She had treasured each picture Beth sent of them. She had loved the little notes Tresa used to mail. Around the ages of eleven to thirteen Tresa had gone through a period of correspondence. Several times a year she had written to Pam, telling her about her friends, school activities, home life. Tresa would never know how Pam had reread those little letters. They were with her now, still in the suitcase she hadn't completely emptied.

Pam helped Beth with the supper. She made salad and set the table in the dining room. All the while, as Beth prepared vegetables and sliced a ham roast, she filled Pam in on her children's lives. Her talk was breathless and nervous, and Pam nodded,

387

and spoke appropriate replies. She heard how neither kid could really make up his or her mind about what they wanted to do with their lives, so both had taken degrees in business. Justin worked now as manager of a discount store. Tresa had gone to work as a secretary for a lawyer.

"Now she's talking about going on to law school, after she gets her family started. She and Blake want children. Two, I think. They're building a house. Instead of a honeymoon, they're putting their money into the house. Did I tell you? I think Justin and Zenoa are simply going to—"

Pam interrupted. "Who?" She stood with her knife poised above the cutting board. The odor of chopped onions wafted up toward her. *Zenoa?* She must have misunderstood.

Beth's eyes met hers, puzzled, almost blank, as if the interruption had destroyed her chain of thought.

"Justin's fiancée," she said. "Zenoa."

Pamela couldn't stop the frown. She repeated the unusual name softly. "Zenoa."

Beth went back to work on the ham. The electric knife sliced neatly with a faint buzz.

"A very sweet girl," Beth said.

What an odd coincidence. Pam had felt a tightening of the skin on her shoulders and the back of her neck the moment Beth spoke the name. She was tense and anxious now. She stared out the wide windows over the sinks. The roses, the bird bath, and feeder, were only a background of blurred colors for her thoughts. Beth's continuing adulation of Justin's fiancée a blur of words she didn't hear. *Zenoa.* The name of the doll. Didn't Beth know that? No. She probably wouldn't have known.

"Strange name," Pamela said. "I've heard it only once before."

"Oh really? I don't think I ever heard it. Unique, like the girl herself. Justin couldn't have pleased us more." She paused, took the knife apart and put the blades in hot water in the sink. "Well, me anyway."

Pam continued chopping the onion bits into smaller bits. She had done all Beth had instructed her to do, feeling as ill-at-ease as Beth acted.

"Ross," Beth said, "Well, Ross usually never criticizes anyone. You know Ross. You remember Ross, how good-natured he always was, how ready to accept people with all their faults. Even those little twits who used to call Justin at all hours, Ross just laughed. But . . ."

She stopped. Pam waited a moment. Then Beth started talking about the wedding, coming up so soon now, just two more days, and Pam was left only with the impression that Ross for some reason had not really approved of this fiancée.

"She has no family, so she wasn't interested in a big wedding. She's a very unusual girl. There'll only be a few of us."

"You don't have to invite me," Pamela said. "I don't want to push myself onto you."

"Of course I have to invite you! I want you to come."

Beth's answer was so spontaneous that Pam felt she was sincere. Maybe then, after tonight, they would feel more at home with each other.

Pam asked, "Do they know?"

There was a slight pause before Beth answered. "I assume so," she said. "The kids were here a few nights ago, and I told them you were home now. They know they'll be meeting you, of course."

"I mean . . ." About the murders, the prison.

"Yes, I'm sure they must. I — uh, I'll take this to the dining room."

She had been going to say something else, Pam felt certain. *I told them to tell Blake and Zenoa?* They would have to know, sometime. She could only speculate. Pam had to give Beth credit for trying really hard to bring her back into the family.

When Beth returned to the kitchen, Pam said, "I'm not staying, Beth."

"Not staying? What do you mean?"

"I mean, as soon as I finish my business here, I'm leaving."

Beth stood silent, looking at her. A range of emotions crossed her face. All difficult to read.

Then she asked softly, "But where will you go?"

"I don't know. Florida, maybe. Down on the coast. It sounds like a nice place."

"Bugs. Sand fleas."

Pam smiled, shrugged. "I'll sell the house, if it's all right with you."

"I told you, the house is yours. Of course you can sell it. Take the money, buy a smaller house."

Did she sound relieved, or was it only Pam's imagination? Her voice had grown softer, more relaxed, though there was a deep sadness in her eyes. The memory, Pam knew. She understood. With her gone, the memories would recede again, and Beth could go on with the life she had made with her husband and kids, her friends, her church, those things that had been a comfort to her.

"I worry about you," Beth said. "I hate to see you all alone."

"It's all right. Ultimately we have to be complete within ourselves. As much as possible. Cats are allowed in prison. Did you know? On a limited basis. There was one in the library where I worked. She grew old, and last year she died. She had gotten where she followed me. She slept on my desk during the day, and went with me to bed at night. She slept beside me. Animals can be a great comfort. It's nice to feel that warm body, hear something alive breathing beside you. So I'll get a kitten, maybe two. And a dog. I won't be alone."

Beth put out her arms suddenly and drew Pam to her. They stood together, hugging tightly, as they hadn't done in all their lives. Pam realized Beth was weeping.

"I'm sorry," she whispered, drawing away. "I'm so sorry, Pam."

Pamela patted her on the shoulder. "It's okay. I understand, really I do. You can always come to visit me, you know."

Beth nodded, wiping her eyes. "Sure. Sure. Maybe Florida would be nice. I'll be down every winter, all winter long."

They laughed.

At that moment the back door opened and a lovely young woman with long dark hair entered. Her eyes, as brilliant blue as Ross's, found Pamela immediately. She smiled. The face was beautiful, and Pam saw her mother there, in the curve of the mouth, the dimple high in the cheek. Only half noticed was the man behind Tresa, medium height, husky, with light brown hair, he looked like the type of man a girl like Tresa would have chosen to fall in love with. He reminded Pam a bit of Craig.

"Aunt Pam!" Tresa cried, smiling, coming immediately, to Pam's surprise, to give her a warm hug and a kiss on the cheek. "I'm so happy to meet you. This is Blake, Pam, my fiancé."

Tresa held onto Pam's left hand. Pam noticed the softness of the young hand, and the warmth. Not in a million years had she expected so warm a reception. Nor, she could see, had Beth. Beth was looking as surprised as Pam felt.

For a few minutes the kitchen was filled with voices and friendly confusion. Blake's handshake was firm, his eyes accepting. Ross came in, the newspaper still in his hand. Tresa released Pam and went to hug her dad as if she hadn't seen him in a month. As he looked at his daughter, Ross's eyes revealed where much of his adoration lay.

The voice came from the front of the house, the deep, resonant voice of a man. "Anybody home?"

He came through the hall, guiding the petite young woman in front of him. Pam's first glance saw the tall Justin, the strong lines of his face, his jaw bone prominent, high cheek bones, eyes a lighter blue than Tresa's, but just as intense. Then her gaze fell upon the girl, and became a stare.

Cold terror whipped over her as if she had suddenly been exposed to the horrors of a death beyond death, of a universe godless and cold and impossible to escape.

Zenoa.

The doll. The face. The same as the doll. The dress she wore, small, short. Hers. From her closet at home. But most of all was the disbelief within herself. The feeling that she had gone mad, that somehow nothing she had ever believed was correct. This was not a doll, but a girl, a young woman, smiling at her with that same strange, half-smile she remembered, looking at her with her dark brown eyes, round, slightly quizzical, with that strange expression of innocence, or of silent laughter as if she knew something that no one else knew.

Pam heard Justin saying, "You're Aunt Pamela, there's no doubt about that. You look just like your high school picture. Aunt Pam, I want you to meet my fiancée, Zenoa."

With his hands on her shoulders he pushed the incredibly

beautiful girl closer, and Zenoa put out her hand. Zenoa's smile widened and became a real smile.

"I'm pleased to meet you, ma'am," she said, sounding oddly old-fashioned, her voice fine and soft, like a little girl's.

Pam automatically put out her hand. Against everything within herself she found herself offering her hand to Zenoa. Within herself she cringed. Her skin felt tight and cold across her face. She became aware that Tresa was staring oddly at her, but no one else seemed to notice how she felt as she accepted the hand of the girl who was, who looked exactly like, the doll. Whose name was, coincidentally, the same as the doll's.

Didn't anyone else notice? No, Beth probably hadn't taken that much notice of the doll. Nor would Ross have remembered the doll that well, nor probably ever heard its name.

Act naturally. Don't make a fool of yourself. Yet this young niece and nephew didn't know her, she remembered, didn't know that naturally and normally, long ago before her life had come to a halt, she had been outgoing and chatty and filled with laughter. In her heart she felt she knew Justin and Tresa the way she had known Nicky and Kit, so she had to remember they didn't feel close to her.

She heard her voice saying, "Hello. I'm so glad to meet Justin's fiancée." But she quickly drew her hand back. The touch of the girl's hand had made her feel as if she had touched snake skin. The hand seemed too smooth, too silky. The cool feel was more than just a normally cool hand, it was inhumanly cool. Was she the only one in the family who had noticed that?

Or was she losing it upstairs totally, and this thing about the doll existed only in her imagination? She was glad to be able to turn again to the preparation of the dinner, helping Beth, and now Tresa also. Zenoa went with the men to the living room and Pam stayed with Beth and Tresa, though she felt in the way. She helped finish the table, only half hearing Tresa talking, to Beth, and now, as they were left alone in the dining room, to herself. But what had she said?

"I beg your pardon?" Pam raised her eyes to Tresa and saw the young woman smiling curiously at her.

"I said, have you met her before, or something? It seemed to me you acted as if you had met her before."

392

"The — Justin's fiancée?"

Tresa nodded, her eyes glancing from Pam's face to her hands. A look of sympathy settled on her face. "What's wrong, Pam? I hope you don't mind if I drop the aunt. I've always thought of you as being my peer, and having to call you Aunt Pam seems formal and awkward."

"Of course, it's great to be called anything by you." Pam tried to laugh lightly, but failed. At that moment Beth came back into the dining room.

"Tresa, if you'll get them all in here we'll eat."

"Sure."

Pam stood awkwardly behind her chair, waiting. She was so out of place in this nice dining room. Though it was not the dining room of wealthy people, it was lovely and modestly elaborate. There was a chandelier above the table. A lace tablecloth was set with pale blue china trimmed in thin vines of gold. The tableware looked as if it were gold plated. The glassware was very thin and delicate. The furniture in the room was deep cherry, a tall breakfront, a long buffet, a long table and high-backed chairs. Pam wished she could become invisible. This was what she had been afraid of. She had been away from this kind of life for so long that she felt horribly out of place. She loved Beth, Tresa, and Justin with all her heart, and yes, she loved Ross. She had known and liked him when she was sixteen years old, the year Beth had become engaged to marry him. He had treated her like a little sister. But the girl she was then, was not the person she had become. That girl was gone.

She waited for Zenoa to come back into the room. She had to see her again. Her first impression had been wrong. This girl was just a girl, twenty years old, hadn't Beth said? It was ridiculous that in her exceptionally pretty face Pam had seen the image of the doll.

Tresa had seen the leaching of color from Pam's face when she first met Zenoa. In the confusion of voices, the meetings, the other activity in the kitchen she had wondered if only she noticed Pam's reaction. Now, at the dining table, with everyone seated and eating, Tresa watched them.

She noticed that Pam hardly ate. In that way she was like Zenoa. Every time there was a family dinner, which usually happened once a week, the only times she had eaten with Zenoa, she had noticed that Zenoa really ate nothing. After that first dinner, she had said to her mother, "Mom, look at her plate. She didn't eat anything." And Beth had answered, "That's the way I was the first time I went to Ross's folk's house. I was so scared I couldn't swallow. Don't worry, she'll get used to us."

Since that day there had been four or five meals here at home with Mom and Dad in which Zenoa was part of the family, and every time Tresa had noticed that Zenoa really ate nothing. "Look," she had told Beth, "she really doesn't eat. She only rearranges the food on her plate to make it look like she's eating."

"Tresa," Beth said, "you watch her too much. I don't think you like her. Why don't you try to get acquainted with her? Take her out to lunch?"

Beth had no idea how that had stung. "I wasn't really being critical. I was just . . ." Then, she had said, "Do you notice how she looks at Blake?"

"I think she looks at all men in that way. I think she's just being herself."

Tresa never again discussed Zenoa with her mother. For the first time in her life it seemed Beth had taken sides with someone against her. There was no one with whom she could talk about her feelings. Her . . . revulsion? Her fear? *Fear?*

Yes, she thought now for the first time as the voices of the men and her mother swirled lightly around her. Yes, it was fear. Each time Zenoa's childlike voice tinkled like breaking glass among the other voices, something in Tresa cringed. More than jealousy. More than the fear that Blake was hopelessly drawn to her. It was simple fear, as raw as skin peeled back.

She hadn't recognized it until she had seen Pam's reaction to Zenoa.

Tresa listened to the conversation at the dinner table. Like herself, Pam was silent. Tresa could see that her aunt felt painfully ill at ease. Also, when she looked up her eyes went to Zenoa and she stared. It was a stare of recognition. Pam had seen the girl before. She stared at her as if she couldn't believe her eyes, but Zenoa acted as if she didn't notice. Nor, it seemed to Tresa, had any of the others noticed. For the first time Tresa wondered if Zenoa had been in prison. If so, she must not have been there long, and obviously she didn't remember Pam. Or if she did, she didn't reveal it.

Pam, Tresa could see, was glad when the dinner was finally over. Tresa too was glad. She had plans. Tomorrow she was going to run a check on Zenoa, see if she had been in prison.

She helped Beth clear the table and put the dishes in the dishwasher. Pam came with them into the kitchen, making excuses to the men when they invited her to join them in the living room. Tresa saw she wanted to be in a less social setting, probably only wanted to go home. She tried to help Pam by saying, "You guys go on. Zenoa can go with you. Mom and I need Aunt Pam with us."

Pam gave her a grateful look.

Tresa didn't mention Zenoa and Pam's reaction to her. She didn't want to ask in front of Beth.

As soon as the dining room was back in its pristine order, and the dishwasher humming, Pam said, "I hope you don't mind, Beth, if I say goodnight. It was a lovely dinner."

"So early? Why don't you join us in the living room?"

Tresa said, "Maybe she's tired, Mom. Can I drive you home, Aunt Pam?"

Beth said, "Oh, didn't you know she got her old car running? I'd say it would be a good advertisement for Volkswagen, after twenty-four years she —" Beth stopped, obviously thinking, *she came home from prison to find her old car still started.*

Tresa jumped on it immediately, hoping to take that white, strained, bloodless look from Pam's face. "Really? Tell me about it, Pam."

"Like Beth said. It was still in the garage, you know. So are the other cars."

"No, I didn't know. Do you know I've never been in that house? Justin and I used to ride over there and up into the driveway, but it never occurred to me that the cars were still in the garage. Why didn't you tell me, Mom?"

"You didn't ask."

Tresa laughed. She saw Pam almost smile. Her face seemed less—*frightened?* She wondered how Pam could bear to go back into that house, because Mom *had* told her it had never been cleaned up.

As if Pam picked up her thoughts, she said, "I'm having new carpets put down in the upper hall, Nicky's room and Mom and Daddy's, as soon as I can get a carpet layer. Everyone seems so busy." She paused. "Maybe no one wants to work in that house."

"You're going to keep the house, then?" Tresa asked.

"No, only until . . ." Her voice faded away leaving the sentence unfinished.

Beth said, "She's searching for something that must have been stolen."

"You mean the house was broken into?"

Beth said, "No window was broken out or anything, but it seems someone had been living there."

"You're kidding! Who?"

Pam said softly, "I didn't see her clearly. I heard her moving about in the middle of the night. My clothes, you see, had been taken from my closet and moved into Kit's room, across the hall. And I heard a noise. It woke me. I looked out to see a girl with long curly hair going through the light that came in the glass of the front door. I think she was wearing my clothes. I thought at first she must have had a key—"

Tresa cried, "Where would she have gotten a key? Didn't Mom have the only set of keys?"

Beth asked, "What do you mean, you thought at first?"

"I put chairs under the knobs. But last night I thought I heard someone again."

"Good God," Tresa murmured. She had a vision of that large house, buried in its deep lot behind the tall trees. It had always looked haunted to her and Justin, and they had discussed as they sat on their bicycles the mysterious murders that had taken place there, and how it now looked so . . . dangerous, as if something evil lived within. And once, when Justin was about thirteen, he had sworn he saw a face in the attic window. It really had scared him. He wasn't pretending. He refused ever to ride into the driveway again. He didn't even want to ride past it. So they had started bicycling toward the park instead where they had winding paths on which they rode.

"Aunt Pam," Tresa asked, "why don't you come and live with me? I have a sofa that makes out into a bed. You're welcome to it."

Pam looked at first as if she were going to cry, but she smiled at Tresa and said, "That's so generous of you, Tresa. Thanks. But I can't. I wouldn't. And there are things I have to do at home, before I can leave."

"Leave? Where are you going?"

Beth said, as if trying to end the conversation, "She's thinking of moving to Florida, and I think that's a marvelous idea. Now we should go in and be with the others for a while. Thanks for your help, girls."

"I really should go now," Pam said.

Beth answered, "At least come in and say goodnight."

Tresa ached for Pam. She saw how difficult it was for her to go into the living room, say goodnight to each man and to Zenoa. Especially it was difficult for her to speak to Zenoa.

In a carefully modulated voice she said, "It was a pleasure meeting you."

"You'll be here for the wedding Sunday, won't you," Zenoa said, a statement more than a question.

She stood beside Justin, coming only to his shoulder, her long hair bright, almost artificial looking, as if it weren't real human hair. The half-smile that was always on her lips, that was now to Tresa only the expression that was Zenoa, seemed even more pronounced, as if there really were silent laughter, inner contempt. A knowledge of something kept to herself, as if she were laughing inwardly at them all, and especially now at Pam. Tresa saw Pam's glance, as she turned away. It went down over the short little dress Zenoa wore. An odd thought came to Tresa's mind. *She said someone was wearing her old clothes.* It was followed immediately by a chill. The dress was short, princess style, with a little flared skirt, and a small round collar. The style of the late sixties?

Tresa followed her mother and Aunt Pam to the front door. She waited until Pam was gone, and Beth had locked the door, then she said, "Mom, I'm going into the den for a few minutes.

397

There's something I want to see."

Beth returned to the living room, and Tresa went into the den and closed the door. A few months ago Blake would have joined her within minutes, seeking her out, wanting to be with her. But tonight he was enthralled with Zenoa. He would stay where he could watch her, watch every move, be there to catch her eye whenever he could. The pain was still deep and raw, but there was something added. Resignation? Also, there were things now she had to know.

One entire shelf in the storage closet was filled with old picture albums, starting from the year of her parents' engagement. Through these albums Tresa had known her mother's family. Grandma and Grandpa, a handsome couple in their forties. She had known Nicky, forever a preteen, and Kit, the little sister. She had also known Pam. The girl who had been sentenced to thirty years for the murder of that family. The sentence actually was light for such dreadful murders, it seemed to Tresa as she grew older, so therefore the judge must have had some doubt, some sympathy for the accused eighteen-year-old.

In the silence of the closet Tresa pulled down one of the old albums. She was looking only for Pam.

She found her, standing with the family. Pam, sixteen, seventeen. Finally, in another album there was Pam again, eighteen.

She was standing behind Kit, so that only part of her dress was visible. But Tresa could see it was a princess style, with a small round collar and flared skirt. It was floral, but the colors were dimmed.

It could have been the very same dress that Zenoa was wearing tonight.

Eleven

Don't think about it.

Pam lay in bed staring at the rectangle of pale light that was her window. A pale glow from a street light down on the corner beyond the house next door angled obliquely through the trees, absorbed mostly by leaves. Bits of moonlight and starlight further outlined the window. But the room seemed dungeon dark.

That was the way she wanted it. After she came home from having dinner with Beth and her family, she had carefully checked the downstairs doors and windows to make sure they were locked, then she had closed herself into her own room and slipped the chair under the knob. If it were true that the girl who had been coming into the house and taking her clothes was Justin's fiancée, then she knew the girl was not in the house at least at the present. She was with Justin and the family. It had taken Pam only minutes to get home. Zenoa was still at Beth's.

Don't think about it.

It was the only way to retain her sanity. If she weren't already insane. During her years in prison she had not been under psychiatric care. She hadn't needed it. She understood reality, even though she believed with all her heart that something inanimate had been imbued with movement, if not with life as it was known and partly understood. Had been able to move and to kill. Had motives of its own, which, Pam believed, were somehow almost human in that the doll had seemed to want possession of something. Of Kit's room. Perhaps of the whole house. Of Pam's clothes, later . . . as it grew . . . and more, it wanted penetration into the family where it could . . . gain further possession? Where it could destroy . . . kill . . .

NO, don't think about it!

She turned onto her back and stared at the ceiling. She could see, faintly, the light fixture. If she let her imagination go she would think it had legs, and eyes that stared down at her. She almost laughed. The dark streaks on four corners were the gold-colored metal decorations that held the globe, and the two spots that looked like eyes were flowers in the glass globe. Although they weren't visible she knew that thin, trailing vines and leaves connected the flowers. She had looked at that fixture every night for many years when she was a girl. She knew it by heart.

She turned onto her right side, facing the door. Even the outlines of the chair propped under the knob were faintly visible now from a rising moon.

Her mind wandered, edging around the face of Justin's fiancée. Had she been searching so hard for the doll, so puzzled by its disappearance, that she was ready to see a resemblance where there really was none? Perhaps, she thought, tomorrow she would go to the animal shelter and choose a couple of dogs and cats from the pets that were scheduled for the gas chamber. It would give them another chance at life, and give her company. A presence in the house other than the ghosts that haunted the halls. The presence of something who looked like a young woman, but who seemed to be able to enter the house without keys.

On the other hand, perhaps she should just put the house up for sale and leave. Forget everything, leave it all behind. The cars had to be sold. Probably separately, but the house could be offered with the furniture.

No, I can't. She had never left home in spirit. Every night in prison when she closed her eyes she saw her old room. In memory she wandered through the house, going to each room, seeing the faces of the people she loved. Nicky in his room, Kit in hers. Mom and Daddy. They were always in the den, Daddy with his paper. Mom with a magazine, her feet up on the sofa.

The wedding is only two days away. It has to be stopped.

"You've lost it, Pam," she whispered to herself. Go to sleep,

400

forget it. It's only a terrible coincidence. There's no way you can stop that wedding, nor should you.

She pulled one of the pillows over her head.

In the darkness she saw again the dress the girl had been wearing, and there was no way she could make herself believe she had been deluding herself. It was her dress. She had bought it with her own money when she went to work at the supermarket twenty-five years ago. She had worn it only once.

The girl who had been living in the house, who had taken her clothes, was Zenoa. The name of the doll had been Zenoa. The face of the girl was the same as the face of the doll.

But who would ever believe her?

Not even Detective Jefferson, the one person who had stood by her, would believe that. Though he had come to her many times in the past, quizzing her obliquely about the doll, she had told him nothing. It was important to her that he not believe her insane. She cared what he thought about her.

Through the years he had continued to come to the prison to see her, and had wanted to be the one to take her away from the prison. But she had not called him. Even now he might not know she had been released. She had a job to do first, then she would call him, if she could. He had been talking about retirement lately. He would be sixty on his next birthday. "Time to do something else," he had said on their last visit. "I've learned that some cases can never be solved, so I might as well go and see if I can find a place that's peaceful." Then he added something that stunned her to a heart-racing silence. "The thing is, I'm waiting for you, so you can come along." He had smiled, as if he might be teasing. But afterwards she thought, no, Jeff doesn't tease. She carried his image with her. His hair had turned silver, but he was still strong and straight.

Maybe he could be part of her life, now.

No. Why would he want to be?

Just go, she told herself. Don't try to understand any of this. We are looking at the universe through incredibly small, incredibly limited human eyes. Forget the big bang, forget any attempt to find a beginning. Our hearts pulse, nature pulses. Why is it so difficult to believe the entire universe pulses? The expansion of the universe will be followed by a contraction, and on and on forever. What was there before the big bang? The contraction that was traceable? Other residues, floating through space, parts of which came to earth, and, perhaps, became such creatures as *Zenoa*.

Pam knew herself, her own mind. Only she knew she was not wrong the night she saw the doll move. She saw the blood on its face and hands and clothing. She saw the ice pick where the doll had dropped it. She saw the doll walk, alert, and she saw it drop as if the light from the sun had killed it.

But when she tried to tell, Beth looked at her as if she had totally lost her mind. Even Gramma Vee had not believed her. Within her own mind she knew, but no other living human mind would believe. *Why?* she could cry out to them. Why don't you believe? How can you say *anything* is not possible? Conversely, how is a smallest thing possible, or a largest thing? How can there *be* a beginning or an end? And within that scope, how was anything not possible?

Before she slept she knew there was one more person she would tell.

Tresa had overslept. She had stayed up late, thinking, sitting up in bed with her knees drawn up and her arms hugging her legs, wishing she dared call her aunt. A lot of crazy thoughts had been going through her head, and she wasn't sure but that some of it was wishful thinking. Zenoa had a police record, she was sure of it. But there was no way to find out until Monday. She wished she had made friends with someone who had access to police files, someone she could ask on a Saturday to check Zenoa out for her. If her boss weren't going to be out of town she could ask him.

She had to work Saturday morning. She was going to be late. Not that her boss would even know, since he wouldn't be there. But she had some depositions to put on the word processor before noon. The earlier she got through, the earlier she could go talk to Pam.

She'd call her, ask her to have lunch, maybe. She wondered if Pam had problems being in public, out around people.

She hadn't had a chance to ask Pam about her years in

prison, what kind of life she'd been able to lead. She wasn't sure that she should ask her. Had she been with people, or had she been mostly alone?

Tresa had seen how uncomfortable Pam was last night. How difficult it was even for her to eat. How pale she'd been after she met Zenoa. If she knew something about Zenoa, why hadn't she told? Instead she'd run off as soon as she could after dinner, pale and silent. Tresa had wanted to go after her, but they'd started a game of cards, and Tresa was forced to play, hoping it would end and she'd get home early enough to call Pam. She hadn't.

Tresa was just stepping out of the shower when the phone rang. So early? She looked at the clock. A few minutes after eight.

Dripping, trying to absorb the water with a big towel, she ran barefoot into her bedroom and picked up the telephone.

"Tresa, this is Pamela. Did I wake you?"

"Pam! No, you didn't wake me. I was going to call you. I wanted to call you last night, but it was past midnight when I got back to the apartment, and I was afraid it would be too late."

"I'm sure I was still awake, but I wouldn't have heard the phone. It's downstairs. I want to talk to you, Tresa. Could you come to the house?"

Pam would have thought she wasn't working today, of course. Saturday. The day before Justin's wedding. Tresa's mind ran rapidly over the depositions she had promised herself she'd get on the processor. What the heck? She could squeeze them in Monday.

"Sure. If that's what you want."

"You've never seen inside the house, you said. I thought you might like to see it."

"I'd love to! I'll be there as soon as I can get ready, okay?"

"Thank you, Tresa."

"Is there anything I can bring?"

"No. Just yourself."

Only after Pam had hung up did Tresa begin worrying. She had sounded . . . sad? Frightened? She wanted to talk, but in her excitement Tresa hadn't even asked what about. It was serious, Tresa sensed.

She hurried, throwing on jeans and a loose knit top, and sandals. She brushed her hair and pulled it back into a single barrette at the back of her neck. Without bothering to make up her face she ran out, grabbing her shoulder bag and car keys.

When she drove into the driveway of the old house, the gloom of the place made her shudder. She sat a moment in the shadow of trees and the high, Victorian angles of the house and wondered how Pam could stand returning there.

Tresa got out of the car. The grass was mown, but no one had kept the shrubs trimmed, and they had grown tall in the spaces between sidewalks and the walls of garage and house, almost hiding windows. It increased the silence, the sense of oppression.

At the closing of the car door Pam appeared suddenly, coming from a door that connected a long, one-story garage to the rear of the house. She was dressed as simply as Tresa, and like Tresa had tied her hair back. She stood smiling as Tresa went toward her. Tresa had no feeling of having just recently met this person. It was like an old friendship, of a soul close to her own, someone she would always be able to trust. This person would not scold her, as her own mother had, for seeing between Blake and Zenoa something dangerous. Pam was, instantly, a friend.

"Thank you for coming," Pam said, receiving her hug and returning it warmly.

"I was just thinking . . . you're not afraid here? You have to be really brave to come back here."

Pam shrugged, her gaze flicking over the shadowed places, going up the angles of the house toward the peak at the top, toward the attic window and the slope of the roof beneath it. She smiled again, the same small smile with which she had greeted Tresa, as if no smile would ever reach her heart again.

"Not brave," Pam said, "Just determined."

"Determined?" Somehow that didn't fit Tresa's idea of reasons why Pam would have returned to this terrible place.

"I had a job to finish, you see." Pam's hand was warm on Tresa's elbow as she guided her toward the door. "Come in and have a cup of coffee with me. Do you drink coffee?"

"Oh sure."

They went into a hallway that had a door at both ends and

404

windows that looked out into a backyard that Tresa had never seen. It appeared to be almost a forest, filled with the shade of trees, and many more shrubs that had grown beyond their allotted spaces.

"This used to be a breezeway," Pam explained. "We moved into this house when I was a little girl, and there were only railings here where the walls are now. When it rained and blew, the roof over the breezeway wasn't much protection, so Mom and Dad had it enclosed. This door goes into the utility room. Our maid, Alice, had just ironed some of Kit's little dresses. They're still hanging there."

Pam opened the door and Tresa stepped into a large utility room where there were a washer and dryer, a deep sink and a regular double sink, a row of cabinets, an ironing board still standing with an iron, as if the iron had just been used. But the sight of the little girl's clothes hanging on a metal support at the end of the board depressed Tresa. For the first time she was entering the reality of what had happened in this house.

"You left the dresses there," Tresa said wonderingly.

"Yes. I cleaned the floor, and swept down the spiderwebs, and brushed the dust and webs off the dresses, and hung them back."

The oppression Tresa had sensed from the outside settled within her. Quietly she went ahead of Pam into the large kitchen where a table and chairs stood by double windows. She saw where her mother had tried to recreate her childhood home, now that she was here. The same kind of large family kitchen, the same warm atmosphere, though here, in this house, the warmth was gone. Left was the space and a sense of the past, of one night in which horror had moved through the house. The fragrance of freshly made coffee did not dispel the sense of horror.

"First, we'll have the coffee, all right?" Pam said.

Tresa noticed the cups were already on the table. So were cloth napkins that matched the tablecloth, and a plate of bakery goods, donuts, apple fritters, Danish rolls.

"Then," Pam continued as Tresa sat down, "after I've told you—what I have to tell you—I'll show you the rest of the house."

Tresa watched the dark stream of coffee from the pot as Pam poured. Steam rose in the cool air of the kitchen.

"Is it about Zenoa?" she asked softly, not looking at Pam.

Pam paused. "How did you know that?"

"Well . . . I've wondered about her. And I saw the way you looked when you met her last night."

"You wondered about her?"

"Yes — uh — everyone in the family is so enthralled with her. Even Mom. And, I'm sure you noticed, also Blake."

She waited, giving Pam a chance to say something, but she remained silent. She finished pouring the coffee and put the pot back onto the stove. Then she sat down, and put sugar and cream into the cup, turning the coffee pale.

Finally she spoke as she stirred. "But you wondered. What? Why?"

"She came so suddenly into our lives. Justin brought her to the house, and everybody just *fell* for her. Except me, of course, and I'm not sure about Dad. Then, less than a month later they had set their wedding date. Aunt Pam, I want you to know it's not just jealousy on my part. I mean Blake . . . never acted that way around anyone, but that's not the reason I have always felt there was more to Zenoa than anyone knew. She doesn't have any family. No relatives are coming to the wedding. There won't be anyone there but us. Now isn't that rather odd?"

Pam continued to stir.

Tresa faced her, watching her eyes even as they watched the coffee. "Then last night I saw your reaction to her. I knew you'd seen her before. Therefore she must have been in prison."

Pam raised her eyes abruptly, staring into Tresa's. Surprise? Caused by her observation, or what? Still, Pam said nothing.

Tresa continued, "That might explain why she claims she has no family. Maybe she doesn't want them to know where she is."

She waited. Pam's eyes moved away from hers. She picked up the plate of sweet rolls and offered Tresa one, then put the plate down without taking one for herself. Tresa continued to wait, nibbling the roll. She had no interest in it, and soon laid it down on her saucer. A joy in food seemed to have left her. It coincided with Zenoa's entrance into her life.

406

"I didn't meet her in prison, Tresa," Pam said gently.

Not prison. Well, thank God. Tresa was surprised at her feelings of relief. For Justin, she told herself.

"The truth is, I never met the girl before in my life."

Tresa struggled to understand, trying in her impatience to read between the lines. "Then . . . your reaction to her? Oh! It must have been the dress." She paused again to give Pam a chance to explain, but Pam still hesitated, as if she were no longer able to express herself. Tresa spoke for her, "You said someone had been living in the house, that they'd even stolen your clothes. I looked in one of the old albums Mom has and there's a group picture taken on a lawn. Here, probably. And you were in it, and the dress you were wearing looked as if it could have been the same one Zenoa had on. Is that it?"

Pam took a long, deep breath, and sat back in her chair.

"Partly," she said. "If that were all, I'd just laugh it off. I'd say that Justin must have shown her this house, and maybe told her what happened here, and so she knew the house was unoccupied. Maybe she even got the key from Beth. That is, maybe she saw it, and had an extra made. Then, maybe she just came in, alone, found the clothes, and began using them. I can't say she *lived* here, but there is indication someone has been sleeping in Kit's bed."

She paused. She even smiled at Tresa. It increased Tresa's bewilderment. Was that all? Then why had she reacted as she did last night?

Tresa said slowly, watching her, wondering, "You've really figured it out, haven't you?"

"In my position you do a lot of thinking, Tresa. I've been doing a lot of thinking for a long time. A lot of reading too. I worked in the prison library, which saved my sanity, I'm sure. I actually enjoyed the work. Of course my dreams of a normal life had to be left behind, along with everything I loved. My parents, Kit, Nicky. Beth too, in a way, because you see she never believed in me. And I had a very special grandmother. I lost her too. They said she committed suicide."

"Yes," Tresa said softly, "Mom told me. I want you to know though, Pam, I think you're innocent."

"You do?"

"Yes. When I started working for this law firm, I learned how to do some digging. So I read your trial transcripts. And I just don't think you did those — that."

"I didn't. But, I know who did."

Tresa's breath caught in her throat. Her heart began to pound. "And you never told?" she whispered. A vision passed swiftly through her mind. Young Pamela going to the door in the deep of night to surreptitiously let someone into the house. But the vision made Pam guilty though she didn't do the actual killing, and Tresa rejected it immediately. Pam's next words surprised Tresa as much as her admission had.

"Yes, I told. I told Beth, and I told Gramma Vee."

"For God's sake! Mom knew? All this time?" Beth had never indicated to Tresa that she knew Pam was innocent, that she knew who was the actual killer. Indeed, Beth had allowed Tresa to believe that she thought Pam guilty.

"Beth never believed me," Pam said in a low voice. "Neither did my grandmother. I never told anyone else. My lawyers knew, because Gramma Vee had told them, but of course they didn't believe it either. I vowed never to tell another soul. And I would have stuck with that. But last night, after meeting . . . *her,* after . . ." She paused again and moistened her lips.

Tresa waited, her bewilderment turning to consternation. All those people knew Pam was innocent of the murders, yet all of them doubted her. Why? *Why?* She didn't realize she had whispered aloud until Pam glanced at her.

"Last night I knew I had to break my vow to myself. I had to tell you. I have a reason. It isn't entirely selfish. That is, of course I want you to know I didn't do those terrible things, I loved them, loved them all. I wouldn't have hurt anyone, anything. But the reason I have to tell you, and beg you to keep an open mind and try to accept this thing, is that she is there. Zenoa. And she's . . . dangerous."

Twelve

Zenoa—*dangerous?*

Tresa had heard the growing urgency in Pam's voice as she spoke, but Tresa was more confused than ever. She had difficulty keeping it straight. Zenoa? A girl who hadn't even been born twenty-four years ago. What did she have to do with Pam having been found guilty of the murders of her family?

Zenoa dangerous? How could Pam know, when she herself had said she'd never met her before? Dangerous in what way?

Pam said, "I have to take the chance that you're going to think I'm crazy. That's what happened then, I think. What else was Beth and Gram to think? I understand that. But, you see, when I was in prison I thought of ways and ways in which to destroy—the—the killer. Then when I got out—" She stopped again and looked pleadingly at Tresa. "In order to make you see it as I saw it, I have to go back to my little sister's ninth birthday. Kit's."

Pam took a long breath again. Tresa heard it in the quiet room. The occasional car that drove by on the street was muffled almost to silence by the trees, shrubs, walls. She listened to the faint sounds of the house, a creak in the floor, a rattle at the stove as Pam got up and renewed their coffee.

"Kit was the most precious little girl," Pam said. "She was the blond in our family. Her hair was long and lovely. She was quiet, a natural artist, I think. Anyway, Gramma Vee was exploring an antique store over in the heart of the city, close to where she lived, when she found a doll. It was large, a hundred years old, and had been in the back room of the store since the original owner bought the doll back in the eighteen hundreds. The doll had belonged to two little girls. One of the girls, though she was only six or seven, was said to have stabbed to death both her sister, and her aunt, with whom they lived. She had used an ice pick."

An ice pick. Tresa noticed the similarity in the murders instantly. But those had happened . . . when?

Again she saw she had spoken aloud when Pam said, "To be exact it was eighteen-sixty-nine."

One hundred years before the other ice pick deaths.

"The little girl was found with the aunt. The doors were locked. She was mute. She never spoke again. She died in an insane asylum a few years later. Also in the house was this large doll. It had been a very beautiful doll, but had been pretty much destroyed, its eyes gouged, its hair pulled out, scratches on its face."

Tresa had just given up trying to understand. She too sat back in her chair, as Pam had. She listened carefully, her eyes never leaving her aunt.

"Gramma Virginia bought the doll and took it to a doll restorer, to have it fixed for Kit's birthday. Gramma and I had lunch together, and she told me the history of the doll. I didn't tell Kit, of course. The doll was incredibly beautiful. It had long reddish blond hair, curly, parted in the middle, with little ribbons holding back small sections on each side of the part. It had large, round brown eyes, which were unusual in a doll. It had a strange expression on its lips, not quite a smile. It had a small overbite, and the corners of its lips kind of tucked into dimples."

As Tresa listened to the description of the doll she felt goosebumps rise on her arms. Pam was describing Zenoa.

She said, "That sounds like . . ." She let her voice drift to silence. But Pam seemed to understand.

"Yes." Pam's eyes met Tresa's briefly. "It was an unusual looking doll. Also, the coincidence of the old ice pick murders, and—those in my family—it's difficult to accept. I know."

"It's very confusing," Tresa murmured. There was more to the story, she knew, and she didn't want to distract Pam, though she sensed nothing would. The murders were connected, somehow. It was like a thread that Pam was slowly revealing to her.

"Kit didn't like the doll. She was afraid of it. She didn't know its history. No one but Gramma Vee and I knew. I think I told my boyfriend — but even though he was very important to me then, he isn't really a part of this. Anyway, strange things began to happen in Kit's room. She came to me. She was afraid."

Tresa listened, incredulous, as Pam described a little sister who she believed then was having mental problems.

"There was something about the doll that made Kit do these things, I thought. Instead of going to our mother, who was a child psychologist, I just tried to fix it myself. I called Gramma Vee and asked her if she'd take the doll back. Of course she would. But that was at eleven o'clock that night. I was going to take it over the next day on my lunch hour. I worked in a supermarket. But that night Kit came again to my room and said Zenoa had gone downstairs again to the powder room. The doll, Kit had been telling me, was fascinated by the powder room. She even put makeup on herself. She'd sit in the vanity chair and look at herself in the mirror, as if admiring herself."

Tresa leaned forward, her stomach pressed against the edge of the table. "Kit thought the doll *walked?* That she came alive at night?"

Pam nodded slightly. "She was terrified of the doll. The doll had ripped up her favorite Barbie dolls and their clothes, she said. She really believed this, Tresa."

"I don't understand why you didn't go to your parents. After all, your mother was a child psychologist."

"That's the very reason I didn't go. Kit was afraid she'd be put in an insane asylum."

"Like the last owner of the doll," Tresa said. Things were coming together in this confused mess. Kit had an overactive imagination, and it had turned rabid on her. "She was afraid the same thing would happen to her that happened to the other little girl."

"But remember, Kit didn't know that story."

"Then . . . ?"

"She knew that sometimes children were put into places to get well, and that she would be considered delusional at best."

"Oh."

"Anyway, that night, the night of the murders, Kit came to me again. So I told her I'd take the damn doll to the attic and lock it in there, until the next day. Then I was taking it back to Gramma Vee. So we went downstairs to the powder room, at three in the morning. The doll was there, on the vanity stool. I thought the same thing you're probably thinking. Kit put it there. She had even put some makeup on it. It didn't matter. I took the doll and went up to the attic. You've never been up there. It's a large room, with a solid floor. Some old things are up there. Among those old things are a tall chest of drawers, some baby beds, boxes, stuff like that. In one old box that was there when we bought the house was some old-fashioned stuff from a kitchen. Among the junk was an ice pick."

The ice pick of the murders. It was a chilling thought. Inwardly Tresa cringed. This was real life, and death. She wasn't sure she wanted to hear it. But she also thought of the other person Pam had known about, the real killer. Pam seemed to be leading farther and farther away from it. This thing, all this stuff about a doll. What did it have to do with the actual murders? She wanted to say impatiently, *forget the doll.* Then she remembered the strange coincidence of the doll's history, and she knew Pam was leading her down paths strange and twisted. She didn't want to go. But she couldn't walk out and leave Pam alone with this.

With difficulty Pam continued, her voice sounding strained, her eyes intense, staring at something only she saw.

"I told Kit to wait at the foot of the stairs. I carried the doll up under my arm. My left arm., I was going to lay it in a baby crib. But I was so disgusted I decided to put it in a drawer of the chest and shut the drawer. I was going to the chest when . . ."

Pam paused, looked down, then raised her eyes to Tresa's.

"I felt the doll move. It twisted under my arm, shoved at me with its hands. I dropped it. It gave me a hard shove, that threw me off balance. I fell against the chest. My head struck the corner of the chest. I blacked out."

What? Tresa wanted to cry, as if she hadn't heard. But she was unable to say anything.

"I didn't know," Pam said in a softer voice, "I didn't know I

412

had blacked out until I came to. It's that way. Consciously you're transported from one moment to the next. I knew I had been unconscious. There was a sickening pain in my head. There was blood on my forehead, sticky, partly dried. I stood up. The sun had risen, and the house was very quiet. I could see the light of day. I remembered the doll. It wasn't there."

Pam had told her the doll shoved her. It was like a nightmare her aunt was telling. Something not real. She said nothing in the brief pauses as Pam hesitantly told the story.

"I went down the attic stairs." Pam's eyes lowered, her voice trembled. "Kit was there in the hall, face down, the back of her pajamas tattered and dark with blood. It seemed to be everywhere, soaking the carpet, like tears on the walls. I don't know if I started screaming then. I don't think so. I think I went in complete silence through the upstairs. Nicky was just like Kit, in his room. Mom and Daddy were both on the floor too. Their room was like the hall."

She took a deep breath. Tresa said nothing.

"I went down the stairs. I was going to the door, going for help. It didn't occur to me to try to use a telephone, I was only thinking about our neighbor, getting her to help. In the foyer I saw the ice pick on the floor. The blade was rusty, dark with blood, the handle smeared. I picked it up. Can you imagine my horror? Yet I picked it up. I couldn't believe what I was seeing. Then I noticed the powder-room door was partly open, and I saw the doll sitting there on the chair smirking at herself in the mirror. As I stood watching, only a few seconds, it turned, got off the chair and came toward me, out into the hall. The sun wasn't exactly shining in the glass of the door, but the light was there, and a reflection of the sun on the carpet. The moment the doll came into the light, it fell. It changed in that moment. It became just a plain doll again. I'll never forget the way it looked. It lay there, on its back, its arms slightly raised. There was blood sprinkled on its face, its clothes, all over it. I ran out of the house screaming. I was holding the ice pick. Of course, everyone thought I had done it."

Pam paused again, as if she were exhausted.

"Thank you, Tresa," she said. "For not stopping me, for not running away from me. For not telling me I'm crazy. I told

Beth, and I told Gramma Vee this story, and neither of them believed me. Gramma told my lawyers, and wanted them to plead an insanity defense. They refused. They went instead with the intruder defense, saying someone had come in the attic window . . . but you said you read the transcript, you know how the trial went."

Tresa nodded. She was still unable to speak, or turn her eyes away from Pam. She didn't know what to say. It was too unbelievable. Pam took another deep breath.

"That isn't all," she said, looking at Tresa wearily. "The doll's name was Zenoa."

If Pam had thrown her hot coffee into Tresa's face, even after the terrible story she had told, she wouldn't have been more shocked.

"Zenoa!" she whispered.

"Yes." Pam stood up.

"You think . . . the doll . . . where is this doll? Now? Where is it now?"

"That's why I came back, Tresa. To get the doll, to destroy it. Beth told me she had put it in the attic, that she'd locked the door. It isn't there. Another thing—Gramma Vee had taken the doll home with her the night she supposedly killed herself. A detective, Detective Jefferson, noticed strange small footprints that had been made by the doll, and he couldn't understand. He thought someone had 'walked' the doll after the murders, yet he didn't think I had committed the murders. Jefferson has remained, or become, one of my few friends. But I never told him the truth about the doll. But he took it to Beth, back then, and Beth brought it over here."

"Yet it's gone?"

Pam picked up a large album from the kitchen counter and brought it back to the table. She laid it where Tresa could see it and opened it to a page already marked with a small slip of paper.

"I searched the whole house, Tresa. I couldn't find it. Then those strange things happened about the girl in the house, and my old clothes. Then, I met Zenoa at your house."

Tresa shook her head. She knew now what Pam was going to say, and she couldn't accept it. Her mind wasn't capable of taking a fantasy that far. "No," she whispered, more to herself than to Pam.

Pam pointed to a snapshot on a page of similar pictures. Tresa could see without leaning closer that it was a family gathering of some sort.

"We took pictures on Kit's birthday, just as we always did on every gathering. There's a picture of Kit's birthday cake," Pam put her finger on a slanted picture that clearly held nine candles and contained a birthday greeting and the name Kit.

Reluctantly, with robot movements, Tresa rose and leaned over the album where she could see clearly. Pam's finger moved back to the group of people and pinpointed a little girl with long blond hair holding a large doll. Tresa stared incredulously at the face of the doll. *Zenoa.* Though the picture was not terribly sharp or clear, the face of the doll resembled the face of the girl so completely it was shocking. Tresa pulled back.

Pam sat down, her hand flat on the open page of the album. Her eyes, looking across the table at Tresa were deep and sad.

"That was the doll, Tresa."

They sat in silence. Tresa tried to think.

She finally said, "I don't understand. The doll is gone. In its place a girl came. She looks exactly like the doll. The doll was dangerous."

"Very. Extremely. All the more so because no one in his right mind could ever attribute those—*actions* to something manmade. Nor motives. It seemed to have a motive. Where did these things come from?"

"Motive?"

"Kit—Kit knew. Zenoa, she said, wanted her room. She destroyed the other dolls Kit had. That was her first act. Another thing, Tresa. She moved only at night. In the daytime she was—seemed to be—only a doll."

Tresa felt the quick frown on her face. Her mouth opened. Memories tumbled one on the other.

"Yes," she said. "I hadn't thought of it. We all work, so it really hadn't come to my mind before. I mean, it was only one of those things."

"What?" Pam urged.

415

"She doesn't like sunshine She refused to go out into the sunshine that one day she came for Sunday dinner. She only came once. The rest of the time Justin has made excuses for her, and so we had our family dinners and gatherings in the evening."

Pam got up, closed the album, and laid it back on the kitchen counter. She came back to the table and sat down.

Tresa asked, "What does she want, Aunt Pam?"

"I don't know, Tresa. But you must stop the wedding."

"It's tomorrow! Tomorrow evening at eight!"

There again, an evening affair, after the setting of the sun.

Pam stood up. "Where does she live, Tresa? I came home to destroy the doll. I won't stop until I have. Where does Zenoa live?"

Thirteen

"Aunt Pam," Tresa whispered harshly, "That's *murder.*"

A flicker of pain crossed Pam's face. She looked off across the kitchen, and her eyes fell for a moment on the album. She stood at the edge of the table. Tresa sat still, looking up, her hands flat on the table top. Yes, murder. Murder had been done twenty-four years ago, and a hundred and twenty-four years ago. But this involved Tresa, and she couldn't.

"I don't know what she was," Tresa said, watching her aunt, feeling her pain. "But I know that Zenoa is flesh and blood, a real person. I can't help kill her, Aunt Pamela."

Pam sat down, her head lowered. Tresa thought she was going to cry, but when she lifted her head and looked at Tresa her eyes held only terribly deep, deep pain.

"I would have never thought any of this possible, Tresa," she said. "But I saw what happened. I know Zenoa is something that goes against all the laws of nature, but she exists. She killed. She will kill again."

"But—if this is true," Tresa cried desperately, "if Zenoa changed and became human over the years—maybe she also has some human feelings, Aunt Pam. Maybe she feels love. Maybe she's . . . *human,* now."

Pam laced her fingers together and looked in misery at Tresa. Her fingers worked together, nervously, as if they outwardly expressed the jumble of her thoughts.

Tresa found herself talking hastily and anxiously. "It's true there are some very strange things about Zenoa. She just seemed to have appeared out of nowhere. Mom wanted me to

417

have lunch with her, get better acquainted with her, because I—I felt a weird revulsion toward her right from the start."

Pam nodded, as if she understood. Tresa hadn't understood, now she felt as if she were seeing Zenoa with the eyes of a different reality. Her human reaction to Zenoa had been revulsion, instantly. Beth had thought it simple jealousy. So had Tresa, she realized, deep within, even as she knew there had to be more to it than that.

Tresa went on, "I suggested lunch. But there was nowhere I could call Zenoa. She said she'd call me. She never did."

"Where does she live, Tresa?" Pam asked again.

Tresa said, "I don't know, Aunt Pam, and that's the truth. Of course she's going to be living with Justin after tomorrow."

Pam bit her lip. "I hope you're right, Tresa. That she has become human, with human emotions. Because otherwise, there's only one solution. She has to be destroyed."

"I can't be a party to that. And you know, Pam, I don't think you're capable of murder either."

Pam closed her eyes tightly. Tears eased out. She wiped them away.

They sat quietly. Pam laced and unlaced her fingers. Then she said, surprisingly, "Maybe in the daytime she reverts to a doll. Maybe then—if I knew where she lives—"

At that moment Tresa saw her aunt in another light. She saw madness. She saw a woman who, perhaps in her hours of derangement from a fall, had murdered her family. She saw a woman who had met a young woman who had a startling resemblance to an old doll that was now missing, and who also carried the same name. Perhaps Pamela was, after all, capable of murder, then and now.

For the first time Tresa felt uncomfortable with Pam. She wanted to leave.

"Aunt Pam, I must go. I have some depositions to put on the word processor—"

Pam stood up quickly. "Don't you want to see the house first?"

Tresa hesitated. Then she said, "Yes, why not?"

Pam led the way and Tresa followed, going through a door into the front hallway.

Pam opened a door. "This is the den. We used to gather here to watch television. That chair over in the corner was Daddy's."

It had a haunted look. An old newspaper that had turned a sickening yellow drooped over the arm of the chair. As if Pam saw the direction of Tresa's gaze, she said, "I didn't even move his newspaper. I couldn't. That was Daddy's favorite place in the house. He was an attorney, as Beth has probably told you. A tax lawyer. He was good, he was a great father, solid gold. I've missed him daily. Mom too. All of them, even Beth. And you. You were an adorable baby then, and I loved babysitting."

She walked through the room and pointed out the favorite chairs of others of the family, and the sofa where her mother liked to sit.

Then she moved out into the hall again, and said unexpectedly, "Of course, I'm sure Zenoa had been living here, going out only at night, moving about only at night. Even though I've taken extra precautions about locking up, I still have heard sounds in the house, as if she still comes back. That's probably why she never told you where she lived."

Yes, Tresa thought, that's logical. But she had no desire to speak in this roomy house that had not moved forward in time. The light was gloomy, the air chilly. Vines and shrubs nearly covered the windows. Only the front door with its clear, etched glass seemed to draw light. Rays of sunshine reflected somehow into the front hall.

Pam opened a door on the inside of the hall. Tresa saw a small room beneath the rising staircase.

"This is the powder room."

It needed no other explanation. Tresa's eyes immediately found the vanity stool with the small woven metal back, and the tufted cushion. The room had a long knee-hole vanity and a wall mirror above it. The mirror had a series of cracks that lifted away from a shattered core where something had broken it.

Pam pointed to a couple of small spots on the white vanity stool cushion. "I didn't see these of course until I came home. I didn't even go in here the day I found them. *It* was in here, the doll. Zenoa. She got down and came toward me, as I told you. That was the first time I saw that Kit was right and it actually

419

did move. If she had been lying inert in the hallway, the way she fell when she came into the light there, I would never had known who, or what, killed my family."

Tresa looked closely at the spots on the cushion. Dark brown. "Blood?" she whispered. That awful coldness that gripped her since she came into the house intensified. For the first time she was seeing signs of the murders that had been so distant from her life.

"Yes."

Pam led the way up the stairs. Halfway up she pointed silently at small dark blotches on the rug. "I didn't even try to clean those, yet. The only thing they can be is her footsteps as she came down. See, they grow lighter, and finally disappear."

"And the detective asked you why the doll had blood on her shoes? Why didn't you tell him?"

"Don't you see, no one believed me. So I decided to say nothing."

There had been moments when Tresa didn't believe her. There had also been moments when she allowed her belief in the natural order of things to be suspended and in which she did believe. Now, more and more as they went through the house, Tresa believed. She saw the ruin of the carpet in the master bedroom, where Pam had tried to clean it up and make the room neat again. She saw the bloodstains in Nicky's room and the hall.

"The carpets have to be replaced," Pam said. "But I only want to do what I have to do and get out of here. I'm going to sell it at whatever price I can get."

Tresa nodded.

Kit's room was like a small jewel in the house. Pink and white, it was almost like new. There were no edges of dust, no webs in the corners, as there were in some of the other rooms. Pam opened the closet door and showed Tresa where Kit's clothes had been.

"I folded them and laid them on the shelf. These, evidently, are things Zenoa didn't want. She left them hanging. They were in my closet when I lived here, of course."

By the time they were climbing the attic stairs Tresa was beginning to feel as if she were going to suffocate. She wanted to leave. How could Pam bear to stay here even one night? She couldn't break and run now, though. Now that they were almost finished with seeing the house.

The attic was large, with dormers dark and windowless. The center of the room with the peaked ceiling overhead, had board floors and one finished dormer with a window that let in a thin light, enough, with the help of a single bulb, to see the webs that had woven across the peaks and dips of the ceiling, over the furniture, the boxes of things saved.

A tall chest stood in the center of the room.

"Is this the chest?"

"Yes," Pam said, and reached up to her forehead. "I have a small scar."

When she pushed her hair, Tresa saw the white line, almost invisible, in the edge of Pam's hair. How could a jury have found that young girl guilty? Tresa wondered.

Suddenly Tresa was anxious to talk to Justin. Minutes were passing, taking him closer and closer to the wedding, only a little more than twenty-four hours away. Yet she was perplexed.

"Pam," she said, "why do you suppose she wants to marry Justin? Could it be just a legitimate way to become . . . maybe owner of this house? Is that what she wants?"

"I don't know what she wants. Beth put the house in my name. Of course, if I were dead . . ."

"I don't understand why she took the chance of staying in the family. Why didn't she just leave? No one would ever have known. If she changed, and became like us, then why stay where there is even a picture of her as she once was? Why not go away where no one would ever know about her?"

Talking like this made Tresa feel as if she were part of the madness in this house. She suddenly remembered the strange feeling of suffocation as she entered the stairway to the attic. It was as if she had crossed a division between two realities.

Pam said, "Maybe she can't leave. Maybe it's *here* that keeps her as she is. Maybe in this house is some kind of energy that rejuvenates her. I don't know, Tresa. Don't you think I have tried to understand? I can't. I don't know. I only know what happened, and I'm terrified of what might happen. I think not only Justin is in danger, but all of you."

Tresa saw Pam's pale face in the twilight of the attic, with the chest behind her. It was Pam, Tresa suddenly thought, who was most in danger, if all this were true.

"You should get out of here, Aunt Pam. Don't stay here."

"I have to stay. If she comes back — I have to be here."

"Aunt Pam, if it's true that she is not — is what you believe she is, what chance do you think you'd have against her?"

The answer Tresa had demanded didn't come. Tresa saw Pam knew, but she couldn't put it into words. Suddenly Tresa knew what she had to do. She had to find Justin and talk to him. If she hurried he'd probably still be in bed in his apartment. She knew he and Zenoa partied every night until almost daylight, and on weekends Justin caught up on his sleep.

"May I use your phone, Aunt Pam?"

"Of course. But the only one that's connected is downstairs."

"Fine. I'm going to call Justin and arrange to meet him. I want to call before he leaves his apartment."

Her slob brother. She could almost see him sprawled toward all four corners of his sleep-sofa, which took up about half of his one-room pad when it was extended. Otherwise, the room wasn't too bad.

It was such a relief to get back downstairs that she felt as if something vital had been pulled out of her. She leaned against the wall as she dialed the old-fashioned black wall phone. She had noticed, though, a dainty little blue princess phone in Pam's bedroom, so a girl in 1969 had not been so much different from a girl in the nineties.

"Huh?" Justin said sleepily, then rousing, added, "Hello."

"Wake up, sleepy head," Tresa said tenderly.

An image of Justin at age eight came to her. His hair had been blond then, and curly, his face round and dimply. Though she was only a year and two months older than he, she'd always felt so much older. He was such a baby. Now she had to look up at him. His face had gone from round and dimply to firm and angled, with high cheek bones and a strong chin and jaw. But his hair was still wavy and had a habit of falling down onto his forehead.

"Zat you, Tres?"

"Yeah. Sit up, put your britches on. I'm coming over. Okay?"

"Sure. I guess. Bring something."

"All right. Be there soon. Well . . . give me an hour, okay?"

"An hour? Where are you?"

"At Aunt Pam's."

"What? Why?"

"I'll tell you later."

She didn't ask Pamela to go with her. She had to talk to Justin alone. It would take a lot of warm, sisterly convincing to get through to him. Even if that were possible. He was so much in love with Zenoa. Zenoa had woven a spell around him as tough and firm as the cobwebs in the corners of this old house.

Fourteen

Tresa left the elevator on the sixth floor, her handbag under one arm, the strap over her shoulder, and three white paper sacks in her hands. A mixture of aromas wafted around her. She grinned apologetically at others in the rising, quiet elevator but gave no explanation. She was glad to leave the confined space.

Justin opened the door for her as if he could smell her coming. She teased him as she unloaded in the tiny kitchen area in the corner where there was a minuscule sink, an eighteen-inch square counter and one wall cabinet over a two burner hot plate. A microwave took up most of the room. There was a table for two, with two chairs.

She had even brought coffee. She was going to soften him up with food.

"You must want to borrow my fortune," he said, peering into sacks not yet unpacked. "You're after something, I can see that."

"Rolls, coffee, and fish and chips with hushpuppies. How's that for breakfast?"

He sat down and elaborately tucked the corner of a paper napkin into his collar. He hadn't worn such a bib since they both were in high chairs. She laughed at him, but it was a laugh hiding the strain she was feeling.

She sat down. He began to eat, not bothering to remove the food from Long John Silver's styrofoam tray to a plate.

"What's the honor?" he asked. "Aren't you eating?"

"Just coffee. I ate with Aunt Pam."

424

"How was it there? The house and all. I can't imagine anyone just going in there to stay. It must be in a terrible spidery mess. She been doing a lot of cleaning?"

"I think so. But some rooms are still closed. The master bedroom, for one." She paused, then watching him, said, "You should go there, Justin. It's weird going into those bedrooms. Our grandparents' clothes are still in the closets, the bed was still unmade. The carpets are stained horribly and the walls have blood blotches. She said she's going to replace the carpets, and give all the clothes to charities."

"Then she's selling?"

"Maybe. Probably."

"Good." He ate half a donut in one bite.

Tresa said carefully, "I'm here Justin because I have to talk to you."

Responding to the suddenly serious tone, Justin slowed down and looked up. "Yeah?"

"She told me all about that night."

"The night of the murders?"

"Yes."

He leaned back in his chair. "Creepy."

"Yes, very. And surprising."

"How do you mean?"

"You know I told you I read the transcript of her trial, and I became convinced Pam is innocent."

"Yeah, right. So who do you think did it?"

Tresa said nothing. She looked into her brother's eyes for a long moment. She saw him squint slightly, a suspicious narrowing.

He said, "You're not going to tell me it was somebody else in the family, someone she was covering for?"

"Not exactly." She reached for her purse. "First, Justin, I want to show you a couple of old pictures that came from an old album. The last of Grandma and Grandpa's albums. Some of the last pictures taken."

He pushed aside his food, and put his elbows on the table. Leaning forward he looked curiously toward Tresa removing the snapshots from her purse. She laid them flat on the table, facing him. Praying he would at least look at the pictures, at least listen, she pushed them closer. First the one where Pamela was wearing the dress Zenoa had worn last night at dinner.

She put her index finger on the picture of Pam. Justin smiled slightly.

"Yeah, Aunt Pam. Doesn't look a lot different from now, does she?"

"Notice the dress, Justin."

He stared hard at the dress, and his smile disappeared. But he said nothing.

"Doesn't it look familiar?"

He shrugged. She knew by the look on his face that he recognized it, but he wasn't going to step into that trap.

"You remember hearing that someone had been living in the house, Justin? Did Mom tell you? Some girl had sort of made herself at home there, coming in, wearing Pam's old clothes."

"So?"

"Doesn't this look like the dress Zenoa wore last night?"

Anger flickered on Justin's face. "You're crazy. It only looks like Zenoa's dress." He shoved the picture away and turned sideways in the chair. His face hardened, a muscle tightening in his cheek.

The picture Pam had given Tresa from the album was a better, clearer picture than the one in the album at home. Pam standing farther forward in the group, the colors more distinct. There was no doubt it was the same dress, but Tresa didn't want to argue with Justin. She wanted to convince him, not fight with him. She pushed the other picture forward, but he didn't look at it. Suddenly he smiled.

"Even if it were. So what? So sometimes we go over there and walk around. Zenoa thinks it's a lovely old home to go to waste, to just sit there. I told her no one lived there, and hadn't since the murders. Maybe she decided to take a look inside, and maybe she found something she thought was really neat, and borrowed it. So what?" He grinned a little and shrugged. "I think it's kind of cute, actually. She found something that was neat. Nobody was using it."

"Look at this picture, Justin."

Justin glanced at it, frowning quickly, looking away, irritably. "What for?"

426

"It's Kit. You've heard about Kit. You know who she was."

"Sure. Kit, nine years old. Murdered with multiple stabs from an ice pick, just like the rest of them. Why are you dragging out all this old stuff?"

"This was taken on her ninth birthday, just a week or so before she was killed. Justin, she's holding an antique doll her grandmother gave her for her birthday."

"Yeah? So?" Justin, clearly puzzled now, didn't look at the picture, but turned his eyes steadily on Tresa.

"Had you ever heard about that doll?" Tread gently, she warned herself. *Be careful. He has to believe you.*

"No," he said. "I don't think so."

"There's quite a story behind it." She told it as she remembered it, that the doll was found by their great-grandmother in an antique store, that it had been almost destroyed at one time long ago. She told him the history of the doll. The ice pick murders in which a little girl six years old had never uttered a word of explanation, and had died at a young age in an insane asylum.

"That's weird," he said, the puzzled frown deepening on his face. He stared at Tresa.

"Right. A coincidence, too, wouldn't you say?"

He said nothing. His gaze flicked from her right eye to her left as if to see beyond this seemingly absent rambling.

"So then," she said carefully, "it came into our family. Pam and Mom's family. The grandmother gave the doll to Kit. Kit was afraid of the doll. She kept telling Pam she was afraid. She'd come to Pam in the middle of the night and tell her things the doll had done. The first thing that happened was the big doll went into Kit's walk-in closet and tore up her favorite Barbie dolls and their new clothes—"

"Hey, wait a minute! What the hell is this? You mean this antique doll was carrying around some kind of curse, and whatever kid that owned it went over the cliff?" Disbelief was written all over his face, yet it was mixed with apprehension. "I don't like what I'm hearing. Who the hell told you this?"

She opened her mouth, but didn't get a chance to speak.

"Of course," he said. "Aunt Pam. Trying to come up with an excuse or something?" He turned his chair away from the tiny table and rested one ankle on his knee. His hand caressed the bent knee absently.

"Aunt Pam is not insane, Justin. And she's not guilty of the murders."

"So this little girl Kit did the killing then stabbed herself in the back? Get real, Tresa. This is not like you."

"So you're so logical you can't see beyond the end of your nose, right? You're not ready to admit there might be a few things, perhaps a very few, very strange things that do not move to our accepted laws of logic, right?"

He fixed his gaze on her again. "Okay, so what're you saying? The doll did it?" He added a sarcastic smirk.

Surprised, it took her a moment to answer. By that time he had answered for her.

"I knew the minute you walked in that you were up to something. I was afraid when that woman popped up so unexpectedly, right before my wedding, that it was bad news. But I'm not going to let it spoil my wedding, Tresa, and you can bet your life on that."

She felt as if he had slapped her. At the end of his small tirade his voice had lowered, softened, and become very cold.

"Justin," she admonished, "this is your sister you're talking to! You know I wouldn't do anything to hurt you, not ever."

He looked down, and finally nodded. "Yeah. Sorry. But Tresa, I really don't want to hear about this stuff today."

"Did I interrupt some plans?" she asked carefully. "Were you and Zenoa going to do something special today?"

"We're not even seeing each other today. Today I'm going out with a few guys. Zenoa's idea. I don't want to, but she insisted. We'll be together the rest of our lives starting tomorrow evening, she said, so tonight she wants me to be a bachelor, for the last time." He smiled tenderly, rubbed his knee and twisted his shoulders slightly, like a little boy. "She's really special, Tres, you know it? So considerate, so sweet. She's the best thing that ever happened to me. Sometimes I feel like I'm too lucky."

"So the fact that she was wearing one of Pam's old dresses doesn't bother you at all?"

He shrugged. "I'm not at all sure it was Pam's dress. Whose word do you have for that? Pam's?"

428

"I have the picture, Justin."

He glanced toward it, and away. "So they're similar."

"Justin, tell me something. Have you made plans? For after you're married?"

"Well . . . yeah, I guess."

"Do those plans include living in the old house?"

His gaze leaped to hers and locked in. It seemed to Tresa he turned a shade paler. "So?"

"I'm just asking," she said, trying to put him at ease, wondering if Pam were right.

"Well, yeah, sort of. Zenoa really likes it, and it is a damn shame that it's going to waste, just a nice big place. She thinks it would be a great place to raise children." The tender expression crossed his face again. That look of wonder and disbelief that always accompanied anything to do with Zenoa. "You said Pam wants to sell it, right? Do you suppose she'd make a deal with us?"

Tresa felt a jolt of understanding. Now Zenoa's motive was becoming more clear. She wanted the house. She wanted a human, legal possession of it, and the only way she could get it was to marry Justin.

After marriage, after getting the house in her name, then what? Tresa wasn't ready to see Zenoa as a killer, not now. Yet she had no doubt that Pam had told the truth. She didn't understand it, but she believed it. Justin had to know. What he did with that knowledge was up to him.

She heard him talking on and on about their plans for the house, and was more convinced than ever. Obviously they had parked there many times.

"Justin, do me a favor, okay?"

"Yeah, sure."

"Look at this picture."

He scratched the back of his neck. "I did." He shrugged again. "So maybe Zenoa wanted to see the inside of the house, and maybe she borrowed Mom's key. Maybe she saw the clothes and took some. Is that a crime?" Hastily he added, "I mean considering she's my fiancée? Nobody knew Pam was going to show up so soon."

"*This* picture, Justin. The one where Kit is holding the doll."

"Oh. Okay."

He picked up the picture and looked at it, then positioned his stare at one point. Tresa knew he was looking at the doll.

"There are more very strange coincidences, Justin," she said softly. "The name of that doll was Zenoa."

He threw the picture down. "You're crazy," he said, his stare slamming against her, his frown deep. "What is this, anyway, some kind of conspiracy?" He tried to laugh, but failed.

"The doll's name was Zenoa. A very unusual name. Its footprints were through the blood, spotted along the hall. A detective saw them, but couldn't explain them. The bottom of the doll's shoes were bloody. The doll was downstairs in the powder room when Pam went down that morning. She had been carrying the doll into the attic to lock it away until the next day. She was going to take it back to her grandmother because Kit was so afraid of it. The doll jumped in her arms, shoved her so hard she fell against the chest and hit her head. It knocked her unconscious. When she went downstairs after she came to the next morning, a couple of hours later, the doll walked out of the powder room. *Walked*, Justin. The ice pick was on the floor. When the doll reached sunlight it fell, inert, just a doll. Zenoa was the killer, Justin. Not Pam."

Surprisingly, he hadn't interrupted her. When she finished her quiet and hasty explanation her heart was pounding as if she'd been running. She was desperate that he believe her, because as she had repeated what Pam had told her, she had begun to feel the danger that was among them. Justin had to listen. Justin had listened.

But he began to shake his head. "So you're bringing me this story, and you believe it? I can't believe you're so gullible, Tres. That woman, obviously, belongs in an insane asylum. Whose word do you have for any of this? *Think*, Tresa."

Her hopes plummeted. "Justin, look again at the doll's face. Her name was Zenoa. Look at her."

"I looked at the goddamned doll's face! I saw it! So what? So it favors Zenoa. Whose word do you have that its name was Zenoa? Huh? Pam! Whose word do you have for anything? Pam's! And she's nuts, Tres. She's off the wall, man!"

He stood up, his voice loud and angry. He reached down and

thumped the table so hard it slid a couple inches sideways. Tresa leaped up.

"I'll tell you this. You tell that bitch she is not welcome at my wedding, do you hear? And while you're at it, just tell yourself the same! I don't ever want to see either of you again as long as I live. Now get out of my place!"

He turned his back to her, his arms folded tight across his chest. She could see the tips of his fingers gripping his biceps. They were white. His shoulders shook. Tresa wanted to put her arms around him and hug him and tell him she was sorry, but she backed away instead.

"Justin —"

"Just leave, okay, Tres?" he said in a softer tone, the hurt in his voice.

"Okay." At the door she looked back toward him. "Just be careful, will you Justin?"

He didn't answer. He was still hugging his chest, his head lowered when she left.

The moment the door clicked shut behind her the tears came. A couple coming down the hall stared wordlessly at her, and she tried to blink the tears back, but they persisted. She kept them brushed off her cheeks as she rode down in the elevator. But by the time she reached her car they were coming full force.

She sat with her forehead resting on the steering wheel, weeping, until the tears finally stopped. What was she going to do now? Would it help to talk to Mom? Mom knew the story. Pam said she'd told Beth and their grandmother. If Mom would back her up . . .

She started the car and drove swiftly through the traffic, changing lanes, getting a few silent angry mouthings from other motorists.

"Let her be at home," she prayed in whispers as she drove into the driveway. This was Saturday. There was a chance she'd be out shopping. But there was an equal chance she'd be cleaning her neat house in preparation for tomorrow's wedding. The attached two-car garage was closed. She couldn't see if either her dad's car or her mom's was there.

The back door was unlocked and she entered the house calling, "Mom?"

Beth came in from the utility room smiling. "Well, what a surprise. Are you alone? Where's Blake?"

"I don't know. I haven't seen him today. Mom, I need to talk to you."

Beth blinked. "Sure," she said. "What's the matter? Have you been crying, Tresa? For goodness sakes, sweetheart, what's wrong? Here, sit down, I'll get you something to drink."

"No, that's okay. Mom, listen. I've been over talking to Justin. It didn't go well." She allowed Beth to guide her to the table where she sat down. She noticed her dad coming into the kitchen quietly. She threw him a thin, apologetic smile of greeting.

Beth demanded, "What do you mean, it didn't go well? You surely weren't fighting!"

They hadn't fought since they were teenagers. And even then they hadn't fought as much as most brothers and sisters.

"Mom, Dad, listen. I don't know how to say this. But before I went to talk to Justin, I went over to Aunt Pam's. She told me the story of the doll. She said she once told you. Back then."

Beth's face changed instantly. She looked suddenly very tired and sad. "Not that damned old doll again!" She almost fell into one of the kitchen chairs. Behind her Ross came a few steps closer. "Oh God, I hate to say this, but why did she have to come home?"

"She gave me these pictures." Tresa said. "Did you notice the dress Zenoa had on last night? This is a picture of Pam in the same dress back in sixty-nine."

Beth turned her face away and stared out the window, but Ross stepped forward and looked down. Tresa saw that her dad was their only possible ally. But he said nothing.

"Did either of you know," Tresa asked, "that the doll's name was Zenoa?"

Beth threw Ross a quick stare. *"I forgot that!"* she cried softly.

"I thought I'd heard that name before," Ross said. "But I couldn't remember where."

"She gave me this picture too. Look, Dad."

Ross bent over the table. Beth too looked at the doll in Kit's arms, and turned quickly away again, her stare going deter-

432

minedly out the window.

"I'll be damned," Ross said softly. "Sure looks like her, doesn't it?"

"It is her," Tresa said. "Pam is positive of it, and I believe her."

For a moment there was silence.

Tresa said, "Pam is afraid of her. She thinks she's dangerous, that she wanted Justin for a reason. I think I know what that reason is. She wanted the house and the well . . . human standing, I guess, the legitimacy of ownership. They're wanting to buy it from Pam. But when I told Justin, when I showed him this picture he ordered me out of his life. Pam is not welcome at his wedding, and neither am I."

Beth stood up. Her voice was loud and angry as Tresa had never heard it before. Like Justin the anger showed in her movements, in the tightness of her lips. For the first time in her life Tresa was seeing fury in both her brother and her mother.

"I don't blame him! Pam is not only not welcome at my son's wedding, she is never to step in my house again! I was afraid she'd start a bunch of crazy stories, and here she's actually got my daughter believing!" She turned on Ross. "Why the hell are you acting as if it's all right? You know as well as I do that these are the ramblings of a crazy woman! And now she's got your daughter convinced? I want you to call Pam and tell her she is not to come here anymore. If I try to call, I'll say too much maybe. Go, Ross, for God's sake! Tell that woman to stay out of our lives and don't ever mention that doll to me again!"

Ross stared at Beth, then he left the room. But he made no comment, no promise.

Beth went back to the table and slumped in a chair, her head supported by her hands, her face hidden. Tresa saw the white tips of her fingers, as she had seen Justin's. Then suddenly Beth reached out and swept the two pictures off the table. They fluttered toward the floor like free-falling divers through the sky.

Trembling, Tresa stooped, picked them up and put them back into her purse

"I'm sorry," she said. "I'll just leave."

She started out the back door, changed her mind and went to the door into the hallway. She had to say goodbye to her dad.

"Tresa," Beth said in a more normal tone.

Tresa stopped, but didn't turn around.

"Ignore what Justin said about you not coming to his wedding. I want you to come. You and Blake. I'll smooth it over with Justin. But promise me something."

"Yes? What?"

"Don't ever mention Pam's name in this house again."

Tresa nodded agreement, then went on into the hall. At the den she called goodbye to her dad.

He turned at her approach. Tresa stretched up to kiss his cheek. His arm came around her shoulder and gave her a warm hug.

"I'm leaving, Dad."

He walked with her, his arm still around her. "You're coming back tomorrow, though, aren't you?"

She hesitated. "Dad. This is tearing me apart."

"Yes. Me too, Tresa. And your mother. Your aunt too, and I expect also Justin."

"But you know Dad, what if Pam is right?"

He said nothing. At the door she kissed him again and went out onto the small porch.

"Don't forget the wedding tomorrow," he said in a voice almost normal, meant to be cheerful. "Come early."

She waved goodbye.

So this was the way it was going to be. Pretend that all was right with the world. Pretend that horror hadn't entered their lives.

Fifteen

The hour of his wedding was approaching.

The sun was down, the lanterns set up in the semi-circle in the backyard of his parents' home were lighted and flickering. The flowers had been delivered, and arranged in vases slightly below the lanterns. Justin was dressed and waiting. The fifty or so guests had arrived. Pamela was not among them. Tresa was there, with Blake, both of them wearing forced smiles. Tresa came to Justin and kissed his cheek, but she didn't apologize.

"You look fantastic," she said, and that was all.

Justin looked over her head. The wedding was set for nine o'clock. *Where was Zenoa?*

Had she changed her mind? Was she going to never be there for him? Was she unreal, something beautiful that appeared only at night, as Tresa had suggested.

Justin had lived since noon the day before with a mixture of rage and terror. Emotions that threatened to destroy him. He had tried to locate Zenoa since Tresa left his apartment yesterday, even though Zenoa had told him she wouldn't see him again until time for the ceremony. He had gone to the clubs. He had called the manager of her apartment house, and was told no such person lived there. In his fury he had almost torn the phone out of the wall before he caught himself and placed it properly on the table.

Then he had gone there, and was not allowed to enter. "If you don't get the hell out of here I'm calling the police!" the manager yelled at him. Then, calming, he pointed at the mailboxes. "Man, do you see that name anywhere?"

Justin left, frustrated, wanting to cry. All evening he haunted the hangouts where he'd met Zenoa in the past, and she wasn't at any of them. The bartenders hadn't seen her. He drank, mostly alone, and realized during the evening that he'd lost all his old buddies. They hardly knew him. With his head feeling as if it were floating in the air above his body, connected by only a string, he'd driven carefully home, about ten miles an hour through four a.m. traffic that was blessedly sparse, and stumbled upstairs to bed. Only then did he remember he was supposed to have joined a few left-over friends for a stag party.

Sunday was little better, plagued by a hangover in which his head had settled onto his body like a ton of bricks. He stopped trying to find Zenoa. She wouldn't let him down. She'd be there.

Sunday dragged more slowly than any day in his life. Finally, in the afternoon, he went over to his folks' house where relatives had been arriving all day. Some of them had come for lunch. Food was going to be catered for a nine-thirty supper. Justin couldn't eat, and his mother worried over him now and then.

In the evening he dressed and joined the group in the backyard. The minister came and went smiling among the people who were mostly strangers to him, carrying his bible.

Justin stared over heads, watching for Zenoa. Yet he wasn't the first to see her. At first he noticed the change in the crowd. A kind of appreciative moan rose, and heads turned. A path opened.

Justin looked. Zenoa stood in the open patio doors at the back of the house wearing a white lace suit, mid-calf, a tiny veil on her bright hair, and carrying a small bouquet. Her eyes found Justin and she smiled.

Justin's heart pounded in his throat. All the others became background for Zenoa. He had been so afraid that Pamela and Tresa had gone to her, and somehow destroyed what he and Zenoa had together. They didn't know, they didn't understand. She was his life now. She was all he wanted. With Zenoa, the world and all that was in it faded away. He and

Zenoa existed on a plane of their own.

The party arranged itself. The minister took his place in front of the lanterns and flowers. Blake, who had been chosen to walk Zenoa across the lawn to the designated spot of the ceremony, stepped forward and gave her his arm. Justin saw the look on his face and was momentarily puzzled by it. Sadness? Tresa must have told him Pamela's crazy story too.

Rage boiled again within him, mixed now with relief. Here she was, the most beautiful bride in the world.

She came forward, walking with slow, carefully spaced steps, the only music that of the night insects buzzing away in the trees. The odor of burning lantern wicks mingled with the fragrance of flowers.

Justin heard a woman whisper loudly, "She's as lovely as a doll."

Something inside Justin lurched at the description, dropping a pall over the moment.

As she approached, as Blake stepped away and Justin took his place and Zenoa's cool, slender hand touched the back of his hand, he tried to bring forth that feeling of delight, of happiness. But the pall remained. He wished he could wave a wand and make it all go away, everything that had happened since yesterday when Tresa came to see him.

He wished he and Zenoa had gone to a Justice of the Peace, as he had wanted to. Where none of this would exist. The wedding was for his mom. She had planned it, bit by bit with Zenoa listening, smiling, accepting.

Zenoa something other than what she seemed? Zenoa? She was the sweetest, dearest, most precious person in the world. She was beside him now, at last, forever.

"Until death do you part," the minister was saying, "I now pronounce you husband and wife."

Pamela sat on the back step looking into the dark shadows of the trees in the backyard. The night air was growing cool, but she continued to sit, scrunching tighter into herself, leaning against her legs for warmth. The phone call from Beth yesterday afternoon thundered in her heart, intermingling with Tresa's voice, mixing with voices from the past, with memories fresh as the blood that once flowed, that now was crusted dark and old. Pamela had stayed near the phone yesterday, expecting to hear from Tresa. She had spent the hours walking from a window where she could see out into the driveway, to the kitchen where she could hear the phone. When it finally rang, it was Beth, not Tresa, and Beth's voice trembled in fury.

"If you ever speak to either one of my children again, Pamela, I'll . . . I'll . . . Oh Lord, why did you have to come home?"

Pamela couldn't speak. She gripped the phone, feeling the connection between herself and her sister finally breaking.

"Listen," Beth said in cold and precise tones, "let me put it this way. Tresa came to me and told me all that crazy stuff you told her. I am furious with you, Pam. More than that, you are out of my life. I don't ever want to see or hear from you again. The invitation to Justin and Zenoa's wedding is withdrawn. Please leave us alone."

Pamela stood by the phone trembling, her hands covering her face. Then she went out to sit in the sunshine on the back step, trying not to think about all that had happened.

She'd call Jefferson, she decided, and ask him to come and see her. She was ready to tell him everything. Still, she was afraid he'd walk away, convinced of her guilt after all. Not able to accept the truth. She didn't call.

Maybe Tresa would call her.

But the phone didn't ring after Beth's call, and the friendship Pam thought she and Tresa had formed waned in her mind like the sunshine that had warmed her body.

The night passed slowly. There were no sounds in the house other than natural creakings and the whispers of old wood. No footstep on this night before the wedding. No door closing mysteriously, no window found open in the morning.

She couldn't eat. The house was chilly, and she went out again to sit in the sunshine on the back porch.

At noon the phone rang, and she went to answer it with terrible visions of death flitting through her mind. Someone was calling her to tell her Tresa had been murdered with an ice pick . . . or Justin . . . or Beth. All of them, dead. But no, she told herself, it wasn't done that way. A policeman wouldn't call, he would come to her door.

It was Tresa on the phone. Pam felt such relief that she slipped weakly to sit on the floor beneath the wall phone, the cord stretched.

Through the hours of the afternoon and into the cool of the evening the call repeated itself in her mind, like the buzz of the katydids in the grass and trees.

"Aunt Pam," she'd said, sounding close physically, yet remorsefully distant, "I'm sorry for waiting so long to get in touch with you again. I would have come over but I have to help Mom today. Getting ready, you know." She sighed deeply.

"I understand," Pam said. "It's all right."

"Aunt Pam, I talked to Justin. He only became very angry. He doesn't want us, you or I, at the wedding. Mom insisted I come anyway. She eased it with Justin, I guess. Anyway . . ."

"Beth told me," Pam said. "It's all right. From her point of view, it's understandable."

"I just don't know what to do."

After a pause Pam said, "Have a good time. Forget everything I told you. Enjoy yourself. Maybe it will all turn out fine."

"Oh, Aunt Pam. I'm sorry. I'm sorry you won't be with us."

The phone call ended, but like a refrain from a song it continued through Pam's mind, repeating itself over and over. She stared into the darkness of the backyard.

Maybe it will all turn out fine.

Forget everything I told you.

The hour of the wedding had passed.

Sixteen

"I don't want a wedding trip," Zenoa had said to him when they were planning their wedding. "I just want to go home with you."

After the wedding, as they slipped away and were close in the privacy of his car, she said it again. His right hand gripped hers as he steered with his left. She leaned against him. Her single suitcase was in the backseat. He had seen it when he opened the door and the interior lights came on. She had smiled at him and explained the taxi driver had put it there for her. "That's it," she'd said. "My dowry. Okay?"

He squeezed her to him. "Dowry? You're so cute, Zen. As if you're really serious. All I want is you, anyway."

As he drove the streets back to his apartment he asked again, "Are you sure you only want to go back to my dump? We could at least go to a nice hotel somewhere."

She snuggled against his arm, her free hand caressing the back of the hand that held hers. "Why? Your place isn't a dump."

"How do you know? You'd never come up to see it," he teased, kissing her on the lips with a series of quick little kisses as he tried to stay off the curb. "When I get you up there I'm going to keep you."

She giggled. "That's why I wouldn't go up with you until we were married. I wanted you so *you* couldn't get away."

"I don't want to get away."

"That's nice, because you never will."

Her voice was low and whispery. Always. It was her natural way of speaking. He had to listen carefully to hear what she said. Did it now hold a warning, or was the chill that passed over him just an extension of this weekend? Filled with anger, fear of losing Zenoa, frustration of not being able to get in touch with her, it had been the worst weekend of his life. Then finally, the wedding, and the culmination of his dream to have her with him. Forever. That was all it was, that awful darting fear that went through him. The worst weekend of his life, and the best.

"I'm hanging onto you too, baby. Now that I've got you, that's it. But I have a problem."

"Baby will fix all your problems. What is it?"

"Do I carry you over the threshold of my dump?"

"No! You wait and carry me over the threshold of our house."

"I'll carry you all the way. From the parking spot to the elevator and down the hall. I'll carry you in my pocket when I go to work. Now that I've got you, I'll take you with me everywhere I go. The wedding band is your chain. Get used to it."

She had a tinkly little laugh that was childlike and appealing, as so many things about her were. She had given her age as twenty, on the marriage license, but at times a niggling concern made him wonder. Was it possible that she was younger? What proof did he have that her background was anything that she'd said it was? Wasn't it rather odd that she was so alone in the world?

He threw the thoughts away. Damn that woman with her crazy story. No one with a right mind could believe that, but . . . Since then, he'd been wondering. Wasn't it odd, that Zenoa didn't have so much as a cousin with whom she communicated? But on the other hand, what did he know? She had kept herself so private from him. He'd never been in her apartment. He'd never even been in her place of work. What did he really know?

Crazy. *Don't think.* Maybe that had been part of her appeal, the reason he had fallen so hard so fast. She needed him to take care of her because she was so vulnerable in this modern world. So old-fashioned, with her old-fashioned morals, her way of pulling back at the last moment.

In the shadows of his parking slot he kissed her long and passionately, and she didn't pull back. His hand slid from her firm, small waist down to the curve of her leg and hip. The feel of the lace suit was as smooth and slippery as the sex act as it eased over silk or satin beneath. He could hardly breathe in his excitement as he pushed her back against the seat, his hand slipping beneath the skirt to feel the round thighs, one crossed over the other. When he tried to push his hand between her thighs she moved, drawing away, as she always had.

In her whispery voice she said, "This is the parking lot, Justin. Don't I even get to see this so-called dump of yours first?"

He sat a moment, forcing his mind away from her. Upstairs he had put a bottle of wine in the fridge this afternoon in case she just wanted to come straight back to his apartment. He got out of the car, reached for her suitcase, then offered his hand to help her out. She always waited. Unlike most girls he had dated she never opened her own doors. She had a way of helplessness that made him feel strong, as if she needed him desperately. Her soft, brown eyes looked up at him, and she smiled faintly. Her eyes caressed . . . or did they probe? Reading her expressions were sometimes as impossible as understanding her past. It was part of her, of Zenoa, the mystery of Zenoa.

He held her hand as they went upstairs, as he always held her hand when they'd strolled in the park, as they danced in a crowded club, or sat together with drinks. He tried to think of something clever and lighthearted to say, but was mute, for one of the first times in his life. A strange sadness gripped him. A feeling of depression so foreign to his nature. He gathered her closer to him and waited for the elevator to stop.

At the door to his apartment, as he released her hand in order to unlock the door, he asked, "Were you serious about me not carrying you over this threshold?" Such an insipid question, but suddenly he was incapable of anything bright or magic.

"Yes."

He pushed the door open. She went ahead of him into the one room apartment, looking around.

"Why, Justin," she said, "this isn't so bad. It's even nice and neat. The way you talked about it, you had me thinking you were a real slob."

"I cleaned it up for you."

She turned and smiled at him, her head tipped slightly to one side. "I don't believe that. Sit down, let me pour you a drink."

He obeyed her, amazed at the commanding tone of her soft voice. It was the first time she had taken this position. She went to the refrigerator as if she had seen him put the wine in, and removed the bottle. On her wrist she'd carried a small, white, beaded bag that matched her lace suit, and now she removed it and laid it on the counter beside the bottle of wine. She stretched up and opened the correct cabinet door and removed two glasses. With her back to him she slowly poured wine.

"I noticed your Aunt Pamela wasn't at the wedding," she said.

"No."

"Why? Was she ill?"

"No." He stood up, removed his coat and tie and hung them over the back of a chair. He felt compelled to tell her, at least part of it. "She said some things I didn't like."

"What?"

He pulled out the sleep-sofa and straightened the sheets. He had carefully cleaned up the bed, laundered the sheets, and put them back on again. Everything was clean for his wedding night. He sat down on the edge of the bed. He not only didn't want to talk about Pamela, he didn't even want to think about her.

"She had this idea you'd been living in the old house."

She came to him carrying two glasses of wine. He took the one she handed him. With her head tipped again, a teasing look in her eyes and on her lips, she said, *"What?"*

"I know. A ridiculous idea. She even thought you were

wearing one of her old dresses."

She looked down at her white suit in so comical a way that he laughed. Holding her glass of wine out to one side she visually examined her wedding suit.

"Not that one," he said, laughing.

"Then which?"

He shrugged. It was beginning to sound so silly. "The poor, crazy woman saw the one you had on the night of the dinner and thought it was hers."

"What on earth made her think that? Is she . . . not well?"

"Obviously not. What did you expect, someone who butchered her whole family. Good thing Mom had already moved out, or she'd been gone too. Anyway, don't worry about it."

Zenoa sipped her wine delicately, then sat down on the corner of the bed away from him.

"Justin, perhaps it was really bad for her to come home to that house, where she murdered her family so horribly. She shouldn't be in that house at all, should she?"

"I don't think she'll stay long."

"She probably won't sell it to us now, now that you fought with her."

"I didn't fight with her. She told Tresa, and Tresa came and told me. I didn't say a word to Pam."

"But she knew you were angry. She knew you didn't want her at the wedding."

"That's right, I guess."

"Justin, I hope you haven't let your temper ruin things for us. Such a silly thing to do, get angry because of that silly little thing about a dress."

"There was more to it than that."

"What?"

He deliberately took a couple of drinks of the wine. She needed to know how crazy the woman was, he decided. "Well, I guess I'll tell you, babe, because then you'll know to stay away from Pam. Don't ever let her befriend you. She can be pretty persuasive, so it seems. She certainly swayed Tresa into accepting that story."

444

"Stop being so mysterious! What story?" She slid over to sit leaning against him, so trusting, so intimate. With one arm around her he told her about the picture of the doll. He couldn't see her face, but was relieved to hear her childish laughter.

"Me? Look like a doll?"

He kissed the edge of her forehead. Her body, leaning against him was cool. Even her thigh beneath his hand felt oddly cool. He had noticed that before, but never so much as now.

"What else?" she asked.

He told her the story of the doll that had been given to the little girl named Kit. She sat quietly against him, occasionally sipping her wine, saying nothing.

Justin said, "She somehow convinced Tresa that . . ." This was the hardest part. To bring it into the present and connect it with his bride. ". . . that there was more than simple coincidence in you looking like the doll. It happens, according to Pam, that your names are the same."

"Really? The doll's name was Zenoa?"

"Yeah. According to Pam. But that's only her who remembers that. So it's just her word, which doesn't amount to a damn."

"Anyway," Zenoa said, going on with parts of the story he had left out, "you're telling me Aunt Pam thinks the *doll*, made of whatever dolls are made of, was not really a doll? But something terrible and dangerous, right? She was the one who murdered the little girl and the aunt more than a hundred years ago, not the little girl who died in the asylum. Not Becky. And of course she always thinks the doll was the one who did the killing in her house."

"That's about it. Crazy, I know."

Zenoa stood up, took their glasses to the counter and worked slowly refilling them.

"So," she said as she brought them back. "Pam thinks I'm that doll." She smiled at Justin, laughing softly, her eyes catching the light of the lamp just for a moment and sparkling, then reflecting blankly.

Justin managed a laugh. He took the glass she handed

him.

"The bad part, Justin, is that woman would never let us buy her house, right? Not if she's making up all these silly stories about me, and actually believes her own stories. But Tresa? How could Tresa believe? She's a modern girl, she's . . ." Zenoa paused, adding, "is it possible that Tresa has this illness too? This mental thing like your aunt?"

"I hope not. But, I don't know."

"She actually brought this picture to you and suggested I look like the doll?"

"Yeah."

"And you got angry."

"Damn right. I told her to stay out of my life. I told her not to come to the wedding. But Mom called me later and told me Tresa couldn't be left out. Pam wasn't coming, but Tresa must. After all, Blake was part of our wedding. I gave in. I'm sorry, Zenoa, I couldn't see any way around it. But don't worry. That's it. We'll get out of here, go where we never have to see the family."

"Leave?" she cried, alarm in her eyes "No, Justin. You promised me you'd get the house for me, Justin! You promised. So people would know it was *mine*. So strangers wouldn't be coming and mowing the grass. So nobody else could live there! You promised!"

"Baby, that was when it looked like Pam'd be in prison the rest of her life, and there was no reason we shouldn't have it. I wanted to get it for you. I meant to. But we can find one just as good somewhere else."

"Oh no, never! You promised me, Justin!"

"Zenoa, please. What do you want with that old barn, anyway? All creepy, crawling with vines. Bugs too, probably. Blood on the carpets and walls. I can't even stand to look at it."

"That wasn't what you told me!"

"I'm sorry."

Zenoa seemed unexpectedly upset, yet when she sat down on the bed again there was no heightened breathing or any of the signs of anger. Not even as much as he was experiencing. His heart pounded slow and hard as if he were exhausted. He didn't reach out to her.

"Is that all you married me for?" he asked, trying to sound as if he were teasing. "Just to get the old house?"

Zenoa didn't appear to hear him.

"You said Pam owns the house, but your mother's name is still on it too, didn't you?"

Justin couldn't remember having said that, but maybe he did. "I don't know. Mom said she doesn't want anything to do with it, but legally, her name may still be on it."

"Then . . . if your aunt died, who would own the house?"

"Mom would. Even if her name isn't on it. Unless Aunt Pam has made a will."

Zenoa turned her head and gave him a direct look. "A will! What's that?"

He wanted to laugh at her ingenuousness, as he would have even three days ago. Though at times she seemed so knowledgeable, at other times she appeared to have been totally protected from the world. He wondered what her background really was. She did not seem to be world-traveled, a service brat.

"Sometimes, baby, I think you've spent your whole life in some old Victorian place protected from all the nasty things of the world."

She smiled faintly and did that little sideways shrug with her head that went straight to his heart.

"I just forgot a minute. It means she could leave it to someone else, right? Like you."

He snorted. "Not apt to happen."

Justin drank the wine, a sip, then a longer drink. He wished there were something stronger in the house, even though he had never been much of a drinker. Until last night. His head still felt odd. Very odd, in fact. He set the glass aside and leaned down on an elbow toward Zenoa. She edged away and smiled down at him.

"Finish your drink," she murmured in that oddly commanding tone, "and I'll pour you another."

"I'd rather have you. I want to forget the world. This is our wedding night. You don't know how I've longed for

447

this, Zenoa. You've had me lusting like a bull with an overload of testosterone."

She kissed his forehead, and he reached out in an attempt to wrap his arms around her waist, but she stood up out of his reach.

"Are you trying to make me spill this red stuff on my nice white suit?"

"Take it off," he said. "Let me take it off you."

"No, not yet."

She moved away, came around him and took his glass. Though there was still wine left in the bottom, she carried it over to the counter.

He sat watching her, his desire ebbing away. The picture of the doll had lain in the back of his mind like a memory waiting to be brought up by hypnosis. He saw it clearly again, the lovely little face with the rosy cheeks, the slight overbite, the dimple in the chin. The large, questioning brown eyes with the pale eyebrows uplifted, half hidden by the bangs of the reddish gold hair. The almost-smile that could be read a thousand ways.

She glanced over her shoulder at him, the same look the doll had worn. He was suddenly seeing her in a fluttery little dress, wearing little white shoes tied with a bow. He saw her too in a longer dress, lacy, ruffling, her little shoes black, hightopped, laced. A dress of the nineteenth century. One image overlapped the other. When she turned and came toward him carrying a fresh glass of wine, all the images merged. He felt oddly frightened and overpowered as she stood over him, her strange expression commanding him to drink.

. . . *not the little girl who died in the asylum. Not Becky.*

Her words had escaped him at the moment, coming back now to counteract the warm wine. Something dark and cold felt as if it had gripped the back of Justin's brain.

"How did you know her name?" he asked.

"Whose name?"

"The little girl who died in the insane asylum. The little girl who owned the doll a century ago."

"But Justin, I don't know her name. What makes you

think I know her name?"

He said nothing. Instead he took a deep drink of the wine, more than he intended to. He noticed an odd, musty taste, and a swirling, milky look. Or was it the images, distorting everything?

"Is something wrong?"

"Tastes funny. Not very good, is it?"

"You're just used to having your drinks mixed by a professional. I guess I'm not very good at pouring wine." She stood over him. "Finish it, quickly. I'll put it away. Then, I want to undress you."

He glanced up at her, surprised. A strange feeling was beginning to swirl through his head. He hadn't had enough wine for that. Something else, he decided. The anger, the frustration, the crazy thoughts he'd been having. Maybe even the hangover. He tipped the glass up and drained it. One side of his face felt odd, almost as if it were paralyzed, making his attempted grin up at her feel crooked and crazy.

Crazy. Crazy. Too much of it, entering into everything. *Becky*, she had said. Not Becky. The words kept echoing in his mind. Not Becky . . . not Becky . . .

"Lie down," she said sweetly, and he obeyed.

Her face appeared in broken images above him, with its unique little girl hair style, long, curly, with two little ponytail-type deals high on her head, on each side of the center part. Everything, exactly like the picture of the doll.

He felt her unbuttoning his cuffs and rolling up his sleeves. Why was she doing that? She unbuttoned the front of his shirt partway down, then unbuttoned his trousers.

He tried to speak, and his tongue felt as if it filled his mouth. "Why—" he managed "why—is—house so—im-import'ant?"

"It's mine, that's why!"

She continued to loosen his clothes. Then she stood still looking down at him, and he knew. With his muscles so heavy he couldn't move, his tongue growing thicker, the terror came. She had given him something. She was killing him. He couldn't swallow, or turn his head, or lift his

449

hand. He stared up at her, helpless, his mind bringing forth bits and pieces of conversation, images flitting, broken, severed. How could he not have known something was wrong, that first day when she asked him to take her to the house?

"How did you know about this old place?" he asked as he pulled into the shady, overgrown driveway.

"Your mama told me."

He believed her then, but now he believed Tresa, and Pamela. God help them all. Zenoa had come forth to take possession, and he could not stop her.

She moved, the edges of her body moving behind her, like pictures laid upon pictures, each a fraction away from the next. She went toward the bathroom. He saw the light go on. She stood there, looking down at something she was doing. Then she turned and came back toward him.

His eyes followed her hand. He knew why she had been so careful in rolling up his sleeve.

Her eyes smiled ironically into his for just a moment before she inserted the hypodermic needle into his arm.

Her voice was like the images, like the sound of a hundred distant radios.

"Your precious family didn't even know you were a drug addict, did they, Justin?"

Drugs . . . in his vein. NO! NO!

He was aware when she picked up the telephone. She stood over him, looking down, watching, waiting. She wasn't dialing, she was only holding the phone, waiting.

Help me.

In his hazy, unsteady vision she wavered, above him. Her doll's face looked down with unemotional, casual inspection.

Oh God. Aunt Pam . . . Tresa . . . they were right. Why hadn't he seen that? Why hadn't he acknowledged that something wasn't right about Zenoa, that it never had been? From the moment they met he should have seen that it was carefully planned. She had come directly to him, through the men who reached out to her, past everyone, to him. She had watched him, she had stood in the

450

doorway until almost every pair of eyes in the club had turned her way. She had known exactly whom and what she wanted.

He didn't understand, even now. Was it her ascent to a human status? Then, the almost immediate plan to marry him and buy the old house, a further ascension?

Now the wedding having been completed, in her strange, nonhuman way of thinking, she had no further use for him? What had changed her plans? The release of Pamela? Her return to the house?

He tried to sit up. He had to go to Pamela and tell her to get out of the house, let it go, let Zenoa have it. He had to tell his folks, and Tresa. All who stood between Zenoa and her legal ownership of the house. Let her have it. If one thing in this world was so important to Zenoa, don't try to stand in her way. Because, if they did, Zenoa would kill them.

He struggled against his total loss of control. He made an effort to plead with her, to agree to anything if she would only get out of their lives, but he was sinking into the large, black hole beneath. He was distantly aware that she finally started to dial.

He tried to rouse himself, to keep himself conscious. Was she calling for emergency help?

Then he heard her voice, and knew he was lost. As he fell through the darkness that pulled him down, Zenoa made her call.

"Blake," she cried. "Can you come over? Something terrible has happened. I'm afraid Justin took an overdose of drugs. I'm so afraid, Blake . . ."

Seventeen

Tresa sat curled in a recliner in front of her television, seeing colors and movement, her thoughts replaying the wedding and Blake's part in it. She had left early, as early as she could politely get away. Mom had looked pink cheeked and happy, talking to relatives, feeding them, having the time of her life. Dad had looked far less happy, and Tresa remembered seeing him staring off, once, with a concentrated frown. The memory of Blake's face was like a hand squeezing the last dregs of blood from her heart. Blake had been hurting. Tresa knew now, for certain, that he had fallen in love with Zenoa. Even though nothing would probably ever come of his love for her, his wedding plans with Tresa were gone.

Sometime soon she would have to tell her parents. Invitations would have to be withdrawn. Shower gifts returned. The house . . . her dream house, the house she had thought was his dream house too, could be sold. It was the least of the problems. Of course she would also have to talk to Blake. If he continued to deny his feelings for Zenoa, Tresa would have to take the responsibility for calling off the wedding.

The telephone rang. Tresa jumped, then her heart began to beat rapidly. *Blake*, she thought. Calling to tell me goodnight, the way he used to? To tell me he loves me, and can hardly wait until we can be together forever?

Her dad's voice said, "Tresa."

Tresa's eyes sought the digital numbers of her clock radio on the table that also held the telephone beside her chair. Past midnight. "Dad?" the tone of his voice, strangely flat, alarmed her. "What's wrong?"

"I think you'd better come to the hospital."

"Dad! What's wrong?" Images flitted through her mind, a broken morass of tragedies. Mother, sick. Aunt Pam. *Justin.*

"Get a cab and come on over." He added, an afterthought, "Uh—Saint Frances Hospital."

He was gone. She ran to the bedroom, tore off her robe, and pulled on a pair of jeans and a top. She grabbed her keys and purse and left the apartment. Not until she was in her car and headed through the streets toward Saint Frances Hospital, where she, and Justin, had been born, did she remember Dad had told her to get a cab. He had a reason, she knew. He must have felt she wouldn't be able to drive home. She knew then that someone important in her life was ill or seriously injured. She wondered at herself for being able to sit and worry about her love troubles and not know, intuitively, that something terrible was happening to Mom, or Justin . . . or perhaps even Blake.

She entered the large lobby at the front of the hospital. A circular reception station in the center of the lobby had one woman in charge There were only a few people sitting in the rose-colored chairs, waiting. One of them was Dad.

He came toward her, his face almost as white as his shirt collar. He held out his arms and hugged her briefly, then turned and with his arm across her shoulders led her toward the elevators.

"They're upstairs," he said "It's Justin. He's dead, Tresa."

"Dead? *Dead?* But . . . how is that possible?" she cried, seeing him again in his tuxedo, so handsome, so alive, barely three hours ago. "Dad! What happened?" Tears came as if they were controlled by something beyond her will. The outline of the elevator doors, the outline of her father blurred beyond them.

His hesitation seemed painfully long. Finally he said, "An overdose of cocaine."

"*What?* That's not possible! Justin did not take drugs."

"Zenoa said he wanted to try. To celebrate their wedding."

"Oh my God." *Zenoa said.*

Ross's voice broke when he said, "He used—used a hypodermic needle. Zenoa said—he said he wanted—to do it that way. He uh—he'd taken other stuff by mouth. They don't know yet what it was."

She felt as if she were walking through a dark, alien forest as her father guided her toward the room where the others waited. The nurses were ghosts, the few strangers walking along the halls nothing but dark shapes with no faces.

The room they entered was an office with a desk and a few chairs. A doctor in a white coat was present, a man, and present also was a woman in nun's clothing and another in a white nurse's pant suit. Zenoa, still wearing her white wedding suit sat on the edge of a chair. Tresa was not surprised to see that Blake was with her, his hand on her shoulder.

Beth came weeping to Tresa and they stood together, embracing. Tresa repeated what she had told her dad.

"Justin never took drugs, Mama. He was never into drugs. How could this have happened? Could it be a mistake?"

"Zenoa said she begged him not to."

"In accidental deaths," the doctor said, "there has to be an autopsy. We'll know more."

"I'm so sorry," the nun said. "If there's any way we can help, we'll be glad to try."

Ross said, "Maybe something to help my wife."

Tresa was aware of movements, of the continuing weeping of her mother. She saw the nurse bring something from an adjoining room and give it to her dad, as if tranquilizers were kept there for this purpose. The doctor said something about it being enough for tonight, but it might be a good idea if she went to her own physician the following day.

They began to leave. Zenoa stood up, Blake moving behind her, his hand on her back.

Ross said, "Come home with us, Tresa. Ride with us."

"I have my own car, Dad. I'll follow you."

Beth turned to Zenoa, put her arms out and hugged her. "Zenoa, you come home with us too. You're our daughter now, too. Stay with us."

Tresa held her breath. *No, not there. Not in the same house with Mom and Dad.*

"Thank you, Beth," Zenoa said. "But if you don't mind I'll go back to Justin's apartment. That's where I feel closest to him. Maybe Blake will take me home."

"Of course," he said.

Tresa felt such relief that Zenoa was not going to be in the house with her parents that it only briefly crossed her mind to wonder why Blake was here with Zenoa in the first place.

Then Beth said, "But you will come and stay with us, won"t you? Our home is yours, now."

"Thank you," Zenoa said in her sweet, childlike voice, that whispery softness. "There's nowhere else I'd rather be. In a few days." She kissed Beth's cheek.

There were no tears in Zenoa's eyes, Tresa saw, with her own vision suddenly sharp and clear. For the first time, as she looked at Zenoa, and felt the same antipathy she had always felt toward her, she accepted the reality of Justin's death.

Suddenly she knew. Zenoa had killed Justin.

As Blake drove Zenoa back to Justin's place, he remembered that he hadn't kissed Tresa goodnight. He hadn't even told her he was sorry about her brother. From the moment of the frantic call from Zenoa, as he was just going to sleep, he had forgotten everyone else.

Going to sleep hadn't been easy for him. In the dark he had lain with his arm over his eyes, trying to shut out the vision of Zenoa in her white suit, so petite, so perfect, standing with Justin in front of the minister.

He had left the wedding party as soon as he could after Zenoa and Justin drove away. He had looked for Tresa.

She was, after all, his fiancée. It was Tresa that made him a part of the family. Without Tresa, he wouldn't have an excuse to see Zenoa.

The guilt might come later. He knew it was there, as far under the surface of his thoughts and emotions as he could shove it. Shove it down, sit on it, just don't think about it. He'd be a good husband. He'd never stray, because the only woman in the world he wanted was Zenoa, and she was Justin's bride.

Then the call had come.

The apartment door had opened the moment he reached it, as if she sensed he was there. Zenoa was like that. She was filled with strange little mysteries that had intrigued him from the first time he met her, that Sunday night Justin had brought her to the family dinner. She had tipped her head sideways and looked up at him, her dark eyes twinkling almost as if they contained an inner light. "Reflect, is more like it," Tresa had said in a nasty voice later as he told her his impression of Zenoa. Such a doll, he had told Tresa. He had expected Tresa to understand. After all, he and she had been friends before they became lovers. They had always been able to talk.

"I don't like her," Tresa said, that night . . . how long ago? So recent, actually. So many things had happened in the short weeks since Zenoa had come to dinner that night.

"Why the hell not?" he had thundered at her. "You know, Tresa, you're really being catty. I never knew you had this side to you."

After a long pause in which Tresa sat with bowed head, she murmured hesitantly, "I don't—I'm not—I mean, Blake. There's something about her that's not real. She's got Justin enthralled with her, and also, she has you. Dad is the only male in the family who hasn't been drawn in."

They had not discussed Zenoa much after that. What was the use? Tresa couldn't see beyond her jealousy.

They had reached the apartment building in which Justin's apartment was located. Blake stopped the car at the entrance and turned toward Zenoa. She sat looking straight ahead. He wished he could help her, do more for her. She was the kind who held her emotions in. Blake knew she must be devastated, but she hadn't wept a tear. He touched her shoulder. It felt cool.

"Are you cold?" he asked, wishing he dared pull her into his arms and warm her. The poor kid, no folks, no home, actually. "I suppose it's too early to talk about your plans," he added.

"Plans?"

"Justin's apartment . . . when the rent's up, stuff like that."

She nodded, and looked down at her gloved hands. She was still wearing her wedding suit, even to the gloves. Something unwanted within him was relieved she was still dressed. That meant, probably, there had been no sex yet. Justin had liked to tell him how Zenoa was making him wait until their wedding night. Now, she was here . . . and he wasn't yet married to Tresa.

"I'll take care of you, Zenoa," he said, hearing his voice like a stranger's, husky, deep. "You know I will I — I'm in love with you."

"What about Tresa?" She did not sound surprised.

"That hasn't been going anywhere lately. We really haven't been getting along very well. I've been thinking about breaking it off anyway." He knew as he heard the words leave his mouth that it was true. He no longer was in love with Tresa; he wanted Zenoa. And until tonight there had been no chance of that.

He sat back on his side of the car, leaning against the door, moving his hand from Zenoa's shoulder. The man he had been recoiled from that last thought. *Until tonight.* What the hell was wrong with him that he could be glad a man was dead? No, it wasn't true. He wasn't like that. Justin had been a decent guy, mad about Zenoa. Now he was dead. The least he could do was wait until the man was buried.

"I'd better go," Blake said.

Zenoa nodded. "Me too."

She sat still, and Blake suddenly remembered, Justin always opened doors for Zenoa. She wasn't like Tresa, who would have been out the door and halfway home.

Blake got out of the car and hurried around to open her car door. He walked her to the entrance, and stopped there, under the canopy.

"Will you be all right?"

She looked up at him, beneath the little girl bangs, and smiled faintly. "I'll call you," she whispered. Then she was gone, the doors closing behind her.

He returned slowly to his car and started the engine. As he pulled slowly away from the curb he felt as if he were leaving not only his heart but his soul. Nothing about him seemed right anymore. He thought of that homeless, rootless little girl up there in the large apartment building, lost, alone. Why had he let her go? Why hadn't he just said to her, "Look, Zenoa, I want to help you. Tonight. I just want to keep you company. You shouldn't have to be alone on this night, of all nights."

He reached the end of the block and looked both ways along the street. No traffic at the moment. Very little traffic at this hour of the night, well past one o'clock now.

On sudden impulse he pulled a tight U turn and parked in an empty spot among other cars across the street from the entrance to the apartment building.

He slid down, his eyes on the brick building, his head on the headrest. Zenoa wouldn't know it, but she wouldn't be alone this night after all. He would stay with her, as close as he dared. Tomorrow morning maybe she'd let him take her out for breakfast.

He had barely settled down when he saw her again. Like a memory, a vision, she was coming out of the doors, straight out onto the sidewalk.

Puzzled, he sat up. She didn't look toward him. In his dark blue sedan he was part of a string of dark sedans. As unnoticeable as if he didn't exist.

She had changed clothes. She was now wearing slender jeans and a dark top with long sleeves and a high neck. She carried a black satchel with a half-moon handle. She crossed the sidewalk with quick, deliberate steps.

458

Suddenly a taxi swerved in and stopped. Zenoa opened the back door and got in. The taxi pulled away.

Blake sat still, his hands tight on the steering wheel. Where was she going at this time of night?

Blake watched closely, increasingly troubled, and beginning to feel there was something very weird, perhaps even eerie, about Zenoa's behavior tonight.

He started the car and followed the taxi, staying far enough behind that he was sure he wasn't seen.

They came into a neighborhood that at first was strange to him. It was a quiet street with large trees, large, secluded homes. The taxi stopped, Zenoa got out in an area with almost no light, as if she knew exactly where she was. She disappeared up a driveway cloistered in darkness. Heavy trees and shrubs closed out the bit of light from a distant street lamp.

Blake pulled to the curb and turned off his lights, watching the place where Zenoa had disappeared.

He got out of the car and walked into the driveway. The moment he saw the dim light in the downstairs window, he recognized the house.

As he stood in darkness Tresa's words returned to him, and this time replayed themselves in his mind.

She's been living in the old house, Blake. Wearing Pamela's old clothes. Pam recognized them. She saw her, Blake, in the house.

At last, he listened, stunned that he hadn't really heard them before.

Eighteen

Pam woke, heart pounding. The sound echoed in her mind, from a dream, from actuality. She wasn't sure. The house now was deathly silent.

She sat still, listening. Nothing.

Sleep had come on restless, delayed wings, carrying her deep into a haunted world. Kit was always there, sometimes floating in the darkness, a pale ghost, her arms out as if she were trying to swim, or fly. At other times she was sitting at a desk, drawing, painting with the new oil set Nicky had given her. In the background, creeping nearer within the hovering shadows, was the doll, its face never quite seen, its presence venomous, a danger to Kit. Pam was always trying to scream a warning to Kit. Then, something fell. Or a door closed somewhere in the house. Or a window slammed down.

Her thoughts went to the attic window. The window with no lock. But even if an intruder had entered, he— she—wouldn't be able to get into the main house because the attic door was securely fastened with the metal slide lock in the hallway.

For several nights now there had been no sounds of the girl, or anyone.

The house was quiet, except for the creaks of an old building, of wind at the corners, of a tree limb brushing against the outside walls.

Pam turned on her bedside lamp.

She looked at the clock. One-thirty. She had no desire to

try to sleep again. Sometimes when a bad dream woke her in the middle of the night she got up, chose a certain section of the house, and cleaned it. Last night she had dusted the shelves in the den that held the picture albums.

The wedding was long over.

Had Justin taken his bride away for a wedding trip? She knew nothing, nothing about her family. She had only succeeded in driving a permanent wedge between herself and them.

She pulled on the terry-cloth robe she'd hung over the foot of the bed, and tied it securely at the waist. The chair was not propped under the knob tonight, nor last night. She had stopped bothering. What plans she'd had in mind when she came home all seemed ridiculous now. Find the doll, destroy it, sell the house, leave. Now she was just existing, one minute following the next. Zenoa was there, in the family, she was out.

Since Beth had called her and told her she was no longer welcome in her house, since Tresa had called and apologized, Pamela had begun to wonder about herself, and the proof behind her long-held convictions. She wondered, and her mind became more and more uneasy. Maybe she should just seek help from a mental institution. Maybe she was, after all, wrong about it all. Maybe she was the one who had murdered.

Maybe . . .

The phone rang. She heard it distantly, as if it were only part of her delusions.

She opened the bedroom door, and heard the phone ringing down in the kitchen, a sound like the faint buzz of a lone insect in the trees.

She found the hall light switch, turned it on, and hurried downstairs, turning on lights as she went. The phone grew louder, an old-fashioned ring meant to be heard all over the house. She had thought briefly about having her old phone line hooked up, so that she could call from her bedroom if she needed to. But that was just another of the plans that were vague and unimportant.

The phone continued to ring. A wrong number, prob-

461

ably. Or a call that something . . . terrible . . .

She entered the kitchen with a sense of relief assuaging her growing fear of the phone call. Here, the ghosts of the past seemed less prominent, or perhaps they were just happier here. Here where the family gathered to eat, where there had been no traces of the blood that stained the upstairs, the stairway, the foyer.

Pam grabbed the receiver off the wall.

"Aunt Pam?"

"Tresa?" It had to be Tresa's voice that quivered faintly over the phone line, but it sounded like more of her nightmares, those faraway voices that sometimes were Kit crying for help, and sometimes a voice she couldn't identify.

"Tresa, what's wrong?"

"Oh, Aunt Pam. He's dead. Justin is dead. I'm—"

"Dead!" She saw him suddenly, lying in a pool of blood, his back like Nicky's had been, ragged and torn.

"Drugs. An overdose, they said. Mom has been given a sedative, and she's asleep. Dad is going to lie down with her. I'm coming over if it's all right. I need to talk to you."

Drugs.

Pamela hung up the phone, and stood still. Justin, dead, on his wedding night. She felt a deep sense of the inevitable, of fate being fulfilled. Only the method surprised her.

She went slowly to the door that led from the old breezeway to the drive, and turned on the porch light beside the door. With the door open behind her, she waited on the step.

Within minutes a small car spun into the driveway and came to a stop a few feet from Pam. Tresa came running to her, and threw herself into Pam's arms.

Pam held Tresa while she wept, until she pulled away and wiped her eyes.

"Come on in," Pam said gently, "and I'll make us some hot cocoa. That was always one of my mother's remedies. Go to the kitchen and drink a cup of chocolate, or cocoa."

In the brighter light of the kitchen Pam saw that Tresa looked as if she had dressed hastily. Her hair was mussed, her face cleaned of makeup. She looked so young,

462

so vulnerable, so scared.

Tresa talked, her voice spilling the events of the evening. Pam stirred hot cocoa and poured it into cups, adding so many marshmallows they formed a lumpy covering. She listened as Tresa told her of Ross's call for her to come to the hospital.

"I didn't even get to see him, Aunt Pam. No one would let me see him. Aunt Pam, Justin never, never took drugs. Not that I ever knew of. Could he have taken drugs and kept it hidden so well from the family? Why would he choose his wedding night to experiment? Zenoa said he wanted to celebrate. She said—"

The sound was somewhere above, the definite sound of a door closing.

Tresa grew still, her eyes turned toward the ceiling.

"Do you have a window open?" she asked.

"Perhaps in my bedroom . . ."

"But there's no breeze," Tresa added, her eyes coming to Pam.

"I'm going up to see," Pam said. "You stay here."

"Oh no. I'm coming with you."

Pam hesitated. She was afraid to go upstairs, but she was more afraid not to go, to check, to make sure the windows were locked, the attic door secured.

"All right," she finally said, glad, deep within, not to be alone.

With the quick movements of someone very nervous, Tresa got up and followed Pam closely. Pam led the way into the front hall where the light was muted. They passed the closed door of the old powder room. As always, Pam thought of the doll. Would she ever pass that door without thinking of the doll?

She said, "I often hear sounds, like a door closing, or someone walking. Not always at night. Sometimes in the daytime. But after the first few days I began to wonder if it was sometimes in my mind."

"Not tonight it wasn't. I heard it too."

"After that first time I actually saw her, the noises subsided. As if . . . she stopped coming."

463

She started up the stairs, and stopped. The second-floor hall lights were out. The only light on the stairs came from below. Tresa, behind, touched her arm.

"What's wrong?" she whispered shrilly.

"The lights are out." Don't alarm her, she warned herself. Don't alarm yourself. "I left the lights on. But the house is old. Maybe it's the wiring. Also, the circuit breaker is outside. Something might have happened there." Or . . . someone turned them out.

As if she had read Pam's mind, Tresa said in a low voice, "It can't be Zenoa. She's with Blake. Blake took her home."

"How long ago?"

"About an hour—" Tresa paused. "Perhaps longer. I stayed with Mom and Dad. Waiting for them to be able to stay alone before I called. Mom took the capsules and Daddy and I put her to bed. Then Daddy said it was okay to leave. He just wanted to rest. I promised him I'd come back there to sleep, to be there in the morning. So, Blake, I'm sure, is still with Zenoa. It can't be her, Pam."

Pam nodded, hearing the tinge of bitterness in Tresa's voice when she mentioned her fiancé's name. If Zenoa hadn't returned, then they really had very little to fear. Still, to be safe, she wanted to check the lights, and the attic door.

She climbed the stairs, looking into the shadows toward the master bedroom. The door was closed. She could see its outlines, in its dark, recessed setting. The hallway toward the other bedrooms was almost totally dark. She went forward cautiously, her heart pounding, that ghostly cold hand of fear drawing away from her with each step, beckoning her forward.

She reached the hall, and the light switch. The muted overhead light halfway down the hall came on. She felt weak with relief. Then the knowledge hit her. There were no problems at the circuit breaker or with the wiring. Someone had turned out the light here in the hall.

Behind her Tresa whispered, "Perhaps you just automatically turned it out, and forgot. Sometimes I turn them on, and not notice what I've done until later when I realize . . ."

"Yes, that's probably what happened."

It was better to let Tresa think that. And perhaps Tresa was right. When the sound of the ringing phone reached Pam all she thought about was answering it. Maybe she only thought she'd left the lights on because she was used to leaving them burning behind her at night when a sound drew her into another part of the house.

Pam led the way back to the end of the hall. She stepped to the side of the rug that covered the largest of the old dark bloodstains, and Tresa followed in her steps. Pam stopped within a few feet of the attic door.

The latch was open.

Without saying anything to Tresa to alarm her, she stepped to the attic door and pushed the metal latch shut again. Tomorrow, in the light of day, she would go into the attic and check. Tonight, she had to check the rest of the house. Old visions and memories returned. Her lawyers saying, "Anyone, agile enough to climb as most burglars are, could have come into the house. Up the trellis, the drain pipe, to the roof above the utility room, above the roof that connects garage to house, a sloping roof that reaches up within a few feet of another sloping roof above a bedroom, and then to the attic window. That window does not have a lock on it. Anyone can enter there."

Not until then had Pamela known there was no lock on the attic window. Such things as locks had not been important in her young life. Now, they had become a major part of her life. All her years in prison she was surrounded by locks. Now, in her freedom, if the locks weren't in place, she was nervous and jumpy, hearing sounds, feeling drafts. But tonight Tresa had heard the sound too. Somewhere, up here, a door had closed. The attic door?

The illogic of her thinking crossed her mind briefly. If someone had come through the attic window, they could not have come down into the hall, because she was positive she always kept the attic door latched. Whoever entered, if that was the sound they'd heard, had to have entered

465

somewhere else.

Or had she forgotten, somehow, to lock the attic door after her last search up there?

Not Zenoa, Tresa had said. Zenoa's with Blake.

Even her bedroom light had been turned off. She entered the room cautiously, and turned the light back on. She slid her hand beside the door and closed her fingers over the hatchet handle, holding it behind her so that Tresa wouldn't become alarmed. She looked around. Nothing in the room was different. Her bedclothes were thrown back, just as she had left them.

Tresa followed her, every step. She stood in the middle of the room.

"I'll check the bedrooms, Tresa. Why don't you wait?"

"Why don't I help you?"

"Well, all right . . . if you'd like."

Zenoa's with Blake. Was it possible something could have happened, just for a while, with the wiring on the second floor? A strange malfunction? Was it possible that she'd not fastened the attic door? Could windows be open somewhere, bringing a draft that caused a door to slam shut?

Pam said, "If you'd like, you can peek into your mom's old room. I was in there just today, doing a little dusting. Maybe I left the window open." She pointed toward the door where Beth once lived. "I'll check Kit's room."

Tresa went down the hall, and Pamela stepped carefully across the throw rugs on the hall carpet and opened the door to the pink room.

The switch worked, and the ceiling light came on. Its light seemed as muted as a candlelight. Standing there, just inside the door, was like being alone, except for the ghosts that lived here, in the ruffles and the pink. The room smelled musty and old, though it hadn't changed in appearance since Kit had sat at the desk across the room, her head bowed over her drawings.

Pam could almost see her there. Something was on her desk, just as if Kit had only stepped away from it. Pam went softly, silently across the thick carpet, and looked at the top of the desk. A drawing of a garden of flowers lay

466

on the desk, and beside the eight by ten sheet of art paper lay several colored pencils.

Pam stared down at them, at the things that belonged to Kit. Just hours ago they had not been lying there. The top of the desk was bare except for the small wicker pencil holder, the few books, the desk lamp. Pam had carefully dusted the desk, carefully arranged everything on the top, and put away into a drawer the very items that were now spread out again.

She heard the soft sound of movement behind her. Footsteps as soft as her own had been, the whisper of Tresa entering.

"Did you know, Tresa, that Kit was a marvelous artist—"

The pain between her shoulder blades drove her forward against the desk. She gasped for breath, a strange, heavy weight suddenly surrounding her chest. She gripped the edge of the desk and began a slow anguished turn as the pain came again, and again, piercing, driving her down, down. On her knees she turned at last and looked up. She tried to lift the hatchet, almost forgotten in her hand, but it was too heavy.

As if she were plunged back in time Pamela saw the doll, coming toward her from the powder room, as agile as a child, her face sprinkled with blood, her frilly, lacy dress stained with dark red blood. She came forward, closer and closer, larger and larger, and this time sunlight did not touch her, and she did not collapse.

Nineteen

"Aunt Pam?"

Tresa thought she had heard Pamela say something. She wasn't sure. She listened a moment, heard nothing more, and turned her attention again to her mother's old bedroom. The walls didn't hold posters. If posters had ever hung on these walls they had been taken down. But on the bedside table was a picture of Beth when she was a smiling teenager, a pretty girl with her dark brown hair in a center part, the hair waving downward and obscuring the sides of her face. She looked perhaps sixteen, maybe younger.

The room was yellow and orange, a wallpaper with flowers meant to appear artificial, with perfectly rounded or angled forms. The colors had faded over the years, more so in some areas than others. Back in the corners away from the two windows the yellow was cheerful and clean. The furniture was dark. It was free from dust, but high in the corners of the high-ceilinged room were clusters of spider webs, and webs had woven around the chain of the ceiling light.

Another sound came from somewhere beyond the wall. A faint moan, then wood scraping against wood, followed by a dull thud. Alarm raced over Tresa's skin, pulling it tight and cold. She opened her mouth to call out again, then ran instead into the hallway.

The hall light was out. Dim light came from doors down the hall only partly open. Tresa could see that no one stood in the hall.

"*Aunt Pam!*" Tresa cried in low urgency.

Silence answered her. Then, she thought, the soft sounds of movement, somewhere. A soft-soled slipper on carpet. Or a sleeve brushing against a wall.

She tried to speak again, but fear stopped her.

She stood still, in the middle of the hall. Go to Aunt Pam, one part of her mind ordered, find Aunt Pam. While another part demanded, *run*. Run downstairs to the telephone. Call for help. Something has happened to Aunt Pam.

Yet another part of her mind urged her to crouch back, hide, wherever she could. She remembered that she had only her aunt's word for the strange, crazy explanation of the murders. Only her aunt . . . who herself might be the danger.

No. She would never believe that. Pam needed help. Somewhere, there, in Kit's bedroom. *In Kit's bedroom.*

She went forward, toward the angling light on the left side of the hall. Kit's bedroom.

She put out her hand and with her stiffened fingers pushed the door slowly inward.

Her eyes fell immediately on the figure across the room, on the floor, beside the desk chair that had been pulled over. In that first instance she didn't recognize Pam. She saw the figure, the body. She saw the ripped and bloody garment, its colors lost beneath the oozing red. Then she saw Pam's cheek, her face turned toward the desk.

"Pam!" she screamed, and ran forward, going instinctively toward her, reaching down to help.

Then, just as instinctively reacting to the danger that crept so swiftly up behind her. As the light went out she bolted to her feet and whirled.

Another, dimmer light outlined Zenoa, caught in her hair and surrounded her like an aura of evil, like a shadowy, dark ghost rising from her head. Even in the dim light she saw the face of Zenoa, the half-smile, the tips of the two white teeth, like a doll's.

Zenoa held in her hands something with a long, pointed blade. She raised it above her head, holding it with both hands.

Tresa could smell her perfume, the sweet scent of obscure blossoms. She smelled something mingling with it that was old and musty. She smelled the warm, frightening odor of blood.

Tonight Justin had died, and Pam. Tonight she too would die. Why, Zenoa, she wanted to ask. But her voice was frozen in terror, only her mind lived, at this moment, her body already prepared for death.

"Zenoa! Why? Why have you done this to us?"

She heard her own voice with a sense of disbelief. A question in the last moments before death. What did it matter now?

Zenoa paused. An expression flashed across her face, a lost memory, perhaps. She looked startled, as if she'd been awakened.

"No. No," she said. "Heather. My name is Heather."

"Heather." Tresa pulled a breath into her lungs. It was as if Zenoa's hesitation, her strange return to someone named Heather, had given her a second chance. She glanced down. On the floor a few inches from Pam's outstretched hand was a hatchet. Its blade caught the muted light in a dull glint. Tresa was afraid to move, to lunge for it. If she could only further distract Zenoa . . . start her talking . . . change the direction of her gaze . . .

"You're not Heather," Tresa said, hearing her voice weak and tremulous, but growing stronger. "You're Zenoa. You're a doll, Zenoa. You were given to Kit—"

"No!" Zenoa screamed, her beautiful features suddenly twisting into a mask of dark fury. The black halo roiled around her head, turning her hair oddly dark. With both hands she lifted the ice pick high over her head. Yet still she didn't move.

She cried, *"Heather! I am—Heather! Beautiful! Never age, never die. Live—beautiful—rich. This is my house! Mine! I was promised!"*

"Kit! Don't you remember Kit, Zenoa? You were given

470

to her. A doll, Zenoa!"

"Kit! Ellie! Becky! They're all the same! I have no time for them! They ruin my beauty, make me old and ugly. He promised me I would live forever, be indestructible, be beautiful and rich and live in a big house. He promised me! You can't take it away, you, Justin, Pam. You can't— you can never keep me from mine! *I was promised!*"

Tresa felt as if she were two people in one body. Her heart, pounding in her temples, and something else that was growing oddly calm. She saw Zenoa's confusion, her fury and hesitation. She had no doubt Zenoa would kill them all, but first . . . *first* . . .

She eased down, as if to kneel, moving slowly, her hand reaching for the hatchet, inch by inch, along Pam's arm. She had to keep Zenoa's mind on whatever it was that lingered somewhere within her, or within whatever knowledge she might possess of the past. She had to keep her mind on the mysterious Heather.

"Who promised you, Heather?"

"He! It! The—the keeper of the scythe and the darkness . . ."

Her voice trailed away, and it seemed her shadowed eyes stared at something beyond Tresa, beyond the walls. Perhaps even beyond the world.

"The devil!" Tresa cried softly. "Heather sold her soul to the devil!" She knew then she was in the presence of an evil beyond anything she had ever imagined. In her world, there had been no dark negative, no opposite to God. Yet here she was, paralyzed for a moment in terror in the edge of that darkness.

"The most powerful one. The Prince of Darkness . . . it would be mine, always—"

She had to move, though her heart pounded in absolute terror. She had to rise against the evil of Heather.

"Not yours, Zenoa! Heather's! Heather's!" Tresa shouted. Her fingers touched the handle of the hatchet and she gripped it tightly and leaped to her feet.

"No! No!" Zenoa screamed and lunged forward, her shadowed face contorted. With both arms stiffened, she

471

brought the ice pick down swiftly.

Tresa felt it rip into her sleeve. For just a second it caught, its blade nicking her arm as she jumped backwards. With the hatchet in her left hand she swung hard, sideways.

She heard it connect with Zenoa's head. The sound was a sharp cracking, as if she had struck an object hollow and thin. In the half light she saw the right side of Zenoa's head had caved in and split open. The screams that came from Zenoa were high-pitched and eerily distant, yet combined with a deep, guttural cry of fury, of hatred, of darknesses beyond Tresa's understanding.

There was a thin, faraway voice coming from Zenoa, screaming out words, jumbled sentences. Voices streaming, sounds as unearthly as Zenoa herself. Perhaps it was true, Tresa thought. Perhaps Zenoa was indestructible.

The ice pick came down again, held in Zenoa's hands, arms stiffened. Tresa saw it coming, and clutched the hatchet in both hands, steadied it and then swung, stopping the downward jab of the ice pick with her arm.

The blade of the hatchet caught Zenoa directly across the neck, and Tresa watched in a kind of slow-motion horror as the head separated from the body and dropped to the floor.

Suddenly the overhead light flashed on.

Blake screamed hoarsely, "Zenoa!"

Tresa glimpsed Blake in the doorway, his hand still at the light switch.

She stared down at the head on the floor as it rolled, spinning on its back, face upward.

The face held the expression that had been Zenoa's, large-eyed, quizzical, the half-smile set, two little teeth white and pearly, peeking out from beneath the upper lip. As the head had separated from the body and dropped with a strange, horrible thud onto the carpet, it regained the doll-like blankness of Zenoa. The head rolled slowly on, round and round, toward the corner, away from the light as if seeking darkness.

The body of Zenoa remained standing, arms lifting, the

bloody ice pick reaching its apex. A rancid liquid, thick and slimy, eased out of the opened neck and made greenish black rivulets down the shirt, the jeans. The arms began their descent toward Tresa. Swiftly, it came down, aimed at her heart.

Blake cried, "Oh my God!"

Tresa hesitated just a moment, slumping with exhaustion, the hatchet hanging. In disbelief she realized that whatever it was that had been Zenoa, the danger was still there. The intent to destroy and kill as strong as ever.

Hardly aware of her actions, her mind flitting through the names of Heather, Ellie, Becky, Kit . . . Zenoa . . . Tresa jerked the hatchet up, quickly sidestepped the plunging ice pick and struck again, and again, beating down the body that seemed, after all, indestructible. She heard her own gasping breath, and saw her own hands striking again and again with the hatchet, as if she stood apart and watched.

The body cracked open, separating, as the head had separated. The liquid blurted forward. The arms fell, though the hands still held tightly to the ice pick. The torso hung for a moment in the clothing, and the legs moved, turning, as if to attack again its attacker.

It fell, at last.

Tresa stared in horror down at the thing jerking and moving on the floor, as if still it aimed to rise and attack. The hands lifted the ice pick. The feet kicked, moving the torso.

In the corner, like an empty mask, the beautiful face looked up at the ceiling with the expression of the doll fixed forever.

Blake hunched forward, his arms across his middle, breathing as if he were ill. Tresa too felt sick suddenly. And sad. Unutterably sad.

Why, Zenoa? she had asked. And the answer she had been given included a promise never kept, a soul given, perhaps, in return for beauty forever, a life forever. It included names that must have belonged to other children, killed or destroyed, like the child who had died in the in-

473

sane asylum, no longer able to speak or express herself. Was she Heather's child? Was Becky the name of the little girl in the asylum? Zenoa's first owner, with her sister, Ellie. The sister, perhaps, that Becky was said to have stabbed. Even then Zenoa had received within herself something of Heather. The promised life, perhaps, not possible for a human, but possible for something beyond human.

But even if Zenoa could tell her more, Tresa would never understand, because they had been destined for different worlds, and Zenoa somehow became lost in the wrong world.

Tresa dropped the hatchet, stepped around Blake on legs that felt made of rubber, and began to run.

The telephone . . .

Aunt Pam needed help.

Twenty

Pam watched the hospital room door. She had heard Jefferson's voice in the hall, talking to Tresa, who had been with her during the twenty-seven hours she had been in the hospital. His flowers surrounded her in the room, mixtures of wild flowers, garden flowers, lush and fragrant.

I'm getting out of here today, Jeff. Come to me. Hurry.

She hadn't talked at length with him yet. She had regained consciousness in Kit's room, and had seen the horror of what Tresa had faced alone. Tresa, at her side, told her she had called for an ambulance, and she had seen Jefferson's number on the note by the telephone, and had called him. She remembered Pam telling her once, if anything happened to her, call Jefferson. Tresa recalled having read the officer's name frequently in the transcripts, and knew who he was. Pam, with Tresa and Blake's help, had walked from the room, so the ambulance attendants had not seen the horror that was in the room.

Her three wounds were deep, but had entered muscle, not vital organs or bones. Jefferson had looked in on her later in the hospital, kissed her for the first time, and hurried away. "I'll be back," he said. At the door he'd looked back and scolded, "Why didn't you call me as soon as you knew you were being released?" But had disappeared before she could answer, which was just as well. She had wanted him with her. But wasn't sure how he felt. She hadn't wanted to obligate him. There were many reasons he would not accept, so it was just as well he didn't expect an answer.

Now, she felt as though she could breathe again, after long years of holding her breath. Suddenly, with the destruction of Zenoa, she felt as if the weight of the world, of . . . eternity, had been lifted from her. That she could breathe again.

Justin's death was a dark cloud over that feeling.

Tresa too, needed a change. She had said goodbye to Blake. Outside the hospital door they had talked in low voices, but still Pam had heard Blake pleading.

"I can't pick up those old dreams where we left them," Tresa told her minutes later. "He can have the new house. I don't want it."

That was the way Pam felt about her old home. She would never enter it again.

The door opened. Jefferson came in alone, came to the bed, to Pam's outstretched arms. He sat beside her, warm and close. She had almost forgotten the feeling of real security.

"I'm taking you away," he said. "I've been planning this for years. I knew you were being released, but they must have changed the date. I thought it was next month. I bought this place, years ago. A thousand miles away. There's privacy, and a view of the ocean. There are also a couple of cabins that can be used as guest houses."

"For Tresa?"

"Yes, if she wants."

But something had been coming back in her dreams. Something that was growing, threatening and black on the horizon.

"Jefferson, I dreamed . . . I dreamed she came back. I saw her the way I used to. Coming together again. Her fingers working out of the ground, her body going in search of the rest of her, of her head, her hands—"

He put his hand over her mouth.

"It's okay. I promise you those parts of—whatever she was, are so widely distributed there's no chance of anything like that ever happening. I promise."

476

"How . . . ?"

"I got a couple of guys I knew I could depend on. That's all. Don't worry. No one outside you, me, Tresa, Blake, and those two guys know the real truth."

She drew a long breath.

The door opened again, and a nurse entered, with Tresa behind her, bringing new clothes for Pam to get dressed in.

It was time to go, to go forward to a new life, to forget the past.

If possible, forget the past.